URSULA'S SECRET

MAIRI WILSON

BLACK & WHITE PUBLISHING

First published 2015
by Black & White Publishing Ltd
29 Ocean Drive, Edinburgh EH6 6JL

1 3 5 7 9 10 8 6 4 2   15 16 17 18

ISBN   978 1 78530 008 0

A CIP catalogue record for this book is available from the British Library.

ALBA | CHRUTHACHAIL

Typeset by RefineCatch Ltd, Bungay, Suffolk
Printed and bound by Nørhaven, Denmark

For my parents, for sharing their love of reading.

Three things cannot be long hidden: the sun, the moon and the truth.

Attributed to Buddha

1

Edinburgh, June 3rd 2014

Lexy heard the taxi pull away behind her. She'd over-tipped in an attempt to make up for the driver's lost chance at a better fare from one of the other passengers off the London train, but it hadn't worked. The driver had scowled at her as he'd pocketed her money and muttered something she couldn't catch under his breath, although the words *daft wee lassie* had featured in there somewhere. Not an auspicious start to what she knew would be a tough few days going through a dead woman's affairs.

The building towered above her, solid and city-stained. Number 17 didn't look familiar to her, or any different to all the other tenements that lined the short street, but as soon as she turned the key in the panelled front door and felt the chill of the hallway she was bombarded with memories. A fusty dampness mingled with the tang of bleach from cleaned flagstones. A waft of cut grass drifted in through the open arch leading to the garden. The swoosh and thud of the heavy door swinging shut behind her silenced the hum of distant traffic as abruptly as the click of the off switch on a radio. She bit her lip and stood shivering in gloomy half-light, marooned for a moment in the past.

She knew what she would see when she looked up beyond the spiralling stairs to the glass dome in the ceiling: dust peppering the shafts of coloured light splaying down on her. She had stood here before, small hand in her mother's strong one. She could picture Ursula's face beaming down from a long way above as she called them to come on up. How daunting those stairs had seemed to a child who lived in a bungalow. Up and up and up, never-endingly. She'd pulled back, reluctant, shaking her head.

"But look, Lex. The stairs are smiling to welcome us." Her mother bent down and whispered in her ear. "Let's smile back, shall we? Show them we're happy to be here?"

So Lexy had, and she did it again now as she realised the "smile" was just the curve that years of trudging footsteps like their own had worn into the lip of each step.

The stairs were worth it, though, even if Lexy was breathing heavily by the time she reached Ursula's top-floor flat. She paused on the threshold, basking in the light flooding the generous hallway from the sitting room's bay windows. In the distance, she could see the green expanse of the Meadows. Smoke hovered like mist over grass sprinkled with groups of lingering students, exams over, barbecues dying, end-of-year celebrations already in their twilight stages. Smudges of pink and lilac bruised a cloudless sky. Breathtaking, surprising and immediately soothing. Easy to see why Ursula had stayed on long after she'd retired, although for a woman of nearly ninety those stairs must have been a challenge: her fall no real surprise, whatever police protocols might suggest.

Feeling like an intruder, Lexy left her case and bag by the door and stepped further into the hallway. All the rooms opened off this and all their doors were ajar. She pushed open one to her left and looked into a large L-shaped kitchen, a dining table and benches built into the alcove at the far end, in front of the window. She had a view of the Meadows from here too, albeit obliquely and without the glow of the evening sun. The padded window seat behind the table was piled with cushions, a perfect spot to linger in the morning with the papers and cups of tea. Did she really remember her mother sitting there or was it just the kind of thing Isobel liked to do?

The room was tidy, a single plate propped against a mug left to

2

drain on the rack beside the sink, alongside an upturned vase, its thistles and leaves glazed in blues and greens. Lexy recognised it instantly: there was one just like it in her mother's hallway. Had Ursula always left things in such an orderly state or had someone been in to clean since she'd died, thrown out fading flowers, brushed away crumbs, rinsed dishes?

A pile of post on the end of the worktop decided it. But who would it have been? Police? Someone from the solicitor's office? Or perhaps social services did that kind of thing. It would be nice to think so, but she doubted it.

Her phone bleeped as she walked back into the hallway. Text message. Another one. She should answer, but she'd no idea what she'd say. She glanced at her bag, then turned away.

She opened the door to her right and a surge of nostalgia swept through her. Twin beds with matching pink candlewick bedspreads, a small nightstand and lamp, a dark wardrobe flush against the wall by the door, and an old-fashioned dressing table in the corner near the window, itself screened by net. The curtains fluttered, and as Lexy walked over to close the window, she grew larger in each of the three mirrored panels above the dressing table. The glass gleamed.

She pulled the stool from its nook, traced the roses of its tapestry seat with her fingertips.

"Isn't it beautiful?" Ursula's voice was clear. "Your mother did it, for my birthday one year." Lexy heard pride, love, in the soft lilt, felt the warmth that had always been there whenever Ursula told her tales of Isobel's childhood.

Watching her reflection in the mirrors, Lexy hooked a leg over the stool and sat down. There she was, eight years old, lips streaked in red, powder-blue smudges on her eyelids. Her mother appeared at her shoulder, then Ursula behind her, and for a moment Lexy watched all three of them laughing together, smelt eau de cologne, wrinkled her nose at the antiseptic edge of coal tar soap. Then the breeze through the curtains cooled her cheek and the illusion dissolved.

She pushed open the next door and paused, hand resting on the cool porcelain doorknob. Ursula's room. Chintz wallpaper and fifties furniture. This had been forbidden territory to her as a child and even now she was reluctant to go in. She was dreading the prospect of trawling through the remnants of Ursula's life, and above all in here. This would be the greatest intrusion of all, unpicking the intimate details of a private Ursula Lexy had never known. Tomorrow would be time enough.

And then the final bedroom. That was the one that made Lexy's throat constrict, her breathing stall. It was a young girl's room. *Her* room when they'd visited, the one where her mother had lived out her own childhood, dreamt teenage dreams. Lexy ran her hand along the books stacked neatly on top of the chest of drawers, the bookcase itself crammed full, books jammed in horizontally between tight rows of upright volumes and the shelf above. Lexy read as avidly as her mother had ever done, had spent hours of their visits curled up on this bed, devouring stories with the same curiosity, the same thirst for adventure and make-believe.

Ursula had changed nothing in here as far as Lexy could see. She sat down on the bed and smoothed the paisley-patterned eiderdown to either side of her. It felt cool and silky, tiny pinpricks of feathers just apparent through its surface. Slipping her feet from her shoes, she swung her legs up and round and lay back. Eyes closed and she was a child again, listening to the sound of her mother and Ursula chatting in the sitting room at the end of the hall, or chinking dishes as they washed up in the kitchen opposite. Sometimes they'd forget to whisper and she'd hear them talking, making plans for the next day, discussing something they'd already done.

"The zoo," her mother's voice had stated clearly that last time they'd visited. "She's been penguin-mad ever since you introduced her to *Pingu*."

"Has she?" Ursula had sounded pleased. "Right. That's it then. A trip to the zoo on your final day. My treat." A kitchen cupboard door had banged shut. "We'll keep it secret and surprise her." Footsteps in the hallway drowned her mother's response as the women moved through to the sitting room.

Lexy turned onto her side, drew her knees up and rested her hands under her cheek as she let the memories return. Hours spent tucked between her mother and Ursula watching the same videos over and over; squeals and shrieks as the three of them, at Lexy's insistence, waddled or slid up and down the polished wood in the hallway; penguin-speak conversations in the igloo they'd built her under the kitchen table. But, now that she thought about it, they'd never gone to the zoo. That was the trip that had ended early, when they'd taken the sleeper home, and that had been excitement enough to put even penguins in the shade. Until now. They'd been happy, the three of them. What had changed that? Why had the visits stopped?

Lexy woke to the sound of a key turning in the front door. She lay rigid, disorientated, eyes registering 8.31 on the alarm clock. Morning. She'd slept straight through.

Hinges creaked.

She scrambled to her feet, cold despite the sun streaming though the uncovered window. Her stomach growled, but no time for that. She struggled to wake, to grasp that she wasn't alone. A thud, then a grunt. Someone tripping over the suitcase she'd left in the hall. Adrenalin crackled like cellophane.

"Hello? Who's there? Hello?"

She pulled at the bedroom door, shrank back at the stranger's hand reaching out to push it open. "What the—"

"Jeez – who the hell are you?" The stranger's hand dropped. "I . . . I mean . . . Sorry. I'm Jenny. Ursula's help, Miss Reid's, that is. Her . . . her carer . . ." The hand shot up again, extended in

5

introduction now as the woman recovered herself, stretched a smile on her face. "Right. Yes. I'm the carer. Jenny. How do you— Oh, you'll be Isobel, won't you?"

Instinctively, Lexy took the outstretched hand, shaking her head as she tried to keep up. "No, I'm Lexy. Lexy Shaw. Isobel's my—"

"Oh, *Lexy*. Yes, your mother. I know. Ursula talks . . . talked about you all the time."

"She did?"

"Well, no. But a lot. Enough." The stranger rubbed her shin. "Jeepers, that hurt. What's in that case – concrete?"

"I . . . Just some . . . Sorry, who did you say you were?"

"Jenny. I'll make tea, shall I? I've brought the milk." She vanished into the kitchen. Lexy heard a bag clunk onto the worktop, then running water and the clatter of a kettle lid before the woman reappeared, shrugging off her jacket. "Or there's coffee. Not that she drank it herself, but you know how she was. Kept it for visitors. Rare enough those, though, these days." The jacket was flung onto a coat hook and Jenny disappeared into the kitchen again. "So what's it to be?" she called over clinking crockery, clearly at home in Ursula's kitchen and leaving Lexy feeling wrong-footed. It would have been nice to know someone else had a key.

"Tea. Tea's fine, thanks." Lexy followed her into the kitchen and sat down at the table, relaxing a little when Jenny produced a packet of biscuits. No one armed with chocolate-chip cookies could mean any harm.

"May I? Haven't eaten." Lexy was already opening them.

"Oh, but there's plenty of food in the cupboards, yet. And the freezer. Did you not look?"

Lexy shook her head. "Too tired," she explained between bites. "Fell asleep." Watching Jenny bustle around the kitchen, Lexy realised they were closer in age than she'd thought, first impressions thrown off-kilter by speech tics and mannerisms she associated with an older generation.

6

"Well, you *will* be needing to look at this lot, Lexy." The pile of post slapped down on the table. "Not opened anything, of course, although I'd usually read everything for her. Almost blind she was at the end there, with the cataracts. Told her she should pull a few strings, what with her background, get herself moved up that waiting list, but she'd have none of it. She always was a stickler for the rules, wasn't she?"

"I don't . . . I couldn't really say." Jenny probably meant well, and maybe Ursula had been glad of the chatter, but Lexy found it irritating and wished she could think of a polite way to get the woman to stop. Or at least slow down a bit.

"Well, you'd not seen her for a good long while, though, had you," Jenny was saying, "nor had your mother neither." Jenny's sniff was eloquent disapproval. "But she was, you know, a great one for rules. And standards. Oh yes, even at her age she'd not let anything slide. 'Slippery slope, Jenny,' she'd say, 'slippery slope . . .'"

The barrage slowed and Lexy took her chance.

"Look, I arrived last night. The solicitor gave me the key. I didn't know about you or—"

"Oh, don't worry about me," Jenny was revved up and racing away again. "I've been half-expecting someone ever since . . . the accident. Thought it'd be your mother, though, as she'd been planning . . . Is she coming later, then, Isobel?"

"No."

"Really? Well." Another sniff. "I know they'd had their differences . . . but all the same, this was your mother's *home*, and now they were speaking again . . . Still, her business, I suppose."

"My mother . . . she's . . ." Jenny's words caught up with Lexy. "They *spoke*?"

"Of course they did. Closest thing to mother and daughter, weren't they now, and wouldn't you call your mother sometimes even if you did have a wee fall-out now and then?" Jenny reached

7

down for a biscuit and crammed it whole into her mouth, giving Lexy a few precious seconds to try to work out what she was hearing.

"But . . . when? What did . . . My mother never said . . ."

Jenny brushed crumbs from her chest, swallowed, then carried on as if Lexy hadn't spoken as she poured freshly boiled water into the teapot. "I always knew when your mother'd phoned. Ursula was brighter, sharper, you know, and when Isobel said she'd visit—"

"What?"

"Beside herself, she was. Years since she'd seen her, she said. She hoped Izzie'd bring you, too, let her see the woman you'd become for real, not just in photos."

"Photos?"

"She kept them all. Boxes of them there in the press by the fireplace. We'd go through them on a rainy—"

"My mother sent photos?" Lexy lowered her biscuit. "And she was coming here? When . . . *Why?*"

"Well, you'll have to ask her that, won't you now, Lexy? But surely she's told you? It was to be next week, after all. It's there on the calendar." Jenny waved in the direction of the wall beside the door with one hand as she passed Lexy her tea with the other. Three days were circled in thick blue ink. "Which is why," Jenny continued, cradling her own steaming mug and sliding into the bench opposite Lexy, "I thought you'd be her. Ursula had me spring-clean the guest room and I've been keeping it aired and fresh ever since. Then you go and sleep in the *other*—"

"Jenny." Lexy, out of patience, cut across the other woman's prattle. "Jenny, my mother's dead."

After Jenny had gone, Lexy wandered around the flat, listening to the carriage clock ticking away the seconds until she had to leave to get to her appointment with Ursula's solicitor. She'd showered

8

and changed her clothes, even put on some make-up for the first time since her mother's funeral. But still time yawned ahead of her.

She couldn't settle. This was Ursula's flat, not hers, whatever the lawyers might say, and it didn't feel right being there alone. As if she were trespassing in a life she had no right to explore. But she'd have to eventually. She'd have to empty the flat to sell it, go through Ursula's possessions, dismantle her life. Jenny had offered to help as she was leaving, but Lexy had been reticent, politely non-committal, not sure why, except perhaps she couldn't face the endless chatter that would come with the assistance. Jenny's questions, judgements; Lexy's own doubts.

Because now that she was alone, really alone, Lexy's certainties had abandoned her. She was in limbo, drifting, waiting, poised between one version of herself and another. Between child and adult. Between daughter and orphan, fiancée and single woman.

As if on cue, her mobile started beeping again. She pulled it from her bag. Incoming call this time. Danny's name lit up the screen. Guilt and avoidance tussled, but guilt got the upper hand.

"Lexy? Where the heck are you? I've been round to the flat and you weren't there. Mrs B said you'd gone out early yesterday but hadn't come back. When you didn't show up at the crematorium, I was really worried."

"I'm fine, Danny. I'm in Edinburgh."

"Edinburgh? What the blazes are you doing there? And why didn't you answer my calls if you're fine?"

"Sorry, Danny. I didn't want to talk."

"But we were going to collect the ashes for heaven's sake. Your *mother's*—"

"Yes. I know." The righteous indignation in his voice was irritating, but she deserved it. "I'm sorry. I . . . was just . . ." She gave up. There was no excuse so no point in pretending there was. "Did you get them?"

"Yes."

"Where are they?"

"Here. On my desk – and I've got a tutorial starting in ten minutes."

Despite the circumstances, Lexy had to smile at that. At the thought of Danny, junior lecturer with professorial pretensions, conducting a tutorial with his might-have-been mother-in-law's ashes standing watch.

"Sorry, Dan. Can you keep them for me? I'll be back at the weekend and we can—"

"*No.* No, okay? *We* can't anything. I've got plans. We were supposed to do this yesterday. I'd cleared my diary for the afternoon to do this with you. *For* you. The least you could have done is show up."

"I know, Danny. I'm sorry."

"Stop saying sorry, will you? Or at least try to sound as if you mean it." Huffy, now, that note of childish petulance she hated. But, again, she deserved it.

"Dan, I don't know why I didn't call you, or answer your calls, or . . . I . . . Look, something came up."

"Something came up?" Lexy was no musician, but Danny's voice rose what sounded like a full octave. "What could possibly come up that would be more important than your mother's ashes? Oh, you know what? Don't answer that. I'm done. I've tried to support you through this, Lexy, I really have. I know you've got no one else really, and you're useless at asking for help anyway. But we're not engaged any more. I've got Fizz to think about now and she's been great about me spending all this time with you, but I won't let her down by cancelling this weekend. It's important. We're going to her parents'."

"Oh my, meeting the parents? She's taking you seriously, then." Lexy's attempt at light-heartedness sounded snide, even to her.

"It's complicated. She's . . . I mean . . . we're . . ." Danny cleared

10

his throat, and something in his awkwardness told Lexy what he couldn't.

"She's pregnant." It was a statement, not a question. "Wow, that was quick."

"Yes." She heard him sigh, knew he'd be frowning. "I was going to tell you before, but then with your mother and everything . . ."

"Of course. I understand. I mean, great . . . Congratulations. I mean, it is, isn't it? Congratulations? You always said you wanted kids."

"I . . . well . . . I suppose so, yes. Yes, of course. But look, that's not the point. The point is, Lexy, I can't come with you to do the ashes thing, and I don't really want them in my office. It's a bit gruesome, frankly, and I can't take them to Fizz's. So what do you want me to do with them?"

Lexy could picture him there in his office, on the phone, looking awkward and earnest. He was a good man. Kind. But kindness wouldn't have sustained a relationship, a marriage, even if he hadn't been sleeping with one of the department's postgrads. But they'd been beyond salvaging even before—

"Lexy, come *on*! What do you want me to do with her? It. *Them*. Lexy!" His exasperation had developed an edge of panic. Students gathering in the corridor, no doubt.

"Could you drop them round to the flat for me?"

"I don't have a key, remember? You made me—"

"No, I mean could you leave them with Mrs B?"

"Lexy, she'll freak. You know what she's like. Or that malodorous cat of hers'll knock the urn over or pee in it or something." Lexy tried to stifle a giggle, but Danny heard. "Lexy! I'm serious." Didn't she know it. He always was. But that wasn't for her to say any more.

"Sorry. It's all just a bit surreal. Look, I really appreciate what you've done for me. You've been great. I couldn't have got through all this without you. I mean it. Thanks, Danny."

"Lexy . . ." Danny paused and she steeled herself. "Look, Lexy, it's probably not the time and I know things haven't always worked between us, but—"

"Don't, please." Lexy knew where this line of conversation would go if she let it. When he'd turned up at the hospital he'd said no strings, but she'd been on her guard all the same. And she wasn't sure a pregnant Fizz really changed anything. "Danny, thanks. You've been such a good friend to me through all this," she said, picking her words but wincing at the pain she knew they'd cause.

"Not sure I can keep doing that, Lexy." She heard the crack in his voice. "Being your friend."

"I know. I'm sorry, Dan." And she was. Really sorry. She'd miss him. She couldn't remember ever feeling quite so alone.

"Lexy . . ." She could hear him breathing unevenly in the distance between them. Couldn't bear it.

"Look, Danny, how about you put the whole thing in a box? Tape it up to deter smelly cats and nervous neighbours? Tell Mrs B it's just books or something. Could you do that?"

"Sure," he said after a pause, coughing sharply as he cleared his throat. "Fine. Matter of fact, I do still have one or two books and bits of yours. I'll stick those in too and drop it all round later this evening."

"Great. Thanks, Danny." Now was the time for one of them to say goodbye, but the silence still held them together.

"So," Lexy said gently to break it. "A baby, eh?"

"Yeah." She could hear a tiny flicker of excitement creep into his voice. "Yeah. A baby."

She slowly pressed the disconnect button, laid the phone down on the table and stood staring out over the Meadows, arms hugging her chest, not moving until it was finally time to leave.

12

2

Edinburgh, June 4th

Two deaths, two inheritances and two solicitor's offices in as many weeks, although this city firm was very different to the dusty suburban practice Lexy's mother had chosen to use. Lexy perched on the edge of a low-slung leather and steel sofa and looked around her, seeing nothing to lighten her mood. There was none of the comforting chaos of a small family partnership here. Bland Scandinavian-style office furniture which even Lexy knew wasn't IKEA conspired with the burr of discreet phones to create a sense of detachment and distance from the messy business of real life. Behind a desk that looked like it had been designed at NASA, a blonde receptionist with frosty-pink lipstick, a dentally enhanced smile and narrowed green eyes kept vigil. Her sleek perfection made Lexy reach up a hand to smooth her own tumble of curls, though she knew it would make very little difference.

A triptych of commissioned art dominated the wall opposite and Lexy squinted to read the small white panel beside it. It was by an artist she'd never heard of, although no doubt the unpronounceable name was at the leading edge, the very vanguard, of the Next Big Thing. *The Vigilance of Justice, Humanity and Integrity*. Impressive title, but it did nothing to improve Lexy's opinion of the artwork. Childlike naivety was the kindest she could come up with. On balance, she preferred the National Farmers' Union calendar and the Turner prints randomly displayed on the scuffed walls at her mother's Smith & Littlejohn.

"Miss Shaw?" Frosty lips were moving. "She'll see you now."

She. That was different too.

The receptionist indicated a glass wall to the right of her flight deck. As Lexy approached it, a buzzer sounded and one of the panels swung open.

"Straight through please, Miss Shaw, and the conference room is the first on your left. Ms Hamilton will join you there. I've ordered coffee for you."

Lexy was tempted to point out that, like their erstwhile client Ursula, she was not a coffee drinker unless it was guaranteed to be fair trade, but knew that would just sound petty. There was something about this place, though, that brought out the rebel in her. That made her feel more uncomfortable than the high-heeled shoes she'd thought she should wear or the confines of the crumpled suit that hadn't travelled well from London and had responded with indifference to Ursula's iron.

Ms Hamilton, when she finally arrived nearly twenty minutes later, did nothing to improve Lexy's mood. She was crisply dressed, perfectly coiffed and, of course, poised and attractive. A classier and more expensive version of Frosty Lips. The lawyer sat, deftly adjusted her chair to a preferred height and placed a folder on the cherrywood in front of her. Lexy tried to sit straighter in her chair, wishing she'd thought to adjust her own seat height so her feet could touch the floor and give her some leverage. Ground her. But she'd missed her moment. Chances were she'd come off badly if she tried it now, so she'd just have to dangle.

"Sorry to have kept you waiting, Miss Shaw. I was on the phone to our people in Malawi."

"Malawi?"

"Yes, we'd hoped to have all that documented for you, too, for today, but sadly that's proved impossible. Coffee?" A manicured hand waved in the general direction of a sideboard, where the contents of the receptionist's coffee pot would be little better than tepid by now. Unless the coffee pots had been designed by NASA too.

Lexy shook her head, wondering what Malawi had to do with anything.

"Right, let's get to business then, shall we?" Ms Hamilton opened the thin Manila folder and Lexy caught a glimpse of a photo of herself paper-clipped to the inside cover. Ms Hamilton glanced at it and back at Lexy as if to confirm that she was indeed in the right meeting and then extracted a single page, closed the folder again and began to speak.

"Aside from a few small legacies and a recently added codicil leaving a small bequest to her cleaner, Jenny Kennedy, Miss Reid has left her entire estate to you. Well, to your mother initially – my condolences, by the way – but as you are sole beneficiary of Mrs Shaw's estate, Miss Reid's will also pass on to you. We would be happy to continue to handle matters on your behalf just as we handled everything for Miss Reid, should you wish to instruct us to do so, and I know I speak for our associates in Malawi in assuring you that they too would be happy to offer you their services – and absolute discretion – in continuing to manage the interests there and, of course, the financial arrangements between Miss Reid and her son."

Lexy wasn't sure she'd heard correctly. "Miss Reid and her son?"

"Yes. Now unfortunately, as I've already indicated, I'm not in a position to give you up-to-date detail on the Malawi situation, but I hope to have a full and consolidated report shortly. In the meantime, we can discuss the Scottish portion of her estate and what you would like to do with that. That is indeed much more straightforward . . ."

Ms Hamilton's voice faded as Lexy grappled with this new information. Ursula had a son. Alive and in Malawi, it would seem.

15

So why had Ursula left everything to Isobel, her one-time ward, and not to her own son?

Enough. This was all too much. Lexy was exhausted. She couldn't deal with any more surprises. She was still reeling from her mother's death, that pointless, stupid hit-and-run that had set all this in motion and just kept raising question after question. She didn't want secrets and mysteries. She wanted to cling to the certainties of her life before the horror started and find some kind of peace or solace in a familiar world.

"Ms Hamilton, please stop."

The solicitor looked up in surprise.

"I'm struggling to cope with all this, I'm afraid. It's a lot to take in and I'm not sure I'm quite ready to . . . make any decisions or even listen any more. Perhaps we could meet again in a couple of days or so, when I'm feeling a little clearer?"

"Of course, Miss Shaw." The lawyer didn't skip a beat. "I quite understand. You've been through a lot." Lexy was surprised at the note of sympathy in the other woman's voice. "I'll have my PA find us another time. Or why don't you ring when you're ready? I'll do my best to make myself available to suit you." Now that, Lexy was sure, was a real concession on the part of this high-flying, and no doubt high-charging, lawyer.

"I appreciate it, Ms Hamilton. Thank you." Lexy had been too shocked, too numb to cry at her mother's funeral, yet this small kindness was in danger of reducing her to tears. She swallowed hard and looked down at her hands. It was always there, beneath the surface, her grief, that overwhelming sea of sadness, ready to drown her at the most inappropriate and unpredictable moments.

"Not at all. I should have thought." Lexy's head jerked up again at the squeal of Ms Hamilton's chair being pushed back. The lawyer walked round the table, then touched Lexy briefly on the shoulder before stepping back. Legalese for a consolatory hug.

"We always try to act swiftly in these matters, Miss Shaw. For

16

the sake of continuity. But perhaps that's not always appropriate. Look, why don't you take this with you?" The Manila folder was placed in front of Lexy and she stretched her fingers out to touch its nearest edge.

"You don't need me to read it to you, I'm sure," Ms Hamilton continued as she walked over and opened the conference room door. "You can go through it at your leisure. It might be easier to review it in your own time, think things through and then ask me any questions you need to when next we meet. I'll have the Malawi side compiled by then, too; you have my word."

Still fending off tears, Lexy slipped the folder into her bag and followed the solicitor down the corridor towards the reception area.

French-manicured fingernails tapped a code into a panel set on a short pillar in front of the glass door. "You'll find details of the property in Ross-shire in the folder, too. Should you wish to visit it, our receptionist can give you keys and details of how to reach it." There was a buzz and Ms Hamilton held the door back with one arm and extended her other to shake Lexy's hand. "Well, Miss Shaw, I look forward to hearing from you when you're ready."

The door had swung shut again, leaving Lexy on its far side before she could ask what property in Ross-shire that might be, although she knew she should be getting used to the surprises by now.

The late afternoon sun was warm on her face as she stepped out into the quiet heart of Edinburgh's New Town. She walked slowly along the cobbled street before turning left and up the hill towards George Street. She'd seen some pavement cafes there and decided she'd have a glass of wine in the sunshine. There was nothing to rush back to the flat for, and she needed to stop and take stock. There was so much to take in. So much that wasn't as she'd thought it would be, so many questions she couldn't answer – and she didn't know who, if anyone, could. Her mother had let her believe Ursula was dead but had been in touch with her for, it would seem, some time, keeping her up to date with Lexy's own development. And Isobel, so Jenny said, had even been planning a visit to the old woman. A visit she'd not told Lexy about. Would she have, if she'd lived, or would she have kept it secret somehow?

Lexy felt a chill run over her arms. She pulled her jacket off the back of the chair and draped it over her shoulders, shrugged it off again almost immediately. They'd been so close, the two of them, so in tune. She'd been so young when her father died that it seemed it had always just been Izzie and Lexy united against the world. There'd been no one else, no cousins, no distant relatives sending occasional birthday cards, no big family gatherings at Christmas. But it hadn't mattered. They'd had each other. She'd never doubted her mother's absolute love, and she'd never imagined how bereft she would be without her.

The chill returned, and with it a flicker of doubt. Izzie could have tried to make sure Lexy wasn't left alone, that there would be someone else to love her, somewhere else for her to belong should anything happen to Izzie herself. But she hadn't. She'd kept Lexy from Ursula, denied her a grandmother figure in her life. And if she'd done that, what else had she kept from her?

Lexy finished her wine, signalled to the waiter for another one, tried to suppress her growing disquiet. Nothing seemed certain any more, and even the life of a retired hospital matron now looked as if it had been far from straightforward. Ursula, too, had had secrets, it seemed. She had a property in the Highlands and interests in Malawi that had never been mentioned, as far as Lexy could remember, although that was less surprising. Perhaps they were recent acquisitions. She doubted that, though. Malawi was in the past. It was where her parents had met, in the same hospital where Ursula had once worked. That much was part of familiar family lore.

But all of that paled into insignificance in the face of the big one. Ursula had a son. Had Isobel known? With Ursula as Isobel's legal guardian, he would, in effect, have been a kind of brother to Isobel. An uncle to Lexy. Family of sorts, when she'd thought there was no one left. Not a blood tie, true. But the next best thing. Why hadn't anyone told her about him? She felt a flutter of excitement. Hope, really. Hope that there might be someone, some sort of family, that she might still have somewhere to belong.

The second glass of wine didn't make the answers any clearer. Lexy's cheeks were growing warm, and not from the fading sun. Food. She should eat. After an initial burst of hunger that morning when she'd devoured almost half of Jenny's biscuits, she'd had nothing, and wanted nothing, her appetite long gone. No wonder she felt light-headed. Fuel required.

When she got back to Ursula's flat, the post had arrived. She scooped the letters up from the mat. A couple of brown envelopes and one white one which no matter how hard it tried couldn't hide the fact it was a bill. Holding letters addressed to a dead person felt wrong, disrespectful. She'd felt the same way when she'd gone to her mother's house for the first time after she'd died. She hated the way that life carried on without pausing to acknowledge that this person was gone. Unreasonable, she knew, irrational even. How could anyone know what had happened? But it felt cruel, nonetheless. Callous. Unfair.

Suppressing a small stab of unfocused anger, she threw the envelopes onto the table with the rest of the pile waiting to be tackled. She watched it overbalance and cascade onto the tiled floor.

"Bugger." She gathered them up again, picturing the look of disapproval on both her mother's face and Ursula's. "Bugger," she repeated defiantly. She'd get to the post later this evening. Maybe. But for now, she needed a cup of tea and something to eat. Toast seemed simplest. Jenny had said there was bread in the freezer. Time enough to worry about good nutrition when she had less on her mind.

Her phone beeped with a text as she was waiting for the toaster to throw out her supper. Jenny.

Hope went ok today. Remember here to help if U need me.

Kind of her, and above and beyond the call of a cleaner and carer. But then it was clear she'd forged a special relationship with Ursula and seemed happy to extend that to include Lexy. Or perhaps she just wanted to be sure Lexy did right by Ursula in clearing the flat and so on. Remembering the "recently added" codicil, though, Lexy felt a twinge of suspicion and wondered if there was something less wholesome behind Jenny's cheery chat. But if so, what could her objective be? Money, or something that could be turned into it, most likely. Looking around, though, there didn't seem to be much, but then Lexy was no expert. Plenty of paintings on the wall and a few African-looking bits and pieces that could be more than mere bric-a-brac. She'd have to get someone in to value it all.

The toaster popped and snapped her back to the moment. She was being uncharitable. She should just accept that there were genuine, caring people in the world and Jenny was one of them. She was letting the aftershocks of her mother's death cloud her judgement. But it was hard not to, when you knew a stranger had left your mother to die on a quiet suburban street. A drunk, probably, the police had said, classic hit-and-run, and leafy suburbs didn't tend to yield much by way of CCTV or witness statements so best not expect too much. No, not easy to trust in the milk of human kindness after something like that. And especially not after discovering that that same mother, the person you trusted most in the world, had been holding out on you.

20

She dunked a teabag in a mug of hot water just long enough for it to colour into something that passed for tea, splashed in milk and then took it with the toast through to the sitting room. She didn't put the light on immediately but stood for a moment looking out at the long shadows cast by the last of the sun. No one around this late on a weekday evening apart from the odd dog-walker. Yesterday's barbecuing revellers had disappeared. There was a movement at the foot of one of the trees across the road from the flat, at the edge of the Meadows, and Lexy instinctively drew back. Was there someone there, hiding behind the broad trunk of a sycamore? Watching the flat? Watching her? She waited, looked along the shaded path. There was no one in sight, and, when she turned back to the tree, nothing except shadows of branches and leaves, twitching in the breeze. It'd be UFOs and little green men next.

She turned away and sat in one of the old high-backed armchairs, tugging off the ill-judged shoes, stretching her feet and wriggling her toes to get the circulation going again before dragging a footstool closer. Balancing the mug precariously on the arm of the chair and the plate of toast on her knees, she rested her head back. She'd close her eyes for just a moment, let the quiet and the gathering darkness soothe—

She jolted upright at the rattle of the letter box, sending toast and plate skittering across the floor and lukewarm tea splashing into her lap. So much for the smart skirt. Hobbling out to the hallway, holding out the bottom of her skirt to try to contain as much of the milky liquid as possible, she saw a letter lying on the floor inside the door. Its edges were bordered with something she hadn't seen in years: the blue and red chevrons of an airmail envelope.

Intrigued, she stooped to pick it up, hardly feeling the splatters of tea landing on her feet as she let go the skirt hem. She heard the door across the landing close as she read the words *Delivered to*

Flat 8 in error printed neatly in pencil beneath the colourful stamps clustered in the upper corner. She could just make out enough of the frank against their exuberance to see it had come from Blantyre. Malawi.

3

Between continents, June 6th
Lexy stretched her legs out in front of her and flexed her ankles, mirroring the diagrams for health in the air she'd seen in the in-flight magazine, before bringing her feet back to the footrest and realigning her body in the large seat until she was settled and comfortable. She was grinning like a child with candyfloss, but she didn't care. An upgrade to First Class. Things like this never happened to her. But then again, she'd never done anything quite this impetuous before. She'd taken it as a good sign, a sign she was doing the right thing. Not that it mattered if she wasn't. She didn't have to explain herself to anyone any more. Her throat tightened. There was no one left who would expect her to explain.

No. She wasn't going to think like that, feel sorry for herself, feel abandoned and alone. She was doing this so she *wouldn't* be alone. She was going to find ... what exactly? Her mother's ... stepbrother? She wasn't sure there was much of a legal relationship, if any, but Ursula had given birth to one and mothered the other, so there was a connection, and that was all that mattered.

Willing herself to push thoughts of her mother to the back of her mind, she picked up the glass she'd just accepted from the stewardess, held the cool stem and raised it to the window as if tipping a farewell toast to the sun setting over London behind her.

Malawi, here I come.

She sipped the champagne, savouring the froth of bubbles exploding on her tongue, tingling like the excitement she'd felt when she'd walked out of the travel agent in central Edinburgh

23

yesterday with her itinerary in her hand, subduing a sense of alarm at the amount of money she'd just spent by telling herself this was exactly the point of credit cards. This morning she'd been on a train to London, stopped at the flat just long enough to find her passport, pack a bag and put a note through Mrs B's door asking her to hold on to the box Danny had left, and then took the Tube to the airport. Easy. Frighteningly easy.

It wasn't until she'd checked in and gone through security that she'd had a moment to think. Should she be doing this? Why *was* she doing this? Because of a letter from someone she'd never met, to a woman she hadn't seen in more than twenty years? Because she had nothing better to do with the long summer holiday stretching ahead of her than deal with the aftermath of bereavement? Or because she was terrified that if she stood still long enough the full enormity of the last couple of weeks would break over her and bury her in blackness?

She'd stopped dead in the corridor near the boarding gate, paralysed by panic.

"Hey, careful!" someone had growled behind her and then a heavy man sidestepped past with exaggerated effort, turning to walk backwards for a couple of steps so he could shake his head and glare at her. She'd just stood there, petrified, as other passengers navigated their way round her like water round stone. She didn't have to go, she told herself. She could turn around and go home. To her empty flat. To her mother's empty house. No one was waiting for her, just as no one was forcing her to get on that plane. Whatever she did, it was her choice, her decision.

And that was all she'd needed. The recognition that she was in control, was free to choose, calmed her. She chose to get on the plane even if it did feel a bit like running away. So what? No one needed to know. And everything would still be waiting for her when she got back, so if she wanted to go to Malawi, why shouldn't she? It had been where her parents met, where Ursula had worked, where so much of the history of her little family had been forged, and she was curious now, now that there was no one left to tell her about it. Strange that the idea of visiting had never occurred to her before, that her mother had never suggested it, never wanted to return.

Isobel had rarely spoken of her time there, or of her younger life at all, and Lexy hadn't thought to press her. Now, though, she was hungry to know what her parents' early life together had been like before Lexy arrived and took centre stage. She wanted to bring herself close to them again by getting to know something of their younger selves, the people they were before they became defined by parenthood. A ridiculous, desperate notion perhaps, to fight off the loneliness and despair looming in her shadows, to make up for her regret at taking her parents for granted when they'd been alive. Her father she could forgive herself for; she'd only been a toddler when he died and she barely remembered him, just accepted him as he'd been handed down to her by her mother, by the newspaper obituary she'd found tucked in her mother's jewellery box, alongside a heart-shaped locket with a tiny photograph of Lexy as a baby and a faded photo of a young man she'd assumed to be her father, and a lock of baby hair tied with a pink satin ribbon.

But her mother was different. Lexy had made the mistake of not looking, not seeing beyond the maternal to the core of the woman she'd grown up with, of not recognising her mother as anything more than the role she played in Lexy's own life – a mistake she could never put right now. But at least this trip could pay some kind of homage to the woman she wished she'd taken the time to know better, to understand, to befriend. The woman she was furious with for leaving her, but especially for lying to her.

She drained her glass. The champagne had lost its edge. Lukewarm now. Her attempt at devil-may-care spontaneity wasn't really working. She could almost hear Danny lecturing her, as he had so many times before.

"Lexy, why don't you *think* sometimes. Actions have consequences, you know," he'd say in that prissy, patronising tone, as if he were speaking to a student late with an essay because they'd been out on the razzle all night. He could be such a pain at times. Especially when he was right. His lectures always triggered arguments. She'd tell him he was boring; he'd tell her she was behaving like a spoilt child. She'd storm out; he'd shout at her not to slam the door, so of course she would. And then after she'd stomped round the block a few times or kicked the hell out of the leaves in the park, she'd sneak back home again. He'd be reading some academic journal or getting on with his marking as if nothing had happened. Except he'd have to say it. Couldn't help himself. Every time. "You really need to learn to control yourself, Lexy." And they'd start all over again.

But what Danny would or wouldn't have said was, like so much that had guided her life until now, no longer relevant. She was a free agent. She stared at her reflection in the window, clouds beyond her blurring her outline. She was free. She wasn't sure she liked the feeling, but she'd have to get used to it. So, this was a start. Going to Africa to find Ursula's son, an uncle of sorts. And if that letter was right, the fact that it wasn't going to be as straightforward as she'd initially thought just added a little spice. There was a hint of drama, subterfuge even, and she'd always found that sort of frisson irresistible.

The crisp airmail paper crackled as she pulled it from her pocket.

Blantyre Hospital,
May 24th

Dear Ursula,
As you requested, I contacted the Mission on my last clinic tour hoping to be able to put your mind at rest, but I'm afraid the news does nothing to alleviate our concerns. They had recently received

26

a visit from a woman claiming to be the daughter of a German missionary compiling a book of some sort on the history and legacy of European missions in Africa. She was particularly interested in the orphanage and said she was devoting a chapter to the role of the Church in resettling orphaned or abandoned children, but she aroused suspicions when she mentioned a certain name as an example of the work the Mission itself had undertaken in that regard. It is our good fortune that it was Sister Agnes herself who met with this visitor, and needless to say she divulged nothing beyond general statements about past activities, the paucity of records and archives and so on. An invitation to tour the orphanage itself was declined, despite the alleged interest in that area, and the visitor left scarcely better informed than when she'd arrived.

That night, however, there was a break-in at the Mission, the first ever. Malawi isn't what it was when you were here, but it is still safe enough and a crime against the Mission rare indeed, so it seems unlikely to have been a coincidence, especially as it was the archive store that was targeted and vandalised. The whole room was turned over, with papers from files strewn everywhere and paint and bleach poured over everything too, destroying many of the records, or at least leaving them all but illegible. The clearing up and re-filing is proving to be a slow and challenging process and it's difficult to tell yet precisely what's missing, but the papers we are concerned about have not been recovered, at least to date. I fear we must assume they will not be. Sister Agnes clearly blames herself, for keeping them in the first place, but it was what they always did and she was not in a position to break with procedure at the time. I tried to make her see that none of this is her fault, but she seems determined to wear sackcloth and ashes – metaphorically, not literally, we must hope.

Sister Agnes gave me a description of the visitor, but she was cautious as to its accuracy. Not much gets past our friend and she

27

said she was sure the woman was disguised. Most likely wearing a wig, so probably not blonde at all, as she appeared to be, nor German, as the German the woman spoke before they settled on English was, even by Sister Agnes' schoolgirl standards, old-fashioned and stilted, so whatever else she may be, Sister is sure she isn't a native German speaker. The visitor's English, on the other hand, was almost without accent and remarkably colloquial. Beyond that, she was youngish and of average height and build, although loose clothing and heeled shoes could be masking the reality there too, and she had blue eyes. Very blue eyes. Probably tinted lenses, our Sherlock of a Sister suspects. She looked quite suntanned, apparently, as if she'd been in the country a while, but the good Sister again commented that the backs of the woman's hands were paler than her face, so she surmised make-up or fake tan.

In short, the visitor had come disguised and that in itself is enough cause for alarm. But Ursula, perhaps we need to take the initiative here. This is all ancient history and it may be that it's time to bring it out into the open. I don't say that lightly, but times have changed. I understand it would be difficult, that it would stir up painful memories for you, for Gran too, come to that. But surely the lives you both have led are testament to your goodness? You only did what you did because you truly thought it was for the best and no one will blame you for that. I can't see that there's any need to keep these secrets any longer. What would once have been an unimaginable scandal, something that could ruin a career, destroy a business, would be no more than a five-minute wonder now. A headline in one day's paper and forgotten the next. Think about it, Ursula. It may be best for everyone in the long run. Perhaps it's time that the injustices of the past were properly and fairly resolved, or at least some gesture made towards their resolution. No one has to do or be anything they don't want to, after all, but I do feel everyone has the right to be given the choice.

And remember, Ursula, there's no potential for blackmail if there are no secrets.

But know that whatever you decide, you can continue to rely on me to support you. And Gran too, of course, although I've not shared these more recent developments with her. She continues, I'm sorry to report, to fail. But, as ever, she refuses to slow down or make any concession at all to her advancing years or her medical condition. I can see why you two have remained such firm friends for so long – there's more than a little "kindred spirit" shared between you. You share that same formidable determination that just seems to get stronger with each passing year.

There seems to be little by way of good news to send you, I'm afraid. Although there is the possibility that my research application will be accepted and we will be able to expand the programme considerably if that is the case. Malaria is on the agenda again in world health circles, so I am hopeful. Other than that, life in the hospital is as it always is, and Blantyre society continues as always too. I sometimes think we live in a time warp here, and if you were to return, you would find it all much as you left it. But for all that, I'd not be anywhere else. Despite your love and care, those cold years in Edinburgh were proof enough that I need the African sun to keep me warm, although I will try, I promise, to come and visit soon.

I'll leave it to Gran to fill you in on the latest gossip from the Club and your old cronies. She always seems to be well enough to keep tabs on everyone, and besides, I know you'll be waiting to hear what my investigations at the Mission turned up so I'll get this off to you now. But Ursula, please, do reconsider the need to continue with this secrecy. I'm really very concerned for you. You didn't say why you suspected there might have been contact made with the Mission and that bothers me. Is there something you haven't told me? What was it that prompted your enquiry? Whatever it is, please be careful. The threat of discovery is not sufficient reason to put yourself at risk in any way and I worry that you might do that, perhaps without even realising. Would it really be so bad if the truth came out after all this time? I doubt it. It might even end up all being for the best.

Yours, Robbie

Lexy folded the letter again and slipped it back into its envelope. Turning it over in her hand, she reread the black writing on the flap. *Sender: Dr Robert Campbell, Blantyre Hospital, Malawi.*

Campbell. That name as much as the secrets and skulduggery alluded to in the letter had been what had hooked her. It couldn't be a coincidence. Izzie's godmother had been someone in Blantyre, Malawi, called Evie Campbell. They'd not been close, but there'd been Christmas cards and occasional letters that would arrive in similarly chevroned envelopes with the same surname printed neatly, although in a different hand, on the back flap. Her mother had carefully steamed the stamps off the envelopes and Lexy had hoarded them for playground barter, but the letters had dwindled then stopped at some point in her early teens and she hadn't thought about them in years.

Lexy's fingers drummed the envelope where she'd placed it in front of her in the centre of the fold-down table. The "Gran" referred to in the letter could be, *must* be, Evie Campbell. And the secret they were trying to hide must be to do with Ursula's son. It had to be. This 'Mission' must have been involved in some way, and Lexy intended to find out how. She would find Ursula's son and, though they may not know it yet, Dr Robert Campbell and his gran were going to help her do it.

4

The Residence, Blantyre, Malawi, June 7th
As soon as the door clicked shut behind her, Lexy threw herself back on the bed. *Africa*. She'd made it. She was exhausted, but her head was buzzing. Everything around her was new, exotic, exciting. Even the taxi from the airport had been an experience: mismatched colour work, plastic roses in a green Tate & Lyle syrup tin jammed into the drink holder between the front seats and a smell that was not at all the "new leather" aroma her local car wash offered. Lexy doubted very much the driver had insurance, or even a licence, but the daring mood that had swept over her and propelled her on this insane journey prevailed. Life really was too short: her mother's final lesson to her.

Africa. She was here. She kicked off a shoe. *Malawi*. The other shoe slapped down onto the floor, too. The place names were sparking like fireworks in her head. She was actually *here*.

She couldn't help herself. She laughed out loud, drumming her heels against the mattress with sheer excitement. *Africa. Africa. Africa*. For someone who hadn't known where Malawi was until the travel agent had pointed to it on the map, this was incredible.

The sound of her phone was unexpected and alien in this new country and it took her a moment to react. Then, scrambling to her feet, she snatched it from her bag and touched the screen to make it stop, seeing Danny's name too late. Not *again*.

"Danny."

"Lexy, what the blazes are you up to now? Mrs B's in a real state. Says she can't be tripping over your stuff for days and the cat's all upset and keeps mewling at it. I don't need this, Lexy. I really don't."

"I'm fine thanks, Danny. How are you?"

"What? Oh, for heaven's sake. She wants to know what's going on."

"Why's she asking you? She knows we've split—"

"Your mobile was switched off. Again. I've been trying for hours, too. Left a few messages. Not that you're exactly responsive to those."

Lexy hadn't checked. Hadn't realised her phone was getting a signal until it beeped.

"I'm sorry." She was annoyed to find herself apologising, justifying herself, but couldn't stop. "I tried, but she was out and I left her a note explain—"

"Your note, it seems, was vague. She wants to know when you'll be back." Which meant Danny wanted to know. "Saying you'll collect the box when you're back but not saying *when* you'll be back really isn't very helpful you know, Lex."

"This is none of your business."

"You think I don't know that? I'm not exactly thrilled at being involved in all this. I delivered the box, just as you asked, and thought that was an end of it. But then you go and pull another of your ridiculous stunts. Where have you run off to this time? John o' Groats? Land's End? Timbuk-blinking-tu?"

"Close. Or could be. My geography's not too good when it comes to Africa."

She heard Danny catch his breath.

"Where are you, Lex?"

"Not your business, Dan."

"Where?"

"Malawi."

"Where?"

"Malawi. It's in Africa, between Zambia and—"

32

"I know where Malawi is, dammit." He would, too, she thought, more than a little peeved at having her new-found knowledge dismissed.

"Lexy, you've lost the plot, you really have. You've gone on holiday? For heavens's sake, you can't run away like this."

"It's not running away! And it's certainly not a holiday and . . . and it's nothing to do with you anyway."

"I don't know what's going on with you. I can only think grief has unhinged you, or something. Why Malawi? And why now when you've got your mother's estate—"

"Don't really know, okay? Or at least, can't quite explain it. And you'd never understand anyway. Look, like I said, sorry about Mrs B and all that, but I'll deal with it. I'll phone her or send a postcard or something. Just tell her it's nothing to do with you any more, *I'm* nothing to do with you any more, and then you can forget about me and get on with playing happy families with that doting broodmare you've shacked up with."

Lexy heard him gasp, then the line went dead.

She threw the phone down on the bed, then picked it up and threw it down again, harder. It bounced off the bed and clattered onto the polished floor. She kicked it away and threw herself down on the bed instead. Why did he always bring out the child in her? The spiteful brat she'd never actually been. She wasn't proud of herself. She was sickened. She'd hurt him, deliberately, and she didn't really know why.

Maybe because he was a pompous ass. Maybe because he was right. Was she "unhinged"? How could she tell? Grief wasn't something she'd experienced before, not as an adult anyway. How dare he say she was running away? She wasn't. She was . . . she was . . . discovering who she was, who she could be. But she had to admit, she was behaving out of character and all this impetuousness was a little scary. At least she'd managed to avoid telling him she'd bought an open ticket to Malawi. That she didn't know when, or even if, she was going back. She had leave of absence from school till the end of the term, then the holidays, and then who knew? She'd been unhappy there for some time now, not that Danny knew that. He never asked. He'd had no idea what she'd been feeling, even before her mother died.

She ran back over their conversation. The little she'd told him had been enough to provoke his incredulity, his evident disapproval. Judgemental prig. He'd just been using Mrs B as an excuse, probably, a way of keeping tabs on her. Unhinged, indeed. She could feel the stirrings of anger and self-righteousness overcome any lingering panic or fear about her trip. Maybe she had been a bit harsh with Danny, but she'd plead provocation. She could have said she'd come to Malawi just because she could, now she was rid of him, because Danny himself never would have, because she could go anywhere she pleased now that he was out of her life. But that would have been cruel and now she wasn't his lover she didn't want to joust, to score points, to inflict pain.

And yet she had. *Well done, Lexy. Well done.*

She flung her arms wide, struggling to recapture the excitement she'd felt before the phone call, but instead she just felt tired. She'd been too excited to sleep much on the overnight flight. She reached out, stretched through her fingertips, but she still couldn't reach the sides of the huge bed. She could hear crisp linen creak beneath the batik bedspread as she rolled over and propped herself up on an elbow to look out through the open balcony doors to the lush gardens of the hotel. *You can run but you can't hide,* her mother's voice was whispering in her head. Why did everyone assume she was running? She wasn't, or hiding. She was just *here*. On another continent. In another world, and one she was desperate to explore. How could that be running? For the first time since her mother's death, she was looking forward, eyes open wide, instead of looking back, eyes half-shut. And maybe what she discovered here would end up returning a part of her mother, of her past, some of the certainties the last few days had stripped away, with their puzzles and revelations.

Pushing herself up from the depths of the vast bed, Lexy stepped out onto the balcony, where the heat washed over her, as soothing and soft on her skin as cashmere. The balcony was shaded by a climbing jasmine, its tendrils weaving a dense canopy between wooden struts, its white waxen flowers as brilliant against the shadows as stars in a night sky. Beneath Lexy, an immaculate emerald lawn lay like a velvet cushion bordered with hibiscus bushes bursting with blooms in orange and red, yellow and gold. She leant against the balustrade and breathed in the still air, the floral perfumes sweet and cloying, rich and exotic to her hungry senses. She closed her eyes and turned her face to the last of the sun, heard the hum of traffic in the distance, the occasional blast of a horn, the cry of a street vendor, the bark of a dog.

Whatever it was she'd come to find, it was out there, waiting for her.

When Lexy woke, she was disorientated again. After years of waking up in the same bed, with Danny beside her, this was too much change too quickly, too many strange beds and places for her soporific self to take on board. It was the alone-ness. Even when she and Danny were on holiday she'd wake up to the familiar warmth of his body, the sound of his breathing. Or, most mornings, she woke to the sound of his voice and the touch of his hand gently shaking her as she'd slept through yet another cacophony of buzzers and bells. He'd bought her so many different alarm clocks; he couldn't believe her ability to sleep through noise. He'd been beside himself when he'd taken her to the Albert Hall and she'd fallen asleep during the *1812 Overture*.

She shook her head sharply. Danny was the past. Danny was over, a continent away. She was in Africa. She breathed in deeply, stretching her legs out from under her as she sat up, the balcony's rattan sunlounger shifting noisily beneath her. It was dark now and the cricking of cicadas seemed loud in the cooler air. For a second or two she felt panic, the unfamiliar African night intimidating and smothering her like a captor's hood. Then she heard voices below, deep, rich and lyrical in a sing-song English she couldn't quite catch, and she relaxed, feeling a little less alone. She let a tentative smile creep across her face as she stood and stretched more fully, long limbs easing out their cramps and creases, erasing any lingering memories of the long-haul flight.

She was thirsty, so she wandered back into her room and poured water from the jug on the table neatly covered with an embroidered net veil to protect it from she didn't like to think what. She'd slept for nearly two hours. Her suitcase still lay closed on the luggage rack just inside the door, where the porter had left it. She sprung the combination lock and rummaged through the contents until she found her washbag, clothes spilling to the floor as she pulled it out. She stepped over them on her way to the bathroom. She'd unpack properly later. Another couple of hours were hardly likely to make the creases any worse. Packing had never been her strong point. Nor had ironing, come to that.

In the bathroom, the face that peered back at her was pale and dark-eyed. Sleep didn't seem to have helped with that. She ran a comb through tangled hair, splashed water on her face, brushed her teeth and decided that would have to do; it wasn't as if anyone knew her here.

She shrugged one strap of her backpack over her shoulder but caught sight of herself in the mirror as she turned for the door.

"Oh all right then," she muttered, imagining her mother's frown of quiet disapproval. "Lipstick, but that's it."

Still not exactly elegant. She grabbed the end of a cream pashmina trailing from the suitcase and swirled it round her. Better, but surely she could manage the journey to the hotel restaurant without a bulging backpack? Digging deep amongst the travel paraphernalia and the bundle of still-unopened post from Ursula's flat, she extracted her purse, her notebook and the Manila folder the Edinburgh solicitor had given her. She'd tried to go through it on the plane but failed. Perhaps a decent meal and a glass of good wine would help her make sense of it all. She dropped the backpack onto the bed, clutched folder and notebook to her chest like a breastplate and went in search of sustenance.

As she locked her door with the old-fashioned metal key and turned to survey the corridor, she caught her breath. She hadn't paid much attention to her surroundings as she'd been shown up to her room, just concentrated on plodding behind the porter, who'd done his best to pretend her case was feather-light. Perhaps to him it was, but when she'd been hauling it through the airport herself she'd regretted the decision to pack the photo albums Jenny had told her about, as well as the package of papers she'd found beneath them. She'd also thrown in the folder she'd found under the seat of the armchair when she'd been mopping up her spilt tea. There'd been what looked like old letters and diary extracts in that, which had intrigued her. Not her usual type of holiday reading, it had to be said, but then this wasn't her usual type of holiday. In fact, it wasn't a holiday at all, as she'd pointed out to Danny, perhaps a little too emphatically. She still felt bad about that conversation. And the ashes. How could she have done that? Her mother, for goodness' sake. She couldn't, wouldn't think about it. It was like peering over the lip of a deep, dark well and she had no idea what lay at the bottom of it. It frightened her, made her unspeakably sad.

Right now, though, she'd enjoy the moment as best she could. She was delighted to find herself on a wide balcony looking out over a central courtyard, lit softly by lanterns lining the two paths that crossed it like a saltire. Her room, on the upper of two storeys, opened on to one side of this quadrangle, which in turn was open to a purple-blue sky, studded with stars like tiny spotlights and adorned with a sliver of crescent moon dangling over the roof of the wing opposite her.

Wall lamps splashed yellow pools of light over the cane chairs and coffee tables outside each room, mahogany floorboards gleamed, and potted palms and other plants she didn't yet recognise cast living shadows against the plain white walls adorned with occasional paintings of African landscapes. Her footsteps echoed as she walked towards one of the two staircases that swept down from either side of the rectangle, then crossed the patio to make her way back to the reception area to ask for directions to the restaurant.

"Ah, Miss Shaw," the sharply dressed receptionist greeted her as she approached the desk. "We have a message for you."

"Really?"

"It just arrived. We were told not to disturb you but to wait until you came down."

"Thank you." Lexy took the proffered envelope, surprised to see her name handwritten in black ink across its centre. She turned it over, but there was nothing on the reverse to indicate its sender.

"Are you having dinner, Miss Shaw? Barney can show you to the restaurant."

A flick of the receptionist's forefinger summoned a short teenager, resplendent in a bellhop's uniform, to her side.

"Please, follow me, Miss." Lexy followed the boy across the lobby towards a gentle hum of conversation and the muffled sound of piano music playing in the background. He stood back to let her through to the restaurant ahead of him, to the greeting area where a magnificent ornate lectern guarded access to the tables. Double doors opened on to a bar on her right where the pianist's bowed head was just visible beneath the slope of the grand piano's lid. The few occupants of the room ignored him, more interested in each other, or their cocktails at least, than in the music: a lone drinker propping up the bar, a couple of tables taken by elderly, sun-leathered couples, a group of women in cocktail dresses giggling in armchairs by the window. Her mind still on the letter she held in her hands, she stopped in surprise as the lone drinker raised a hand to wave at her, then she lurched forward, dropping the letter as Barney stumbled into her back.

"Oh, I'm so sorry," Lexy said, embarrassed, colliding with the boy again as they both reached for the letter at the same time. "Oh!" She rubbed her forehead, feeling herself blush at the sound of laughter from the bar, surely the lone drinker, amused at the effect he'd had on her.

"My fault, Miss Shaw. Allow me." The boy ducked down, but not before Lexy saw a flash of white teeth as his mouth split into a grin. And she was sure he winked as he handed the letter back to her and ushered her forward again, up to the lectern and out of sight of the bar.

"Sorry – jet lag," she offered by way of excuse, although she doubted the small time difference really made it a very good one. "Thank you."

"No problem, Miss Shaw."

"Barney." A slightly disapproving voice behind her made Lexy spin round to the now-occupied lectern. "That will be all. I'll take care of our guest now." Attention turned to Lexy and the voice changed; its hard edge softened into a slippery obsequiousness that would have put Uriah Heep to shame. "How may I help you, ma'am?"

"I . . ." Lexy was mesmerised by the sheer height of the man, hovering over his lectern like a minister in a pulpit. Or, she thought irreverently, like a vulture. A Disney vulture, straight out of *The Jungle Book*. The hooded eyes—

"A table for Miss Shaw, please," Barney prompted.

"Yes. Sorry. Yes, a table. For one, please."

"Enjoy your meal, Miss Shaw." Barney bowed and was gone before she could thank him.

As she walked the length of the busy dining room, aware of conversation slowing at the tables she passed, their occupants looking up to take in this newcomer, she became increasingly self-conscious. She was glad she'd ditched the backpack but knew it would take more than a pashmina to lend her the air of sophistication such opulent surroundings seemed to demand. At the far end, the restaurant extended out onto a long verandah alongside the same immaculate garden her room overlooked.

"Inside or out, madam?"

"Oh out, please. Definitely out." There were fewer occupied tables on the verandah and these were interspersed with plants and carved fret screens, which offered greater privacy than the expanse of the inside room. As if intuiting her desire for concealment, or deducing from her appearance that she might cause less upset to the regular clientele if tucked discreetly away, the maître d' led her smartly to a small table at the far end of the verandah, beyond the view of the other diners. He held a chair back for her, sliding it gently beneath her as she sat, then snapped a white linen napkin open and sailed it down onto her lap.

"Something to drink, Miss Shaw?" he asked as he laid an open menu down on the table in front of her. "One of our special cocktails perhaps, or might I suggest a glass of champagne as an aperitif?"

"You most certainly might," Lexy said with feeling. She'd earned it after running the gauntlet of that dining room. A slight raising of an eyebrow led her to reappraise him. Not Disney at all. That look was pure Vulcan, all those nights with Danny watching *Star Trek* reruns . . .

"Um, yes." She realised he was waiting for her to speak. "A glass of champagne, please." Champagne? Again? Her conscience pricked her. Hardly appropriate for a grieving daughter. Anyone would think she was celebrating, which she wasn't, or rich, which she most definitely wasn't, but she'd worry about budgeting tomorrow. Besides, she hated to think what would happen to the Vulcan's eyebrows if she ordered a pint of cider.

A slim flute was brought over by a waiter who took her order and then left her in peace to contemplate the still-unopened message she'd tucked inside the cover of her notebook. She was intrigued but reluctant to open it, didn't want to disturb her sense of isolation and distance. Not running. Or hiding, of course. Who was she kidding? Danny had seen straight through her bluster.

But this message. No one was expecting her. No one even knew her here, or knew what had happened to her mother, or to Ursula, which was a big part of why she'd come. Had she even told anyone she was coming? Danny, but this wasn't him. And the lawyer. She was going to contact the office here, but this hardly looked like an official letter. Besides, Lexy hadn't said when she was coming, or where she'd be staying.

She was rattled. She'd been relishing the feeling of anonymity, of freedom. That someone had found her, had seen fit to communicate with her already had dispelled that all too quickly. She'd open it after dinner. *Procrastination, thy name is Lexy*. She tucked the note away at the back of her notebook again and pulled the Manila folder towards her. This too she'd been putting off, despite carrying it with her since the lawyer gave it to her. But that didn't mean she wasn't going to face up to her responsibilities and sort out Ursula's affairs. And then her mother's. How dare Danny think she was running away? She flicked open the folder and started browsing through the pages of numbers and legalese. A foreign language, in black and white and—

"Miss Shaw?"

She swept up the folder and sat back, expecting a plate to be placed in front of her, looking up when it wasn't. A tall, fair-haired man sporting a blazer and what had to be a regimental or old school tie smiled down at her. The lone drinker.

"Yes?" Lexy managed, remembering the wave, wondering if she should know him, certain she didn't.

"Forgive the intrusion." He paused, as if expecting her to say something, but she had no idea what.

"Pendleton," the man continued, smoothly. "Hugh. Consular service. Saw you come in. How do you do?"

"I'm sorry . . . Do I . . . Is there a problem?"

"Good heavens, no. Didn't mean to alarm you. No problem at all. I always try to make visitors welcome, you see, show them around, help them get the most from their time in Malawi and so forth. Make sure they know who to come to if they need a hand, which is me, of course. Pleased to meet you."

"Oh, I see," Lexy said, shaking his damp hand, although she didn't see at all. Surely this level of attention wasn't normal from a consular service. Even somewhere like Malawi. More likely some lounge lizard ploy to chat her up. She'd stop that in its tracks. "Thank you, but I'm fine."

"Nonsense." Hugh's free hand waved dismissively. "All part of the service. Anything I can do and all that. Join you for a moment, shall I?"

Releasing her hand, he crashed heavily into the seat opposite, sending a shockwave across the table that upended Lexy's champagne glass, its contents frothing over the notebook and Manila folder she'd just laid back down like spume from a breaking wave.

"Oh I say!" He snatched up the notebook and Lexy grabbed the folder. Waiters with cloths appeared almost immediately and a flurry of wiping and rearranging of linens and cutlery ensued.

"Awfully sorry about that. No harm done, though, all salvageable." He was flicking through the notebook to let the pages dry without sticking together, but a little too slowly, as if trying to read what was written there.

"I'm sure it's fine now, thanks." Lexy reached across to reclaim the notebook, giving him no choice but to drag his eyes up from the page and hand it over. As he did so, the envelope she'd tucked inside the back cover fluttered down onto the tabletop between them. Hugh picked it up, turned it over and back, studied her name scrawled on the still-sealed envelope and frowned.

"You don't seem to have opened this. Forgot it, did you?" The affable, cultivated bonhomie reappeared, but she could feel his eyes watching closely as she took it from him.

"It's just arrived. I haven't had time."

"Don't mind me. Might be urgent."

"I very much doubt it." Lexy looked around for a waiter. Vulture or Vulcan, she was relieved to see the maître d' acknowledge her from deep within the restaurant and start off in her direction.

"Won't know unless you open it."

What was the matter with the man? "Look, Mr Pendleton—"

"Oh *Hugh*, please."

"I don't wish to be rude or unsociable or anything, but I really am rather tired."

"Anything I can do for you, ma'am?" The maître d' cast the briefest of glances in Hugh's direction. "Sir."

"No, we're fi—"

"Thank you, yes," Lexy cut in. "I wonder, could you arrange to have my supper sent up to my room? I think the jet lag's catching up with me."

"Of course, ma'am. Right away." He melted away as smoothly and swiftly as he'd arrived.

Lexy stood and Hugh stumbled roughly to his feet.

"I say, nothing I said I hope."

"Not at all, Mr Pendleton." Lexy saw a sudden scowl crumple his face.

"*Hugh*."

"It's just it's been a very long day and I think I was a bit overambitious coming down for dinner. Please excuse me."

She smiled as best she could as she struggled to mask the irritation she was feeling. All she'd wanted was a quiet dinner, alone, looking through her notes and planning how she'd spend the next few days. Which, whatever else, would not be in the company of Mr Humongous Pain Pendleton.

"Another time, then. Spot of supper perhaps. Could show you some of Blantyre's—"

"Thank you, but I've got quite a busy schedule ahead of me. Goodnight, Mr Pendleton." Cheap shot, but she couldn't resist. Lexy smiled sweetly as the scowl returned to his pink, fleshy face. She sincerely hoped that was the last she'd see of it.

Lexy was relieved to return to the sanctuary of her room, even though she'd forgotten just how much of a mess she'd left behind her. It looked like a crime scene, as if she'd been burgled or a spook from MI5 had ransacked the room looking for that missing microchip or whatever. But no. She knew she was quite capable of creating this level of turmoil all by herself.

Her backpack had fallen from the bed, where she'd flung it before going down for dinner, and Ursula's unopened post was now scattered over the floor along with Dr Campbell's letter and the other paraphernalia of travel. Her suitcase, too, seemed to have developed a will of its own, maliciously tangling clothes and papers and spewing them randomly from its open jaws. *More haste less speed.* Her mother's voice again. Her mother had had an amazing repertoire of proverbs and sayings, something for every occasion. Even now.

She flipped open the suitcase and started to shake out clothes. Her mother was right, of course. If she'd taken the time to unpack properly rather than just rummaging and yanking out what she'd needed, it wouldn't be such a chore now. In fact, if she'd taken the time to *pack* properly in the first place . . . She wished she could tell her mother she'd always known she was right, but it was just that teenagers didn't admit to stuff like that. But she couldn't. She wouldn't be telling her mother anything ever again.

She shoved the last of her underwear into a drawer and slammed it shut. She wouldn't be sad. Not on her first night here in Malawi, the place her parents had met, where she'd been conceived. Happy thoughts, not sad ones, were more suited to memories like that.

She ate her supper on her balcony, with cicadas and moths for company. Far more amenable than Pendleton. She left the tray outside her door, locked herself in for the night, then curled up on the chaise longue on the balcony with the first of the photograph albums. A trip down memory lane could be dangerous territory after she'd been drinking champagne, albeit not very much before that man knocked it over, but nonetheless she'd chosen carefully. This one was labelled *Africa*, so she was unlikely to be hijacked by any unexpected glimpses of herself growing up with her parents. She couldn't face anything like that yet.

The album had been painstakingly assembled, each photograph fixed in place with corner mounts, with a brief description inked beneath it or to one side in evenly spaced copperplate handwriting: *Zomba, May 1st 1947, Danish Embassy Upper Shire River Orphanage Fundraising Event, Helen and Ursula seated, Frederik Stenberg (Cultural Attaché) and Jurgen Axelsen (Director) standing.*

Or later: *Blantyre Hospital, March 22nd 1949, Outpatients' Clinic Opening Ceremony, L to R: Dr Campbell and his wife Evelyn, Matron Proudfoot, Sister Reid, Padre McFee.*

Or later still: *Lake Nyasa, August 1949, Helen's Birthday Picnic. Standing L to R: Cameron, Fredi, Douglas, Gregory. Seated L to R: Evelyn, Helen, Ursula.*

Lexy smiled at Ursula's sense of propriety. She never said "me" but always gave her name as if the album had been compiled by some absent hand, her own presence in any of the photos nothing more than a happy coincidence. Nor did she use diminutives unless the occasion allowed it. *Fredi* on a picnic became *Frederik*

45

Stenberg (Cultural Attaché) if photographed in his formal capacity, and *Douglas* was most definitely *Dr Campbell* when he appeared professionally.

As Lexy turned the heavy cartridge pages, she began to recognise the faces peering dimly back at her in the flickering light of the citronella candles she'd lit to keep the insects at bay. She began to understand the relationships between the names, the parts they'd played in Ursula's life, to recognise the recurring faces of Ursula's inner circle. Evelyn and Helen appeared more frequently than any of the others; Gregory and Cameron only a little less often; then, a little less prominently yet, Fredi and Douglas, Evelyn's husband. Tennis games, croquet, picnics all featured regularly, as did cocktail parties, fundraisers, balls. But so too did the hospital. Ursula, it seemed, had been, even then, the dedicated professional of Lexy's childhood, and only occasionally a young socialite Lexy barely recognised.

Somewhere in this circle, this smart set of bright young things, lay the answer to the mystery of Ursula's son. The frequent recurrence of the Campbell name alongside the photographs gave Lexy heart. The Dr Campbell of the letter she'd brought with her could not, of course, be the same Dr Campbell in the photographs, but he had to be related in some way. Grandson, perhaps, if Evelyn was "Gran". But she'd find out more tomorrow when she visited the hospital. Returning the letter to Dr Campbell would be the first step towards the answers she was seeking.

Lexy wandered back into the bedroom. She'd risk a look through Ursula's folder, the one she'd found under the armchair cushion, intriguing simply because it had been in such an odd place. She'd piled most of the paperwork from her backpack on top of the chest of drawers. She couldn't see the tea-stained folder at first, but before she started to search, her attention was caught by the other two photograph albums. One was clearly marked Edinburgh, which she was not up to just yet, sure it would contain pictures of her mother, maybe even of Lexy herself on one of their visits. But the other had no identifying label, so she decided to take it to bed with her. The diary could wait, her wilting brain more likely to make sense of pictures than words, anyway.

As she lay back against the padded headrest swaddled in crisp linens, she opened the album, and immediately wished she hadn't. Izzie in profile, laughing, her head tilted back in a pose so familiar Lexy's stomach contracted and the picture blurred as tears sprang with raw suddenness to her eyes.

She turned the page quickly and immediately realised her mistake as she recognised the faces staring out at the camera in the next photograph. Ursula and Helen, standing in front of a white wall, a house of some description. Lexy could just make out an edge of window to the right, and to the left, a thick bank of flowering bushes. Even though the print was only black and white, she knew it would be a blaze of colour, like the banks of azaleas and hibiscus around the hotel's lawns. The women were looking straight at the camera, holding a baby between them, their hands clasped over the baby's chest, their clothes and hair screaming 1940s.

Lexy sighed. Perhaps young, happy women all look like each other and she'd seen her mother in someone else's features because that's what her subconscious was most afraid she would see. She turned her face up to the ceiling and let the whirring ceiling fan dry the moisture from her cheeks. She closed her eyes, but a different picture burned brightly on her eyelids now, like a slide from a projector casting its image on a plain wall in a darkened room. Izzie. It wouldn't fade.

The damage was done, and she wouldn't sleep now. The shock had rippled through her and left her shaken and wide awake. She turned her attention back to the album open in her lap.

Her breathing deepened and calmed as she studied the image, but then her heart thudded again. Whose baby was it? Hard to tell, the way they stood shoulder to shoulder, each embracing the child. Was it Ursula's? Or Helen's? Or someone else's? Anyone's. The person taking the picture, or perhaps they were visiting the orphanage and it was one of its babies. It didn't have to be Ursula's just because she was one of the women holding it. Lexy peered closely, but there was no way of telling if it was a boy or a girl. No telltale pink or blue in a black and white, now sepia-tinged photograph. No ribbon in the bonnet-covered hair. No frilly dress to be seen beneath the plain knitted baby blanket swathing the sleeping child.

Her hand trembled slightly as she turned the page. More of the baby, but on its own this time. Surely it was the same one: it was hard to tell, but it had to be, didn't it? And as she looked at the photos of the baby growing up, turning the pages as the child progressed from passive bundle to active toddler, it became clear it was indeed a boy, so it had to be. It had to be Ursula's son.

Impatiently, Lexy continued to flick through the pages, looking for more of the precise copperplate, a word, a name to give her a clue, to confirm her growing certainty that this was Ursula's son, but there were no notes, nothing. Nor were there many adults in the pictures. In fact, there was hardly anyone else at all—

There she was again. The ghost of her mother. Grief playing tricks on her as exhaustion tightened its hold on her crammed mind. She blinked, rubbed her eyes, refocused on the picture of a woman sitting in a high-backed rattan chair like the throne of an Indian maharajah, with the infant standing beside her and another baby held in her arms, woman and young boy both staring down at the unseen face adoringly. Helen. It was Helen, but that still didn't mean the children were hers. The boy could still be Ursula's son.

Clinging to hope, Lexy continued to turn the pages, saw both children, both boys, playing together as they grew up, more and more people appearing with them. Still there were no captions, no dates, places or names, but having recognised Helen, Lexy began to recognise most of the others populating these captured moments, remembering them from the other album she'd reviewed. Helen and Gregory, Cameron, sometimes Evelyn and occasionally Douglas, even Fredi once or twice. Other children came and went, as did birthday parties, Christmas celebrations, first school uniforms, sports days, school plays and so on through the years. All the usual childhood landmarks were recorded, the boys taller, clearer as time passed and traits of the men they would become began to be chiselled into their faces. Here a photo of Helen and Gregory either side of the boys seated on bicycles; there a photo of Cameron teaching the elder boy to hold a golf club; and yet another of Cameron buried in sand with both boys standing to attention either side of him, spades held like rifles against their shoulders as they laughed at the camera, the family resemblance strong.

It was clear this was a close circle of friends, the boys as much a part of it as each of the adults. Ursula herself had only appeared in that first photo. Had she returned to Scotland by the time the rest of these were taken? Had someone sent them to her as a way of keeping her up to date with . . . what? The life she'd left behind? The children growing up? Her son? Lexy felt her disappointment bite as she accepted the two boys were clearly brothers, and given Helen's regular appearance as the one tending to them, holding them, hugging them, she had to conclude they were Helen's boys.

The first of the colour photographs removed any lingering doubt, or hope, that she'd stumbled so easily on Ursula's son. It was a formal family portrait, with Helen sitting in the centre, Gregory and Cameron standing side by side behind her chair, and her two sons, one on either side of her, like smaller, younger versions of the men, the elder boy of his uncle Cameron, the younger of his father Gregory. A matching pair of brothers in each generation. History waiting to repeat itself, Lexy thought, and wondered if it had. Gregory disappeared from the photos shortly after that, as did Evelyn and Douglas, and the last few were mainly of the two young brothers, Helen and Cameron appearing only once or twice, before the photos stopped altogether. The final photograph, again a formal portrait, showed the two boys, now almost teenagers, standing side by side, the elder of the two awkwardly holding a baby, which this time, judging by the profusion of crocheted lace tumbling from his arms, was a girl.

Lexy flicked through the final, blank pages of the album. Stuffed in-between the last page and the cover were a handful of newspaper clippings, all about the Buchanan Trading Company, and all dating from the last ten years. David Buchanan-Munro, CEO, and his uncle Cameron Munro, chairman, were pictured in one, opening a new wing at Blantyre Hospital, the Helen Buchanan Wing, in memory of a much-loved wife and mother. Others, older, reported that the company had successfully expanded their South African operation, won a new contract to supply the Church of Scotland Missions, to supply government schools, launched a new transport division. That Cameron had been awarded an honorary doctorate from the University of Zomba, that David had been appointed president of the Chamber of Commerce. The family and their company seemed to be going from strength to strength, although no mention was made of a brother or sister to David and Lexy wondered what had become of them and, indeed, of their mother, Helen, to have merited the hospital wing in her honour. Her curiosity would need to be curbed, however. Fascinating though the Buchanans seemed to be, she was here to find Ursula's son, and find out anything she could about her own family.

5

The Residence, June 8th

"Lexy, are you listening to me? Lexy!"

Danny. Danny's voice. Why was she dreaming about Danny?

"Lexy. Answer me!"

Phone. She was holding a phone. Danny was on the phone. Oh, for God's sake, again? She sat up in bed, heart thudding so hard it kept the irritation she wanted to feel at bay.

"Danny, yes. Danny. Sorry. What did you say?"

"The flat. You've been burgled. Mrs B phoned me."

"What?"

"They'd kicked in the front door. Mrs B was at her whist club but came back to find your flat door open. She was pretty much hysterical when she phoned."

"But what . . . I don't understand."

"Burgled, Lexy. Keep up, for crying out loud."

"Back off, Danny! I was asleep. Do you know what time it is here?" Her anger turned into mild embarrassment as she looked at the clock and saw it was mid-morning.

"Hey, no need to shout. Of course I know what time it is." He would, she realised. "Listen to me, Lex. Someone broke in to the flat. I've been round and it's a mess. They've emptied out all the drawers, cupboards, you name it. Turned the whole place over."

"Well, I didn't leave it particularly tidy . . ."

"No, Lex. This is beyond even you at your best. Really. Someone's been in there. You've been burgled. Well, I say burgled, but . . ."

Lexy was wide awake now and conscious of a creeping nausea.

"When? When did this happen?"

"I just told you. When Mrs B was at her whist. The police have been round, but—"

"The police?"

"Mrs B called them before I got there. And anyway, of course the police. It's a crime and you'll need to have that reference number or whatever for your insurance claim, although . . ."

"Although?"

"Well, the police were asking if I thought anything had been taken, and I said I couldn't be sure, of course, but . . ."

Lexy's heart was still thumping hard, blood roaring in her head, arms tingling with pinpricks of adrenaline. Her flat. Her *home* ransacked. And she was on the other side of the world. She realised Danny had stopped talking.

"But what, Danny?"

"The police said it looked as if they were looking for something specific. None of the obvious stuff had been taken – TV, music, that sort of thing, it was all still there. But all your books had been pulled off the shelves, opened, and your files were scattered everywhere. Even the freezer, Lexy. They'd pulled everything out of that, too. The cat was going mad trying to get to the fishfing—"

"Why would anyone do that?"

"Apparently people sometimes bury valuables under the frozen peas or something."

"Dan, for Chrissake, not the freezer. Why would anyone do this at all? To *me*?"

"Look, I don't really know. But if they were looking for valuables, they didn't take them. I checked your jewellery and it looked to me like it was all still there. It had been tipped out onto the floor but there didn't seem to be anything of value missing."

"How would you know that?"

"Because I gave you half of it. And I was the one who got it all valued for you for the insurance, remember? You said I was fussing, but perhaps now—"

"Not the time, Danny."

"Well, just saying. Oh, and the cash you keep in the kitchen drawer?"

"Still there."

"Yes."

"But what could they possibly have been looking for, then?"

"No idea."

"What are the police saying?"

"Not much. Asked a lot of questions about you."

"Like?"

"Just like who your friends were, what you did, you know. Where you were." Lexy heard the disapproval in that last one.

"I see."

"I don't think you do, Lexy." He was off again. The lecturing.

"Danny, I'm in Malawi. I haven't run off to a terrorist training camp or set up a drugs cartel in Colombia."

"They asked me if you'd been behaving oddly lately." He sniffed. "And I had to say you had been acting a bit strangely. Not been yourself—"

"My mother's just died. Of course I'm not myself."

"Well, quite. But not turning up to collect her ashes, even."

"I explained about that!" She could feel her pulse quickening, her colour rising.

"No, you didn't. Not really. And then running away to—"

"I haven't run— No. No, Danny, I won't do this."

"Do what?"

"Fight! Argue with you. Explain myself to you."

"If only you would. Instead of leaving me to pick up the mess you leave behind."

"I didn't ask you to—"

"What am I meant to do? Mrs B didn't know who else to call

53

and I can't just leave your flat like a bomb site or tell the police I know nothing and pretend I don't care!"

They both fell abruptly silent, the words quivering in the air between them. She took a deep breath. This kept happening. It had to stop.

"Danny, I don't know what to say. I'm sorry. I . . . Look, I'll come home. I'm not sure when I can get there, or how, so it'll be a few hours before I can organise anything, but if you could just hold the fort for me until . . ." Lexy sighed. She felt bad asking him, but she didn't know what else to do. Didn't know how to deal with this.

"No, don't. I've arranged for a locksmith. Should be here soon. And I've calmed Mrs B down." Danny was all practicality again, the emotion of a moment ago buried but, Lexy knew, not resolved. "I'll tidy things up a bit, too – the police say it's all right to do that now they've been in and done what they need to. And so there's not really much else you can do even if you do come home. So stay. You might as well."

"But Danny . . . I probably should . . ."

"I don't understand why you went out there in the first place, Lexy, but you clearly felt you had to, so stay. Do whatever it is. I'll take care of things here. It's okay."

"But what about Fizz? Won't she—"

"No, she won't."

"But I thought you said—"

"Do you want my help or don't you?" Lexy was silent. "Right. So. I'll keep you posted if anything develops."

Lexy tried to thank him, but the line was already dead. She hugged her knees into her chest, protecting herself against a chill that had nothing to do with the temperature in the room.

The hotel was tranquil and cool after the frenetic activity of the street outside. In a burst of enthusiasm, Lexy had ventured out on a brief excursion in an attempt to get her bearings. It had been fascinating, challenging and exhausting in equal measure. She'd seen enough to be sure already that she was going to like it here. There was a lightness, a light, that was special. But Malawi's exuberance would take a bit of getting used to, she realised. After only an hour, hot and flushed and a little unnerved by the persistent attentions of street hawkers and shopkeepers alike, she'd returned to the hotel to regroup, the retinue of small children she'd acquired only hesitating for a moment before following her up the Residence's driveway, giggling and gambolling towards the facade.

"You need to go now," she said, turning to them. "I don't think you should come in ..." But the children were laughing and pushing each other and paying her no attention at all. Just like her class at home.

Barney appeared beside her, clapped his hands and rattled off something she couldn't understand and they ran, laughing and shouting as they raced each other back out to the street.

"Thanks, Barney. I tried ignoring them, but they just kept coming."

"They don't mean harm, Miss Shaw, just nosey."

"Oh, I'm sure. My fault really. Probably should just have gone for a walk in the hotel grounds."

"Yes ma'am, but not so much fun, eh?"

"No," she admitted, "not so much. Right, tea, I think." Lexy stepped into the shade of the portico, but Barney quickly moved in front of her.

"On the verandah perhaps, Miss Shaw? You can come this way." He indicated that she should step back outside and led her to a path that ran round the hotel. "The lobby's very busy this afternoon. Lots of people, waiting for certain guests to come back."

"Ah." Lexy thought she understood. "Some of our consular officials possibly?"

"I think so, ma'am." Barney, it seemed, was a useful ally.

Settled comfortably as before at a corner table out of sight of any casual glance from the hotel dining room, Lexy ordered her tea. She would have liked to have showered or at least splashed water on her face first, but the thought of running into the Pendleton man again, who, if she was to understand Barney correctly, was lying in wait for her in the lobby, was more than ample reason to put up with feeling a little limp and grimy.

Her walk had been more arduous than she'd expected, true, but it had been dazzling. She'd loved it. She'd seen documentaries and news features about Africa and had an idea of what it might be like, but nothing had prepared her for the full-frontal assault on her senses that hour walking through the town had been. Africa in 3D. The smells of spices and fruits as she'd walked through the market a welcome relief after the rank aftermath of the fish market being hosed down by a man wearing nothing but a loincloth and a pair of mismatched wellingtons, a pack of thin cats watching and prowling in and out of each other, as if dancing a feline cotillion. The noise too. From all directions, an untuned orchestra of instruments jamming together to create a soundscape that lifted her spirits and reminded her of what it was to be alive, to be searching, to be of the world rather than spectating. Colours in motion, swaying bodies carrying baskets and bundles on high heads, buses overflowing like spilt paint pots, batik fluttering like bunting from a washing line. And blazing down on everything, the sun: its heat, the feel of it drenching her clothes, firing her skin, dust drying in her eyes, her throat. She was exhausted, yes, but exhilarated, energised by her walk in a way she'd never been by the drab, familiar streets of her London suburb. Already she knew her mother would have loved it, and she wished Izzie had brought her here to share it with her, let her see it through her mother's eyes. Had her mother walked that street, come here to take tea in this oasis of elegance, just as she herself was doing? She wanted to believe so.

She pulled her notebook from her bag, and as she sipped the last of her tea, she browsed through the pages, edges crinkled from their champagne bath, but the notes she'd made on the plane intact. She'd tried to make sense of Ursula's affairs as summarised in the Manila folder, not to be confused with the tea-stained one she'd found under Ursula's chair. That one looked much more personal and interesting but would have to wait. *The Manila Folder*. It should be the title of a "jolly good adventure for girls" by Enid Blyton perhaps, or a Bogart and Bacall movie, or a Graham Greene novel. Any of them would be much more appealing than what it actually was: the sum total of a life lived by a woman Lexy knew very little about but who had bequeathed her all her worldly goods, along with the story that wove them together – unintentionally, it was true, but Lexy owed it to her mother to take it seriously. It weighed heavily on her mind both as a responsibility to the dead and as a clue to the living. She was sure she'd find the trail to Ursula's son somewhere in the Manila folder if she looked carefully enough.

She started to make sense of her notes. Most of her questions related to three areas. First, and perhaps most straightforward, there was the 'Ross-shire property' Ms Hamilton had dropped in as a parting shot at the end of their meeting. Paperwork documented its purchase and then a few years later a lease had been drawn up, although the copy in the folder was unsigned, the space for the tenant name blank. Nothing since. Did that mean the property had been let for a period, and if so, was it still tenanted? Or had Ursula changed her mind and the lease was just there should she need it at a future date? And where and what exactly was this property? It was referred to by name, Taigh na Mara, but nothing more, and that was hardly helpful. For some obscure, forgotten reason Lexy knew the name meant house of the sea in

Scots Gaelic, but given the miles and miles of ragged coastline in that part of the world, it was likely to be as popular a house name up there as Dunroamin for Scots exiled anywhere else. Not exactly unique, in other words.

Second, Ms Hamilton had also referred to financial arrangements between Ursula and her son. Apart from the obvious question here, as to the son's identity, Lexy had been unable to find any trace of these payments in Ursula's bank statements, the most recent copies of which had been included for each of the three accounts: current, savings and some sort of investment account. In amongst the post she'd brought with her from Ursula's flat, there'd been a credit card statement and some correspondence relating to Ursula's pension but nothing to suggest there was another account of any sort anywhere. So what exactly were these payments? And in which direction did they flow between Ursula and her son? There was no regular unexplained debit or credit to give any clue. But follow the money, they said, and she'd find it somehow. It was her best chance of tracing the mystery man.

And finally, there were a series of what appeared to be share certificates for the Buchanan Trading Company, all dated more than thirty years ago. Lexy had no idea what they might be worth, or what to do about them, or even if she could do anything. A note on the lawyer's summary cover sheet referenced them as 'held in trust for RBM', but she hadn't been able to find any further reference to RBM in the folder. Who or what was RBM, and did this mean she'd become a trustee of some sort through this inheritance? Ursula's inheritance, it seemed, came with responsibilities for someone, or something, Lexy didn't know. But the lawyers would.

She glanced at her watch. Time to go. She could phone Ms Hamilton later. She should probably let her know where she was staying in Malawi anyway. Perhaps their office here would have completed the summary of Ursula's Malawi interests by now and

Lexy could deal with them on that directly, although the thought of yet more lawyers and complexities didn't fill her with cheer. Was this what death was all about, she thought bitterly, lawyers and "interests"? It seemed such a brutal way to package up a life, a loved one. She stood up quickly, snatched up her notebook and squared her shoulders. *Stay focused.* She had work to do, and right now, that meant an appointment with Dr Campbell of Blantyre Hospital.

6

Blantyre Hospital, June 8th

The reception area was cool and calm. Lexy was impressed. She'd expected something noisier, busier, more like A&E on a television programme. But here, on a warm June afternoon, staff in pristine uniforms passed almost silently through the rows of benches and seats, collecting patients, returning them, handling their family and friends in reassuring, well-modulated tones. If all Malawi's hospitals were like this, Lexy wondered why her parents had ever returned to the UK.

"Miss Shaw?" An efficient-looking woman in a black skirt and glowing white blouse stood in front of her. "I'm Dr Campbell's secretary. Audrey Lanakela."

"Pleased to meet you," Lexy said as she rose and extended her hand.

"And I you." Audrey inclined her head, then led the way down wide, tiled corridors. "Dr Campbell's in theatre, but he'll be finished shortly. You can wait in his office."

As they walked, Audrey's polite questions prompted Lexy to explain why she was here, where she'd come from and, Lexy realised, almost everything about the last few weeks of her life. Impressive. CID could learn a thing or two.

They climbed a short staircase that opened onto a balcony running around an interior patio similar to that in Lexy's hotel but more functional, and without the plants and soft lighting. Again, though, doors opened off each side of the rectangle and Audrey stopped in front of one bearing Dr Campbell's name engraved on a brass plate that glimmered like gold.

"Here we are. Please." Audrey showed Lexy in and indicated one of two rattan sofas facing each other across a low coffee table. There was nothing on the glittering glass surface, not even a fingerprint as far as Lexy could see. In fact, there was nothing on any of the surfaces in the office.

"Can I get you anything, Miss Shaw?"

"No, thank you. I'm fine. It's amazingly tidy in here."

Audrey beamed at the observation. "He's hardly ever here, so it's easy enough to keep things in order. Dr Campbell spends most of his non-clinical time in his research lab – and that's a very different story. Overflowing with papers and equipment and goodness knows what. No one's allowed to touch anything there – I believe it's a dismissable offence even to try."

Realising it was expected of her, Lexy laughed. "That explains it. Because doctors are said to be the most untidy individuals on the planet, after all."

"I wouldn't know. I've only ever worked for Dr Campbell."

"Really?"

Was that a touch of reproval in Audrey's voice? Had she thought Lexy was being critical or was it simply that humour was not to be reciprocated? Lexy decided to be cautious just in case. "I would say he's very fortunate." Silence. She ploughed on. "And how long is it that you've been with him?"

"Nearly ten years now, ever since—" Audrey stopped abruptly, leaving Lexy intrigued.

"Since . . . ?"

"I finished school." Audrey busied herself brushing imaginary dust from the top of a bookcase, then straightening the already straight books on one of the shelves.

"Well, if his office is anything to go by, he's lucky to have you." Lexy knew she'd been fobbed off and hoped the compliment

61

would smooth over any offence her question may have caused. *Curiosity killed the cat.* Her mother was back.

"He's a brilliant man, you know." Audrey's features were relaxed and smiling again. "He's been so good to my family. Without him . . ." She trailed off and again Lexy's curiosity rumbled like hunger, but before she could think of a tactful way to find out more, Audrey was leaving.

"Well, I must get on." Audrey clicked a switch and the ceiling fan began to stir. "Will you be comfortable here?"

"Yes, thank you. Perfectly." The door shut quietly and Lexy was alone.

So this Dr Campbell was something of a hero, to the devoted Audrey and her family at least, Lexy mused, deciding that the efficient Audrey was suffering from a monumental crush on her boss. The passion of those tight-laced PAs should never be underestimated. He *had* to be related to the Dr Campbell in Ursula's photo album, didn't he? Too much of a coincidence, otherwise. Lexy had to find a way of asking without appearing to interrogate him before he'd had a chance to take on board the fact that Ursula was dead. Exercise tact, restraint. Neither were her strong points.

She wandered round the empty office looking for clues to the man she was about to meet. But there was nothing. No photos, no ornaments, not even a discarded scrap of paper in the bin. The adoring Audrey's hand, no doubt.

Well, nothing else for it: she'd just have to be patient. Something else that didn't come naturally. *Patience is a virt—* Lexy shut off her mother's voice. Oddly comforting how vividly all her mother's homilies were coming back to her. It made her feel her mother hadn't left, was still with her. Perhaps that was what happened when someone died: you absorbed a part of them into your own self. A spark from the eternal flame.

Lexy shook her head to stop the thoughts. Wicker creaked and groaned as she settled back into the depths of one of the sofas. So much of this furniture everywhere. No chance of a quiet sit-down. She let her mind drift, the soft whirring of the fan soothing and lulling her into drowsiness as the heat and the travelling and the roller coaster of the last few days took their toll.

Lexy started and snapped her eyes open at the sound of footsteps outside the door. Audrey's, and the heavier tread of someone else.

"Wait, Robert – you have a visitor!" Audrey's voice dropped to a whisper, but Lexy was still able to make out the words. "Miss Shaw is waiting in your office."

"Shaw?"

"Yes, she's from Brit—"

"I know. What does she want?"

"Something about a letter. She said it was personal. I'm sorry, I thought you'd want—"

"It's fine, Audrey. I'll deal with it."

It? Lexy was wide awake now, annoyed at his tone already. She tried to make sense of what she'd overheard. Dr Campbell knew of her. That meant she was right. She had to be. This Dr Campbell must be connected to the same family as the Campbells in the photo album. She had no time to speculate, though. A click of the door and a figure in a white coat was silhouetted against the afternoon sunshine, the face in shadow.

"Oh!" Her hands scrambled for purchase, as she pushed herself up from the deep cushions. "I'm sorry . . . I was just . . . I . . ." Finally, she was on her feet. She tugged her rumpled skirt back down to a respectable length, flicked her hair back and squared her shoulders.

"I'm Lexy Shaw."

"Lexy?" He sounded surprised.

"Yes, for Alexis. Dr Campbell, I presume." She winced. Stanley greeting Dr Livingstone? Well, it was Malawi.

63

"You presume correctly, Miss Shaw." There was a hint of amusement in the smooth, low voice. "Sorry to have kept you waiting."

Dr Campbell stepped out of his sunlit halo and into the room. Able to see him clearly for the first time, Lexy was surprised and a little flustered to find that he wasn't middle-aged and stuffy, as she'd expected, but young, handsome and, yes, clearly amused by her.

"So, what can I do for you, Miss Shaw? I take it this isn't a medical matter." He shook her hand, gestured for her to sit again and dropped down opposite her, all in one easy, fluid motion. This was a man who didn't waste time.

"N-no. Not medical," Lexy stammered, unsettled by his purposefulness, struggling to recalibrate her expectations of the man watching her, a hint of wariness in his face. "I have something of yours that I want to return."

"Really? How unexpected."

Lexy was galled that he didn't appear to be taking her seriously. Even more galled that she was behaving like a smitten teenager. She couldn't remember the last time she'd blushed like this.

"Yes. Well, I'm afraid it comes with sad news." Lexy hadn't meant to snap, but he was getting to her.

The professional smile slipped a little. "I see. And what might that be?"

Lexy was struggling for words. She hadn't envisaged the scene playing out like this. She was supposed to be in control, but the man sitting opposite her had her flustered and wrong-footed and she didn't really know why. Or at least she didn't want to admit to the effect he was having on her.

"Miss Shaw, what is it?" Dr Campbell prompted, concern rather than amusement or wariness now evident in his pale features. How could you live in a climate like this and still have pale skin? Her own was already sun-kissed, and she'd only just arrived.

"Miss Shaw?"

"Sorry. Yes. Sorry." She scrabbled in her bag for the smooth envelope, its edges rubbed to the velvet texture of peach skin by her hands turning it over and over since it had come into her possession.

"It's a letter of yours. To Miss Reid—"

"What on earth . . . ?" His gaze hardened. "Have you read it?" He leant forward and snatched the envelope from her to check the seal. "I see you have. You shouldn't have done that, Miss Shaw."

"I had to! I mean, it arrived after . . ."

"After what? For goodness' sake, spit it out, whatever it is."

"Yes. Right." The rattan complained again as Lexy shifted. She was uncertain where to start and disturbed by his reaction to the letter. "Sorry. I know you must be busy."

"Extremely."

She was stung by his impatience, but she could see herself reflected in his dark eyes and knew how idiotic she must seem. How slight. How could she explain that she'd come all this way to return a letter, and one he clearly would much prefer she hadn't read, when she could have simply dropped a brief, polite note telling him of Ursula's death in a postbox and been done with it? That she'd used his letter as a catalyst, a talisman, to spur her into action, into tracing a dead woman's son, her own fam—

"Miss Shaw?" There was steel in his voice now.

"It arrived after I . . . Miss Reid . . . She had an accident, a fall, and went into hospital and she didn't . . . I'm afraid she . . ." Lexy dragged her eyes up from her lap to meet his as she trailed off, and he nodded slowly.

"Died," he finished for her.

"Yes. And I've inherited, you see. I'm her . . . or rather my mother . . . Well, it's complicated, but I decided to come to Malawi anyway and I brought the letter with me. I thought you might want to know if she'd read it or not and . . . and she didn't."

She stopped, appalled at the mess she was making of this and the mixture of emotions her limping explanation seemed to be summoning in Dr Campbell. Sorrow, incredulity, surprise, shock all flitted across his features until anger swept in and washed everything else away.

"Are you sure it was an accident?"

"Yes, of course it was. She fell. The stairs at her flat—"

"Were the police involved?"

"Yes. Her carer called 999 and they came as well as the ambulance."

"Was she there when it happened, this carer?"

"I don't know. I suppose so, unless she arrived and found her. I'd need to ask her. Why, though? Does it matter?" He was staring at the letter in his hands. "Oh. Goodness, sorry. Yes, of course it matters. I'm afraid I don't know, but I . . . I hope so. I mean, it would be awful if she'd died alone without anyone . . . I'll ask when I get back. Or I could call—"

"No."

Lexy's rambling was halted by the sharpness in his voice. "Well, if you'd rather I didn't . . ."

"No need. It really isn't important."

Lexy had the feeling, though, that it was.

Dr Campbell stood and strode across the room to his desk. Pulling a key from his pocket, he unlocked a drawer, pulled out a blue folder and slipped the letter inside. His fingers drummed its surface for a moment before he dropped it back into the drawer and slid it shut. He rested his hands on the desk and dropped his head for a moment. When he looked up again, the professional mask had returned and he spoke calmly.

"Miss Shaw, why have you come here?"

"I just wanted to return your letter and . . ."

"And what?"

"Ask you a few questions. About the letter and my family. Look,

66

I can explain . . ." Lexy offered, though she wasn't really sure she could.

"Please do."

Ignoring the sarcasm in his voice, she took a deep breath to calm herself. The whole thing seemed preposterous now that she was faced with explaining herself to a stranger. To a doctor, a man of science and facts who would be unlikely to understand the emotional reaction she'd had to the letter, to the mystery of its foreign address and colourful stamps, to the hint of spice she'd smelt when she first held it but which had long since faded. To the clues she was sure it held about Ursula's past, and her own.

"I'm afraid I don't have time for this." He started towards the door.

"Wait, please. I'm sorry. Ursula was my mother's guardian. I think Ursula knew my grandparents when they were all here in Malawi in the forties; my mother's parents were missionaries, apparently, and Ursula was a Sister here in the hospital. But you know that, don't you? I mean, you knew her."

His face was giving nothing away and Lexy's discomfort grew.

"Ursula was back in Scotland but stepped in as legal guardian when my grandparents died, and so my mother grew up with Ursula. She was the only family we had, really, especially after my father died. But you know that too, don't you?" The briefest of nods, enough to encourage Lexy to continue. "So it's probably not surprising that she, Ursula that is, left everything to my mother. Only now I think it is a bit, because I've discovered, or I think I've discovered, that Ursula had a son and in your letter I think you're talking about him and I can see it's meant to be a secret but you don't think it really has to be any more so I wondered if you'd help me . . ."

Lexy stopped. She was gabbling. What was this man turning her into? Whatever it was, the look on his face made it clear he wasn't impressed. And that he was unlikely to help. Not today, anyway. As if to confirm her fears, he turned away and looked out the window, arms crossed across his chest.

"I'm sorry," Lexy said to his back. "I should go." She snapped her bag shut and stood. "I don't blame you for being angry with me, suspicious or whatever. I can see this all looks wrong. I only read the letter because I had to, and I haven't discussed it – *won't* discuss it – with anyone. But, you know, if I hadn't read it, you wouldn't even have known she had died. Or how. Look, I really am sorry. Sorry to have broken the news so badly, if nothing else." She of all people should have been more considerate in breaking the news of the death of someone close. She wished she could think of something to say that would make amends.

Dr Campbell's attention remained fixed on whatever it was he was watching through the window. She wasn't even sure he was listening any more.

"I'll leave you in peace." She paused in the doorway. "If there's anything else I can tell you when you've had a chance to take this all in, then please let me know. I'm staying at the Residence—"

"How long?"

"Sorry?"

"How long are you staying?"

"Well, I haven't quite decided. It depends on what I can find out and—"

"There's nothing to find out. You should go h—"

"Dr Campbell!" The shout ricocheted around the courtyard outside and Audrey burst into the room, bumping into Lexy, pushing her so she stumbled back down again onto that noisy sofa. "Rob— Dr Campbell, it's the Ellory boy!"

He sprang forward, all his attention now focused on Audrey.

"He's bleeding again, they're struggling—"

Dr Campbell strode towards the doorway. "I'm sorry Miss Shaw, I have to—"

"Of course. Go, please." Lexy followed them to the doorway

and watched as he and Audrey disappeared down the stairs. She started to pull the door shut behind her, wondering if it would lock by itself or if she should—

Her eyes fixed on the desk. He hadn't locked the drawer. Looking around her to check she was alone, she slipped back into the office and closed the door quietly. The drawer opened easily. The sound of her breathing filled the room, her blood awash with adrenalin. She had no right to do this. She should leave.

God helps those who help themselves. Her mother was right. Lexy pulled out the folder and slapped it down on the desk in front of her. A small scrap of yellowed paper fell from between the cardboard flaps and floated to the floor. One edge was frayed as if torn from a book and it was blank but for a few scrawled marks at its centre. In black ink.

Blantyre 144.

She couldn't be sure but … She scrabbled in her bag, remembering the still-unopened note she'd received at the hotel the night before, *Miss Alexis Shaw* in scratchy writing across its centre—

Footsteps in the corridor. She scooped the folder back into the desk drawer, already turning towards the window as she slammed it shut, her breath shallow and fast.

"Miss Shaw." Audrey's voice had lost its polite warmth. "I'll show you out, now."

Chizumu & Chizumu, Blantyre, June 9th

Lexy sat waiting in yet another reception area, waiting to see yet another lawyer. She could have been anywhere. Money cocooned you, muffled you.

As the quiet car that brought her here had slid forward like a shark through teeming waters, she'd watched the tumble and chaos of the African streets roll past, a fundraising documentary with the soundtrack turned down, Lexy herself some kind of voyeur at a peep show, tinted windows sealed to protect her anonymity.

Looking around, she could see money also introduced an element of blandness. Different continent but same bland furnishings, same bland receptionist, same quiet burr of distant phones and muffled clacking of keys as the receptionist typed whatever it was receptionists typed when they weren't intimidating visitors. Lexy had been assured Mr Chizumu *was* on his way, but as she was just that bit early she'd understand if it took a few minutes? The subtext was clear: any discomfort Lexy felt was her own fault.

Lexy didn't mind. It gave her time to collect her thoughts, run through the notes she'd made last night, the questions she wanted to ask. She'd come to expect surprises, but she'd no idea what these lawyers might have in store for her, what the "Malawi interests" Ms Hamilton in Edinburgh had referred to might reveal. Or who. There'd been nothing in the bank statements. She'd gone through them again in detail, concentrating hard to stop herself dwelling on the debacle of her meeting with Robert Campbell. Still nothing. No trace of money going in or out that might represent these financial arrangements between Ursula and her son. So that clearly was a question she had to ask, just a breath behind who this son might be. Ms Hamilton had claimed her office had no details, as it had all been set up over here. But Lexy had the feeling that even had she known, the formidable Ms Hamilton was not one to give anything away.

"It was all set up to remain confidential," Ms Hamilton had pointed out, her voice still crisp and efficient over a crackling phone line, "so there's every possibility only third parties can be traced and that the son's identity may not be retrievable, even by our Malawi associates."

Retrievable? She'd made him sound like data in a corrupted computer file.

"I *am* Miss Reid's sole beneficiary," Lexy had pointed out, doing her best to sound authoritative, but if she'd succeeded, Ms Hamilton wasn't a woman to be cowed and remained, regrettably of course, ignorant on the subject. Lexy didn't buy that, but she'd decided not to push unless the Malawi associates were less than forthcoming too; then she'd have to launch a more sustained attack.

There was a whoosh and a slight stirring of air as the doors slid open and a tall, slim man in a crisp suit stepped up to the reception desk. Steely-grey hair belied the youthful vigour he seemed to project, the purposefulness of his movement. Lexy frowned. There was something familiar about him.

"Richard Chakanaya. Here to see Daniel Chizumu. Tell him I'm coming through."

The receptionist jumped up, came round the desk and all but curtseyed to the visitor. The plane. Hadn't he been in the First Class cabin? Lexy couldn't be sure but couldn't think where else she might have seen him.

"Of course, Mr Chakanaya. He's expecting you. Please follow me."

Mr Chakanaya, though, seemed to know exactly where he was going and strode down the corridor to the right of the reception desk, leaving the flustered woman no choice but to totter in his wake. So she wasn't entirely unflappable, then, Lexy was amused to see. Worth remembering. Who did you have to be, though, or what did you have to do, to get away with that? If Lexy tried it she'd be chased round the building by burly men with walkie-talkies. You had to be rich, clearly. Was he a politician, maybe, or a celebrity? Certainly he had the looks of a movie star.

"Ms Shaw? Christopher Chizumu. Senior Partner. Delighted to welcome you to Blantyre." Lexy stood and let her hand be squashed and heartily pumped by a pot-bellied man who'd stepped straight out of Dickens.

"As I'm sure Ms Hamilton will have explained," he continued, flapping his arms to shoo her down a short corridor to a meeting room of far lesser grandeur than their Edinburgh counterpart's, "my brother and I represent her firm here and as such have managed Misss Reid's interests for many years. I never knew her personally, of course, but I admired her greatly. Her reputation, you see, and her generosity to the children over the years. Yes, indeed. Inspiring. May I offer you my sincerest condolences? Do please sit."

It seemed Lexy wasn't required to speak, so she didn't. She sat where he indicated she should and waited, impressed by the way he transitioned seamlessly from small talk to business.

Two hours later, she was again being shepherded into the back of that silent car, before the door closed, cutting her off from reality once again. Only this time she was glad of it. She needed an oasis. The noise and the bustle of the streets that she'd found so

72

exhilarating yesterday would have overwhelmed her now. Her brain was jammed. Too full to take in anything more. Christopher Chizumu had been unsettling, particularly there at the end.

He'd started out much as Lexy had expected he would. He'd been friendly, open, helpful even, but no, he didn't know the identity of Ursula's son. Or if he did, he was every bit as practised a dissembler as Ms Hamilton. But he'd still been able to help Lexy fill in some of the other gaps, including in which direction the payments between mother and son flowed, and she'd got one strong lead to pursue, even though she was sure the old lawyer wouldn't approve of her doing so.

"An intermediary set up the arrangements, Miss Shaw," he'd told her. "The payments are made through us to our associates in Edinburgh. Miss Reid herself collects – collected – the money twice a year directly from Ms Hamilton. And I'm not surprised you've found no trace of these payments. Cash, you see."

"Cash? But surely that's a little . . ."

"Irregular, yes. But not unheard of, even for such a large amount."

"How . . . large?"

"Five thousand a month, sterling, paid twice a year."

"But that's . . . that's a *lot* of cash. Why? It doesn't feel quite . . . well, above board."

"I assure you it was, Miss Shaw. We wouldn't be involved were it not."

"Of course, I'm sorry, I didn't mean to suggest—" His raised hand halted her faltering apologies.

"Not our business to demand explanation from our clients, Miss Shaw. Not perhaps a payment method we would advise, admittedly, but our client was insistent and most particular we follow the instructions to the letter."

He'd gone on to discuss her share income, but Lexy had been wondering where all that cash could have gone. Ursula had lived comfortably enough, but not extravagantly. Did she gamble? No. Ridiculous idea. Nothing like that, Lexy was sure. There'd been nothing she'd found so far to suggest Ursula was any wealthier than her pension would have made her, and nothing at all to suggest she had some extravagant secret addiction or indulgence.

"Mr Chizumu," she'd interrupted as a new thought surfaced. "This intermediary . . . Are you able to tell me more about that aspect of the arrangements?"

"Hmm." He hesitated a moment, flicked through the papers on the table in front of him and paused to scan a document near the bottom of the pile. "Yes. Yes, I think I can."

She'd waited. He continued reading for a moment, then dropped the papers back into place and squared the pile up neatly.

"Chakanaya. Richard."

"*Chakanaya?* But he's here. I've just seen him come in; he's with your brother right now. Can we talk to him? I—"

"Ms Shaw. You have to realise we lawyers must run with the hare but hunt with the hounds."

She'd no idea what he meant by that, but it was clear he wasn't going to introduce her and he wasn't going to discuss another client's business either, even obliquely.

"Suffice to say, Mr Chakanaya has wide-ranging interests." Lexy was sure there'd been distaste, if not disapproval, in his voice. "Our firm does not represent him in them all."

With that, the subject was closed, and he moved on to outline the rest of Ursula's estate in Malawi. Lexy wasn't really listening, though. She was thinking about how she was going to engineer a chat with Mr Chakanaya, whether the lawyers would help arrange it or not.

The meeting rumbled on in legalese she struggled to grasp, although by now she'd have thought she'd be fluent. There were a couple of small legacies left to faithful retainers, housekeeper Adela Kamanga, gardener Joseph Kamanga and so on, donations to the hospital and a generous allowance to a Mission orphanage in the north. That last one sounded more interesting. Lexy had made a mental note to look into that more closely.

Then things had taken an unexpected turn. As he was winding up their meeting, Christopher Chizumu had closed his folder, opened a French window onto a small roof terrace peppered with pots of jasmine and hibiscus, and invited her to step out and admire the view. They were at the rear of the building, looking down on to a well-tended park.

"Do you know anything of the flora and fauna of our country, Ms Shaw? Our birdlife perhaps?"

This conversational gambit had caught Lexy unawares and she shook her head, wondering where the little man was going with it. Already she had enough of a sense of him to feel that the slightly blundering manner was a well-honed front to hide a very deliberate nature.

"You would find it a most rewarding study, Ms Shaw. Most rewarding," he'd continued, nodding his grey head for emphasis. "Take the honeybird, for example. An unprepossessing little thing but remarkably adept at survival. Some call it a honeyguide and claim following its call will lead you to honey, but there's no proof of that, much as we greedy creatures may want to believe it."

He'd paused, as if searching for words. "It has a sweet call, our honeybird, and of course a sweet name, yet it is drab and vicious. Like your British cuckoo, it is a brood parasite, leaving its eggs to be incubated in another's nest. Then as soon as the intruder hatches, it murders its nest-mates, ensuring survival at the expense of all others. It is born with a sharp mandible hook, you see, and even before it opens its eyes, it uses this to stab repeatedly at the shells or bodies of the other chicks, killing them, before the hook falls off after a few days. It always puts me in mind of that riddle of a perfect crime where the victim is stabbed with an icicle, which then melts away: the murder weapon that can never be found."

He'd looked back into the building behind him before adding softly, "Beware the honeybird, Ms Shaw. Don't follow its song."

Back at the hotel, there was a short message for her. Ms Hamilton requested that she call at her earliest convenience. Lexy did, but, predictably, Ms Hamilton herself was unavailable. *Let the telephone tag begin*, Lexy thought, as she was put through to the lawyer's assistant instead to leave a message. She was surprised to find herself talking to a young man, but then she probably shouldn't have been. Not how they did things at Smith & Littlejohn's of course, or indeed at Chizumu & Chizumu here in Malawi, but the Edinburgh firm was in a whole legal league of its own.

"I'll make sure she gets your message as soon as she's free, Miss Shaw, and I assure you she'll either call back promptly or brief me to call on her behalf."

"Thank you. I wonder, though . . ."

"Yes, Miss Shaw? Was there something else I can help you with?"

"Miss Reid's property in Ross-shire. I'd like the address and also just wondered if there's anything you can tell me about it. Did she go there often or . . . I don't know, really. Anything."

"We wouldn't know Miss Reid's movements, of course, although it is rather remote and Miss Reid was getting increasingly frail, so common sense would suggest it is unlikely she'd have visited much in recent years. But if you'll bear with me, Miss Shaw, I'll fetch the file."

Common sense would indeed suggest. Stupid of her. Of course they wouldn't know when, or even if, Ursula visited the property. Who would? Jenny perhaps? Another question for the list. Lexy had pulled out her notebook and was tapping it sharply with her pen by the time the assistant returned.

"Yes, Miss Shaw, I have the full address. We also hold a key should you wish to visit the property. Do you have a pen and paper?"

Common sense, Lexy thought wryly, would suggest that of course she did. She took down the address, having to ask him to spell out the unfamiliar names. Not a part of the country she was familiar with. They'd never gone further north than Edinburgh on her childhood trips to Scotland.

"Can you tell me anything else about it?"

"Well, there are some photographs, and it seems to be an old croft house." Lexy wished she could see the photos for herself. "Another view shows the sea and some small islands in the distance, and this one seems to be from the other side. There's a hillside rising up behind it. Quite steep." Lexy's frustration grew at his lame descriptions. He wasn't exactly narrowing the field for her. "That's odd."

"What is?"

"It seems we prepared a lease for the property some years ago."

"Yes, I know. I have a copy." She took a deep breath. She was sounding snappy and she knew that wouldn't help her get what she needed. *Patience is a virtue.*

"Miss Reid has signed it, but there's no tenant signature, or name."

I know, Lexy screamed inside her head, sick to death with the ponderous ways of the legal profession. *Get to the point.* "So . . . ?" she prompted with a restraint that would have made her mother proud.

"It leads me to believe it's never actually been put into use. So I'm not sure why we have retained it in the current file."

"Just for your records, perhaps?" Lexy suggested.

"That would be in another file. Our archives, in fact, given how long ago it was drafted. Unless . . ."

"Unless?" The end of Lexy's pencil broke as she stabbed at the doodles that were in danger of obscuring the hard-won address.

"Well, it's possible Miss Reid had been planning to do something with it more recently. But I don't understand why we wouldn't have just drafted a new one. I find it hard to believe terms and conditions from so many years ago would still be relevant to a tenancy today. Perhaps Ms Hamilton will be able to shed some light."

Perhaps, but unlikely, Lexy had thought as she'd wound up the call. Ms Hamilton would have been a child at the time the lease was drafted, no doubt holding mock trials with her Barbie dolls or something suitably career-focused, but hardly likely to have any insight into Ursula's intentions of over twenty years ago.

Wishing she'd asked when she might expect to hear back from Ms Hamilton, Lexy decided against a dip in the hotel pool in case she missed the call. She was sure the lawyer wouldn't leave important information as a message with a hotel receptionist, nor would it be the kind of call Lexy wanted to take dripping wet or lying poolside slathered in protective slime.

The rest of the day stretched ahead of her and she debated her options, which were limited but all came down to the same thing in the end. More of the paperwork. She opened the desk drawer where she'd stashed the photo albums and papers she'd brought with her and saw the tea-stained folder she'd found beneath the cushion of Ursula's armchair. She'd been surprised to find it there and would have dismissed it as an old woman's idiosyncrasy until she saw, written in pencil in the top-right corner, the words *For Isobel.* That had been enough for her to scoop it up and drop it in with the pile of post and other papers needing her attention.

She pulled it out and placed it on her lap, swinging the desk chair round to face the balcony doors, now finding herself a little reluctant to open it. It was addressed to her mother. It didn't seem right, somehow, this prying and peeking into the affairs and correspondence of her elders.

But it had to be done, whether she felt comfortable doing it or not. It might hold the answer to the identity of Ursula's son. Although that wasn't the only reason she had to read it. She needed her own answers, needed to understand what could have happened between Ursula and Izzie to make her mother deceive her. And they were hardly in a position to complain. Ursula had wanted her mother to read it, and if her mother, then why not Lexy herself? Besides, her mother would have shared it with her. Lexy felt a stab of resentment. Well, at least her mother *should* have shared it. Qualms quashed by the reminder of her mother's betrayal, she settled herself on the bed, cross-legged, leaning back against the pillows and preparing herself for more riddles.

The folder wasn't unduly thick, but contained an assortment of documents and scraps culled from different sources, different times. Lexy flicked through. Torn pages from diaries, letters, handwritten notes and occasional newspaper or magazine clippings, all dated and with brief explanations in that precise writing she had first encountered in the photograph album. She glimpsed names she'd seen in that album too, as she'd suspected she would. With the exception of the first page, everything was dated, again in that same meticulous hand, so it was clear that Ursula had intended it to be read in a particular order. Resisting the temptation to jump ahead, pull out pieces here and there, Lexy tapped the papers together into a neat pile and started at the beginning. She would be patient and thorough in her research, working meticulously, just as she'd seen Danny at work so often in the past, marvelling at his ability to plod on steadily. She was the sort of person who flicked ahead to the last page of a novel, something Danny found incomprehensible. And infuriating when she'd share it with him if it were a book he hadn't already read.

She steeled herself when she saw the first page was a handwritten note to Isobel, the penmanship neat, precise, with just the odd tremor evident in some of the longer strokes. Recent, then? The writing of an aging, failing woman, perhaps, but there was no date and no real way to tell when it had been composed. The smoothed sheen of the folder suggested it could have been under that cushion for years. Shuffling herself further back on the bed and rolling her shoulders back and down, she began.

For Isobel

I should have told you all this years ago, but couldn't. Not wouldn't, as you thought, but couldn't because it wasn't my story to tell. And he was still alive, then, Cameron, who, as you will see, had more than a hand in all of this. So much I didn't tell you, even that awful night. I still don't know what it was that made you question the truth we'd always lived by. What it was that made you so sure there were secrets. Made you doubt me.

What little you forced out of me was enough to drive you away. I can still hear the harsh slam of the door behind you, as final as a gunshot. What, I wonder now, would you have done if I'd told you all of it back then? Could it have been any worse than not having you and little Alexis in my life these last years? How you've punished me! But I couldn't tell you then, even if I'd dared.

No more secrets, I promise. No more pretending it was right, what we did, no matter our reasons. It wasn't just me, you see, although I was at the root of it, and the others only did what they did to help me, despite my stupidity. I haven't tried to paint any of us in a better light than we deserve, but just to show you how it was. We do not appear at our best, me least of all. My diary will show you what a fool I was, so hopelessly gullible and naive; the letters will show you the true and trusting friends I was blessed to have and who helped me. They suffered too, immeasurably. Such a mess, all of it. My fault.

I left so much behind when I came back to Scotland. Thought I'd lost everything. Until you came to me. And then when you left, it felt as if it was happening all over again.

Oh Izzie, I'm so very sorry. How could I not be? I had the joy of you all those years, and yet you were right. There could have been, should have been, so much more for both of us, if I'd been stronger, braver. But I've always been a coward, worried about what people think. They say there's no fool like an old fool, but believe me, there's no hypocrite like an old hypocrite, either. And that's worse: much, much worse.

I'm old now, but still frightened. I've been afraid all my life, of something or someone, of my own feelings, and now I'm afraid I'll die without seeing you again. Without having the chance to explain. To be forgiven.

But at least I must try. Bear with me, my darling child. At my age it all gets jumbled. That's why I've pulled these papers together. I will do my best to tell you all of this when you're here and fill in any gaps, but I am afraid the excitement, the joy of seeing you again, of having you beside me, will overwhelm me. I'm afraid that when it comes to it you might yet change your mind and not come at all. Might still want to punish me. So this will be here for you one day, if you ever want it. If I'm gone by the time you do. If you don't come, I'll give it to my lawyers to keep safe.

So here it is, dearest Izzie, everything I didn't tell you that night, in our own words as far as I can assemble them. Please don't judge us too harshly, my darling. It was fear and love that made us do what we did. Made me do what I did. Which serves as no excuse, I know, but may go some way towards explanation. Forgive me if you can, Izzie. Please.

Ursula

Twisting her head from side to side to release the tightness that was gathering in her neck, Lexy leant back against the bedhead for a moment. Her mind buzzed with questions. She threw the papers down on the bed. None of it made things much clearer. No insight into what "that awful night" had revealed, what exactly

Izzie had found out, why Ursula had abandoned one child and taken in another.

Lexy struggled to make connections to the photographs she'd seen in the albums. Cameron. He'd been married to Helen, hadn't he? Or was that Gregory? They were brothers, she remembered that much. And the friends. Helen? Evelyn and Douglas? Fredi? All of them, or none?

She pushed herself up from the bed and stalked out onto the balcony in exasperation. *Calm down. Think.* She needed to tackle this more systematically. She would do a Danny and chart it. Plot out the relationships between the people in the photographs as far as she could. But first she'd see what else was in the folder.

Pausing to let her eyes readjust to the darker shade of the room after the bright sunshine of the balcony, she saw the still-unopened note she'd been given at reception on her first night lying on the floor under the desk. It must have fallen when she slammed her notebook down after speaking to the lawyer's assistant. How could she have forgotten about it? Jet lag. No, that excuse had been lame to start with. She needed a new one. She stooped to pick the envelope up, sat on the edge of the bed and slipped a finger under the flap. She ripped it open, parted the envelope's ragged edges and pulled out a small square of paper, black ink scrawled across its centre: *Go home.*

8

Blantyre Hospital, June 10th

Evie was restless. She'd been here long enough now, spent each night lying sleepless in this coffin of a bed, to know the rhythms of the hospital. She could tell when shifts changed, when night took over from day, when they reached the dying hours, those small hours of the morning when so often a patient would silently slip away. One night it would be her. But not yet. Not yet. She had too much still to do. She'd yet to dance on Cameron's grave as she promised Helen one day she would. For Ursula. For all of them.

And there was so much still to tell. Or, rather, to sift and select before telling. Lexy was coming and Evie had better be prepared. The past was spooling through her mind like an old film, creaking and jumping in parts, blurred and discoloured in others. Which version should she share with this young woman Robert had asked her to see? Dear Isobel's daughter. Lexy. How very modern. Ursula's nose would have twitched a little at the abbreviation, but Alexis or Lexy, no matter. Poor child. She must be feeling very alone. No wonder, really, that she was searching for Ursula's son.

And Ursula herself dead. Nearly sixty years they'd been friends, Helen too. All three of them tied together by their secrets, placing their trust in each other unreservedly. Sharing those secrets with no one for all those years and then only with Robert as they became older and frailer, less able to manage the responsibilities alone. He was a good boy, young Robbie. More like a son than a grandson, so like his father, yet he'd chosen to stay in Malawi when Edward and Susan had left. Evie sighed softly, trying not to waken the wheeze in her chest. She missed him, her Teddie, but the last time, the only time, they'd visited he'd sounded more Australian than his wife. He'd settled. He wouldn't be coming back. But he'd left her Robert. Malawi had that boy's heart, just as it had hers.

She arched her back, pressed palms against the mattress as she tried to shuffle herself back up straight against the pillows. The effort exhausted her, so she slumped back down again, head dropping forward onto her chest. She shut her eyes. This getting old was a tiresome business. Now, think. She and Robert must tread carefully. There was so much at stake. They could tell Lexy enough, just enough to satisfy her, to send her safely home. Tell her the son was dead, perhaps.

No. Not worth the risk. It raised more questions than Evie wanted to answer. Better to say nothing. Nothing at all. Feign surprise at the suggestion of Ursula having had a son. Or just trust her instincts and decide what to say and what to conceal when she saw the cut of her young visitor's jib.

She strained to lift her head up again and rest it back on the sagging pillows, took deeper breaths as she recovered from the effort, heard the rattle in her chest like a snake's warning. Robert had said it must be Evie's decision and so it would be. She hated to lie, but in the circumstances . . .

She'd set Evie to remembering, though, even more than usual, this young Lexy. As she lay imprisoned by her body in this gloomy room, she found herself thinking about the old days more and more. The reward of old age, a kindness of sorts, to return to one's youth in memories more vivid than the events of today. Perhaps she'd feel more grateful if the memories weren't so painful.

What did Lexy already know, Evie wondered; what had her mother told her, or Ursula, even? Evie had held her breath for two long years when Izzie had come to work in this very hospital.

Blantyre was too small for their paths never to cross and she was certain one day her god-daughter would see him and pick up a hint, a resemblance in a gesture or an expression, and come and ask, demand, to know the whole sorry story. Or worse still that she'd come not to Evie but go directly to them. To Cameron. He'd been like a cat watching a mouse and Evie was terrified that one day that paw would swipe, the claws would scratch and he'd leave Izzie on Evie's doorstep as a gift. A reminder. A punishment.

But their dear girl never did. Why should she, really? She knew nothing, then, and it was only Evie's own guilt, and Ursula's persistent, anxious letters during those interminable years, that fuelled her fears. Their darling, inquisitive, precious Izzie. Then she'd married Philip and returned home, neither of them knowing he'd already contracted the malaria that would kill him. So very sad.

Evie had loved the time she'd spent with Izzie, and then with Philip too, but had been so relieved they'd gone, Ursula almost giddy with excitement that they were back. Now Evie had to find a way of making sure Izzie's daughter left Malawi too, before she came to any harm.

Lying open-eyed in the darkness, scenes from her earlier life played before her eyes over and over again. Was there anything that could have warned her, the slightest clue that could have let her steer them all safely onto another course? But there was nothing, there had been nothing that could be done differently. The die had been cast by another's hand and all they had done was play his game.

"How unlike the others to be late," Evie mused to Ursula as the maître d' seated them at their table.

"Oh." Ursula's face creased in puzzlement. "Only five places have been set. We should call the may ... mader ... that man back."

"Strange," Evie agreed. "I'll speak to him when he brings the others over. Let's not make a fuss."

"But they really shouldn't—"

"There's Helen, now. And Gregory at her side, of course." Evie dipped her head in the direction of the door. She watched the couple start to make their way across the floor, stopping to talk to other diners as they went.

"Always someone wanting to talk to our Helen," Ursula muttered, tugging at the lace sleeves of her borrowed gown, then pulling its scooped neckline a little straighter, higher.

"Well, she is delightful, our sophisticated friend, and just look at them together. So charming. And so very kind of her to lend . . . I mean, I'd no idea we'd be dressing for dinner, but then we neither of us have much experience of society, do we?"

Evie felt Ursula tense beside her and feared she had offended her, but when she looked round she saw Cameron had arrived, pausing in the open doorway to survey the room, although Evie felt sure the pause was more to let the room survey him. He was undeniably handsome, arrestingly so, but his conceit and arrogance made him unattractive in the extreme. She thought again of her dear Douglas, short, round and florid of face, already balding at the age of twenty-eight and no doubt even less hirsute now than when she'd last seen him nearly two years ago. No. Not a patch on Cameron to look at, but worth twenty of him.

Ursula was rearranging the cutlery at her place setting, her hands twitching so that the knives tinkled against one another.

"Do be still, Ursula. Don't give him the satisfaction of seeing how upset you are."

"What? Nonsense. I'm perfectly fine and I don't— Oh!"

Again Evie looked over to the door. Cameron was bowing over the outstretched hand of Gertie von Falken, his lips briefly touching its back. Allowing herself to be uncharacteristically uncharitable, Evie hoped he'd cut his lip or snag his thin moustache on one of those ostentatious rings the young widow sported. However, he straightened up to full height unharmed and offered the simpering woman his arm to lead her across the floor. As they approached the table, Evie put her own hand out and grabbed Ursula's restless one to stop her picking at the linen tablecloth, squeezing her friend's cold hand as she laid it firmly in Ursula's lap.

"Chin up, old thing," she instructed out of the side of her mouth, tilting her own chin and squaring her shoulders. She was unsure quite what was happening, but whatever it was, she'd confront it full on.

Cameron and Gertie were leaning into each other, the merry widow whispering something into Cameron's ear. A second later he threw his head back and laughed, making people at the nearby table stop talking and look up. Gertie looked around her, clearly delighted at being the centre of attention. They held their pose for a moment, then they leant their heads together again and continued their passage across the room.

Evie's heart was racing. This was too much. The arrogance, the insensitivity of the man. She knew Ursula beside her was in agony. It was unbearable. She stood as the couple came towards the table, determined to save her friend any further humiliation. At the periphery of her vision she was aware that Gregory and Helen were looking over at them.

"Cameron, I do think—"

"Evie, darling. So sorry I won't be joining you this evening, but Gertie absolutely insists I sit with her and you know I can't possibly refuse a request from a beautiful woman." Gertie's smirk turned Evie's stomach. "I do hope you can spare me, ladies." He nodded in Ursula's direction, then swept Gertie on towards her table, next to the captain's, a burst of laughter coming from the widow's scarlet lips as he whispered something in her ear.

Before Evie could recover herself, Gregory was beside her holding her chair. "Please, Evelyn, do sit down."

Helen appeared at Ursula's side. "Why don't I sit next to you this evening, darling?"

"But that's Cameron's place . . ." Ursula's blushes had faded and she was now as pale as the starched white of the table linen.

"Cameron will no longer be joining us," Gregory said in a tone that suggested the subject was not open for discussion. "Just waiting for Fredi now, are we? So, ladies, what have you been doing with yourselves today?"

Evie took the cue, grateful for the opportunity to divert attention from Cameron and to give Ursula a moment or two to compose herself, although as she ran through the highlights of their unexceptional afternoon of deck quoits and tea on the sun deck, she knew no one was listening; everyone was adjusting themselves mentally to the absence of Gregory's younger brother.

"Oh, so sorry to be so late!" Fredi arrived looking as debonair as he always did but with something a little more agitated than usual about him. "I was talking to the entertainment officer," he gushed, "and just wait till you hear what he has planned for our final night at sea."

Instantly the mood was lifted. Fredi had the ability to turn the most mundane situation into high drama or high excitement. Evie loved him for it, and never more so than now as he described the fancy-dress party that would mark the end of the voyage. They had three days to prepare themselves and, according to Fredi, the stewards would be only too happy to assist in costuming the guests.

"So what shall we all be? I can't decide for myself. But Ursula, you" – Fredi turned the full force of his pale-blue eyes to her, clasping his hands together in front of his chest – "you, my dear, should be something marvellous. Marie Antoinette, perhaps – oh, and I can be your Sun King."

"No, no, Fredi," Helen interjected. "That's the wrong Louis, isn't that right, Ursula? Marie Antoinette was married to—"

"Oh details, details, my dear Helen. Who cares? Imagine, the opulence of gold, the richness of velvet, the stunning entrance we shall make, darling Ursula, you on my arm like the priceless treasure you are. Why" – he struck a pose – "we shall be divine." Evie was relieved to see the hint of a smile on Ursula's face as Fredi teased and tended to her, a little colour returning to her cheeks. He was no fool. Beneath that frivolous banter he was doing his utmost to protect and distract Ursula without ever alluding to the empty chair opposite them.

"And you, Helen," he said as he summoned a waiter to fill their glasses, "you, my dear, can be Mary, Queen of Scots, visiting our court at Versailles! Yes, that would be just splendid."

Evie was quite sure Fredi's carelessness with history was deliberate. Helen, however, was looking serious as she tried again to correct their Danish friend. Evie took the chance to turn to Gregory.

"Well?" She raised her eyebrows.

Gregory didn't do her the discourtesy of pretending he didn't know what she meant. "I spoke to him. He won't be joining us again, and I have suggested he stay in Cape Town for a while after we dock. Not travel on with us to Blantyre. Something I think he'll be happy to do." They both glanced over at Gertie's table, where cocktail glasses were chinking, their contents fuelling extravagant and loud laughter.

"That must have been difficult for you."

"Not at all. What's difficult is seeing him behave so shoddily. I am embarrassed to call him my brother." He looked over at Ursula, at her still-full plate, her still-considerable pallor.

"Gregory, it's not your fault. No one holds you in the least bit responsible. You are not your brother's keeper."

"But I am, you see. I promised our mother I would do my best to keep him out of trouble."

"Your best, yes, but no one can achieve the impossible and, I'm sorry to say, I think your younger brother will always find trouble. Or make it. Forgive me. I don't mean to be rude. It's just . . . puzzling. You're so very different."

"We have different fathers. My father died shortly after I was born, leaving my mother still young and a wealthy but, it has to be said, a rather naive widow. She didn't stay that way long. Cameron's father was . . . well, not perhaps the steady hand that my own father had been. We were bankrupt in less than a year and my stepfather long gone before Cameron was even born."

"I'm so sorry. I had no idea."

"My uncle took us in, brought us up. He taught me how to manage a business, how to plan and invest, balance books. All lessons my younger brother chose to absent himself from entirely."

"You sound as if you don't approve."

"I don't. Not at all."

"No, no, no!" Helen's laughing voice interrupted them as she turned and laid her hand on Gregory's arm. Evie saw how quickly Gregory's attention shifted to focus entirely on Helen's animated face.

"Gregory, help us. Who was Mary, Queen of Scots' husband first? Darnley or Bothwell?"

"Darnley, I believe."

"There. Thank you, Gregory." Helen turned back to the others. "I was right. So Fredi, as I was saying, you can't . . ."

"Then why is he travelling out with you to Africa?" Evie asked, picking up the thread of their conversation.

"Hmm? I beg your pardon?" Gregory seemed reluctant to turn away from Helen, but good manners got the better of him.

"Surely this was the opportunity to put distance between you and your brother?"

"It wasn't my decision. My mother begged me to take him." He picked up his wine glass, held it to the light, then put it back down again, untouched. "I gave her my word I'd watch out for him. I'd hoped he would be grateful and perhaps attempt to . . . modify . . . his behaviour at least. After all, after what happened in Edin—" Gregory stopped, reached for his glass again, sipped quickly, then banged it back down clumsily, a few drops of red wine staining the pristine tablecloth. "I'm sorry. I don't mean to burden you with this, Evie."

"You're not burdening me, rest assured. I'm a minister's daughter and a doctor's wife. There's not much I haven't heard or seen before." She pressed on, hoping he wouldn't be offended by her persistence. "So?"

"There was a woman. A married woman. Cameron . . . She . . ." He picked up the glass again, drained it this time, then put it down slowly. "She died."

"I'm so sorry."

"My mother was distraught, mortified. Appalled, really. The woman was . . . had been . . . one of her closest friends. It was best that Cameron leave Scotland."

"Yes, I can see that."

"You'd think he'd have learnt . . . but look. Just look at him."

The suave younger man was pulling Gertie to her feet, leading her out to the dance floor as the band struck up, drawing her in close, too close.

"Well, at least Gertie isn't married . . ."

"Not yet, no. I have it on good authority, however, that our young widow is on her way to South Africa to join her new fiancé. A very wealthy man, by all accounts. I fear this won't end well."

"Evie, darling," Fredi called over to her as he darted round to the side of her chair, "we simply must dance to this. It's a new one for you – the cha-cha."

"Oh Fredi," Evie laughed, "I know I asked you to teach me, but—"

"No, no. I insist. You'll have to dance in Blantyre. We can't have you being a wallflower simply because the latest music passed your Highland parish by. Come on, darling!"

"Yes, go on, Evie," Helen encouraged. "We three will watch you mesmerise the ballroom."

"Gregory, I'm sorry, I—"

"Go on, Evelyn." Gregory was already turning away and pulling his chair nearer to Helen, beaming at her as colour tinged his cheeks. Evie knew when she was beaten.

"Very well, but Ursula, it's your turn next. I can't possibly keep up with Fredi and you know he'll want to dance all night."

Evie let herself be pulled into the music, glad that its volume made conversation impossible. She had a lot to think about.

★

"Dr Campbell rang," a voice was saying as the door pushed open. Crockery rattled on a tin tray. "Said he'll bring your visitor later today if he can."

"Good morning, Celia."

The nurse banged the tray down on the table beside the bed and turned, hands on hips, to look at Evie.

"Morning, Mrs Campbell. How you today?"

"Fit as a fiddle, my dear, sharp as a tack and bright as a button. Ready to go home, in fact."

The nurse grunted what passed for a laugh at Evie's familiar morning greeting and turned to pull the table over the bed.

"Best get you fed, then get you fancied up some in case this visitor comes. All the way from England, Dr Campbell said. Not many in here gets visitors from that far off. Royalty be coming next!" The nurse chuckled, her ample torso rippling with her mirth.

Knowing she meant no real harm, Evie tried to join in with a gentle laugh but ended up coughing instead.

"There, there, Mrs Campbell." The nurse handed her a glass of tepid water. "You sip this, be right as rain."

Evie did as she was told, wondering, as she so often did, why people imagined a declining body signified a decline in mental age.

9

The Residence, June 10th

After a restless night, Lexy was feeling a little calmer as she sipped iced tea in the shade of the verandah outside the hotel restaurant. The fruits she'd ordered over an hour ago as a token gesture towards a healthy breakfast were already wilting as they sat untouched on the plate in front of her, her mind still preoccupied with the note. It had unnerved her, but she wouldn't let it throw her off track. She would just have to be wary. Trust no one. Yes, it was scary, but she wouldn't allow herself to be bullied. It might just be a prank, a . . . a . . . She couldn't begin to think why anyone might do something like that. She remembered the figure she thought she'd seen in the shadows of the trees outside Ursula's flat in Edinburgh. Was someone watching her, following her after all? If so, it had to be something to do with Ursula, and the only thing that could be was something to do with her mysterious son. Retired hospital matrons of exemplary character hardly merited such cloak-and-dagger attention otherwise. No. If anything, Lexy should look on this as evidence that she had a good chance of getting to the bottom of all this and that was why someone was trying to frighten her off.

Well, top marks for the pep talk, Lex, she thought to herself, and before she could start picking holes in her spurious reasoning she pulled Ursula's folder from the backpack she'd brought down with her and which was bulging once again. She wasn't letting any of this out of her sight now. She was no longer sure the mess she'd discovered when she'd scuttled back to her room to avoid the odious Pendleton had been of her own doing. She could easily believe someone had searched her things. So far, she'd discovered nothing missing, but then she couldn't be sure. She had no idea exactly what was amongst Ursula's papers, something she now intended to rectify.

She had the verandah to herself this late in the morning, so she kicked off her sandals and curled her feet up under her in the wide winged chair, no longer surprised by the creaks of wicker that accompanied her movements. She put Ursula's note to Izzie to one side and picked up the next batch of papers, held together by a paper clip in the top-left corner. It had rusted a little, leaving a brown imprint on the top page when she pulled it off. Fanning the papers out, she saw some were headed by dates and place names; all were written in that same copperplate she recognised from the photograph albums, but not all were as neatly composed, nor as well preserved. Some pages were splattered with exuberant punctuation, capital letters, underlinings; others appeared water-stained and blotchy; or creased as if they'd been crumpled and then smoothed flat again. There were scratchings-out in some places, as if the writing had fallen prey to some wartime censor's pen. All the pages, she realised, had been ripped from a notebook, clearly a diary or journal of some sort, and even though they were now all bundled together, variation in the colours of papers and inks showed Lexy they hadn't all been torn from the same book. Selected extracts from Ursula's diaries?

Lexy remembered her mother telling her how Ursula wrote every day without fail and then locked the diary in her desk drawer. As a child, Izzie had been intrigued by them, desperate to read these secret stories. One day she'd seen the key left in the lock and, unable to resist, she'd just been opening the drawer and reaching in when Ursula's hand had landed heavily on her small shoulder; she spun her round and shouted at her, for the first and only time Izzie could remember. Izzie never said what it was that Ursula had actually shouted; the shock of the angry voice enough, the lesson learned.

"You see, Lexy, everyone can shout and be angry. That's easy. It's much harder, but much more effective, to exercise control, judicious use of your temper."

The young Lexy had been puzzled. "What does that mean?"

"If you shout all the time, no one hears you."

Perhaps if she'd remembered that when she was with Danny, he might have understood her better. And, of course, if you're shouting, you're not listening, either.

Lexy sighed, then chuckled softly as she remembered herself rummaging through the drawer in Dr Campbell's office. *The fruit never falls far from the tree.* She was indeed her mother's daughter, although Ursula's wrath, she was sure, would have been far more terrifying than Audrey Lanakela's polite disapproval.

"Can I get you anything else, Miss Shaw?" A waiter had appeared to clear the table.

"More iced tea, perhaps." She suspected it could be a long day going through the folder. He flapped a cloth across the table to remove the last of the crumbs and disappeared to do her bidding. She could get used to this.

As she started to read, she realised these were indeed extracts from Ursula's diaries, but not an Ursula she – nor her mother, she suspected – had known. As Lexy read the inner secrets of this young Ursula, truly an innocent abroad, she found herself warming to her in a way she hadn't expected. This was a giddy, excitable, daydreaming Ursula, one Lexy was sure she would have loved had she known her, just as much as it quickly became apparent Ursula's new-found friends Helen and Evelyn did. Ursula's fears and insecurities were familiar: was she pretty enough? Why wouldn't her hair curl like Helen's? Were her dresses smart enough? Would her manners, her speech, show her up as out of place in this smart set she couldn't quite believe had taken her into their fold? She was clearly captivated by their collective glamour, and by none more than the wealthy heiress at its centre, Helen Buchanan, daughter of the owner of the Buchanan Trading Company. Even Lexy, who'd had no time for history in school, had heard of that.

To her relief, the diary pages started to make more sense of the names in the photograph albums. Gregory and Cameron Munro, brothers from Scotland. Gregory was about to take up the post of General Manager at Buchanan's and was escorting Helen on the journey at her father's request. Cameron's purpose in travelling was less clear, Ursula simply referring to his "special" role with the company. Evelyn Campbell was a distant cousin of Helen's on her mother's side, and so was travelling with them on her way to join her husband, Dr Douglas Campbell, who had already been in Africa for two years. Ursula had joined them because she would be working with Dr Campbell, so it had been arranged that she and Evelyn share a cabin. And then there was Fredi Stenberg, a Danish diplomat on his way to take up his new post, who didn't seem to have any particular reason to join their party other than to make up numbers at their table, as far as Lexy could tell. But that didn't seem to have mattered. They'd all obviously forged friendships that had lasted far beyond the voyage.

Lexy swallowed back a tear or two as she read, as she learned how dazzled Ursula had been by the company she found herself keeping, and discovered more about the origins of the woman whose heir she had become, without even knowing anything of the woman's early years. One passage in particular touched her:

When I think of those sad, small stories we would tell each other in the dark, whispering our fantasies from bed to bed in case one of the Sisters heard us and we were marched down to the dining hall in nothing but our nightgowns to stand with our hands on our heads until our arms hurt and we started to fall asleep where we stood . . . Those stories full of the light and colour and laughter and warmth that we conjured up to escape from the stark, relentless grey of that awful place, the bone-eating cold, the thin soups and meagre stews ladled grudgingly into chipped bowls day in day out. When I think of all that, I want to stand up tall and shout, "Look! Look at me now! Look at the people who are my friends! I am not an unlovable monster!" Oh, if only I could have foreseen this, this magic, it would have made those dark years so much more bearable.

I look at my new friends sometimes, though, and the old doubts return. Am I worthy? Why would people like that want to spend time with someone like me? Evie knows, I think, how I feel. And she helps. This life is new to her, too. She's the daughter of a Highland minister, a widower, I believe, so she had no more time or opportunity than I to learn the ways of this charmed world we find ourselves in. Yet she has such confidence, such poise. I wish I could have that, too. Perhaps being married helps. She knows she is loved. That her husband has chosen to spend the rest of his life with her. How must that feel? To be loved like that. To know there will be someone beside you, to take care of you, always. Would it be too much to hope that one day, I . . . or is that just too silly of me? And yet, does it do any harm to hope? I've come this far, a fully qualified nurse, a *good* nurse, on my way to a position in a hospital in Africa. If an orphanage brat can manage that, who's to say what else might be possible in that far-off land?

So Ursula had been an orphan, too, just like Lexy herself now was, but, whatever else, however betrayed she felt right now, at least Lexy had grown up knowing she was loved.

Lexy's tea had arrived without her noticing, and she reached for it, wondering how Ursula could have abandoned her child to an orphanage, if indeed she had, given her own difficult experience.

The ice in her tea had melted and the glass was slippery with condensation. She sipped slowly, holding it firmly in one hand as she turned pages with the other. After the first few breathless days, Ursula's records became briefer, more obscure, as if she were distracted, or . . . or hiding something. Slowly Lexy began to understand. This was a woman whose dreams were coming true and who hardly dared write about it for fear it would all dissolve. It was a woman who was falling in love, who was being courted and wooed, enchanted by words and glances, a woman whose vulnerability was raw and evident even beneath the careful words. The question was, who was her suitor, the object of her growing affections? The diary was oddly silent on names at this point. One of the Munro brothers, perhaps, but which one? Or Fredi? Or someone else altogether, maybe even one of the no doubt dashing officers employed as much for their ability to charm the guests in their charge as for their nautical skills?

And then abruptly, the diary extract ended. Despite her intention to be methodical, to rigidly stick to the chronology of the documents, Lexy flicked past a couple of pages of a letter to the next paper-clipped batch of torn pages. Even a quick glance showed that by the time Ursula had returned to her memoirs, the party were well established in their new lives and Ursula was hard at work in Blantyre Hospital. Lexy could see the dedicated, meticulous woman she had known emerge from the pages as hospital routines, professional concerns and observations, not always complimentary, on local practice filled the pages. No more blotches or exclamation marks, no more frantic crossings-out or sentence fragments. Precise words and orderly sentences conveyed a sense of calm, the cocktails and dancing, the excitability and extravagance of the voyage replaced with starched uniforms, ward rules and demanding schedules. Lexy missed the effervescence and awe of the earlier pages and wondered—

"Miss Shaw?" It was Barney. "Sorry to disturb you. You have a visitor."

"Really?" Her heart hammered. "Who?"

"Dr Campbell. He said he wasn't expected but hoped you would see him anyway. He is waiting in the lobby. Shall I show him through?"

"No," she said quickly, remembering how trapped she'd felt by Hugh Pendleton plonking himself down in front of her at her dining table. "No, tell him I'll just be a moment and I'll come through."

Lexy gathered the folder and her notebook together and jammed them into the backpack, angry at his presumption that he could just turn up and expect to see her and at the same time acutely aware she looked a mess after her sleepless night and annoyed to find herself wishing she'd had time to freshen up.

Lexy glanced in the bar as she passed, and then surveyed the clusters of chairs in the lobby, looking for Dr Campbell. He was sitting in the far corner near the hotel's open, canopied entrance, resting his chin on hands clasped in front of him, as if deep in thought. Just as Lexy began to walk over to join him, a flurry of activity from the driveway outside made her falter. Barney and one of his colleagues sprang into action, and the receptionist clattered his bell and came out in front of the desk. A long white car with tinted windows had drawn up in front of the hotel steps. Barney got to the car first and opened the rear door.

Lexy was surprised to see she recognised the man getting out. Richard Chakanaya. He swept in through the open doors, bellboys running in his wake, and the receptionist stepped forward with bowed head to welcome him. As the object of all this attention passed Lexy, he nodded at her, a brief smile twitching at his lips before he dismissed her and disappeared into the bar.

Lexy continued over to join Dr Campbell, who was now standing and watching her closely.

"Do you know that man?" Again, Dr Campbell was all purposefulness. No pleasantries.

"Good afternoon, Dr Campbell," Lexy held out her hand. "How nice to see you again."

He didn't turn to take her hand, didn't even look at it. Annoyed, Lexy sat down, expecting him to do the same, but he stood staring towards the bar for a moment longer.

"'That man' is Richard Chakanaya, I believe," Lexy said, to draw his attention back to her.

"So you do know him."

"Well, not exactly. I know his name, that's all. I saw him at my lawyers', and I think he may have been on my flight. I presume he's some kind of local celebrity given the interest and attention he seems to generate."

Dr Campbell's laugh was short, more like a bark than an expression of amusement. "A celebrity. I suppose you could say that."

Lexy's irritation with him increased. She'd handled things badly when they'd met previously and she was sorry about that, but he really wasn't an easy person to get on with. Still, she was determined to maintain her dignity, to conduct this meeting, whatever its purpose, on her terms.

"You wanted to see me, Dr Campbell."

"I'm sorry. I'm doing it again aren't I? I don't mean to, you know. Be rude."

Oh, well that's okay then, she thought, but managed to keep her face calm and the smile in place.

"Look, can we start again?" He sounded almost sheepish. "I'm not always this boorish."

101

"Of course, Dr Campbell." Lexy was enjoying feeling socially superior. Not something she was used to feeling given her own tendency to overreaction.

"Robert. Please."

"Robert." She inclined her head slightly. See? She could do magnanimous, too.

"I wanted to apologise for running off like that when we met. It really was an emergency. And Audrey told me you were still waiting for me when I got back. In my office. I'd assumed you'd realise I'd be gone some time."

"Oh really, it wasn't a problem. I do understand." The altitude of that high ground she'd been standing on was decreasing as she remembered what she'd been doing when Audrey had found her.

"I hope you were able to keep yourself occupied while you waited."

So, he knew. She felt her composure begin to slip. He knew she'd been rummaging through his desk, trying to read the folder.

"As I said, it really wasn't a problem. Was that all, Dr Camp— Robert? I have a busy afternoon ahead . . ."

"Really? Well, please don't let me keep you. Although I had hoped . . . You see, there's someone I hoped you'd be able to meet. My grandmother, Evie. Evelyn Campbell. I told her about your visit, about your news. She was very close to Ursula, as we both were, and I know she'd like to meet you. We both knew your mother, too, of course. She was a regular visitor at the house when she was working here, your father, too. But if you're *busy* . . ."

"Oh, no, I . . . Nothing I can't rearrange." He smiled. Lexy cringed. Was she really so transparent?

"I could take you to her this afternoon, if you *were* able to rearrange your schedule, of course. Three o'clock perhaps? She's usually brightest in the afternoons and prefers to have visitors then. She's in hospital, you see."

"I didn't realise. I mean, I knew she wasn't well—"

"Yes. My letter will have told you that." Ouch. Not one to let bygones be bygones, then.

"Three o'clock would be fine," she managed.

"I'll be waiting in the car outside." He stood, nodded and walked away.

So much for running things on her terms.

10

Evie had spent so many years protecting Helen that it was second nature to her. She and Ursula had been her dearest friends, until Cameron had cast his shadow over them all. They'd outwitted him in the end, but it had cost them dear. What they were forced to do had bound them close, yet separated them forever. Evie lost her closest friends, stayed on without them. Missed them every day. All she'd wanted was for them all to be happy. Evie had her darling Douglas and she'd wanted Helen and Ursula both to marry and be as happy as she was. She used to fantasise about them bringing up their children together, running in and out of each other's houses, helping and laughing, caring and sharing. Ursula would have fallen for some rising star of a doctor, or perhaps one of the steadier consular attachés. Helen: well, that was easy. All that was needed there was a little nudge, and she'd been sure she was just the person to provide it.

She'd watched them together before, but that particular day it was more poignant than ever: their heads almost touching, hands dancing around each other's as they pored over the plans Gregory had spread out on the top of the piano. Their voices were indistinct from where Evie sat outside on the verandah looking in through the open French doors. But she could see, could sense their excitement, feel it buzz like static through the still air in a ripple of rising and falling speech. She didn't need to hear the words, or understand them. They were of no real consequence, the plans for the new warehouses not really what held the couple's rapt attention.

"Helen! Helen, I have them!" Gregory's voice had boomed through the hallway from the moment the front door had opened to admit him. Helen had almost knocked over the silver tea tray as she'd leapt up, and the flush that had sprung equally suddenly to her cheeks had nothing to do with the abruptness of the interruption, Evie was sure.

Gregory had stopped midstream when he'd lurched onto the verandah and seen Evie there, sitting in the shadows.

"Evie! Hello. Forgive me, I had no idea—"

"Don't mind me, Gregory," Evie said, fluttering a hand as if shooing away a fly, amused rather than hurt at his evident disappointment in finding Helen had company. "I'm sure Helen is as anxious to see the plans as you are to show them to her."

That was all the permission either of them had needed. They'd forgotten Evie in a second as they retreated inside and Gregory opened the charts and spread them out on top of the piano, Helen hastily removing the silver-framed photographs that peppered its surface.

Evie had felt old and wise, worldly even, watching them. Evie, the innocent daughter of a minister, saw their love long before they acknowledged it themselves. She wondered that neither of them would admit to it as its strength radiated from them when they were together, or was Evie truly gifted with some mystical insight that allowed only her to see it? Despite his illness, Helen's father must be blind not to realise what was going on between his daughter and his General Manager, and if he'd done nothing to keep them apart, surely that meant he must sanction it or at the very least have no objections?

Evie resolved to meddle. Not something she would ordinarily allow herself to do, but they'd been in Africa nearly three years by then and she cared about them both too much to watch them dance around each other, crippled by shyness the one and delicacy the other. Even Helen, with all her worldly ways, didn't believe a

105

woman should be the one to declare herself, to make the first move. But Evie couldn't forget the bruises she'd seen. When Helen's father died, as he would surely do before too long, then she would be a wealthy woman, and an unprotected one. More desirable than ever, and more vulnerable. Not even Cameron would dare to touch his brother's wife.

It was some weeks later that the opportunity arose. Again Evie was at Helen's, but Helen was upstairs with her dressmaker having a final fitting for whatever stunning gown she'd wear to the Club's Annual Ball. Evie was downstairs on the verandah in her usual spot, sipping lemonade in the shade of the mimosa watching the shadows from its branches dance across the manicured lawn and the polished teak of the verandah floor.

Evie heard the door and Gregory's familiar voice greeting the housekeeper and asking for Helen. Helen must have heard him too, so Evie knew she would be chivvying the dressmaker to hurry up, as she'd be anxious to come down again and join them. Gregory declined a glass of lemonade and sat down opposite Evie, his fingers twisting around themselves, clasping and unclasping, a sure indication of his impatience.

They discussed the weather, and the Club and the forthcoming ball. The silence then hung heavy between them, as both strained for the sounds of Helen descending the staircase, until Evie realised this was her opportunity.

"Gregory, why don't we take a turn around the garden? The bougainvillea are so beautiful and it's hard to appreciate them from here."

No one could ever accuse dear Gregory of inscrutability. Evie could see him struggling to find a reason to refuse, to stay here waiting for Helen to appear so as not to waste a single precious second of her presence.

"I . . . well of course, if you like. But isn't it too hot? Wouldn't you rather stay in the shade, where it's cooler?" A desperate attempt, but Evie was ready for him. Reaching down let her hide her smile.

"Oh, dear man, how thoughtful, but don't worry. I have this" – she wielded her parasol in triumph – "and you have your hat so we really won't be bothered by the sun at all." Trapped. He knew it, so with a swift glance back through the open verandah doors, he gave in with characteristic gentle grace.

"If you're sure, then." He was such a charming man, Evie almost felt guilty at forcing him to do this when he so clearly didn't want to, but she was sure he'd appreciate it in the long run.

As they strolled along the path that bordered the lawn, he chatted as best he could about the flowers they passed, the neatness of the grass, the skill of Helen and her gardener. On this last subject he was happier, of course. When they reached the bench at the furthest point from the house, Evie suggested they sit and again saw him struggle with his impatience to return to the house, before he agreed and humoured her.

"Dear Helen," Evie said, following neatly on from his most recent proclamation on Helen's many talents. "And she is, isn't she?"

He looked confused and so Evie continued. "Dear, that is. To us both."

He nodded slowly and Evie's own heart lurched at the pain that swept into his face, his eyes holding hers briefly before turning back to the house and looking up at the upper floor, where Helen would be standing behind the closed shutters of her room, tapping her toes no doubt as she urged the dressmaker on.

"Yes, she is," he whispered.

"Gregory, I know it's wrong to interfere in other people's business, and I wouldn't except that you both are so very dear to me. We've a bond, I think, forged on the journey out here, no doubt, and our shared experiences of arriving in this beautiful but strange country." He was still staring at the house, but now he was nodding slowly. "And that strangeness, I think, is a good thing. It means we too can be different, a little, that the same strictures and rules don't apply."

He turned to Evie, eyebrows gathering in that frown he wore when trying to follow an argument or understand one of Cameron's faster witticisms.

"Gregory, she loves you."

His eyes widened, hope flickering briefly before he turned away, leant his arms on his knees and clasped his hands so tightly Evie could see the knuckles blanch beneath the tanned leather of his skin.

"No." The single word was tight and painful.

"Yes, Gregory. She does. I can tell. I've seen you together."

"But she . . . I'm just the . . . It couldn't be."

"At home, maybe not. But she *does* love you, and here, Gregory, anything is possible. Would you rather see her carried off by one of those young idlers at the Club, or a titled diplomat? Have her languish as a spinster or sent home to find a husband? Or worse, have her fall prey to some honey-tongued gold-digger the moment her father dies and she's left vulnerable and alone?"

"What I want is irrelevant. She's the owner's daughter, and I'm an employee. Her father would never allow it, even if she were to agree . . . to return my feelings, I—"

"Stuff and nonsense, Gregory. She isn't your typical Edinburgh young lady, you know. She insisted on coming here and, just as importantly, her father allowed it. That says something about both of them, doesn't it? That they aren't answerable to the matrons of Morningside and redundant codes of behaviour?"

"But it wouldn't be right. I'm so much older than she is, so much duller—"

"Gregory, stop. Trust me. Tell her how you feel. And do it now. Her father won't last much longer and when he goes it will be harder—"

"There you are!" Helen was standing on the verandah waving at them. "Shall I come down to you or will you come to me? I've ordered tea."

"Do it, Gregory." Evie squeezed his forearm as she stood. "Just coming, darling." Evie walked back to the house, leaving Gregory on the bench behind her. She could only imagine what was going on in his mind.

"Helen, darling," Evie linked her arm through Helen's and led her back into the house to give Gregory time to recover himself. "I need to go. I'm so sorry. I forgot entirely about Douglas's visiting ladies, the Friends of the Hospital. They're coming to the house to discuss rotas for teas at the clinic. Can you imagine anything duller."

"Oh poor you," Helen groaned in sympathy, but not before Evie had seen the delight in her eyes.

"I know; you can see why I forgot, can't you?"

Helen laughed that tinkling little laugh she had.

"But Gregory's here to keep you company."

"Yes," she smiled, her face tingeing pink as she looked back over her shoulders at the man still sitting on the bench, staring down at the ground between his feet.

"Helen, before I go . . ." Evie looked into her eyes. "You love him, don't you?"

Her chin tilted slightly, as if she felt the need to be defiant. "What if I do?"

"If you do" – Evie took her hand, squeezed firmly – "you should find a way to let him tell you that he loves you too."

Evie didn't know exactly what happened next, as she left to see to the supposed horrors of her husband's tea-serving acolytes, but she could imagine. And she felt, even now, the warmth of knowing she'd had a hand in engineering their happiness. For they were happy. They radiated it. The gossips had their moment of course, whispering of inappropriateness and suspected scandal at the Club, over lunches, behind fanned hands as the couple were fêted and their engagement celebrated. But no one really had much heart for mischief-making; it was so clearly a love match. And Helen's father was their staunchest supporter. Evie had never seen the old man so happy. He even seemed to rally briefly.

But then he collapsed one hot afternoon some months later in the yard outside the new warehouse. He should never have been outside in that heat. No hat, no shade, no sense. At least it was quick, and Helen and Gregory had both been with him at the time, although Evie failed to see that there was really too much comfort in that. He would, though, Evie was sure, have died reassured that his daughter, and his business, his life's two loves, were safe in Gregory's protection.

And not a moment too soon, as it turned out. Cameron was about to arrive, and that would change everything.

11

The Residence, June 10th
Back up in her room, Lexy showered, selected the least wrinkled of her clothes, and went the extra mile with a stroke or two of lipstick and a brush of mascara. When she was satisfied she looked respectable enough for hospital visiting she glanced at the clock. Still more than an hour until Robert the Rude would be here. She looked over at the backpack. The more she could read, the more she knew before she met Evelyn, the more use the old lady would be to her investigations.

Although she was keen to find out more about Ursula from her diaries, she reminded herself Ursula had assembled the contents of the folder in a particular order for a reason and she might miss something if she didn't follow her path. She put the first batch of diary pages to one side and picked up the next item. A letter. A *long* letter, from Helen Buchanan.

Zomba, 12th April 1949

Dear Ursula,

I hope this letter will find you well and happy. It seems an age since we were all together, although I had hoped to find myself in Blantyre again long before this, but many things – of which more later – have kept me here in the capital. And, of course, we'd both hoped you would have been able to come to the wedding, although we do understand how you must put your responsibilities to the hospital and its patients first – your diligence is commendable. How lucky they are to have you, and it came as no surprise to either of us to hear of your appointment as Ward Sister – congratulations, dear Ursula. Such an achievement so young! Oh the joys of living in a country where merit is the only thing that matters, where the old conventions can be flouted!

But back to the wedding. What a day. What a marvellous, marvellous, MARVELLOUS day. You'd have loved it. We most certainly did, and we knew you were thinking of us even before your telegram arrived. Thank you, my darling; it meant so much to us. Evie, of course, will have given you all the details – spared you none, I'm sure, in her meticulous way, so apologies in absentia if we inadvertently bored you! I will not risk doing the same all over again, but I did want you to have this, the enclosed photograph of our small gathering, and to know that we raised a glass to you with much, much love. Was it really only on the voyage out that we met? I feel we've been friends for so much longer, know we will be now, for life. Perhaps that's what adventure does to you. Binds you, ties you fast to one another. I count myself fortunate indeed that we three have become so close. I can't imagine life here without you and Evie to share it with.

But enough. I must get to the point of this letter, as I have little time this morning for correspondence. We have a new shipment arriving and Gregory has just left for a meeting with the Missions along the Shire River so I must oversee the docking and unloading on my own. And then I must go home and make preparations for our guest. There is no gentle way to say this, Ursula, and I know it will be unpleasant news for you, as it is for us all. Cameron is coming.

I know we've never really talked about what happened between you, but I can guess enough of it to know that this will be a shock to you, so I wanted you to hear it from me, first, before the gossip mills start grinding. Cameron will always be a source of delight to them, such is his charm and notoriety. We expect him this evening.

His letter was slow to arrive and there is nothing we can do to deter or delay him.

I do not know what his plans are or how long he will stay, but I do know Gregory is of a mind to employ him and I will not stand against him in that. For all that I would rather Cameron disappeared from our lives forever, he is Gregory's brother, half-brother at least, and Gregory promised their mother he would watch out for him. My husband is a man of his word, and I wouldn't have him otherwise, so please, dear Ursula, forgive me for allowing him that.

I feel I must also share something of the reasons behind Cameron's unexpected visit, again better you hear it from me. Cameron is once again in the thick of scandal. He took up, it seems, with that widow he flirted with so outrageously on the boat. You remember her, surely? Gertrude von something she was then, his darling Gertie as he called her, Gertrude Steencamp as she now is. She married not long after arriving in Cape Town – money, of course – but her husband was a good deal older and it seems she was soon looking for diversion, just as it seems Cameron was only too happy to provide it. I'm sorry if I sound judgemental, harsh even, but after the trouble he has caused I struggle to be charitable. We all of us would be better off without him in our lives. But I will put a brave face on it, out of love for my husband, and hope we find a way of sending him far from our lives here in Zomba, to the remoter districts perhaps. It is a little against my better judgement to have him out of our sight, but I do not want him tainting our life here or, worse yet, yours, if we send him to the Blantyre office. I won't let that happen, I assure you my darling friend. Although I know you hardly have the time to socialise at all these days, I wouldn't want you coming face to face with him if you are out and about, nor avoiding visiting us here in case you do.

More encouragingly, perhaps, Gregory tells me Cameron

113

claims to have made useful contacts for Buchanan's in Cape Town and to have found a young native there from Zomba whom we should employ to coordinate matters on our behalf. A certain Richard Chakanaya. I've heard the name but can't quite remember where. Most likely he is one of the ubiquitous Chakanaya clan who seem to have their pick of official postings from chief of police to head of export and trade. If so, then I'm sure his connections could be beneficial. Cameron is giving little away at this stage, however. Information is currency to a man like him.

So. There we have it. Not the best of news, I know. But forewarned is forearmed, my dear. And on the subject of the best of news, the news Gregory and I are so anxious to be able to impart, I have nothing to tell. We long for a child but are yet to be blessed. Believe me, though, when I tell you that you and Evie, as godmothers-in-waiting, will be the first to know!

Dear Ursula, I do so hope we'll see each other soon. And Evie too. It would be such a joy to have you both here for a few days. After Cameron has gone, of course. Why not think about it? Tell me when you can spare some time and we will send a car for you – and before you protest, let me assure you there's always something or someone travelling between our offices so it would be no trouble. Please do come.

Your loving friend,
Helen

Lexy put the letter down, thoughtfully. Cameron. Cameron and Ursula. So far it would fit. And Richard Chakanaya. Intriguing. She was more convinced than ever he could give her the answers she wanted. She just had to work out how to get to him. Christopher Chizumu might yet change his mind. Or there was Robert. He seemed to know more than a little about the mysterious Mr Chakanaya. She glanced at the clock. Still plenty of time, so she pulled out the next tranche of diary pages and lost herself again in the swirling emotions of the past.

Blantyre, April 15th

There is something comforting about the African night, rich and black, air lush and warm as velvet on my bare arms. Most times I cannot sleep I sit out on the verandah in the old rocker Evie found for me in the market, let it soothe me in its arms till I'm ready to sleep. But not tonight. Tonight I am too impatient for gentle rhythms. I can hardly sit at all, am struggling to keep myself pinned here at my desk, hands still and steady enough to write. The pages of Helen's letter are strewn over the floor where I threw them earlier. I don't want to touch them, to read those words again, but I can't undo knowing what now I do. Why did she have to write to tell me? Why did I have to hear he was coming back from *her* of all people, the very woman I want to hate even though I know that's irrational and unfair. She has done nothing. But yet, yet . . .

It's so hot in here even with the ceiling fan silently turning above my head, the doors open to catch whatever breeze the night may offer. I can barely breathe with my heart so swollen and heavy in my chest. Cameron. Oh God. *Cameron.* Back here. And staying with Helen! I can't help it. I am jealous. Of her, and most especially of the way he feels about her. It doesn't seem to matter that she cares not one jot for him. Nor does it matter that I know he's a scoundrel and a rogue, dishonest, dishonourable. A liar, a cheat, everything I despise in the human character, but somehow in him, I forgive it. I am drawn to it. What is it in me that makes me want him so badly? Perhaps the Sisters were right – I'm bad, unworthy of love.

Even now, after more than four years, *four years*, I can feel his hand light and warm on my back, strong fingers gently rubbing my vertebrae, setting my skin alight through the silk of the evening gown Helen had leant me. He spun me round and round the ship's dance floor, making me giddy in a way I'd never been before. No man before or after has touched me like that. Touched me at all. Claimed me. And there's nothing I can do to stop myself falling all over again, even after these four long years of suppressing every flicker of emotion. I fell in love on that ship and I'm in love still. It makes no sense. Me. Sister Reid, in love with a society playboy. Who would believe it? I can hardly believe it myself.

He said he loved me. No one else has ever said that to me. Not like that. Whispered it in my ear as he burrowed into my neck that night on deck. *Kissed* me. He must have known she and Gregory would find us as they took their turn about the deck after dinner, as they so often did. And of course that's what he wanted. So obvious now. We sprang apart at the sound of the approaching voices. I was mortified, but he seemed almost elated, I thought because he'd declared himself to me. Fool, fool, fool. It was because he knew she'd seen us.

I couldn't understand it. Why he dropped me as suddenly as he'd picked me up. I'd never known how much disdain a passing glance could convey. Had no idea how much pain it was possible to feel in that split second of his eyes flickering past me. How much pain it was possible to feel and still be alive.

That next evening as he came towards us, the three of us sitting together with the ever-faithful Gregory at a table, chatting and listening to the band, my heart was in my mouth. I'd thought he'd claim me, let the world see he'd chosen me, *me*. I stood to reach for his outstretched hand, sure it was reaching for me even as his eyes skittered over me.

"Evie," he said, arm outstretched towards her, "would you care to dance?"

Evie. He might as well have stuck a knife in my chest. I sat down heavily, cheeks burning. I could feel Helen's rage at my humiliation radiating from her narrowed eyes. Gregory's hand dropped comfortingly over mine as Evie tried to decline but finally let herself be led away to the dance floor, too stunned, she told me later, to refuse him.

Dear Gregory. He tried. "Perhaps, Ursula," he said softly, "you would care to dance with me?" I couldn't speak, so he'd left us there, Helen and me, no doubt thinking he was being tactful, that a woman would know better how to soothe me. She'd tried. Moved immediately into the empty seat beside mine. When she'd reached for my hand, though, I'd snatched it away, all my anger coming to a head, turning to her, irrationally, unreasonably. But I couldn't blame Cameron, not him. I knew even then that it wasn't her fault he'd fixed on her. And to be honest, beautiful and charming though she is, I did wonder if Cameron would have desired her quite so strongly had Gregory not plainly been in love with her. He was always jealous of his older brother. Had to try to outdo him in everything. Wanted, expected, everything Gregory had, and more. I know that now. But that night, I blamed it all on Helen. Dear, kind Helen. For being too beautiful, too rich, too sophisticated. Too everything I was not. I still find it hard not to be jealous of her.

That night, when she'd tried to speak to me I'd turned my head away and ignored her, so she'd just sat there quietly, loyally, beside me as we watched the twirling couples, their motion hypnotic and the music covering our silence. Until Evie's scene.

I'll never forget Helen's laugh at Cameron's "comeuppance", as she liked to call it when she joked about it afterwards. So out of character for her to find amusement in anyone's discomfort but shows just how much she despised him. And I'll never forget the horror on Evie's face, either, as she slapped him and walked off the dance floor, stalked in fact, leaving him standing there surprised, holding one hand to his cheek before smiling and making light of it to the dancers who'd stopped in shock around him. Evie disappeared to her cabin and refused to come out for anyone. Such unexpected melodrama from a daughter of the manse, but I was glad of it; it diverted attention from me. Helen – wasn't it always? – finally talked her way in and calmed Evie down. Cameron and his hand again, it seemed, venturing down a back where, this time, it wasn't welcomed. I pretended to be as outraged as the rest of them, but really I just felt an ache because I wanted that hand again on me. Fool. To think he'd been taken with me. But I did. I did! And I think, for just a brief moment he was, or could have been, if he hadn't been besotted with Helen. And by the time I realised he was only toying, playing with Evie and me simply because we were Helen's friends and he wanted to get her attention, it was too late. I'd fallen. As blindly as a duckling, I would follow wherever he led, this, the first man I'd fallen in love with. The only man.

Later, I fled out on deck, leaving the ballroom to the revellers and the cabin to Evie, thinking I'd be safe there. I can smell that salt air again, feel the sting in my eyes and my heart as I heard them. Cameron and Helen. He was laughing as she scolded him, rebuked him with words I've never forgotten: "She doesn't understand your kind of games, Cameron. She isn't like us." I hated her then, for presuming to defend me like that, and for making Cameron say he'd done it to make her jealous. I'd never have had to know that, if Helen hadn't interfered.

I remember the disdain in her voice as she told him she would never, could never, feel anything for him but contempt. And I heard his voice change too, as he swore he'd make her his. I couldn't see, of course, from where I hid in the shadows, but in my mind's eye, I play it over and over. I hear the crack of flesh on flesh, her gasp of pain as he catches the wrist of the hand she'd slapped him with, the muffled noises as she struggled from his kiss.

Then that next night. Any hope that might have been left was dashed, splintering like crystal with every shriek of laughter from that blousy widow . . .

There's a green tinge in the sky just above the horizon. Dawn is on its way. I am a fool to brood like this. No better than a schoolgirl suffering her first crush. I must be stronger than this. I'll fold up Helen's letter, pin up my hair and put on a clean uniform. And then I'll work. Work is what I'm good at. My salve, my consolation. I must, *must* find a way to be strong. I have to. I don't think I could survive him twice. Oh Cameron. Why couldn't you stay away?

Blantyre, April 30th

I hardly dare write this. I'm frightened it will dissolve if I set the words down on the page, frightened it will vanish like a forgotten dream if I do not. He's been here. He's back. He wants me. Cameron. Cameron, my love! My only love.

He was waiting for me on the verandah. I'd started up the steps still thinking about the patients I'd left behind, the nurse I'd had to reprimand, the theatre schedule for tomorrow, when a small movement startled me and I saw a figure in the shadows. But it wasn't until he stood, said my name, that I knew. Such a wave of mixed emotions swept over me. The world quivered, hummed around me, my skin tingled as blood roared through me. My legs buckled under me, but before I fell, he was there, catching me, holding me, pulling me in close, stroking my hair and saying my name over and over in that way no one else can. I breathed him in and felt the strength of him and knew this was what I wanted. It was where I belonged, and the time since I last was in his arms vanished, the pain worthwhile if it had brought me to this moment. Why had I even tried to pretend I could forget him? He is my heartbeat, my pulse, my breath.

I don't know how long we stood there like that. Eventually he led me to the sofa, left me for a moment to call in to Cassie to bring out drinks, food, whatever, to revive me. Then he sat next to me, leant forward so our knees were touching and took my hands between his.

"Forgive me, Ursula, my darling. Can you forgive me?"

His *darling*! Did he need to ask?

Blantyre, May 3rd

He's gone. He came tonight to say goodbye – "*Au revoir,*" he said. And although I feel my heart is breaking without him, he's right: he always is. *Au revoir,* indeed. One week and we'll be together again. One long, long week. But I can do it. I will go to work and come home again and write to him, go to bed and think about him, then get up and go to work again until the days are past and I'm back in his arms. I am beyond happy. I am. I just am. I am the woman I am meant to be when I'm with him. To love and be loved is everything.

These last three days have been a revelation. So much has happened. I'm still reeling. Not just from Cameron's return and his love, although that makes me positively giddy, but I'm reeling from the truth. I was stunned, shocked, when he told me. Couldn't believe it.

But it all makes sense.

How could I not see it before, even though my instinct, my

120

intuition was screaming it at me, that Cameron would never want to hurt me! When I'd found it hard to forgive Helen, truly forgive her, I thought it was my fault, my jealousy getting in the way. How wrong I was! *She's* the jealous one. To think, the glorious Buchanan heiress, jealous of *me*. I should have had more faith. More trust. It's the very basis of love itself, and I nearly lost that. Oh, I have so much to learn about love. But Cameron will teach me, show me. And to think I doubted him, almost started to believe what Helen wanted me to believe. But he forgives me, says it was inevitable, that that's what makes her so dangerous, her ability to manipulate and control.

She'd had him sent away. I should have realised, but even now I can hardly believe she'd be so brutal. But she was behind it all. She poisoned Gregory against him – his own brother! – and made him leave Cameron in South Africa, told him to ingratiate himself with the smart set there to develop business contacts. They'd already had him cultivate that Gertie woman on the boat as their "entrée to society", Cameron said, so that's where he was instructed to start. Helen, Cameron said, had recognised Gertie straightaway as the sort of woman who'd insinuate herself into society in Cape Town – and wouldn't Helen know, after all? Isn't she just the same herself? He was horrified at the tales Helen had told me of scandal and affairs. Didn't I know he loved me, only me, and anything he did was only for his brother's sake, for the good of the business Gregory was charged with running, and that Cameron had never, never, betrayed our love? I can't believe I let her taunt me like that. What kind of woman would make up lies like that, knowing the hurt they'd cause someone who called you friend?

Whatever she's done, though, I should pity her. It's me Cameron loves. Me. She must make do with the brother, the

121

older, duller, diligent brother. Oh, Gregory's nice enough, but he's not like my Cameron. Perhaps she thought marrying him would keep Cameron close, or at least allow her to control him, to make his life miserable. A woman scorned. Oh Helen, and I thought you were my friend! But I will rise above it. Show compassion and dignity, just as Cameron says I should. Say nothing and make my love proud of me.

Cameron, Cameron, my life, my love! You're so right! None of that matters. The past is past and all I care about is that soon we'll be together again. We'll hide ourselves away, eat dinners somewhere quiet under the stars, walk hand in hand through parks and streets, pick our way through the market or watch the world go by from the sanctuary of our hotel room balcony. Can this really be happening? I can't believe it. But I knew, I did. Deep down, despite everything, I knew he had to love me. How could he not when I love him so much?

Oh I don't know what to do with myself! I won't sleep, that's for sure. But I won't need to. I feel as if this strange energy will carry me through anything, keep me buoyant and awake, alive, day after day after day, until Friday when the car comes to take me to him and we'll be together again. He loves me!

The phone at the side of the bed rang, and Lexy reached for it as her eyes raced down to the bottom of the page.

"Yes?"

"Miss Shaw, it's Barney. Dr Campbell said to let you know he's waiting outside."

"Oh!" Lexy glanced at the clock, then relaxed. Still only five to three. "Thank you, Barney. Tell him I'm on my way down, would you?"

"Very good, Miss Shaw."

As Lexy turned away after dropping her key into the box on the concierge's desk, she glanced into the bar and stopped short. Richard Chakanaya was still in there, sitting at a booth talking to someone she couldn't see. As she watched, he looked up and stared at her before letting that slight smile hover over his lips again, and nodding his head in her direction. To see who had caught his attention, his companion twisted his head round the side of the booth, and Lexy was shocked to recognise the florid features. Hugh Pendleton.

Ignoring the hand he raised, she hurried across the lobby, wondering what on earth those two could have in common, but before she could reach any kind of hypothesis, a car horn tooted and Robert drew up. Barney appeared from behind her and opened the passenger door.

"Hello," Lexy said, sliding into her seat. "You're early." The door had barely closed before Robert was pulling away.

"Sorry," he said, "bit of a rush. I've been called back to the clinic so need to drop you and leave you with Gran, I'm afraid."

"I could have got a taxi. You didn't have—"

"I know. But there wasn't really time. And anyway, gives us a few minutes to talk."

"About?"

"Gran. She's very frail, you see, and I don't want her upset, any more than she already has been, that is. She and Ursula were very close and—"

"You hope I'll be a little more tactful with her than I was with you."

"I wasn't going to say that."

"No. But it's what you meant." Less than a minute and he'd riled her already.

"No it isn't. I was simply going to say they were very close and she might be able to help you with your quest. I'm sure she'll want to, but you have to understand she's weak, so don't push her. She'll tell you what she can, but it probably won't be everything you want to know, so please don't expect her to have all the answers."

Lexy knew she deserved the warning. He was clearly very fond of the old woman and she'd done nothing so far to suggest to him she would be considerate and gentle. Tactless and pushy was more the impression she'd have given him.

"Thank you," she said. "I'll keep it in mind. I won't push, I promise."

"Good."

She watched out the window as Robert guided the car through the chaotic traffic of central Blantyre. The streets were heaving with cars and people and animals and bicycles. Her mind drifted back to Richard Chakanaya and Hugh Pendleton. An unlikely pairing to say the least. Perhaps she needed to be a little more cautious than she normally was.

"Robert, why did you want to find out if I knew Richard Chakanaya or not?"

Robert hesitated before answering, as if unsure how to proceed.

"He's not a celebrity, is he?"

"No. Not exactly." Robert smiled briefly. "Although he is notorious. He has a reputation for being a bit of a 'fixer', for being able to make things happen that wouldn't otherwise, in ways it's best not to investigate too thoroughly. It's made him, and his clients, a lot of money over the years."

"Well, is there really anything wrong with that? Making a lot of money?"

"You might not think so, but if some of the rumours are to be believed, it's not always within the bounds of ... acceptable practice, let's say."

"He seems respectable enough."

"Oh yes, he certainly *seems* to be. He works hard to *seem* to be the very picture of propriety. But believe me, he isn't. Steer clear, would be my advice."

"You sound as if you have reason to say that. Do you know him?" Perhaps this would be her way in to Richard Chakanaya after all, to finding out who he was acting for when he arranged the payments to Ursula.

"I know him. I wish I didn't. But Blantyre's a small place."

Lexy decided to bide her time. She'd work out how to engineer an introduction later. For now, she needed to get Robert on side. Make a friend of him and ignore the fact he irritated the hell out of her.

"So," she said, breezily changing the subject, "tell me a bit about yourself. I don't really know much about you, or your gran, except that you used to write to Ursula and your gran was her friend. And, of course, she was my mother's godmother."

"Not much to tell, really. What do you want to know?" This was going to be hard work.

"What about your family, your parents? Are they in Blantyre?"

"No. Australia."

"Brothers? Sisters?" she persevered.

"No."

"Well, Ursula then. How well did you know her? What was she like when she was younger?"

That seemed safer ground, and by the time they'd reached the hospital Lexy had learnt that Robert had lodged with Ursula when he'd been studying in Edinburgh, had still visited her once or twice a year if he could manage it, and that Evie and Ursula were thick as thieves. They'd come out to Africa together and been part of the same close-knit circle of friends, as Lexy already knew. And all of which made her even more certain Evie would be able to help her trace Ursula's son.

In return, Lexy had volunteered some of her own background,

but none of it seemed to be news to him. He even knew of her father; he admired his work and hoped to do his own bit to further the research the esteemed Philip Shaw had begun. She wanted to know more, but they'd arrived.

'Right," he said as he pulled up to the hospital entrance. "Easier if I drop you off here. Ask at reception, they'll direct you up to Gran."

As Lexy waved to the disappearing car, she felt she'd made a reasonable start in getting Robert on her side. Now she just had to be sure she didn't upset his gran.

"Mrs Campbell?"

Lexy pushed the door open and hesitated, not wanting to venture further into the room until she was sure the elderly woman sitting upright in the narrow hospital bed was ready to see her.

"Yes?" An immaculately coiffed head turned and surveyed her. "My dear. Do come in."

The voice was crisp and clear, strong even, and quite at odds with the frailty of the body that housed it. Or the strength of the warning Robert had issued.

'I'm Lexy—"

"I know dear. Alexis Shaw. I've been expecting you. Robert said he'd bring you. Where is my grandson?"

"He said there was an emergency at the clinic . . ." It felt awkward making Robert's excuses for him.

"Isn't there always? Well, no matter. I'd much rather have you all to myself anyway, if truth be known. Now come in and sit down, here, on this side of the bed, where I can see you properly. And draw over that curtain there if the sun's in your eyes. I was so very sorry to hear about dear Ursula."

"Yes. I'm sorry. It would have been unexpected news for you."

"My dear, at my age, such news is never, sadly, completely

126

unexpected. We are all in the waiting room, so to speak. Just look at me."

"I . . . you look well . . . well . . . no, I don't mean *well* . . . or you wouldn't be in hospital. Obviously, but . . ." *Oh, shut up, Lexy. Great start.*

"Quite." Evie laughed. "Oh, don't worry, my dear. I'm sure I'll last the afternoon. Dear Ursula, though. I thought she'd outlive us all, such a will of iron she developed in her later years. I thought Death himself would cower and bow to her authority. A fall, Robert said?" Lexy nodded. "Go on, my dear. Tell me all. I'm not about to faint or fade before your eyes, I assure you. I'm quite up to hearing the worst."

So Lexy told her about her brief visit to Edinburgh, the little she knew of Ursula's demise. Mrs Campbell, Evie, as she quickly became, listened attentively, prodding her with a question now and then, finally asking about Lexy's own mother, clearly upset to learn that Izzie too was dead. Once again Lexy had broken bad news badly. She had forgotten Robert hadn't known that so couldn't have forewarned his grandmother.

"She was such a delight, your mother. Ursula adored her, as did we all. I am so very, very sorry, my dear. What a dreadful shock for you. So much to deal with on your own. I understand now why Robert said you had questions about your family, their time here. I can't promise I'll have the answers, but I did know them both, your mother and dear Philip, and I'll help you if I can."

"Thank you, Evie. I do have questions about my parents and their time here, but I also . . ." Lexy took a deep breath. "I also want to find Ursula's son. I'm sure he's still here in Malawi."

"My dear girl, whatever do you mean? Ursula didn't have a son. She was quite the career woman, no time for family, except your mother, of course. And once she had Izzie with her she had no need for anyone else, she used to say. A son? Nonsense."

"No, Evie, it's not. I know she had a son. He was making regular

127

payments to her through solicitors here in Malawi. Through an intermediary, Richard Chakanaya. For some reason this son seems to want to be anonymous, but he's the closest thing to an uncle, to family, I've got now, and I'm sure if he realised that, he'd want me to find him."

Evie was silent, turned her head away to stare at the window, even though the curtains were drawn. The sun had moved on, though, and the curtains no longer glowed with light as they shielded the room from the searing rays.

"You could open those now, if you would, Lexy dear."

The day flooded in, and Lexy remained where she was, letting the warmth wash over her, looking out over the hospital car park below, her back to the woman in the bed.

"Evie, I don't know why Ursula and her son weren't together, why she never mentioned him or why there was no trace of him in her flat. There's nothing, you see. No record. Nothing. But I can guess, I think. She never married. And I understand that years ago, that mattered. But really it doesn't now and I'm not judging anyone. I just want to find family, if I can, or near family. I just want to belong somewhere. I have no one else left."

There was a long silence and Lexy had all but given up hope of an answer. Of a clue, a hint, anything from the old woman that would help her find Ursula's son.

"What if you find something you don't like, my dear? *Be careful what you wish for,* Ursula would say."

"Yes, she would," Lexy agreed, as a surge of nostalgia flooded her thoughts, "and my mother would have done too."

"Poor child," Evie whispered, her voice rich with compassion. "You must miss them so much."

All Lexy could do was nod as she struggled to brush aside the sadness, stop it derailing her.

"He was an absolute cad, you know. A real bounder, as we used to say."

128

Evie's voice sounded distant, far away in the past, and Lexy froze in case any movement or sound would break the spell her memories seemed to have cast over the old woman.

"We met on the boat coming out to Africa, you know, all of us. That's where it began. And he never loved her, I'm sure of that. Just played with her. Broke her heart. Then came back and broke it all over again. And then, as if he hadn't done enough damage already, he married Helen. Tried to break her too, but she was not the innocent dear Ursula had been. But even she, in the end . . ."

"Cameron," Lexy whispered.

Evie leant back against her pillow and turned her head to the window, the light like a stage lamp illuminating the strain on her features.

"Yes. Cameron. The only person I've ever truly wished dead. Now, at long last, he is."

12

Lexy had been evicted from Evie's room by an officious doctor, resplendent in his starched white coat, trailing a posse of acolytes behind him. She shouldn't have been surprised that Evie had agreed to her illness serving as a case study for the next generation of Malawi's doctors, but much as she admired the older woman's altruism, she'd been annoyed at the interruption. After a frustrating half-hour in the hospital canteen nursing a cup of tea she didn't want, trying to imagine what Cameron could possibly have done to induce such clear loathing on the part of a woman Lexy could tell was by nature magnanimous and forgiving, she was informed by one of the acolytes that she could return.

Evie's eyes were closed, but she seemed to sense Lexy's presence and smiled her greeting. Encouraged, Lexy pulled her chair closer to the bed and took the frail hand in her own firm one. She waited. Evie sighed, turned her head away towards the window, eyes still shut, and then began to speak.

"Evie, darling? Be an absolute dear and help me with this, would you?"

Helen's elegantly manicured hand held the two ends of the necklace behind her, unable quite to make the connection. Evie could hear the undertone of exasperation in Helen's voice and was, as always, only too pleased to be asked to do this small task for her. Helen was like an exotic bird to Evie's starling, and Evie was constantly amazed that she was her dearest, closest friend. "Don't judge a book by its cover,"

Ursula would have said, and how very true. All three of them had been able to see beneath each's exterior to the person within and to find they were kindred spirits at their core.

Evie could never quite believe her luck. Evie, the doctor's wife, taken up by this worldly, fashionable woman, and all because she happened to have booked passage on the same boat. Just think. A month earlier, or a month later, and she might never have met Helen Buchanan, even though there was a distant, very distant, family connection through their mothers. Nor would she have met Gregory Munro or his alarming brother Cameron, or even the slightly frightening but hugely capable Nurse Reid. Dear Ursula. All that professional proficiency and all that hopeless naivety. Sad, though. Brought up in an orphanage. Never knew what it was to be loved.

Evie could be in awe of them, if she let herself. She had been brought up in a remote Highland manse, been courted by her father's godson and found herself married when she'd hardly turned nineteen. Then she was left behind for two long, long years while her new husband established his position before sending for her to join him.

They'd been in the country only a few days then, the evening of the necklace, the passage not long behind them, but shipboard romances done and dusted. Or so she'd thought.

"Of course, darling." Evie reached in, took the ends of the rope of pearls and slipped the hook into its clasp. It clicked firmly into place, the hook sitting tightly in the diamond-crusted shell. Helen leant forward, starting to stand before Evie had removed her hands and that's what made the dress gape away from her skin. Evie gasped. She prided herself on being unshockable, but there was a fading bruise the size of a saucer on Helen's right shoulder, its greens and yellows mottling her perfect skin.

"Darling?" Helen asked. "What is it?" The dress fell back against her milk-white skin and the discoloration disappeared as she turned to face her friend.

131

"I . . . Your . . . There's a . . . Nothing," Evie stammered, turning away as Helen looked at her, one eyebrow cocked in that self-assured, amused way she had then. Evie felt her cheeks flush and her heart beat faster. What had happened? Such a bruise! How had she—

"Cameron," Helen said, her voice flat, her shoulders rising in the slightest of shrugs.

"Cameron?"

"The bruise. Yes, Cameron."

"*Cameron?*" Evie repeated like an idiot. "He did that? How on earth . . . Why?"

"I turned him down, again, you see."

"I don't understand." And in truth, Evie didn't. The very thought of a man hurting a woman, even *touching* a woman who wasn't his wife, was so alien to her. Douglas hadn't so much as held her hand before they were engaged, and certainly hadn't ventured to kiss her until they were all but married.

"He declared himself again, as they say, that last night in Cape Town. Told me he loved me, wanted me and so forth. Couldn't live without me. Said he'd tried with Gertie, but it was impossible. He couldn't get over me. Nonsense, of course, and I told him so, just as I had on the voyage. I told him I'm in love with someone else and that in any case I'd made my feelings about him very plain that night on the ship and nothing had changed. We will continue to be thrown by circumstance into close proximity and I have no wish to make life awkward for any of us, so I will be civil but nothing more. I despise the man, if truth be known."

Helen turned to the mirror, smoothed the powder-blue chiffon of her dress, leant in and puckered her lips. She looked divine. She always did, but tonight there was something ethereal about her. Perhaps it was the light, but she looked so fragile, so delicate. Perhaps it was knowing how badly she was bruised beneath such a sleek and stylish exterior that made Evie feel Helen could break,

132

could be broken, despite the strength of her spirit. Evie was afraid for her.

"So . . . he hit you?"

"No, darling, of course not. I'm sure he didn't *mean* to hurt me. He was upset, embarrassed, I suppose. He pushed me. That's all. And there was a hook on the wall behind me. For the fan cord, you see, and I stumbled and hit it rather hard when I stepped back from him."

"But he had no right to push you! That bruise is dreadful, it must have been so . . . Did he threaten you?"

"Oh, it doesn't matter, darling. It was nothing. Looks worse than— Oh, darling, look! I've a run in my stocking. I can't possibly go out like this. Would you be a dear and pop down and distract the gang while I change? I'll only be a few minutes, but I do so hate to keep them all waiting."

"Oh right. Yes, of course. Absolutely." Evie knew the subject had been closed, so she did as she was asked.

The men were waiting outside, laughing and smoking. A couple of the younger hospital doctors and the new dentist were clustered around Fredi, who was, of course, looking flamboyant and louche with his scarlet cravat and matching handkerchief. She was drawn to their laughter as he regaled his audience with a story that involved much hilarity and posturing.

"No Douglas this evening?" She turned, surprised. She hadn't noticed Fredi's new friend Jurgen Axelsen sitting in the shadows to her left.

"Oh. No. Douglas is upcountry again. The clinics."

"Of course. Tireless, that husband of yours. We're so lucky to have him."

They both turned back to Fredi as another burst of laughter erupted from his small entourage.

"Dear Fredi," Evie laughed. "He's incorrigible. Don't you just love him?" She turned back to the man at her side, surprised to see him blush, cough, look down quickly at his feet. "Jurgen? Are you—"

"Here I am, darlings!" Helen's voice called all attention to the doorway behind Evie and Jurgen and they stepped quickly aside to allow her her entrance. "So dreadfully sorry to keep you all waiting. Were you awfully bored?"

Evie watched the men swarm towards her glamorous friend, saw their faces light up when she descended the steps to join them, laid a hand lightly on an arm, turned a smile to one or other, kissed a cheek in passing, accepted a cigarette.

As they made their way to the waiting cars, all in such high spirits, laughing and joking, excitement entwining them, binding them all together, tethering them to one another, the shadow that Evie's fleeting glimpse of Helen's bruise had cast on her spirits quickly dissolved. Gregory was first to the car, and as he held the door open for Helen to glide elegantly in, Evie saw the look they exchanged. Nothing had changed since the boat, that much was clear. Evie hadn't asked who the "someone else" Helen had told Cameron she was in love with really was, because she already knew.

*

The room was in shadow now and Lexy's face was hidden from Evie until the glare of sudden light and the crinkling popping of the fluorescent strip above the bed building to its full incandescence shook them both from their thoughts. An officious nurse Evie didn't recognise was fussing around her, plugging something into the cannula that dug painfully into the back of her hand, then squeezing a bag that hung from the spindly frame beside her bed like an over-ripe mango drooping from its tree.

"Your grandson phoned to check on you," the nurse was saying in a tone Evie found disagreeable. "He'll be along later, but he got to do his clinic first. Busy man, that one. And you" – the nurse jabbed a finger in Lexy's direction and nodded her head towards the door – "he said time you were gone."

The nurse pulled the sheets taut and tucked them in like a girdle around Evie's chest. Bandaged breasts on a pantomime star couldn't have been strapped any tighter. Then she took Evie's hands and straightened them too as she laid them down on top of the bedclothes. And like a fool, Evie let her, amused at how subservient she seemed to have become. How helpless.

"Water, please," Evie croaked. She swallowed hard and her eyes smarted as the dryness cut her throat like glass. A sigh at the interruption, a clatter and splash, and a plastic beaker was thrust into Evie's hand.

"Lexy," Evie's voice was clearer now. "Don't go."

"I won't. I—"

"But Dr Campbell said—"

"I need to talk to her."

"But you need to be strong for your operation and no talking—"

"Thank you, nurse. That will be all."

The nurse's disapproval was clear, even before she snapped the door shut behind her with brisk efficiency.

"Are you sure you're able to go on, Evie? I could come back tomorrow."

Evie could hear the reluctance in the younger woman's voice, knew she was desperate for Evie to continue. Lexy was more inquisitive than her mother had been and Evie recognised tenacity when she saw it. She would have to tell her . . . some of it. Not everything, of course. Tell her enough to make her realise she wasn't safe, to make her understand why she had to leave Malawi.

Cameron had been home less than a month, but already he was causing Helen concern, even though he'd finally taken a house of his own. That day in May 1949 Evie had just returned from

135

the annual review of the hospital's rural clinics with Douglas. She'd met Helen at the Club for tea on her first day back and it was Helen's gasp and exclamation that had made Evie turn. She couldn't believe it when she saw them come in together, her arm linked in his, her face brighter than Evie had ever seen it. Even from where she and Helen were sitting in the Ladies' Drawing Room, Ursula's euphoria was clear. She looked almost frivolous. But then it was a long time since Evie had seen her out of her nursing uniform, although that afternoon there was more to her lightness than could be attributed to her wardrobe.

"Has she no sense?" Evie hissed under her breath.

"Has he no shame?" Helen had responded.

The couple lingered in the hallway, then he bent and kissed her hand lightly before disappearing in the direction of the Members' Bar. Ursula watched him go, then turned to see her two friends sitting staring at her. She laughed and tripped, yes *tripped*, there really was no other word for it, over to join them. She plopped down in a chair, eyes shining and face glowing.

"Well?" she challenged the silent women. "Aren't you going to scold me, tell me I'm a fool, a respectable professional with a reputation to consider?"

"Darling," Helen began, then looked to Evie as if she should be the one to respond. Picking up the mantle, she tried, but truly was at a loss.

"Ursula, we've been here before. Four years ago on the boat and—"

"And people change." Ursula's hand waved in dismissal. "And deserve to be given a second chance. Isn't that the Christian thing to do, Evie? Tell me, Evie, as a minister's daughter, isn't that the Christian thing to do if a man repents?"

"Not if that man is the devil incarnate," Helen retorted. "And that one is."

"No, he's not. He's changed. His time in South Africa, he says, has reminded him of the importance of values, and morals. Of loyalty and love."

Helen's laughter was as sharp as it was unexpected. "No, a leopard doesn't change its spots. And that man is more of a predator than any big cat. Believe me, he's been living under my roof until this weekend, so I know. Don't fall for it. You'll be sorry if you do."

"Of course. You'd know."

Evie was shocked at the venom in Ursula's voice, the way she sneered at Helen, her friend.

"Ursula, I don't think you should—"

"What's the matter, Helen?" Ursula cut across Evie's attempt to intervene. "Jealous?" Ursula's smirk made her homely features ugly.

"Sorry?"

"Find it hard to accept a man like Cameron might abandon his infatuation with you for something deeper and more meaningful with me?"

"What?"

Evie couldn't bear it. Not her two closest friends. "Ursula," she tried again, "I really don't—"

"This is nothing to do with you, Evie. This is between Helen and me. We all know Cameron was infatuated with her from the moment he set foot on that boat. What we didn't know is that she encouraged him."

"I most certainly did not!"

"We only have your word for that, don't we? Perhaps we should ask Gregory. Cameron told me how awkward it was that the daughter of his brother's new employer was behaving in such an unseemly way towards him. Imagine. How difficult for him."

Evie was horrified by the sheer idiocy of Ursula's words, the depths of her gullibility.

137

"Ursula, even I know that's nonsense." Evie put a hand on her friend's arm in an attempt to stop her. "Gregory was the one who called Cameron to account for his behaviour. Who told him he was no longer welcome to sit with us at dinner. Gregory almost pushed him towards that Gertie, for goodness' sake, anything to keep him away from us."

"Think that if you like, Evie." Ursula shook Evie's hand off, crossed her arms and leant back in her chair. "But Cameron only took up with Gertie to try to stop Helen's advances. If he'd really wanted Gertie, why didn't he stay with her in South Africa?"

"Because Gertie's married—"

"He thought Helen would leave him in peace when she realised he wasn't interested in her. Once she'd started making eyes at his brother instead." Ursula's cold stare was fixed on Helen. "But you couldn't leave him alone, could you? You had to find a way to hurt him, discredit him and have him sent away again. Never mind the pain it might have caused me, your *friend*. That's the truth, isn't it, Helen?"

Helen was quite pale. Evie thought again of the horrendous bruising on her skin that night she'd fixed her necklace for her. Of how Helen had tried to dismiss Cameron's unwanted advances as nothing to worry about, his brutality as unintentional. And she was frightened. Ursula had no idea of the darkness in the man she had allowed to seduce her, for it was very clear that that was exactly what he had done.

Helen, with remarkable dignity, picked up her wrap and wound it around her set shoulders.

"I'm not going to pick an argument with you, Ursula, nor am I going to take offence. He's spun his web around you again; anyone can see that. Just remember that we tried to warn you. And that we'll be here to pick up the pieces when he hurts you once again." She leant over and kissed Evie lightly on the cheek and bent to do the same to Ursula, who turned her head away with a snort of disgust. Evie heard Helen sigh as she walked away.

Ursula looked at Evie, challenge in her eyes, then shrugged before reaching for the teapot and pouring herself a cup.

"You could at least try to be happy for me, take my side for once. I knew you, remember, before you even met our grand heiress. I'm as much your friend as she is. More so. I don't lie."

"Ursula, dear," Evie said, trying to strike a placatory note. "We all just want you to be happy. And he *did* behave appallingly before, so you can see why we might worry." Her smile was forced as she held her tongue and patted Ursula's hand.

"It wasn't his fault. It was hers. And he won't let her ruin his life with her games any more."

Evie felt a shiver, a premonition. This was not like Ursula at all, and she feared it could only end badly.

*

When Evie woke, she didn't need to open her eyes to know Robert was sitting there in the armchair beneath the window. She could smell the coffee he always brought in with him as he stopped to check on her on his way to his early morning clinic.

She smiled, and was rewarded with a soft chuckle.

"So you're awake are you, Gran? And how are you feeling today?"

"Old, Robbie, my boy. As I do every day."

"Well, at your age, what can you expect?"

It was hardly Ealing comedy, but they both enjoyed the familiar routines.

"So what did you make of her?" Never one to beat about the bush, her grandson.

"Delightful. Just like her mother."

139

"Only she's not, is she? Her mother didn't go around asking difficult questions. Dangerous questions." He drained his coffee, slapped the cup down on the windowsill. "What do we tell her, Gran?"

"The truth. She knows Ursula had a son. There's no point in our denying it. I've tried; she doesn't believe me. The best we can do is try to limit her enquiries. She knows more than she seems to realise already, and you, dear boy, need to find out *how* she knows and exactly *what* she knows. Then we can work out how best to protect her."

"Protect Lexy?"

"Protect Helen."

13

Lake Malawi, June 12th

Lexy had been astonished when Robert had called to invite her out yesterday. Well, not *out* in the sense of a date or anything, but to accompany him on a trip up to one of the clinics on the shore of Lake Malawi. She had hesitated for only a few seconds before agreeing. Apart from it being important to keep him onside after getting off to such a bad start, she was excited at the thought of getting out of the city and seeing the famous lake. Just for a day she would try to forget all the shocks and surprises, loss and sadness and just ... relax, which, after another day spent fruitlessly trawling through Ursula's affairs as assembled by the lawyers in that tedious Manila folder, she felt she totally deserved, even if she had done a fair bit of the trawling poolside. She'd gone to bed early so was rested enough despite the early start to remain unruffled whatever the provocation and she would simply rise above any irritation Robert's abrupt manner might cause.

She found herself wondering what she would have said if he *had* been asking her out. He was infuriatingly difficult to read, but then so were her own feelings. Ridiculous even to be thinking like that. With bereavement and break-up featuring heavily in her recent past, she was in no state emotionally even to *consider* ... But he was darkly handsome, charismatic, decisive, a man of action ... the complete opposite of Danny. Perhaps exactly what she needed to help her move on. Her rebound man.

"Oh, grow up, Lexy Shaw!" she scolded herself, throwing a

crumpled blue shift dress onto the growing mound of rejected clothes on the bed behind her. Precious little left in the wardrobe now. But what *was* the dress code for a Sunday non-date picnic trip to Lake Malawi via a clinic, for goodness' sake? Nothing too smart, but then again nothing too casual, which in Lexy's world was usually a euphemism for scruffy anyway, and she had to look as if she'd made a bit of an effort, be rude not to, but not *too* much . . . Oh, this was impossible!

Jeans.

Or would they be too hot?

Tough. She'd suffer. White linen shirt. Sandals. Smear of lipstick, SPF higher than she thought existed until she saw it in the hotel lobby shop, and hair back in a ponytail. Job done. *And don't even think about looking in the mirror again, little miss sweet sixteen going on thirty-one.*

She was downstairs waiting in the lobby on the dot of seven despite her dithering. Robert arrived fifteen minutes later, by which time she was breathing deeply and working hard to give the outward appearance of nonchalance. Keeping her cool wasn't going to be as easy as she'd hoped. But she pinned on her brightest smile and walked across the lobby to meet him.

"Robert, hello. This is so good of you. I can't tell you how much I'm looking forward to seeing something of Malawi other than city streets."

"My pleasure, Lexy." And, to her surprise, he smiled as if he meant it. He was obviously going to make the effort too. Good. "And please, accept my apologies for keeping you waiting." Even better. "I was with Gran first thing and she . . . well, she took a turn for the worse so I didn't want to leave until I was sure things were back under control."

"Oh, of course. I'm so sorry." Lexy was genuinely concerned to hear about Evie but couldn't help feeling a little annoyed that he had a valid excuse for being late, making her feel petty

142

for beginning to get huffy waiting. Score one to Robert. Not that this was about point-scoring, she reminded herself. "How is she?"

"They're probably going to bring forward her operation."

"Shouldn't you be with her? I mean I quite understand if you—"

"No, no. Not at all. She's settled now and will sleep most of the day, and they won't operate until tomorrow afternoon at the earliest, and I'm not sure she'll be strong enough even then. I can't let the clinic down anyway. Some of them travel miles to get there. Shall we?"

Lexy followed him out to the car, letting him tell her about the clinic, prompting him occasionally with the odd question. As they drove out through the quiet streets, she found herself warming to Robert, forgiving his abrupt manner. He was clearly a man who was passionate about his work and his patients. Passionate about Malawi too, she discovered as they escaped into open country, leaving the buildings behind, and he launched into a running commentary on the landscape, the wildlife, the climate, even, becoming increasingly animated as they left the motorway and tarmac behind and rattled along a narrow, dusty track.

"Sorry," he said, stopping abruptly. "I must be boring you to death."

"On the contrary. It's fascinating. I've never been outside Europe before and this is just so . . . so vast. So beautiful. Although that hardly seems to do it justice."

Robert's smile was warm, genuine. "Some people hate it. But some of us . . . some of us just get it. And I think you might turn out to be one of those, Lexy, what do you think?"

Their eyes met for a second but then the jeep hit a pothole and lurched drunkenly to Robert's side and they bounced hard and high.

"Oh!" Lexy grabbed the handrail above her door as Robert's eyes snapped back to the road and he wrestled with the wheel to bring the vehicle back under control.

"Sorry. Didn't mean to frighten you. When the chances of meeting another car are as slim as they are out here, you can get a bit lax about watching the road, but then these potholes can be treacherous. Other traffic isn't really the problem."

Lexy watched his profile as he drove, thinking over what he'd said. Might she be one of the ones who "get it"? She certainly loved what she'd seen of the country so far, and this landscape, this was breathtaking. She'd been conceived here, so perhaps it was in her blood, somehow. Perhaps, when she found Ursula's son and her proxy family, this would come to be where she belonged.

She found herself flung sharply forward as the jeep skidded to a halt.

"There!" Robert was pointing through the windscreen on her side to a small clump of trees, his face animated and excited.

"What?"

"Elephants – see them?"

Lexy shook her head slowly, straining to see where he was pointing.

"Binoculars in the pocket of your door." She pulled them out, looked at them, not quite sure which end was which or what exactly to do with them, but she needn't have worried. He grabbed them from her and scanned the horizon, twiddling a knob in the middle of the two lenses with one hand as he pointed with the other. "Yes!" He was triumphant. "And antelope too, I think . . . yes! Sable antelopes."

Well, great, thought Lexy, *as long as you can see them.* She could see nothing and felt a Danny-style huffiness creep over her. How rude, just to snatch—

"Here." Robert pulled her closer to him and handed her the

144

binoculars. "I've focused them for you." She felt herself blush and hoped it was just because of her discomfort at how easily he'd wrong-footed her again. Nothing to do with being pulled into what was very like an embrace. He had turned her in the right direction and left one of his arms dangling over her shoulder, pointing out the animals with the other. She felt her breath stall. She could see them; brought close by the binoculars, she almost felt she could touch them.

"Amazing, eh?" She knew Robert was smiling, could hear it in his voice. "Come on, let's get closer." He was already opening his door.

"Oh, I . . ." Lexy didn't want to admit to a reluctance to leave the safety of the jeep. "No it's fine, I . . . We should get on . . . The clinic . . ."

"Two minutes. Come *on*."

His door slammed and he was jogging round the car, opening her door for her and tugging at her arm like an impatient child. She hesitated for a second and then laughing, jumped down from the jeep and let him pull her behind him. She could see the animals without the binoculars now, and Robert slowed their pace, brought them to a halt, turned to her with a finger to his lips. They crept forward. Lexy's heart was pumping hard. She had never seen anything like it. Her mother had taken her to the zoo to see "wild" African animals – fluffy, friendly monsters in cages – but this . . . this was something else entirely. She raised the binoculars again, felt him take her hand, guide it to the focusing dial and showing her how to move it. The animals blurred, sharpened and came into focus: a tall black antelope. She tightened the focus further and dark eyes looked straight at her. A predator contemplating a kill. She dropped the binoculars and gasped. Robert looked at her, puzzled. He frowned, then took the binoculars from her and led her back towards the jeep. She sensed his disappointment. As they neared the vehicle, she stopped.

145

"It was looking at me," she said. "Right at me. It was incredible." She was relieved to see his face break into a smile.

"Yes, aren't they? And all herbivores, despite all those tusks and horns."

"Really?" Lexy was surprised. So not quite the predator she'd imagined, that antelope. She wasn't sure whether to be relieved or worried that she'd been so quick to imagine the worst.

"Yes. Use them for defending themselves only. We could learn from that. I'm so glad we got to see them." Robert laughed. "You know, I thought for a moment there you were frightened."

"Oh no." Lexy attempted a light laugh in return. "Not at all." It was a fib, not a lie. She had just been taken a bit by surprise. But no, not frightened. Of course not.

"Sorry I dragged you away then."

"Well," she said, feeling magnanimous, and safe, "there is the clinic . . ."

"Yes, I suppose. Shall we?" He indicated the jeep and they started back. He was grinning. "Don't get too many of those magnificent beasts in Edinburgh, do you?"

"Oh, I don't know. I've come across a few wild bores in the Grassmarket on a Saturday night."

"Yes, and a few stuffed ones in Morningside." They both laughed at the feeble jokes and residual tension evaporated. They were back at the jeep now. He opened her door and closed it gently once she was settled. He walked slowly round to his side, one last glance at the animals before he climbed in, and they set off once again, the silence between them more companionable.

The clinic building was set at the edge of a very small village. It was a long, plain white single-storey structure with a verandah running the length of it. The verandah was already full of waiting patients, and Lexy could see more sitting in groups in the shade of the trees to the side of the building.

146

"Looks like you're going to be busy."

"No more than usual. But it shouldn't take more than an hour or so. The nurses will see to most of them, just vaccinations. Then we can get on to the lake."

"No problem. Can I help?" Lexy saw his hesitation and fought the pique it caused. *Play nice, Lexy, play nice.* "Although I don't want to get in the way. Perhaps I'll just go for a wander, explore a bit, maybe even snooze under a tree somewhere . . ."

"Good idea. Just check the branches first."

"Why?"

"Snakes. They can drop on you and—"

"Oh, don't, please. I hate snakes. I really hate them. Are they pois— No. Don't tell me. I'd rather not know."

"Sorry. But don't worry. They're usually quite shy so probably none this near the clinic. In fact, from personal experience I can recommend that tree there." Robert pointed to a particularly impressive mopane, already sheltering a sleeping dog. "You won't be in any danger from old Rufus there. Deaf as a post and all but toothless. Plenty of room for two, anyway."

Lexy liked this more relaxed, human Robert. But even as she turned back to him, he was all business again, already opening his door and calling to a nurse who had appeared from the clinic.

"Nurse! Nurse Anakele! Give me a hand here, would you? I've brought supplies." He disappeared round to the back of the jeep and started unloading. Lexy knew she'd been forgotten so wandered off to explore the village, which took all of ten minutes, before settling herself under what did indeed look a very inviting tree. She pulled out more of her never-ending papers, spread them on her lap, and read not a word.

"Ow!" Lexy yelped more with surprise than pain as the ball bounced off her leg. She looked up to see a small boy laughing and staggering towards her on plump legs.

147

"George, wait!" Robert came bursting round the corner of the bungalow and swept the boy up high into the air. "Gotcha!" The child giggled in delight.

Lexy scrabbled to her feet, papers scattering over the rug around her.

"Robert, I . . . Are you . . ."

"Finished? Yes." He smiled as he put the child down. "George, take your ball and go in to your mother. You can shoot more goals later." The child took the ball Lexy held out to him and tottered off.

"Nurse Anakele's son. He and I share a love of football, although neither of us is any good at it. Hope we didn't do any damage?"

"Oh no. I was in danger of dozing and it's far too good a day to waste doing that." She bent to gather the strewn papers together.

"Here, let me help." He handed her a sheaf of notes and then sat back against the broad trunk of the tree and closed his eyes. "Now, don't let me disturb you."

Was that a hint of humour in his voice? Surely not, Lexy thought. This was the serious Dr Campbell, after all. She hesitated for a moment, then sat and leant back too, enjoying the touch of the breeze filtering through the leaves above them.

They sat in silence, listening to the rise and fall of voices from the clinic, the occasional snore from Rufus the only outward sign that the animal was still alive.

"I was right, wasn't I?" he said, eventually, sounding almost regretful. "In the car earlier? You do. You get it, don't you?"

"Yes." She breathed deeply, catching scents of acacia and freshly cut grass, the faint musk of the man beside her. "Yes, I do."

The moment was broken by a low rumbling noise from the direction of the sleeping dog, followed by a pungent smell.

"Oh, my . . ." Lexy's hand covered her nose and mouth.

"Time to go." Robert stood, reached down and took her hand to help her up as if it were the most natural thing in the world.

★ ★ ★

148

Lake Malawi was astonishing. Lexy had seen pictures and read a little about it in the guidebook she'd picked up at Heathrow, but she was still completely unprepared for the breathtaking vista that unfolded as the jeep cruised down the gently sloping road to the golden shoreline, the pale water shimmering blue and silver beyond it like shot silk rippling in a breeze.

Robert's picnic was equally astonishing. She was impressed. Very impressed. Until he confessed his housekeeper had put it all together and all he'd had to do was pick it up and put it on the back seat.

"We should have had freshly caught fish and a barbecue, really, but it's been a while since I did that. My father taught me to fish here when I was a boy. There never seems to be time for fishing these days."

"Yes, I can believe that. The hospital, the clinics, your research. And now your gran so ill, too. There can't be much time left over."

"No, there isn't, and then there's the . . . the case as well."

"What case?"

"The Blantyre 144 appeal."

Lexy held her breath. Blantyre 144. The folder she'd seen in Robert's desk.

"The . . . er . . . what?" She tried to sound casual, but his slow smile told her she'd failed.

"How much did you manage to read before Audrey turfed you out?"

"I didn't . . . I mean . . . oh, not very much. Just the title on the front really, and a quick scan of a couple of newspaper cuttings."

"And what did you learn from those?"

"Nothing much. That a lot of people had died, in some major incident, and I caught the name Buchanan once or twice so I'm guessing the company was at fault or implicated in some way."

"Well, that's about right."

"So, what's it got to do with you?" Lexy was eager to deflect attention from her snooping and was relieved when it seemed Robert was going to let it go.

"It was a national tragedy. The scale of it. Not something this country had really seen before: 144 people dead or missing, presumed dead. Very few survivors. Almost everyone seemed to be connected to it in some way, to know someone . . . And of course, my family were too, Gran in particular. Helen Buchanan, you see, and her two youngest, were amongst the missing. Their bodies just three of those never recovered."

"How awful. How really awful. Evie must have been devastated."

"Yes. They were very close. Came out to Africa together, with Ursula, too."

"What exactly happened?"

"There was an almighty storm. Unlike anything anyone had ever known, apparently. Trees coming down, roads flooded and impassable, the lake whipped up into a vicious whirlpool."

Lexy looked out at the calm waters, at the mirror-smooth surface.

"I know," Robert continued. "Hard to imagine, isn't it? But it can be treacherous, this lake. As it was that night. Perhaps if . . . but I'll get to that. So, the storm. There was a landslip, a mudslide over there on the far side; you see the slope? It wasn't always quite as steep as that. The mudslide swept away several houses and took anyone in its path with it. So many people were making their way to the lake to try to get out by boat. The river was flooding further up and everyone thought that was the danger. No one imagined the hill was about to move. Helen's house was destroyed. The mud took out the back wing, crushed like eggshell. Fire took the rest of the house. There was nothing left, apparently."

"Did she . . . Is that what happened? Buried or burnt in her own home?"

"No." Robert picked up a handful of shells, threw them one by one out into the lake. "No, Helen drowned, along with all the other poor souls trying to get on the Buchanan steamer."

"What?"

"There were two boats in, both belonged to the company. There was panic and chaos at the dock, as you might imagine. People desperate to get away. Her husband commandeered the private launch for himself and the family. Wouldn't let anyone else on board. Held them off at gunpoint. So the other boat, the *Blantyre*, even though it was a good deal larger, was very quickly packed, overloaded. Helen saw their housekeeper desperately trying to get on board it and called to her to come to them. When she didn't hear, Helen ran back down the gangplank to the jetty to get her. The mud hit and swept everyone on the dockside into the water as it went."

Lexy was speechless, but it didn't matter, because Robert hadn't finished.

"If the steamer had been properly equipped with safety equipment then there may have been more survivors. And if Buchanan's had maintained the shoring on the slope at the back of their warehouse yard, the slip would not have been able to gather the momentum it did. As it was, the Buchanan's warehouse was utterly destroyed. Although I'm sure they recouped more than enough from the insurance to compensate them for that, and for the loss of the steamer."

She was struck by the bitterness in his voice, but still she said nothing. There was more yet, she could tell.

"Buchanan's were investigated. By an inquiry panel of six, three of whom shared a common surname. One you're familiar with, I know."

Lexy knew where this was going. "Chakanaya."

He nodded. "The very same. Richard has a significant stake in Buchanan's, thanks to Cameron, and he has family and connections at every level of Malawi society. That's why Cameron teamed up with him in the first place. If you want something done, and aren't too fussy about how, he's your man. Some interesting names on the witness list too, even more interesting when you look at the maiden names of some of the married women who came forward to testify. There were a few truly independent witnesses, but one by one they retracted their statements. Other people were happy to talk, off the record, but refused point-blank to testify. The Chakanaya name can have that effect."

"I'm beginning to see why you aren't too fond of him."

He raised an eyebrow. "An understatement, Lexy. I can't stand the man. There were a lot of families left without breadwinners, children without parents. A lot of people who deserved, needed, compensation, insurance money that went to a wealthy corporation rather than those who suffered. But, not surprisingly, Buchanan's and its directors were not held to be culpable in any way at all. There was a memo, you see, that miraculously escaped the destruction. It apparently clearly directed their General Manager to implement full and thorough safety checks on all vessels, to commission a full structural review of the warehouse and its yard. And there were bank statements, belonging to that same General Manager, showing unexpected and inexplicable sums of money going into the account. The General Manager, the courts, in their wisdom, decided, had been embezzling the money meant for these safety measures, and as such was culpable, wholly and individually. Buchanan's got off scot-free. And the Manager went to jail, where he committed suicide."

"Robert, that's . . . that's awful. Are you saying the Buchanan directors *framed* him, their own General Manager?"

"Everything, *everything*, says that's exactly what happened. But it can't be proved."

"This is personal, for you, isn't it? Why? Who . . . ?"

"I can't stand injustice. And particularly not like that. Where it's the rich white man who gets away with it once again, and screw the natives, what ho, old chap. Africa wouldn't be in the mess it is if Europeans hadn't stolen it from the indigenous people."

"You're white . . ." She didn't mean to be provocative but was surprised to hear the vehemence in his voice.

"Yes. White African, third generation, and this is home. But that doesn't mean I think colonialism was right, or a good thing, or a necessary evil, or any of the other justifications you get bandied around. It happened, but Malawi became independent half a century ago, and we have to move on. Besides, it's as much about corruption and abuse of power, or the rich getting richer at the expense of the poor, as it is about colour. I can't stand that kind of injustice anywhere. Certainly don't want it in my country."

He stood and took a couple of steps down towards the shoreline, stood looking out at the calm waters.

"The General Manager: he was Audrey's grandfather."

"Aud—? Oh, your PA." Lexy remembered the look of disapproval on the neat woman's face when she'd discovered Lexy rummaging in Robert's desk.

Robert nodded. "Her own father never lived down the shame, either, grew up being told his family was responsible for 144 deaths. How can you live a normal life with something like that hanging over you?"

"I'm not sure you can."

"No. He couldn't anyway. He spent his whole life campaigning to clear his father's name. Unsuccessfully. It took years to try to bring an appeal and at the last minute it was denied. The Chakanaya clan, again." A stick this time: Robert flung it as far out into the lake as he could, and waited till the splash and ripples had faded away before he spoke again.

"It was the last straw for Audrey's father and he finally took his own life, a little over ten years ago. Audrey came home from school to find him hanging from the tree behind their house. I was the doctor who attended. When I heard the whole story, I couldn't

153

help but get involved. So many innocent people killed, harmed, on into the next generation, and the next, and not a penny paid out in compensation to anyone except a fat-cat corporation. I had hoped that I could help. Speak to David. Make him reconsider, now that Cameron has gone. Our families have known each other since Helen and Gran came out on the boat together. David and my father had been at school together, played rugby on the same team."

"And?"

Robert's laugh was harsh. "What do you think? It ended badly and I haven't spoken to him since. So we're trying the courts again. But if Buchanan's want to block us, I'm sure they'll find a way."

"I'm sorry, Robert. I can't begin to imagine how frustrating it must be. I mean it's . . . Oh, I don't know. It's just . . . *wrong.*"

Robert looked at her strangely. "You think? If you were in David's shoes, what would you do?"

"The right thing, of course!"

"Even if it meant destroying the company that your family had built from nothing into the biggest corporation in this part of Africa? Even if it meant you personally might lose everything?"

"Yes." Lexy was unequivocal. "At least I'd sleep at night. Besides, I'm sure they've all got a private stash somewhere. People like that never starve."

Robert nodded slowly. "Well. Let's hope it gets to appeal and the courts are as clear in their understanding of right and wrong as you are. But sorry. I didn't mean to put a dampener on our day." He looked around him. "And now it's all but done. We'd best get going. Sun will be going down in an hour or so."

Lexy was quiet on the drive back, lost in her thoughts. Robert wasn't at all the sort of man she'd thought. Driven, yes, but not, as she'd supposed, by personal ambition to make a name for himself in the world of science but by something more altruistic. No. Not

154

at all the self-centred prig she'd branded him on first meeting. He'd also turned out to be a good listener. She'd found herself telling him all about the last few weeks, about her mother, Danny, Ursula and as much as she knew about this mysterious son, how she'd worked it out. She'd misjudged him. Maybe finally she'd learn to give people the benefit of the doubt, not make her usual snap judgements.

It was dark by the time Robert turned into the hotel driveway and drew up in front of the ornate portico.

"Thank you, Robert. I've really enjoyed today. We should do it again . . ." Lexy trailed off, hoping she wasn't being too forward, hoping he knew she meant it.

"Mmm, me too. Yes, let's. Maybe with the fishing one of these days." He raised his hand and was off. Watching the jeep drive away, Lexy found herself hoping he meant it too.

14

At breakfast the following morning, Barney brought Lexy a message from Robert to say that he'd been in to see Evie and she was looking forward to seeing Lexy later in the day, if Lexy wanted to go back.

Lexy arrived at the hospital in good spirits, although a little apprehensive that Evie might not be up to continuing with her reminiscences, but she needn't have worried.

"Nonsense, child. What else is there to do lying here waiting for them to cut me open? No. The past, even a sad one like Helen's, is a much better diversion than the thought of that sort of present. Now, where were we?"

"Cameron came back. He and Ursula were back together and Ursula blamed Helen—"

"Foolish girl."

For a moment, Lexy thought Evie meant her, was relieved when the old woman continued.

"For such a sensible and competent nurse – Sister, I should say – our Ursula was remarkably naive. But then that's what an orphanage upbringing can do to a child. The first, slightest suggestion of love or affection and . . . Well, let's just say Ursula hadn't had a chance to develop a tolerance, an immunity, an *awareness*. She was easy prey for a man like Cameron. And, of course, he'd never have looked at someone like her had he not wanted to spite Helen. He blamed Helen's rejection for ruining his life. I think he really came to believe it, too. But the man was ruined before he set foot on that cursed ship. Before he left his mother's womb, I shouldn't wonder. But it would suit him to have Helen as his scapegoat. He made her misery his life's work, you know. And, of course, Ursula believed everything he said, rather than trusting her own judgement. How she could think Helen . . . Well, as I said. Naive. And as for him, some people are just born bad . . . just as some, like Helen, are born good, but fated to have that goodness put to the test time and time and time again . . ."

"I have news, Evie."

Evie gasped and her face broke into a broad beam of delight.

"Oh Helen! Finally, you're—"

"No." Helen shook her head and frowned. "No, not that."

"But I thought . . . I'm sorry. It was just that you said you were going to see Dr Leavenbrook and I just assumed . . ."

"No. But there doesn't seem to be any problem, any reason . . . so we're hopeful. Soon. Maybe. But anyway, it wasn't about that. I'm going back to Scotland, hence the doctor. Seasickness pills."

"Scotland? But why? And what about Greg—"

"Evie, darling!" Helen laughed. "My, but you're impatient this morning. Do let me finish."

"Of course. Sorry. So, Scotland."

"Yes. It seems my aunt's widower has decided to take a post with his Church back in India, so the house in Edinburgh reverts to me. We will of course sell it, but it was home once and there are some pieces there, some things of father's, my mother's too, and I want to sort through them myself."

"But is this a good time to be away? I thought you were opening up the north . . ."

"Yes, we are. But Gregory will do it. If I'm away he can just stay north until the distribution routes are finalised. It will be easier than running to and fro all the time."

"Oh, I see. I assumed you'd go together."

157

"The business couldn't take us both being away for that length of time, so I'll go on my own." Helen shrugged her slender shoulders and fixed on that bright smile of hers.

"My dear." Evie crossed and settled on the sofa next to her, taking Helen's hand in hers. "Is that wise? A rather difficult thing to do, I would imagine, sorting through your family home all on your own. Will your aunt's husband at least still be there to help you?"

"No. He's eager to get back to India as soon as he can. He was never really happy in Scotland. He only stayed because my aunt's health was too poor for the climate out there."

"I see." Evie was concerned for her friend, didn't like the thought of her facing this all alone. "Would you like . . . I'd need to speak to Douglas, of course, but perhaps . . ."

"No, Evie. Absolutely not. You are needed here. But bless you for even thinking of it. Besides, it's easier, sometimes, just to get on with things."

"You're always so strong. I do worry about you. Sometimes it does no harm to lean a little on others. Let them help."

"Well, the housekeeper and her husband will still be there. They can help me."

"That wasn't quite what I meant."

"Gregory's arranging it even as we speak. I leave next Tuesday."

"So soon!"

"And I'll be back in a couple of months."

"I shall miss you."

"Nonsense. You'll barely notice I'm gone. By the time you and Douglas get back from establishing the new clinics in the hills, I'll be home. You'll see."

"I suppose. I do wish Gregory were going with you, though. For support . . ."

"I shall manage perfectly well without him, Evie. And besides, we can't just abandon the business. I will be fine, I assure you. In fact, I'm excited. I can't wait to see what the latest fashions are and I'll take the opportunity to buy new fabrics to send back here for the house and goodness knows what. I might even go to a concert or two. Imagine that! I shall have a wonderful time. Apart from . . . well. But listen, Evie. That was only part of my news. The good part." Helen took a deep breath. "Gregory received a letter from Cameron this morning."

"I don't like the sound of that. Nothing to do with that man is ever good news."

"Quite. And this time he's surpassed himself."

"Please don't tell me he's coming back."

"No. Not that. In fact, that may be the only silver lining. He's back in South Africa and will no doubt be staying there for the foreseeable—"

The footsteps in the hallway interrupted them even before the knock on the door. Evie's housekeeper's face appeared, without waiting for Evie's response, the urgency clear in her wide eyes, but before she could speak, the door burst fully open and the surprised servant sprang to one side.

"Evie, I have to see you. I— Helen! I . . . I didn't know you were . . . I'm sorry am I interrupting? I—"

Both Evie and Helen had stood up in shock at their friend's dishevelled appearance. Wisps of hair drooped from the normally tightly pinned bun and Ursula's face was red and puffy. One of her stockings was wrinkled at the ankle and her blouse was misbuttoned, giving her the look of a lopsided, raggedy doll.

"Ursula! What on earth's the matter?" Evie stepped forward and took her friend's elbow, guiding her back to the sofa as Helen stood aside and reached out a hand to help. Evie ordered the housekeeper to fetch tea, and water, immediately.

Ursula swayed and leaned into her friend, before crashing heavily on the sofa.

159

"Do you feel faint?" Helen reached for the small clutch bag she'd left on the side table. "I have smelling salts, I think."

"No. I'm fine." Ursula's voice was weak, her head hanging down, her hands clasped tightly in her lap.

"You're clearly not. What is it, my dear?" Evie crouched in front of the distraught woman.

"I thought you'd be alone. I didn't mean to interrupt."

"Darling, it's only me," Helen said. "How could you possibly be interrupting? Don't be silly. Just do tell us what's wrong. What can we do to help?"

"I didn't want . . . I . . ."

Evie's housekeeper appeared at the door and Helen took the tray from her.

"Water, Ursula. Sip some of this. It will cool you down."

"I'm beginning to think we need something stronger." Evie started to rise.

"No." Ursula put her hand out to stay her friend. "No. Water's fine." She took the glass from Helen, her hand shaking so much that water splashed onto the pale-blue linen of her skirt, leaving a trail of darker spots across her lap. As the glass rattled against her teeth, Evie and Helen exchanged a worried look. This was so unlike their neat, precise friend.

The water caught in Ursula's throat and she started to splutter. Helen rescued the glass and placed it back on the tray on a side table, while Evie sat up on the sofa and patted her friend gently on the back.

"Come on, old thing. Easy does it."

"I didn't know where else to go." Ursula gasped between coughs. "I don't know what to do . . . I . . . Oh, you have to help me." The shoulders heaved as the coughs turned into sobs. Deep, strangled sobs that neither Evie nor Helen had ever heard from Ursula before.

"Darling! Darling girl, what on earth is the matter?" Helen sat

160

herself on the arm of the sofa on Ursula's other side, looking at Evie over the weeping woman's head. Evie shook her head in puzzlement.

"C . . . C . . . Cam . . ."

"Cameron." Helen's voice was steel. "That man. So you've heard then?"

"Heard? I . . . No. No. He won't reply to my messages. I've been trying to reach him to tell him he has to come back. He has to change his mind. I can't . . ."

"What's he done?" Evie asked. "What's that brute done now?"

"I told him, you see. And that's why he left." Ursula was tugging at the lace border on the handkerchief she had scrunched up into a ball in her hand. Evie put out a hand to calm the twitching, but Ursula shrugged her off, stood abruptly and went over to the open verandah door. "I know he's just scared," she said, looking out into the night. Helen and Evie waited, watching. "It was a shock, of course, but if I could only talk to him again, I know I could make him see that this is good. That we could get married and then he'd be happy. I'd make him happy, I know I would. I would. I love him so much, you see, and I know he loves me too, he is just a little frightened of the responsibility."

"Oh my God." Helen's hand flew to her throat.

"What?" Evie asked. "What is it? I don't under—"

"You're going to have Cameron's baby."

"Helen! Don't be ridiculous . . ." Evie's voice trailed off as Ursula turned and beamed at them.

"He said he didn't want it. That I should get rid of it. But I know he didn't mean it."

"Oh, he meant it. Every word of it, I'm sure."

"Helen, I know this is hard for you. That you love him too." Helen snorted in disgust. "But you could try to be happy for me. It's me he loves. He'll be a wonderful father, and after we're married—"

"Cameron isn't going to marry you, Ursula."

"Yes, he will. Just as soon as he gets over the surprise. I'm having our baby and he'll—"

"Listen to me, Ursula. Cameron isn't going to marry you."

"He is! He is. He has to, don't you see? He has to otherwise . . . otherwise . . . I'm ruined and I . . . I . . ." Ursula's eyes were darting from side to side and her hands were scratching at her head, dragging more hair loose to tumble down over her flushed cheeks. She stood rocking on her heels as she spluttered and the pitch of her voice rose into a louder, shriller shriek.

"Ursula!" Evie's slap silenced the woman, and for a moment all three of them froze, before Ursula collapsed forward into Evie's arms and Evie led her back to the sofa. She soothed the sobbing woman and looked up at Helen, who was standing over them, anger and sadness struggling for place in her pale face.

"Helen, what did that letter say?"

"Cameron's married."

Ursula's sobbing stopped and her tear-stained face looked up at Helen.

"He's married Gertie von Falken, or Gertie Steencamp as she'd become."

"The merry widow . . ." Evie said softly, remembering the journey out to Africa.

"Had become a merry widow again. This time with a large enough fortune to indulge herself with someone more her age. How could Cameron resist? Lasciviousness and wealth. Irresistible to someone like him."

"*No!*" Ursula leapt at Helen, fists flying, "You're lying! It's me. He loves me. He'll marry me!" Evie and Helen struggled to control the flailing limbs to avoid the nails that were reaching out like cat claws. "He can't. He knows I'm having his baby. He can't be!"

"Ursula, he is."

"This is your fault! You! You're jealous of me. You wanted him

162

for yourself and . . . and . . . you always have to spoil my happiness, don't you?"

"Don't talk nonsense, Ursula. Helen never wanted Cameron. And she's telling the truth. Cameron isn't coming back for you."

"But . . . but . . . what am I going to do? I . . . can't have a . . . a baby."

Finally, Ursula slumped back down on to the sofa. "What am I going to do?" The words were a whisper.

"I don't know, darling," Helen said, her face full of pain for Ursula.

Evie was silent for a moment. "I think I might, though," she said.

★

Lexy sat in the hospital canteen nursing her tea and mulling over this next instalment in what was turning into a truly pitiful tale. Her heart went out to Ursula, although it was hard for Lexy to reconcile Evie's account and the image of a lovelorn and abandoned woman with her own memories of the older Ursula, calm, serene, controlled. But also warm, kind, loving. Lexy remembered sitting on Ursula's knee as she read a story to her, or, later, as they read one together. Ursula's hugs and goodnight kisses. The woman had the capacity for love, it was clear. How very, very sad that it had been so abused. She would have loved her son, Lexy felt sure. She'd loved Izzie passionately, Lexy too. So what had gone wrong? What had happened to her son? Come to that, what had happened between Izzie and Ursula all those years ago when the visits had stopped?

"Lexy?"

"Robert!" Lexy felt blood rush to her cheeks as she coughed, spluttering a mouthful of cold tea, hoping he'd put her heightened colour down to that.

163

'Sorry, did I startle you?"

"Yes. No. Well. I . . . I've been with Evie. She's resting now."

"Yes, I know. And I've checked with her consultant. She's not having her operation today. It'll be a day or two yet, he thinks, but we'll see. What are you up to now? Back to the hotel?"

"Oh eventually. Thought I might have a bit of a walk first. Need to stretch my legs after sitting all morning."

"I was just taking my lunch outside." He held up a sandwich. "Join me? I'll give you the guided tour, if you like."

"You did that yesterday – you'll be making a second career of it at this rate. But yes, that would be lovely if you wouldn't mind."

"Not at all. A welcome break from sickness and admin. Come on."

He led her out a side door from the canteen that opened straight onto a large lawn, as immaculate as all the lawns in Blantyre appeared to be, despite the heat, criss-crossed by footpaths and bordered by bushes heavy with orange and yellow bougainvillea and other flowers she didn't recognise but which Robert was able to identify for her. She was again struck by the warmth in his voice as he described his Malawi to her. He loved this country – his country: that was clear. She doubted she would speak with such enthusiasm about her own. But perhaps that had more to do with its inextricable association with the recent events in her life.

They reached the bank of hibiscus in front of the wall at the far end of the lawn and Lexy assumed they would turn around and head back, but Robert pushed aside a few of the abundant branches and revealed a gate.

"What's through here?" Lexy asked.

"Mostly storerooms and suchlike now," he said holding the gate open so she could walk through ahead of him, "but it used to house some of the medical staff before the new quarters across the road were built. Several of the doctors and their families lived here, at one time, before there was a move towards a healthier

164

division between work and home life. Your parents, I believe, lived in one of these after they were married. Your mother would have been in the Nurses' Hostel, of course, as a single woman."

Lexy was intrigued. Again the buildings were single storey, whitewashed and fronted with verandahs in the style that was now becoming familiar to her. Had her parents really lived in one of these?

"Which one? Which one did they live in?"

"I couldn't say, I'm afraid. But Gran would know. You could ask her, if you like. It'll have been commandeered for storage, though, I'm sure, so if you're hoping to find an echo of the past, you'll be disappointed. This one might interest you, though. It's not been changed too much, still used sometimes for courses and suchlike. The old schoolroom, for the compound's children." He tried the door but it was locked. "Oh. It's usually open. That's a shame. You might have been interested to see a good old-fashioned colonial school, given your own profession. Another time."

Yes, Lexy thought, *another time. Or . . .*

"Robert, I . . . I was wondering . . ."

He turned and looked at her expectantly.

"That is, if you haven't got plans . . . I wondered if you'd like to join me for dinner this evening." She felt herself blushing, tried to sound offhand, but her heart was racing. Was she being too forward? Why didn't he say something? She risked a look over at him. He was frowning. Not good.

"Lexy, I . . ." He cleared his throat.

"Oh please, it doesn't matter. I know how busy you are and it was just if you weren't doing anything. I mean, I thought you might be able to tell me more about . . . about my parents or Malawi or . . ." Lexy the gabbler had returned. "Sorry. It's fine. Forget it."

"Lexy, I should probably have said something earlier, but it

165

didn't come up . . . and I didn't think . . . Audrey. Audrey and I are . . ."

"Oh!" Lexy's hand flew to her mouth. "*Audrey*. Your PA? Well yes, of course, she is, and you and she. I see, yes . . . But she's bla— I mean, col—"

"Coloured?" He was angry, that was evident. "Not one of *us*?"

"No, no, that's not what I meant." Lexy said, although she was horrified to think it just might have been. Not intentionally of course, but why else had she not even considered their having a relationship a possibility, despite noting Audrey's evident adoration for her boss. But now it was just so *obvious*. "It's just . . . just that she's, well, quite young and . . . but that's no reason. No. Not at all. She's lovely. I'm sure you're very happy." *Shut up Lexy, just shut up*. Five days in this country and she'd turned into some kind of colonial idiot.

"I'm sorry, Robert," she tried again. "I didn't mean to offend you and I didn't mean to proposition you either." She tried to make light of it. "It was just a thought, just a bite to eat and really, it's fine. Unless you'd *both* like to . . . No, no of course not," she finished quickly as his face told her very clearly that wouldn't be a good idea. "Well." Bright and breezy now. "I think I should probably—"

"Yes," he cut in hastily. "Yes and I should be getting back, too."

They walked back to the hospital entrance in silence, Lexy squirming with embarrassment at having so badly misread the situation. What *had* she been thinking? *Any port in a storm*, perhaps? Her mother and her homespun wisdom were back, although *a still tongue makes a wise head* might have been a more helpful homily.

15

The Residence, June 13th

A taxi ride, a brief shower and an iced tea later, things looked a
little better. She picked up the tea folder again. Perhaps reading
about someone else's humiliation would help lessen her own.
Although a turned-down invitation to dinner was hardly in the
same league as Ursula's anguish. Flicking ahead, Lexy was
surprised to see that the next diary extract was brief, blotchy and
untidy, Ursula's usual instinct for order and tidiness washed away
by her plight. Adrenaline surged at the sight of extracts from
Scotland, more letters from Evie, too . . . but she needed to be
patient. Follow the trail as it had been laid down, step by steady
step, to be sure she didn't miss anything. She sighed. She was
turning into Danny.

Blantyre, September 4th 1949

The night I once found so comforting is now torment, a
punishment. It is endless and black and hopeless and dark
and I cannot see how I can get through this. I told him and
watched his face for the light, the joy I felt sure would come.
I told him and waited for his arms to circle me and pull me
close, for his laughter, tears, anything. He had to be happy.
~~Why wasn't He would be~~

He said he loved me. These few precious weeks he said it
over and over.

~~I can't bear to live if~~
He does love me. I know it.

167

He must.

I feel hollowed out and empty and that's the very thing I am not. One minute I'm filled with wonder at this miracle we have begun, the next I'm crying again like the fool I am.

He needs time. He'll come back.

Perhaps I could have told him more gently, but I was so excited. Perhaps he's worried about what people will say, but it's not so unusual, during the war it was

~~and if we marry soon~~

We might even disguise it, premature baby or

Some of them will enjoy it if they

My reputation will help us.

No one would ever suspect me, Sister Reid, of something like that. We could hide the dates after and oh I don't know but something. Impropriety. Scandal. How strange to think those words might be for me. Matron Proudfoot is unlikely to approve. And she'd know. She I'll lose my position. But I could we could go away. I could work in another hospital. ~~Maybe I won't work after the baby and Cameron looks after~~

He called me a stupid girl. Didn't I know how to take care of things, he said. Surely with all my medical expertise And he laughed. But not how I'd hoped he would. Then he left.

He's not coming back.

What am I going to do?

Cape Town, September 11th 1949

Another sleepless night. One I want to remember. The last under the velvet African sky. For some time at least. Perhaps forever. I can't imagine returning to life in Blantyre. I am not the woman I'd wanted the world to believe me to be. I am a fallen woman. An abandoned one. No better than a Leith slut. About to become a deceiver, a liar, too. My friends as well, to save me.

168

These last few days have gone by so quickly. This is the first opportunity I've had to write, but now I don't know where to start. So much has happened. I see it all so clearly in my mind but don't think I can bear to see it on the page in front of me, permanent. Real. And after all, what is there to say? I'd try to find excuses, justifications. No point in that.

Evie left us yesterday and Helen is asleep in the bedroom behind me, so I'm finally alone on this narrow, flowerless balcony looking out over a dark sea. Tomorrow we embark. Then Scotland. Home. Only I'm not sure it will feel like that any more. If it ever really was. And we sail on the *Aurora* again. Full circle. Back to where I started, no better for my journey.

Upper Shire River Mission House
November 28th 1949

Dear Ursula,

I can't tell you how pleased I was to hear from you, to know that you and Helen are safe and well and haven't frozen to death back in the chill of our Scottish Highlands. You are both – or should that be all? – in my thoughts and prayers every day. It's good that you have each other, but I miss you desperately. I wish I could be there too, to help and support, although pregnancy is something none of us knows much about, and even as a doctor's wife, my exposure to childbirth is limited by the misplaced sense of decorum of the Mission clinic's doctors. Idiots. Women need women around them at times like that. Still, you at least are a nurse so the medical aspects I'm sure will be familiar to you. Let's all be thankful for that.

I smiled when I read about the morning sickness on the boat – how fortunate it was deemed nothing but seasickness by the ship's doctor, although rather worrying in a broader sense that for all that time at sea one's health might rest in the hands of someone who doesn't recognise a pregnant woman when he sees one! Helen, no doubt, had plenty to say about that, and would have found it hard not to say it in public, I'm sure.

Reading your letter made me quite homesick, even though we only ever visited my mother's croft for two weeks each summer. I used to love long walks on that beach as a child and then later as a newly married woman pining for my absent husband. I'd allow myself a little melodrama. I'd walk the shoreline in all weathers, letting the sea spray sting my face and the wind pull my hair and loving the way it made me feel so alive, so connected to myself, if that makes sense. What a place to be born.

Gregory was here last week for the Mission meetings. He was beside himself with happiness. He couldn't stop talking about his plans for Helen and the child – he is, of course, convinced it will be a boy, so heaven only knows what will happen if it's a girl. Although a man with Gregory's capacity for love will adore and cherish whatever he is given. His face when he talked of it!

He will make an exceptional father, Ursula, my dear; you mustn't ever worry about that. And he is utterly convinced by our subterfuge. I did feel guilt tug a little at my resolve, but really, I found myself wondering, does it matter so very much? Your child will be dearly loved. Gregory and Helen are desperate for a child and have not yet been blessed – and at the risk of sounding a little indelicate, it's clear to look at them that their love is such it will not have been for want of trying! Such a gift this child will be, to us all.

Gregory was full of news from Blantyre and Zomba, but little of it really merits repeating. The Clubs continue, the gossip comes and goes, the trade fair for the Missions a huge success – clearly went a good way to alleviating any concerns the recent rumours may have caused as to Buchanan's probity. The sooner Cameron's association with the company is forgotten the better.

Dear Gregory works so hard. He is personally visiting each of the Missions to reassure them that everything is above board and

170

that their trust in Buchanan's is justified. And he looked so much better than when last I saw him. I put that down to the news of the baby. So we must, after all, be glad that business concerns keep him here because if he could, there is no question he would be on the next passage home to be with his beloved Helen and his unborn child – oh Lord, forgive us our deception.

So, we must be strong, all of us, and we must be silent on the truth of it. Helen will love your child as if it were her own and you will be godmother, as much a part of your child's life as it's possible to be, as anyone would expect one of the mother's closest friends to be. And that too is something that gives me great pleasure, dear Ursula. Whatever the circumstances of the child's conception, this child will be loved by us all, and it is through love of that child already that the rift between you and Helen has been mended. My two dearest friends, dear friends themselves again. How could we not love the child that's brought us that?

Gregory did bring some less pleasant news which I feel I should impart to you, and I'm not sure he will have shared this with Helen. Indeed, I can see he is ashamed, but really it is nothing to do with him and we all know that. Cameron and his new wife are under investigation and she has started proceedings for divorce. It appears that Gertie's husband's death may not have been straightforward. Some talk of poisoning, or incorrect dosages of some sort with his medication. There is rather a lot of money at stake, and it seems there is a son from the man's first marriage who has raised concerns over his father's death and a new will made shortly before his demise, leaving everything to Gertie. Cameron has been interviewed by the police, I believe, and told not to leave Johannesburg, which can only be good news, as anything that keeps him as far from us as possible would be. I know this must be painful for you to hear, and truly my heart aches for you, Ursula. For all his wickedness, I know you loved that man, so I tell you this only to help you steel your heart against

171

him, and if nothing else, it may make the prospect of returning to us a little less daunting, knowing he will not be here. Fear not, however. That man has more lives than a cat, and I am sure no harm will come to him. I cannot believe even Cameron would have a hand in murder. And in any case, that Chakanaya man is with him, and if anyone knows how to get around the authorities, it's him.

Of life here at the Mission clinic, I have little to tell you. The orphanage continues to thrive, the clinic to be well attended and the new church is almost complete – how lovely a place it would be for a baptism! But enough – I'm getting ahead of myself. We hope to be here for a few more weeks, then return to Blantyre so will be there to celebrate your return in the autumn.

Stay safe in your Highland hideaway, dear Ursula, stay well. Know that I am with you in my heart and you are with me in my prayers.

Your loving friend,
Evie

Glasgow, May 21st 1950

She's gone. He's gone. I stood at the dock and waved, smiled, as if I were happy to see them go. Helen. Once again I find myself overwhelmed with jealousy for her and yet I should be so very, very grateful. But she again has what is dearest to me. Only this time it isn't the love of a scoundrel, it's my son. My son! Dear God, how could I have agreed to this? How will I live with it?

She expected me to return with her, and in truth, I believed I would too. It was only yesterday, as we made the final preparations, that I realised I couldn't. I couldn't watch her take my son to Gregory, tell him my boy is hers, his. I couldn't watch them become the happy family I thought might have been mine if Cameron had really loved me. If Cameron had

172

had an ounce of honour in him. Honour. There's a thought. Hardly for me to cast that stone. Not me, a coward of the highest order, not even brave enough to keep her own son. I can hardly cast aspersions on another's behaviour. But it wouldn't work, even if I had more courage. How could I keep my baby and my job, and if I didn't work how would we survive?

And now I have neither. I don't know what I'm going to do. Where I'm going to go. I'll have to work. No reference from Matron Proudfoot will make it hard to find a position. She won't have forgiven me for my abrupt departure. And too late I remembered she would know my ailing mother was a lame excuse. It would have been on my records, of course. No parents. No family as next of kin. Orphan. Dr Campbell, dear Douglas, might help me I suppose, if Evie asks.

But I can't think of any of that yet. I have abandoned my child. Given him away. What kind of a woman does that? I'm every bit the monster Cameron is. What chance would any child of ours have? Better to be with Helen and Gregory – the faultless, perfect couple. They will give him a far better chance than he would have with me. And this pain, this wrenching ache, so raw, so . . . this is my penance. I don't deserve to forget. I won't forget. The curling grip of those small fingers, the perfection of his tiny toes! The soft warmth of his breath on my cheek as I held him against my heart, the gentle rise and fall of the coverlet as he slept. Oh dear God. There can be no forgiveness for what I've done, but please don't let him be punished, my beautiful, beautiful boy, for the sins of his shameful mother.

Taigh na Mara, July 29th 1950
I won't come back here, again, despite Evie's generosity: her insistence on signing it over to me, that it should be my home.

I don't deserve it. I'm going to leave all of it behind me. Lock it up and keep it from seeping its poison into my new life. Perhaps I should throw away the keys and just leave it all to rot. A derelict memorial to my sinfulness.

But that's an indulgence I can't afford. The cleaning and clearing has been therapeutic in a way, and knowing that someone new will live here, someone who has no idea of the agonised ghosts that haunt its walls, will help. The solicitors said it will take time to find someone who wants to live out here, but that's good. It will give the ghosts time to settle, move on, find me in Edinburgh. I could sell it, of course. But something holds me back. I don't quite know why. Perhaps because it would seem ungrateful to Evie. Or perhaps because it feels too final to do that. Maybe, just maybe, one day things will be different. I'll bring him here and show him the place where he was born and we'll laugh and cry about it together. And heal. Oh that we might!

Helen sent me a picture of him. I know she means well, keeping her promise to share every step with me as best she can. But I can't help myself. The jealousy runs so deep. And now too I am beholden to her for life. His life. A debt I can never repay and which makes me hate her.

Blantyre
September 27th 1950

Dear Ursula,

I write this in haste at Helen's request and will write a fuller account later. We both want this to reach you as soon as it can, though. Such news – Helen is pregnant with a child of her own! Soon your dear boy will have a sibling, a playmate, someone to look up to him and love him as much as we all do. Oh, you can't imagine how happy they all are – Gregory and Helen are wonderful parents and now with another child on the way it will make our secret all the safer. With children of their own, our little honeybird is less likely ever to be found out.

And fear not, my dear friend. Helen loves that boy of yours as if he were her own, as does Gregory. She promises me she will love him no less when her child is born, and such is the size of that woman's heart, we know she will be true to her word.

I know there will be a small part of you that this news will hurt, but Ursula, what's done is done and your boy really couldn't be happier or better cared for. You wouldn't want him to grow up a lonely child, I'm sure, so try to rejoice at this news. It will be good for him to have other children around him.

More next time, I promise. Till then take care, and know we think of you often.

Much love,

Evie

PS: Do so hope the Edinburgh position is turning out well for you. Douglas was sure you'd be perfect for it and was glowing in his reference – of course!

16

Blantyre Hospital, June 14th

Lexy had slept little so was at the hospital earlier than planned, thinking to have a coffee in the hospital canteen or a walk in the grounds until her appointed time with Evie. Her head was swimming, though, with what she had learned from the tea folder, and it had driven her back to the photo albums, where she'd scrutinised the faces of the women, the men who'd played the central roles in the drama that was unfolding in Ursula's documents. It was so hard to reconcile what she was reading with her memories of the staid, respectable Edinburgh matron of Lexy's childhood. With the warmth and love there had been for Izzie and Lexy herself, whenever they visited. That Ursula had been a caring, loving mother in everything but name to Izzie was evident. So how could that same woman have given up her own son, given him away to another woman . . . or was it because she'd abandoned one child that there was such an outpouring of affection for another?

Such an outrageous plan, and yet one, it would appear, that had succeeded. And Evie had been the one to suggest it. Ursula's son had grown up loved and wealthy, so did it matter to the child? Had he known? The payments. Surely that was why . . . But when had he found out, and how? And how did it make him feel? Lexy's own sense of betrayal, her anger at her mother withholding information from her paled into insignificance in the light of what Ursula's son must have felt when he discovered his birthright, his true identity, had been stolen from him. And yet, he'd grown up more comfortably than he ever would have had his birth mother kept him. But Lexy couldn't help but feel it was fundamentally wrong to lie, to deceive, and particularly about something as central to a sense of identity as the circumstances of one's birth . . . and yet . . . and yet . . .

By the time she reached the hospital her impatience had gained the upper hand. She struck a deal with herself. She could go straight to Evie's room and if the old woman was awake and would see her, so be it. But Lexy had to keep tight control of her emotions, remember that Evie was about to have major surgery and that whatever had happened all those years ago, Lexy couldn't begin to know the full circumstances, or the toll it might have taken on all three women then and through the years that followed. In short, she must not judge. She would listen with an open mind, gather information impartially, academically. Danny would be proud. If she succeeded, that is.

As she walked down the corridor towards Evie's room she could see that the door was ajar. Raising her hand to rap her knuckles lightly on the wood, she was surprised to hear Evie's voice, just catching a few words before the door swung open at her touch.

"Remember what we agreed. Nothing about—"

"Hello?" Lexy's smile stalled and she felt a lurch in her stomach as she realised Robert was in the room. Yesterday's humiliation came flooding back. "Oh, I'm sorry. I hope I'm not interrupting?"

"Lexy, dear, you're early."

"Yes, I know. I was . . . I can come back?"

"No, no. Not at all, do come in child. Robbie boy, jump to it. Clear that clutter away and let the dear child have a seat."

"Thank you, but really I can come back—"

"Nonsense. Robbie doesn't mind sharing me. Now, how are you, dear? Why, you look exhausted. Our Malawian sun perhaps too much for you?"

"No, not that. I didn't sleep much last night."

"Really? You're not ill are you, my dear? Robbie could give you something if—"

"No!" Lexy was appalled at the thought of Robbie tending to her, was beginning to wish she'd mastered the art of patience and was sitting sipping coffee downstairs. "I mean, thanks, but really I'm fine. It was just that I was thinking about what you'd said, Evie, and looking through the photos and reading more of the folder I found under Ursula's chair and . . . well, it was quite overwhelming really. And then I was trying to put it all together with what the lawyers said and make sense of it, but I just kept coming up with more questions, and I . . . So that's why I couldn't sleep and then I didn't know if you'd have your operation scheduled yet or not so thought maybe if I came earlier you'd be able to rest more before it because I really appreciate you seeing me at all when you . . . but I've so much to ask you and I'm sure you have the answers . . ."

Lexy drew breath, looked up at last, saw their faces still and watchful. "Sorry. I'm gabbling, and I know you have your operation on your mind, but it's just so— Sorry."

"Don't worry, dear. I'm not the frail old stick Robert would have you believe, and I'm only too happy to have something to take my mind off the operation."

"Yes. Sorry. I know. But I shouldn't be bombarding you with—"

"No, you shouldn't." Robert finally spoke, frowning at Lexy in clear disapproval. "You need to remember—"

"That I'm bored rigid lying here all day with only the prospect of a trip to some old sawbones to look forward to, so the longer you can spin out the distractions, Lexy dear, the better."

"Gran, you really mustn't let her—"

"Shush, Robbie. Leave the girl alone. I'm fine."

"No. I'm sorry. I've just jumped in again and haven't even asked you how you are." Feeling a little ashamed, Lexy made a real effort

178

to slow herself down. "Robert's right." Much though it pained her to say it.

"But I'm fine, dear."

"No, she's not, actually."

"Robbie."

"Gran, you're the one who's exhausted. I'm really not sure you should be doing this at all, you know, raking over the past and what have you."

"Robbie, we agreed." Evie looked hard at her grandson, as if communicating something other than the words themselves. "Remember. We agreed. So don't fuss." What exactly was it they'd agreed, Lexy wondered, remembering the snatch of conversation she'd heard as she came into the room.

"I'm expressing an opinion – a medical opinion." He shrugged. "That's hardly fussing."

Evie's hand dismissed him with a flutter. "Lexy, pull your chair nearer. Tell me more about these albums, this folder or whatever. They've clearly got you quite excited."

"Gran, please. Enough. Lexy, you really shouldn't be putting her through this. She's not strong enough."

"Robbie, I think that's for me to decide. And I'm sure it's time you were getting along to your clinic. We will be perfectly fine, and frankly it will be much less stressful talking to Lexy without your well-intentioned but quite unnecessary supervision."

Lexy looked down in case either of them saw the amusement in her eyes. That told him, she thought, and was delighted to see that it worked. Like a sulky adolescent he scooped up his jacket and document folder and swept out, with only a scowl in their direction.

"That's better." Evie patted the bedclothes down around her. "Now, dear, you were saying?"

"Yes, right." *Easy does it, Lexy,* she reminded herself. "So. I'm beginning to piece it all together now, about Ursula's son. I brought some paperwork with me from Ursula's flat. None of it really made sense before, but now it's beginning to, or at least what I've looked at so far is, with your help of course. There are gaps still, and bits that don't make sense, but I'm hoping you will be able to help me with all that. And also, all I'm getting are bare facts and none of the why or . . . or anything."

Evie's eyes had narrowed a little and she was watching Lexy closely.

"I've brought the albums with me. I thought you might like to see them."

"Oh, I would, dear, very much. Always such fun reviewing one's youth."

"And I've got some of the documents – diary entries and letters and so on – that were in the folder. She'd marked it for my mother and it's some kind of record of . . . of . . . Well, an explanation of sorts. You see, they'd fallen out, Ursula and my mother, years ago when I was still quite young. But maybe you knew that. I hadn't really understood what was going on back then, but it's beginning to make sense now. I think they must have fallen out about Ursula's son because that's what the folder seems to be about."

Evie was very still, apart from one thin index finger rubbing at the white cotton bedsheet.

"And there's something odd about the folder. If I hadn't spilt my tea, I wouldn't have found it. It was tucked under the cushion of Ursula's armchair. At the time, I just put it down to her wanting it near her, an old woman's habit, tucking things down the side of her chair. But this was actually under the seat, as if she, maybe, wanted to keep it hidden."

Lexy looked up at Evie, whose face was still giving nothing away.

"But then I thought, why would she want to do that?"

"Well, quite. Why indeed?"

"Unless it was something that mattered very, very much. Unless it would give away the identity of her son, Cameron's son."

"I'm really not sure—"

"Of course, it could be argued that Ursula was deranged when she wrote those diary entries, some sort of postpartum depression or delusion. But there was independent corroboration. There was your letter. Your letter, to Ursula, which she kept all these years and included in her folder: your letter helped me finally believe it, even though it's been staring me in the face on every page of this album since I picked it up." Lexy took one of the albums from her bag and laid it gently on the other woman's lap.

"Really, dear?" Evie sounded uninterested, as if this wasn't anything important at all, didn't even glance at the album.

"I know who Ursula's son is. Even without the diaries of a woman consumed by guilt and grief. Your letter told me, Evie. You told me, so not really any point in pretending you don't know now, is there?"

Lexy leant over, opened the album near the back.

"There he is. David Buchanan."

Evie looked down at the photo, the index finger scratching more frantically at the bedsheet now.

"You and Helen and Ursula tricked everyone, even Gregory, into believing he was Helen's firstborn. I don't know how you did it, exactly, but I know about the time in Scotland, the croft, and the fact that Cameron wanted nothing to do with Ursula and the child and how you've kept the secret all these years. That must have been hard. Really hard."

Evie said nothing.

"It all fits," Lexy continued. "Richard Chakanaya was Cameron's man and he's the one, the intermediary, who made the payments to Ursula. I thought at first Ursula had given her baby to the Mission orphanage, even though that didn't feel right, given her own childhood." Evie's eyes flickered to Lexy and then just as quickly away again. "Was that what you wanted me to think? Were you going to lie to me to make me think that's what happened, to throw me off the scent? I might have believed it. All those donations Ursula made to the Mission got me wondering, and then all the time you spent there with your husband, too: you might have helped her. And Robert's letter, of course, about the break-in. What was that? David getting someone to cover the tracks? Ha! Is David in this too? Are you *all* trying to send me away?" Lexy was struggling to stay calm, to keep her voice even and moderate.

'Nonsense, child. Don't be ridiculous. No one's trying to send you away." But the voice lacked something of its usual vigour.

"I thought it all pointed to the Mission. I was going to go there to try to find Ursula's son, but no need now. Thanks to you, Evie. Because your letter has confirmed it as fact and not guilt-ridden fantasy. It doesn't tell me everything, true, but enough for me to see none of this has anything to do with the orphanage. It was all much closer to home than that. I couldn't believe that Gregory would fall for it, at first, but then I felt so sorry for him. It's breathtaking that you actually got away with it, but then why would a man suspect the woman he adored of tricking him with something as fundamental as that? Why? And with David being his nephew there'd be a family resemblance, any similarity to Cameron quite unremarkable. And there certainly was: you can see it, clear as day."

Lexy turned pages of the album then tapped another photo.

"See? The boys look just like smaller versions of Gregory and Cameron, and that's because they are. It is David, isn't it? And that's why she kept all those cuttings too, about David and Cameron. Not because she had shares in the company, or because Helen was her friend or anything like that. But because David was her son and Cameron was her lover. I'm right, aren't I? I know I am."

Evie inclined her head, the slightest of nods, but, Lexy knew, this was the breakthrough she'd hoped for. Evie would tell her now, tell her everything, she was sure of it. As long as there was time before her operation, in case . . . or before Robert came back and threw her out.

"Does Robert know?" she asked. "Is that what you were reminding him to say nothing about? When I arrived?"

"Robbie knows. We needed his help with . . . things . . . as we got older."

Lexy fought the fury that threatened to undermine all the careful, steady steps she was taking. He'd known. He'd lied. Worse, when he'd taken her to the lake and asked her all those questions . . . Good listener indeed. He'd been playing her, finding out what she knew. She stood, walked over to the window, breathing steadily to keep herself calm. She heard Evie sigh behind her.

"Yes, Lexy. You're right. David Buchanan is Ursula's son. But he won't thank you for pointing that out to him. In fact, you really would be much better keeping all this to yourself."

Lexy turned to face Evie, shook her head. "I want to meet him. I have to tell him I—"

"You have to do no such thing."

Lexy was silenced by the sharpness, the sudden force of Evie's voice.

"Don't you think if he'd wanted to know about Ursula, or her life, or your mother, you, he'd have made contact? He sent money all those years, so he knew exactly how to find her if he wanted to, but he didn't. You may not like it, my dear, but he didn't. He chose not to. And you're fooling yourself if you think he doesn't know about you. Of course he does, and if he wanted anything to do with you, don't you think he'd have been in touch by now? No, Lexy. Leave it alone. You'll only end up disappointed and hurt. Believe me. It really wouldn't be a good idea to approach him."

"But if he meets me, perhaps it will make him wonder what he's missed all these years, not knowing his mother—"

"He knew his mother. Most of his childhood, at least. His mother, for him, was Helen Buchanan, and he wouldn't want anyone to think anything else."

"But that's so old-fashioned. No one cares any more about things like that. So he was born to an unmarried mother? Hardly going to get him ostracised from one of your precious Clubs or send the share price tumbling, is it?" Anger was pumping through her veins, her breathing becoming shallow and fast. She struggled to control it.

"You forget that a lot of the company's business even today is with the Missions. They might not share your more liberal attitudes."

"Why would they even need to know? I'm not going to put an ad in the paper, am I? In fact, why would I tell anyone at all?"

"David might not believe that. He'll just think you're after money, my dear. That's the sort of person he is. And he won't take kindly to it."

"What, you think he might think I'm trying to blackmail him? I'll keep quiet if he pays me? That's ridiculous. This is about me, about me trying to find some kind of family, the family you all decided to steal from me!"

"We didn't . . . Oh, child, it's complicated."

"So explain it!" Lexy had abandoned all pretence of keeping her temper under control. She stood, hands on hips, chin tilted forward, breathing heavily as she glared at the old woman.

"If he is Ursula's son, there would be questions over his inheritance. His right to Buchanan's."

"But surely an adopted child has the same rights as a—"

"He wasn't adopted. He couldn't be. For that to have happened, Gregory would need to have known. And besides, that still wouldn't have been good enough."

"Why not? What—"

The door opened and Evie's usual nurse, Celia, stuck her head in.

"You all right there, Mrs Campbell? Your visitor not tiring you out none?"

"Ah, my grandson's got you checking up on us, I see." The nurse smiled sheepishly. "We're fine, dear. Just fine. Although some tea wouldn't go amiss if you could arrange it for us? Plenty of sugar for my visitor, I think."

"See what I can do."

Lexy was staring blankly ahead as the door closed behind the nurse.

"You've contacted him already, haven't you?"

Lexy nodded. "I phoned his office. I have an appointment with him tomorrow."

"Did you say what you wanted to see him about?" Lexy shook her head. "Good. We need to think of a plausible excuse. A reason for you to want to meet him that has nothing to do with his parentage. He knows who you are, remember, but he doesn't know what you know about him. Better still, you could cancel the appointment entirely, although that in itself might arouse his curiosity."

"But I only want to meet him and—"

"Lexy, listen to me." Evie's patience was clearly wearing thin. "You have no idea what you might be getting into here."

"But I wouldn't *tell* anyone." She sounded like a petulant child.

"He'd never be sure though, would he? As long as you know, he'd never be completely safe. He'd have to trust you. Men like David Buchanan, and Richard Chakanaya, who is still very much a part of things at Buchanan's, aren't . . . comfortable . . . with something like that."

"Oh for goodness' sake! What about me? I just want to meet him, to connect with someone who's almost family, to . . . Oh, I

185

don't know. But is it really too much to ask? So what if David's not 'comfortable'? That's not exactly life-threatening."

"Isn't it? Are you sure? For myself, I can only wonder what men like David Buchanan and Richard Chakanaya might do to alleviate any discomfort they might feel."

17

Buchanan House, Blantyre, June 15th

"Well, well. Quite the detective, aren't you?"

David's voice dripped sarcasm as he slowly clapped his hands a couple of times; then he stood and went over to the silver tray on the top of the sideboard. Lifting a cut-glass decanter, he turned and held it out towards her, pouring himself a hefty measure when she shook her head.

Lexy waited. She'd expected . . . what? Shock, delight, surprise? At least that. At least surprise. But not this. But then he'd known, she realised. Evie had been right about that. He'd known about her all along.

"If you knew," she said, "why didn't you contact me? If not before, at least when I came to Malawi? You must have known why I'd come. Why didn't you just get in touch and tell me Ursula was your mother? Get it over with, as it clearly isn't a relationship you want to develop further."

"Wrong question, little Lexy, wrong question."

"For God's sake, David. I don't understand why you're behaving like this. I thought you might be pleased to find you had a . . . that I was . . . am family, almost. Oh I don't know! I thought you might be pleased to meet me."

David had taken a cheroot from the box on the table beside the green leather club chair he'd settled in. He clipped the end off and dropped it in the onyx ashtray. He rolled it thoughtfully between his fingers.

"Oh, I am, Lexy. Very pleased. It means we can have this little chat. You see, you need to be careful, Lexy," he said as he reached for the silver table lighter. He hefted its heavy weight in his hand then clicked it once, twice before it caught, then put the cheroot in his mouth and lit it. "Play with fire and you're liable to get burnt," he said through a haze of smoke, clicking the lighter on and off and on again, holding the flame in front of his face for a few seconds before extinguishing it and letting the lighter thud down onto the desk again.

Oh, very James Bond villain, Lexy thought, exasperated, refusing to be intimidated, worrying that she might be.

The leather creaked as he leant back, lifted one well-shod foot and crossed his legs. Everything about him groaned money, opulence, confidence, cliché. And yet there was something . . . off, something in his eyes that Lexy couldn't quite put her finger on.

"Are you threatening me, David? Warning me off something?"

"Would it work if I were?"

"No."

David's smile was slow. "Then no, I'm not." He took a sip of the whisky, watching her over the rim of the glass as he savoured and swallowed what she felt sure was a very expensive single malt. Nothing but the best for David. She thought about Ursula's flat – nice enough but nothing compared with this lifestyle. She thought about the money that had been transferred to Ursula over the years. Where had it gone? Had Ursula been too principled and proud to spend it, perhaps? It didn't add up. Why hadn't she ever come forward, taken her place as David's mother here in Malawi, a country she clearly loved. Especially after Helen and then Cameron were gone. Surely nowadays the threat of scandal wouldn't be an issue any more. Unless . . .

"Did you pay her to stay away, was that it?"

"I could pay you to stay away." David flicked ash and looked at her thoughtfully. "Would that work? Money? Get you on a plane out of here and back to Lexyland?"

"No, of course not. I don't want your money. I—"

"*My* money?" David laughed and choked on the thick smoke of the cheroot. He spluttered unattractively, small beads of sweat appearing on his brow, reddening cheeks and jowls quivering. "Oh that's good. You really have no idea, do you, Lexy, hmm? All this time and effort spent tracking down your dear dead Ursula's son, and you really had no idea what you were getting into at all. Oh my." He took out a pressed linen handkerchief and patted it to his forehead, his cheeks, then folded it and slid it back into his pocket.

"All right, Lexy. Here's the deal. I'll transfer five thousand a month to you, just as I did to Ursula, only you'll get to keep it, for as long as you live. But you speak one word of what you know to anyone, *anyone*, the money stops. And the trouble starts."

"You *are* threatening me! Why, David? What harm could I possibly be to you? Who cares if you're Ursula's son? That's ancient history, for heaven's sake."

David's eyes had narrowed and he was watching her carefully.

"And I know you're not legally adopted but any court of law, surely, I mean there must be some sort of common-law equivalent for a son, like a common-law wife or . . ." Lexy stopped. What was it Evie had said? Something about even that wouldn't have been enough . . . legally adopted not enough . . . That was it. It was about Helen, about the Buchanan inheritance . . .

"Blood. That's it! Only blood relatives of Helen's . . ."

"Finally, she gets there. That's right, Lexy. The estate is entailed on blood relatives only. I'm not Helen's child. I am not a Buchanan, and yet here I sit."

"But what happens if . . . I mean, there isn't anyone else. Helen's children died with her— Oh, they *were* Helen's, weren't they, or . . . or . . ."

"They were Helen's all right. Yes. After all that time trying for a child and nothing, within a few months of bringing me into the

189

family home, old Gregory finally started sowing his seed. Ross. My baby brother. Rightful heir to the Buchanan throne, not that it would ever have come to that. Helen would have had to confess to the whole scam for that to have happened and I doubt she'd have done that. No. She couldn't even legally adopt me without telling Gregory, so you can see why it was all a bit . . . shaky, shall we say?"

"It can't possibly matter now, though. Helen's line is finished. There are no more Buchanans, so—"

"Sure about that, are you, Lexy? Perhaps rather than spending all that time working out who Ursula's son was, you'd have been better asking yourself who your own mother was."

Lexy felt a worm of anxiety twitch in the pit of her stomach.

"What do you mean? You know who my mother was. Isobel Sh—"

"After she married, yes. But that's not what I said. I wasn't asking for her name. I said you should ask yourself who she *was*."

"I don't understand. What's that got to do with . . . Look, I'm not interested in the rights and wrongs of your inheritance. What matters to me is that you're Ursula's son, and for better or worse that gives us a kind of connection, makes you a virtual uncle—"

The boom of David's laughter cut Lexy off.

"Oh dear child," he said wiping tears from his cheeks, "you really are priceless. You see I *am*. I *am* your uncle, or at least your grandmother would have had the world believe so." He dissolved again into laughter.

Lexy's mind was blank. She had absolutely no idea what he meant. Was he drunk? Mad? She looked at the door. It seemed a very long way away from the low sofa she'd sat back down on. And David was standing now, still laughing gleefully, going back to replenish his glass, to the sideboard between her and the door.

"I'm going to tell you something Lexy, for all the good it will do you. You won't be able to prove any of it and I will deny it if you

190

try. And believe me, no one in this country will take your word over mine. I've spent a lot of money over the years making sure I'm always believed, that history is always written and recorded in the way I decide. Sure you wouldn't like a drink? You look a little pale; it might revive you."

Lexy shook her head, her brain still refusing to understand what David was saying. How could he possibly be her uncle? That would mean . . . what? Ursula was Izzie's *mother*? Or . . . or . . . Cameron . . .

"Well, now, little Lexy, I can see you're struggling with this. And perhaps I'm being a little . . . elastic . . . with the strict legality of the relationship, but suffice to say I'm more of an uncle than you clearly ever imagined. A kind of connection, indeed. Rather more than that."

He was enjoying this, she could tell. She really wasn't sure she wanted to hear any more, doubting already the wisdom of tracking down this smug, overbearing man, subjecting herself to what she was sure was going to be an unpleasant discovery.

"Let's see, where shall I begin?" He dragged on his cheroot, watched the smoke rise as he exhaled. "None of us is ever quite the person we seem to be. And in our family, that's especially so. You're right that I'm Ursula's son, and Cameron's. And that Helen was a sort of *de facto* mother to me, even if the arrangement was never ratified in the eyes of the law. But she and Gregory went on to have a son of their own."

"I know. I've seen photos of you both as small boys with Helen and Gregory."

David nodded. "Touching, those family portraits. Helen loved having them done, would fuss over our hair and shirts and goodness knows what. Odd that she discontinued the practice after she married Cameron. Sad, really, because it meant there were so few of our beloved sister."

The worm of anxiety turned into a snake, a boa constrictor

winding itself around Lexy's windpipe, cutting off the air, stilling her breathing.

"Oh, dear God, no . . ."

David's smile split his face like a knife slash.

"Oh yes, Lexy. No photos of our lovely Isobel. Tragically lost with our mother, Helen, and my brother, Ross, in the mudslide tragedy. The tragedy that was reported to have caused 144 deaths but in fact should more accurately have been reported as a mere 141. The same tragedy that they tried to lay at the door of this company, at the time Helen Buchanan was at its helm. Imagine that. The saintly Helen Buchanan accused of such dreadful negligence, so many innocent souls lost on her watch."

Lexy couldn't hear that syrupy voice any more. Blood was rushing through her head, thrumming in her ears. Izzie. Her mother. Helen's daughter. Which meant that she . . . Lexy was . . . oh God. This changed everything. She looked up at the man opposite her and realised she was the one person left who could take it all away from him. *She* was blood. She was the rightful heir to Buchanan's.

David was watching her with those small eyes, tapping his signet ring against the whisky glass like the tick of a clock. Why would he tell her this? Why? What would he do to stop her telling anyone else? Lexy forced herself to stay calm, to hide her alarm, her fear.

"You're . . . you're saying my mother was your sister. Stepsister. That they survived the . . . But *how*? And why didn't—"

"I adored her you know, your mother, when we were small." David ignored Lexy's questions, a real smile playing on the fleshy features as he remembered. "And she adored me. *Daydid*. That's what she called me. Never did master my name before . . ."

David stood and went over to a picture of a baobab tree, two birds in its branches. He took it down from the wall and Lexy realised it covered a safe. He spun the dial swiftly and, after a

192

series of scarcely audible clicks, pulled open the small heavy door. This was becoming more and more like a B-movie, the whisky and cigar fumes, the safe. All it needed was David in a white tuxedo, stroking a cat. She half expected him to pull a gun from the safe, was relieved when she saw it was a large Manila envelope.

"My father continued the tradition of family portraiture. Helen found it too painful to join them, of course, after her beloved Gregory had passed away, so she is absent from the picture. But here are the rest of us, outside the house in Zomba. Don't we look happy? And the resemblance, my dear, is remarkable between you and your mother, even given the difference in ages."

Lexy was looking at a faded print. She recognised Cameron and the boys, but they were joined by a young girl of four or five with abundant curls and large dark eyes. Her mother's eyes. Her own eyes. And, she now realised, Helen's eyes, too. The similarities between the generations were remarkable.

Lexy reached forward to take the print.

"No. I don't think so. I'll hold on to this, if you don't mind. It means so much to me. I shouldn't worry about it quite so much, I know, when we have the negative safely secured out of harm's way."

Lexy was beyond confused, now. She was in a state of shock. There was no doubt that was her mother. No doubt at all. And similarly, there could no longer be any doubt that Helen was her grandmother. The shock she'd had when she'd opened Ursula's photo album and looked into a young Helen's eyes should have told her. She couldn't believe she hadn't accepted it earlier. But she'd thought she was here to find Ursula's son, a surrogate family, not a real one.

David had put the print back in the safe, replaced the picture and was now pouring whisky into another glass.

"Take it," he said, not unkindly. "We need to talk, now, seriously talk, don't we? Come on, Lexy, there's a good girl. Drink up. I don't want to have to slap you out of it."

Lexy shuddered and coughed as the fire hit the back of her throat.

"Good." David sat again. "Feeling better? You'll be wondering why I've told you this. And perhaps you're also already thinking of speaking out about this, staking a claim to Buchanan's, even. But that would be very foolish, in so many ways. Dangerous even. And would all be for nought anyway, as there is no way you will be able to prove anything I've said. I have spent a good deal of time and money ensuring that the past stays buried. One of the joys of a country like this is that we have a small and close-knit community that takes care of its own, for the right . . . motivation. There are, unfortunately, no official records, no birth certificates or suchlike, available to the public that would help you prove your story, if you were indeed driven to try to do so. No. Nothing at all."

"So why . . . why even tell me . . ."

"Two reasons, Alexis. One you'll believe, I'm sure, and one you may not, but it's true all the same. Pragmatically, I believe in controlling as many variables in life as possible. My father taught me the importance of that, of keeping one step ahead of the other players on the board. And you, whether you knew it or not, are most definitely one of those. I have been following your progress, just as I followed your mother's throughout her life. I hoped you wouldn't, but I knew you'd have to come to Malawi to find me, and I knew the chances were you would probably succeed. Eventually. So I decided to let you do so, and that I would tell you who you are, to stop you stirring the hornet's nest any further. Damage limitation. If I am the one to tell you, to control the information flow, I contain the situation, and when I tell you more of the circumstances around your family background, you will, I'm sure, come to agree with me that the best course of action is for you to disappear back to your life in London. Although the £5,000 a month offer still stands, so you might not have to return to that grim little school you've been working in. Up to you."

Lexy waited, trying to work out what he meant by containing the situation, and what exactly it was in her family background that he could be so certain she'd be complicit in concealing.

"I don't want money, I told you."

"Well, we'll see."

"And the other reason?"

"Ah yes, the one you most likely will choose not to believe. I wasn't always the man you see today. There was a time when I was an innocent, too, a happy child. I truly believed Helen was my mother and I adored her. And I adored my siblings too. None more so than little Izzie when she came along. For a few short years we were a happy family. Then Gregory died and my childish world started to unravel. Gregory was barely cold in the ground before the man I believed was my uncle married my mother. It was not a happy union. I knew he beat her, but I was still young, and lacked the guts to intervene. I would have done. I wanted to but . . ." He shrugged. "Then it became a matter of survival of the fittest. Cameron took it upon himself to toughen me up. Successfully, I should add, although his efforts with Ross bore far less satisfactory results, and Izzie he simply ignored, thank God. But despite all that, I retain a good deal of affection for the old days, the days when I believed I was truly a Buchanan, and was proud of it. So, let's just say it's the whim of a lonely man. I never intended any harm to come to any of my family. It was all orchestrated and put in place while I was still a young boy. For good or bad, I am simply the inheritor of it all and have never found a reason to change what Cameron put in place. I have the Buchanan company, even if I don't have the Buchanan family, any family. But that's enough for me."

Lexy watched him drink deeply from the crystal tumbler, saw something akin to sadness flicker across the ruddy face, thought she heard the softest of sighs as he lowered the glass.

"I have a sentimental attachment to my younger years." David swirled the dregs in his glass. "Your mother was a part of that. So for her sake, I'll help you, Lexy, with money, if you'll take it, and you should, but with advice too. I was curious to meet you, to help you. And believe me, my dear, the best advice I can give you is to go home. Do not dig further into this whole sorry affair; it will do no one any good. You and your grandmother least of all."

"My *grandmother*? What could it possibly matter to a dead woman—"

"Her memory, Lexy. Her reputation."

"What are you trying to say? That you're trying to buy me off out of some sense of family loyalty? That's rich. And what about Helen's reputation? Is this about the accident? The mudslide? That she might be guilty of . . . But Robert says you've got the courts sewn up, so why—"

"It could still impact on the company. Scandal is never good for business. Murder accusations even less so."

"So we're back to Buchanan's, back to money. Not 'sentimental attachments' at all."

David shrugged, drew on his cigar. "Don't be so scathing, my dear. Money takes care of things. And I did use some of it to take care of my mother, not to pay her to stay away. That was her choice, although I'll admit as time went on it suited me."

"She chose not to use your money. Didn't want you to 'take care' of her." Lexy wanted to hurt him, knew she was unlikely to succeed. "So whatever salve to your conscience splashing out five grand a month might have been, it wasn't wanted."

David laughed his humourless laugh. "You'd know that, would you?"

"Yes. I don't know what she did with it, but there's nothing,

196

nothing at all to suggest she spent a single penny of it. Nothing to suggest she lived on anything other than her own hard-earned pension."

"Really? Maybe you just didn't know where to look." David's twisted smile was annoying Lexy. She hated being patronised, manipulated, played for a fool. And she hated most of all having to learn about her birthright, her family from this odious man.

"Of course I knew where to look. I went through everything, spoke to her solicitors, her bank. Nothing. Her flat was modest, her lifestyle no more than you'd expect of a retired matron, so if she did spend it, I don't understand where it went."

"Well, you wouldn't."

"Why wouldn't I?"

"Because the money wasn't for Ursula. You forget, my dear, I had two mothers."

She didn't like being on the receiving end of his cryptic remarks.

"What do you mean?"

"Oh come, Lexy dear. We've just been through this. Do I really have to spell it out? My mother, the woman I *called* my mother, was Helen. Helen Buchanan."

Lexy felt as if she'd been thumped in the chest. "But she . . . Helen . . . she's dead."

"Is she?"

Lexy fell back into the sofa, its springs squealing at the force of her landing on the leather cushions.

David filled his glass again, waved it in her direction. "Top up? You look like you need it."

Lexy shook her head. "Helen Buchanan is alive. That's what you're saying. She's alive."

"Very much so. Couldn't bear that brute of a man, my father – or me, I suppose – so ran out on us both. Taking my siblings with her. At the time, we all thought they'd died in the tragedy. But she always was a clever woman. She'd seen her chance and off she'd

197

gone. Left me behind with dear old Dad. Cheers." He raised the glass to her, drained it, turned quickly back to the sideboard to fill it again so Lexy couldn't see his face. But she'd caught it. A glimpse of . . . what exactly? Pain? Bitterness? Disgust?

"Where is she, David?"

"Good question. I have no idea."

"You don't expect me to believe that."

"Believe what you like. It makes no difference to me." The mask was back, the features hardened once again as he wandered back to his chair behind the desk, another hearty slug of whisky swooshing in the glass as he sat down again.

"You must know. A man with your . . . resources."

He laughed. "That fixer Richard Chakanaya, you mean? Perhaps he knows, perhaps he doesn't. If he does, though, he's kept it to himself. You'd have to ask him, although he doesn't come cheap. Everything has a price, and for him information is the most precious commodity he has to sell."

"But surely you asked him—"

"It's not something we discuss. I have as little to do with him as possible. His type are a necessary evil in parts of Africa. I don't have to like him, just pay him. In any case, Richard was my father's man, really, I simply inherited one or two . . . services he renders the company when I took over. And why would I want to know anyway? My father made these financial arrangements and it's been easier to continue them than not, just as I'll now continue them for you. It's easier than any alternative."

"But why did she do it? Why didn't she come back?"

"She had her reasons. My father made sure of it. Small matter of murder charges."

"The mudslide—"

"Amongst other things."

"But Cameron's gone. And the company's been absolved of responsibility, for now at least. Robert said—"

"Ah yes, Robert again. Our very own knight in shining armour. Intent on saving his little Audrey's family name with his futile crusade. Unlikely, but if he succeeds, well, it will cost a lot of money. And put Helen, as the only surviving director in post at the time, in the dock. She'll stay hidden."

"But she . . . Helen—"

"Is nothing to me. An old woman playing hide and don't seek somewhere all by herself. No one wants to find her."

"But you just said she's your *mother*, you were *happy*. I can't believe you've never even tried to find her—"

"She abandoned me!" The glass slammed down onto the desktop, whisky and spittle speckling the gleaming wood as David's anger burst through his cynical demeanour and he lurched to his feet, leaning over the desk, glaring at Lexy. "Threw this honeybird out of her nest, or rather took the nest away and left me here with . . . with *him*." He was breathing heavily, his face mottled red, twisted and ugly. He dropped his head, then swung his heavy frame round to the window. Despite it all, despite his arrogance, his smug superiority, his refusal to acknowledge the truth openly, Lexy couldn't help but feel pity. She watched him in silence, the broad shoulders heaving as he struggled to bring his breath, himself, under control.

"Helen Buchanan," David continued eventually, his voice now flat and emotionless, "made it perfectly clear she wanted nothing to do with me. No attempt to contact me, even after Cameron was no longer in the picture. I'm merely reciprocating the sentiment."

"But—"

"But nothing! As far as I'm concerned it would have been better if she *had* died in that mudslide. It certainly would have cost me a good deal less."

"But that's . . . that's monstrous! How can you—"

"Monstrous?" David's eyes were black. "Oh, I'm not the

199

monster here. Ask yourself what kind of mother abandons her child. Or should I say what kind of *mothers* – they both did it, after all. Ursula first, then Helen. They both abandoned a child. They both abandoned me."

18

Blantyre Hospital, June 15th

"How could you, Evie? How could you lie to me?"

Lexy burst into Evie's room, stood shaking at her bedside, hands on hips, anger emanating from every pore. "You *knew*. All the time I was telling you what I thought I'd been so clever finding out, you *knew*."

"I . . . Lexy, I'm sorry . . . I . . . I don't know what you—"

"Don't you dare! Don't you dare deny it. Stop lying to me."

"I'm not lying. I didn't *lie*."

"Don't nitpick. You didn't tell me the truth, which is as good as. You let me think I had no family, that my mother was an orphan. All of you. The three bloody witches, fooling the world and denying me my family. How *could* you!"

The old woman looked pale and frail against the starched bedlinen. Lexy felt a pang of guilt, but really, how could she not have said anything?

"What's going on here?" A nurse had appeared at the door. Lexy spun round and strode over towards her.

"Get out! Get the hell out of here!" Lexy slammed the door, heard the staccato rhythm of the nurse's footsteps beating a retreat down the corridor. Lexy leant against the door, breathing heavily as all the anger and pain and loss rose up and focused its intensity on Evie: the only person she could be angry with, could blame for all that she was feeling right now.

"Why, Evie? Why did you do it? All of it?" Lexy was pacing now, the energy of her anger making her almost manic. She felt she was outside herself, watching this prowling stranger ranging through the room.

"Lexy. Please. Sit down. Let's talk about this calmly."

Lexy could hear the quiver in Evie's voice, knew the older woman was shocked by the violence in Lexy's movements, the rage that was driving her.

"It was for the best. Really. Lexy, I'm sorry. We—"

"Sorry? You're sorry? Not half as sorry as I am. Sorry that I've spent my whole life not knowing who I am—"

"That's enough, Lexy."

She hadn't heard the door or the footsteps behind her and jumped as Robert's hand gripped her shoulder with surprising force, spun her round to face him.

"What do you think you're doing? My grandmother is a very sick woman and—"

"You! You knew too. You're just as bad as she is, as all of them!"

Robert pushed her down into the chair, placed his hands on its arms and leant over her.

"Enough, Lexy. Enough. If you can't calm yourself you're going to have to leave. I will not have my grandmother upset like this."

"And what about me? How about how upset I am? Were you ever going to tell me, hmm? Either of you?" Lexy's head darted from side to side as she tried to look at Evie. Behind her, the old woman began to cough. Robert was at her side immediately.

"Gran, take it easy. Breathe slowly. Look at me, Gran. That's it. Gently does it." Slowly the old woman's coughing eased. "I think you should go now, Lexy." Robert didn't even turn to look at her.

"I'm sorry I . . . ," Lexy wiped her eyes with the back of her hand, ashamed of herself, of her tears, but still so *angry*. She sniffed, breathed deep. "I'm sorry, okay? But this is wrong. What you did is wrong and I need to know—"

"Just go. Lexy. Can't you see what you're doing to her?"

"But—"

"Get out!"

Lexy turned to leave, shame sweeping over her as she cast a backward glance at the frail woman. She knew she had every right to be angry, but she also knew it wasn't fair to attack Evie like that and to blame her for everything, yet she had. But, if she wanted to find out the rest of the story, the bits David had taunted her with but then refused to explain, she needed Evie and Robert to help her and this wasn't the way to go about that.

Restless and furious, Lexy needed to walk, march it off, stamp it out on the paths that wound round the hospital gardens. Realising how ridiculous she would seem to anyone looking out of the windows didn't make her feel any better, but she couldn't face her hotel room, and knew, the state she was in, she'd only lose her bearings and probably end up in some slum backstreet in even more trouble than she was right now if she ventured out into the streets outside.

As she paced through the grounds, oblivious to the glory of the rainbow of blooms all around her, or the welcome shade of the heavy acacia trees, and with even yesterday's embarrassing debacle with Robert in these very gardens sidelined, she ran over everything David had told her. She was Helen Buchanan's granddaughter: David Buchanan's niece, to all intents and purposes. She wasn't sure she wanted to be either of those, knowing what she now did of them. A mean-spirited, bitter, seedy man and a woman who lied to a man she was supposed to love, abandoned the child she'd pretended was hers for years, went on the run and was accused of murder. Had she had a hand in it? The company's negligence? Had she known? Worse, turned a blind eye to scrimping on safety measures in the interest of profits? It didn't bear thinking about.

"Oh!" Lexy stopped short as she remembered Robert's question that day at the lake. What would she have done, in David's shoes? He'd known, known that Buchanan's was rightfully hers, and was testing her, trapping her into all but guaranteeing the compensation—

But it didn't matter. She didn't want anything to do with Buchanan's and its ill-gotten gains. *Tough luck, Robert. Good luck with the crusade.* She was so *angry*.

Lexy flopped onto a shaded bench, swinging her backpack down from her shoulder. It thudded to the ground at her feet, weighed down by the photo albums. How could she have been so stupid? It was obvious they were family. Once you knew to look at things that way. How much had her mother known? And for how long? Was that why Izzie and Ursula had argued? Had Izzie guessed her parents were anything but the missionaries she'd been told they were? Had she met David when she'd worked out here as a nurse, invited him to her wedding to Philip Shaw? Or had she been as ignorant as Lexy herself back then? Had David watched, stalked her, worried that she might claim her rightful inheritance, take away the company and fortune that defined him?

More to the point, did Lexy want to do any of that herself, even supposing she could?

"You'll never be able to prove it, Lexy. I've made sure of that," he'd said before she left. "And you'll save us both a lot of aggravation if you don't even try. Stop asking questions. I'm offering you a generous settlement to get out of my life, out of Malawi, and to go back to being the person you always thought you were. It's the safe option. Take it."

"I don't want money. I want to know about my family."

"I've told you as much as you need to know. Believe me, you will regret digging any deeper. I have to live with the consequences of the past, albeit I'm well compensated for it" – he'd indicated the opulent surroundings – "but you'll just have to take my word that you will not be any happier for knowing the past. Some things are best left buried."

"But Evie knows. She could help me—"

204

Again he'd laughed in her face. "An old, sick woman? How can she help? Who is ever going to take the word of a deluded, dying woman over the head of the Buchanan empire? Especially when I have taken so much care to erase the evidence. And she wouldn't anyway. She knows it's best to let the memory of her friends rest in peace. She will still do anything to protect them, their good name. No, there's no one left who can help you prove this, Lexy. I've made sure of that. And no one left who cares, apart from you. You're on your own. No one will listen. So be a good girl, and just run on home."

Lexy felt her anger growing again. She had every right to know who she was, where she came from, even to be able to call herself a Buchanan, if she wanted to, although she wasn't sure she did. But she had to know everything to be able to choose whether or not to reclaim her family. More than that, she needed to know, to understand, why her mother had been shipped off to Ursula when she still had a stepbrother, a stepfather in Cameron. Still had a *mother*. Why hadn't Helen wanted her daughter? Did that mean she wouldn't want her granddaughter either? How dare they all conspire to keep the truth, her birthright, from her? None of it made sense. There was something wrong with David's story.

She stretched out along the length of the bench, crossed her arms under her head as a pillow and lay back. The branches crisscrossed above her, black lace against the sunlight. Think. She had to think. What was it David knew that made him so sure Evie wouldn't, couldn't, help Lexy prove who she was? And why did it matter so much to Lexy anyway? She didn't want the Buchanan fortune or the company. She'd never been driven by dreams of wealth and riches. She had wanted to believe she had family, to find somewhere to belong. But if David *was* that family, did she really want to claim kinship? And now that she knew, could she forget all this and go back to being plain old Lexy Shaw?

No. Not yet, at least. There was still too much that she didn't know, and she might have just blown her chances of finding it out. She'd been wrong to rush in to confront Evie like that. All she'd succeeded in doing was making Evie ill and alienating Robert. She felt sure he knew more than he was saying, too.

She sat up abruptly, grabbed her bag and stood. Walk. Keep walking. Burn off some energy until she was calm enough to think things through sensibly. As she turned the corner towards the front of the hospital, she saw a long black car draw up and a chauffeur leap out to open the rear passenger door. Robert appeared from the shadows of the hospital's entrance and got in. Lexy drew back behind the hibiscus bushes as the car moved forward and slid past. She had a clear view of the other occupant of the car's rear seat. David Buchanan.

Interesting, Lexy thought. What was that about? The Blantyre 144 appeal, or something, someone, else?

19

The Residence, June 15th

Two hours later, calmer and clearer about what she had to do, Lexy walked up the steps into the shaded hotel lobby. She still couldn't face the confines of her room; sitting quietly taking tea on the verandah would be more to her liking.

"Miss Shaw?' Barney was running after her. "Miss Shaw, letter for you. Hand-delivered an hour ago."

She took the proffered envelope, her eyes immediately drawn to the spindly black letters that spelt out her name in the centre of the cream vellum. The writing looked familiar, or was she just being fanciful? Black ink, again, like the message she'd received on her first night in Malawi, like the notes in the folder she'd found in Robert's desk. But was it really the same hand?

"Did you see who delivered it, Barney?"

"No, Miss Shaw, sorry. I've only been on shift for half an hour. You'd have to ask Thomas when he's back on duty tomorrow."

Lexy nodded and handed Barney a coin. "Thanks anyway, Barney."

She turned the envelope over in her hand as she walked thoughtfully out onto the verandah, so lost in her thoughts that she didn't see the large figure in the winged rattan chair until his words made her lift her head.

"More billets-doux, Miss Shaw?"

Pendleton. Her heart sank.

"Mr Pendleton," she said. "Good afternoon."

He grimaced. "I suppose it's pointless repeating my suggestion you call me Hugh? No matter. Won't you join me? I've just ordered tea. Or perhaps we're not really too far from the cocktail hour, if you'd prefer to get started in on the gin?"

"Thank you, but no. I hope you'll excuse me, but I have work to do."

"Work? Heavens. Thought you were on holiday?"

"Well, yes, I am." Why did she feel the need to explain? "But I still have matters to attend to. Administrative tasks and so forth."

"Of course. The aftermath of bereavement. I was so very sorry to hear about Miss Reid. And your mother too, of course."

Lexy murmured something, but her mind was distracted. How did he know about her mother? Miss Reid, yes, he may well have heard about that. Ursula still had connections in Malawi, after all, but her mother? Lexy was sure she hadn't mentioned her to him on her first encounter with the unpleasant man.

"Perhaps I can help?"

"I'm sorry?" Lexy pulled herself back to the present.

"With the admin. Boring old stuff isn't it, but then it's what we civil servants excel at. Be happy to give you a hand."

"Kind of you, of course, but that really won't be necessary, Mr Pendleton. Now if you'll excuse me, I must . . ." Unintentionally, Lexy waved the envelope she still held unopened in her hand.

"Of course. Mustn't keep you from your mystery message, must I?"

"Mr Pendleton, sir?" Barney appeared beside them.

"What, boy?"

"Telephone, sir."

"Oh for goodness' sake. Tell them I'm—"

"Urgent, sir, they said. Consular matters." Barney flicked a glance at Lexy and she knew instantly he was lying. He was rescuing her. She swallowed a smile as the dapper bellhop bowed and ushered the lumbering frame of Hugh Pendleton ahead of him and out into the lobby, where, Lexy was sure, he'd find his urgent caller had tired of waiting for him to come to the phone.

She took the opportunity to descend the verandah steps and disappear round the side of the hotel to the further reaches of the grounds, more than a little rattled. The man was not a natural diplomat, that was clear. That offer of helping with her admin had been ridiculous, blatant. But what was it he wanted from her? What was he trying to find out? Was he working for David, somehow? Surely David's money could buy him a more expert spy than that lumbering oaf.

When she was sure she was out of sight of the hotel and that Hugh Pendleton had been thrown off her scent, she sat down in one of the pergolas tucked away in quiet corners. She ripped open the envelope and pulled out a single sheet of thin paper.

Dear Lexy,

There are things you need to know. Meet me this evening, 7pm, at the old schoolroom in the hospital grounds.

Robert

So she hadn't burnt all her bridges after all. Her conscience squealed, though. She still needed to apologise to Evie. She had behaved crassly, appallingly. Danny said grief had unhinged her and that latest outburst would suggest it had been an accurate description.

She looked at her watch. Yes. There was time, plenty of time. She'd go back to the hospital and apologise to Evie right now.

20

Blantyre Hospital, June 15th

"You're quite forgiven, Lexy dear. We've hardly been saint-like ourselves in any of this. *You* must forgive *us*, I suspect. It's so hard to know what's best. Please believe me when I say everything I've done has always and only been to help, to protect, those I love. To protect you, Lexy. I am frightened where all this might lead."

"I understand that, but I have a right to know who I am. You don't get to decide who will and who won't be allowed their birthright. Do you even begin to understand how devastating all of this is for me? I thought losing my mother was bad enough, but now to find out that she lied—"

"I do wish you'd stop saying everyone's been lying—"

"Evie, I don't want to fight again. But really, what else is it but lying? Whatever the reasons, the end result is the same. The truth was withheld from me, deliberately, and I've grown up believing I was one person only to find I'm another. With a family. With a very colourful history."

Evie sighed. "Yes. You're right."

"So you have to tell me everything now. You owe me that."

"I'm not sure you'll thank me."

"I have a right to make that judgement for myself. Nothing you can say will be worse than anything I'm imagining. The truth, Evie. That's all I'm asking."

The old woman nodded.

It was late morning, May 1961, Evie remembered. The paper was sitting on the sofa where she'd left it earlier, shocked at what she'd read there, unable to understand why her friend would do such a thing, unsure how to greet her when the housekeeper announced Helen's arrival.

"Evie, I know you're disappointed in me." Helen had sounded defensive as she swept into the room, getting straight to the point.

"No, no, of course I'm not." Evie wasn't sure that was entirely true, but Helen was her friend, whatever she did.

"You are." Helen sighed. "I know you too well – I can tell. You're trying so hard to be loyal and support me. I don't know what I would do, would have done, without you, Evie. You and the children, of course."

"And Ursula," Evie added with a smile. "Don't forget our distant friend."

"Oh no. Let's not forget Ursula."

"Helen? That's a little . . ."

"I know. I'm sorry. It's been a . . . difficult . . . few weeks."

"Well of course it has, my darling. Dear Gregory. You two were so close and it was all so very unexpected and . . . and it *has* only been a few weeks, so no wonder you're not quite . . . yourself. But don't you see? That's why I don't understand, why I'm . . ."

"Disappointed."

"Surprised, let's say, that you and Cameron have . . . If nothing else, it's sudden to say the least. And to have already announced your engagement."

Evie was feeling her way here. She didn't want Helen to know how hurt she'd been when she'd read the announcement in *The Times* that morning. She'd had no inkling of it and she was sad that Helen hadn't said anything to her. Evie had been with her every day since Gregory's death. There'd been ample opportunity.

Helen wouldn't meet her eyes, but Evie heard her sigh. Helen would know she'd hurt her. She must have had good reason, although it was hard to imagine what that might be.

211

"You've never even liked the man, Helen, and he's done nothing at all for the business. You and Gregory spent your time putting right his mistakes, mopping up his scandals, his errors of judgement, call them what you will. In fact, you actively dislike him."

"Dislike? Far too mild. I hate him." Helen folded her arms across her chest and tilted her chin as she turned her head to stare out of the window behind her.

"Then why? I just don't—"

"Because he knows, Evie. He *knows*."

"He knows . . . what exactly . . . ?"

Helen turned back to look at Evie, head tipped to one side and an insincere smile on her face.

"No! Surely not. How could he? No one knows except us and—"

"Ursula. Yes."

"But you don't think she . . . Why would she?"

"I don't know. But she must have done. How else?" Helen was pacing now, heels clicking smartly on the teak floor. "It hardly matters. If I don't marry him, and agree to his 'terms', as he calls them, then he'll tell the world that David isn't mine. Isn't Gregory's. It will ruin Ursula, even now, even with her on the other side of the world, although frankly at the moment I'm so angry with her I really don't care if she's disgraced or not—"

"Don't say that, you know she—"

"I don't care! No. I'm not doing this for Ursula. I'm doing it for David. *My* David, *Gregory's* son. He's the innocent in all of this and I will do whatever is necessary to to protect him and his good name. My Ross too, and Izzie. I don't want any of them dragged down, ruined by the scandal, scandal that could rock Buchanan's and maybe even bring it down. And let's not forget," she said, bitterness sharpening her voice, "I did deceive my husband. For years. What kind of woman does that make me? Hardly a

212

trustworthy one. No. It can't come out now. Ever. It would make Gregory look a fool. I won't have that."

"But isn't there another way? Marrying a man you despise is a little extreme, don't you think? I can't believe Cameron really wants to marry someone who hates him." Evie stood and walked over to Helen, led her back to the settee and pulled her down to sit next to her. "He's taunting you. Playing one of his cruel games. He won't go through with it. It would hardly be a pleasant life for him either. He's disreputable, self-indulgent, pampered and heaven only knows what, so he's not going to deliberately make life difficult for himself, is he? Why would he?"

Helen shrugged thin shoulders, rested her head against the cushions. "Money. And jealousy." She sounded so weary. "Anything Gregory had, Cameron wanted, or wanted something better. Believe me if there was another way I'd grab it with both hands and run a million miles from that . . . that . . ."

"You can't do this. There *has* to be another way. We can find it togeth—"

"For God's sake, Evie!" Helen's head whipped round and Evie could see the anger on her face, her pale cheeks suddenly flushed scarlet with the heat of it. "There isn't. Think about it. It isn't just about good name and reputation. We have Buchanan's to consider. Things are shaky enough as it is with Gregory's death. I'm having to work hard to persuade our customers that I can continue to run the business without him – and to be honest even I'm not completely sure that I can. A scandal like this could bring the whole thing down about our ears. Look at who our customers are. Our whole business has been based on our work with the Missions. If we lose them, we lose everything. Simple as that. You may be a forgiving woman, Evie, but can you put your hand on your heart and tell me the Church, the Edinburgh Elders who hold the purse strings, share your compassion?"

Evie looked down at her hands clasped in her lap, tried to

213

believe that they would, but Helen was right. Of course she was. She knew her business and her customers so well.

"No, I can't."

"So what else can I do? Without the Mission business, Buchanan's will crumble. I've tried offering him money, but that's not enough. He wants everything Gregory had. He wants me." Helen stood again, crossed the room quickly and stepped out into the night. But not before Evie had seen her tears.

After a moment Evie followed her and the two friends leant side by side, resting their arms on the verandah railing and breathing in the fragrance of the blossoms around them, listening to the scratching of insects and the distant sound of the servants' voices from their quarters.

"He laughed when I asked, begged, him to wait. To let at least a year elapse before we announced our engagement, but the thought of the scandal appeals to him, despite the risk that too poses to our business position. Just another way of dragging me down. He says I broke his heart. That I'm the only woman he could really have loved. That if I hadn't rejected him, if I'd married him then, he'd have been a better man. Everything he is, everything he's done, he says, is down to me. My fault."

"But that's just nonsense. It's not rational ... It's ... insane."

"Yes." Helen's voice fell to a whisper. "And that worries me more than I can say."

"I can't let you do this."

"I have to. And I will. But don't think Cameron will have it all his own way. He will have more of a battle on his hands than he can imagine. There are things he doesn't know. Things I can do to protect my children, myself."

Evie shook her head, desperately trying to think of a way out for her friend, of a way of stopping this farce. But she couldn't. All she could do was watch over her.

"Can I help? I'll do whatever I can, whatever it takes to keep you safe."

"You may have to, one of these days. But for now, just be what you always have been. My dearest, most trusted friend. And not a word of this to Ursula. Promise me."

Evie's heart was heavy as she nodded her agreement, knowing now she would be forever caught between the interests of her two closest friends, the rift between them that David's birth had mended now widened beyond repair. And she'd been the one who'd suggested it all those years ago. How different things could have been if she hadn't interfered . . .

★

"You need to leave now, Miss Shaw."

The nurse spoke softly, stepped silently across the room to check Evie's pulse. Evie hardly stirred. "All this talking is exhausting her, and we need her strong for her operation."

21

The Schoolroom, Blantyre Hospital Grounds, June 15th
It was already dark when Lexy left Evie's room, and there was
no point returning to the hotel just to turn around and come
back again. She would be early for her meeting with Robert, but
it was a gorgeous, balmy evening so it would be no hardship to
sit on the schoolroom porch and wait for him. She followed
the footpath round to the right and through the gate Robert
had shown her when he'd taken her to see the bungalows just a
couple of days before. When she'd made such a fool of herself
inviting him to dinner, and then been so surprised that he and
Audrey were together. She was glad they both seemed to have
put it behind them. His note had been surprising, but then
perhaps she'd misjudged him yet again and he really did want
to help her. Had he found out which bungalow had been her
parents'?

Lexy was tired and walked slowly. Could she really face Robert
without squirming with embarrassment? She should apologise.
She'd been an idiot, behaved badly. But then that seemed to
be in keeping with this strange family she was now a part of,
whether she liked it or not. And for all she was already shocked
at what she'd learned of them so far, and had a strong feeling
there was worse to come, she had to know. *Be careful what you
wish for,* her mother would have said. Well, she'd wished, and here
she was.

The schoolroom bungalow was in darkness, so she sat down
on the step, leant her head back against the verandah post. She

stretched her arms up above her and clasped the post behind, hearing her shoulders creak and crack as the tension was released. Dropping her hands back into her lap, she raised her eyes up to the clear sky, stars already bright, twinkling like sequins on a deep-blue velvet cape. A brilliant moon hung low in the sky, its shimmering light casting flickering shadows around her, as leaves swayed in the gentlest of evening breezes. Everything was serene, calm, quiet. The night was hers. She relished being alone in it.

Click.

Lexy spun round towards the door, expectantly.

"Robert?"

Had he been sitting in the dark? The door was slightly ajar now, a key in the lock spotlit by moonlight. She hadn't checked, had assumed it would still be locked. The old boards of the verandah creaked as she stepped up to the door, pushed it open.

"Robert, are you there?"

Silence. Darkness, but as her eyes adjusted she could begin to pick out shapes from the moonlight filtering through the high windows running the length of the two long walls of the single-room structure. Neat rows of desks were divided into two blocks by a central aisle, with a larger desk sitting at the head of them like a general at the head of his army. She smiled. Old-fashioned these days. What would it have been like to teach in a school like this? She could see the blackboard, a shaft of moonlight picking out a dusty stripe across its surface, the faint shapes of letters long-erased just visible, ghosts of their former selves. There were posters on the walls, but it was too dark to make them out clearly, and a row of bookcases and cupboards lining the wall at the back of the room, again too dark for her to see their contents clearly. She pushed open the door with her left hand, searched the wall to her right for a light switch. Two switches. She clicked one. Nothing. She clicked the other and felt air start to move, the soft whirr of a ceiling fan stirring into life. It was cool in here, but she left it anyway, soothed by its quiet hum.

She stepped forward, slowly, feeling her way, trailing her fingers along the desks as she made her way to the top of the central aisle, perched on the edge of the teacher's desk and looked out over the banks of empty spaces, filling them in her mind's eye with pupils from the class she'd deserted so near to the end of term. Did they miss her? Did she miss them? Perhaps. A little. The children were never the problem. It was the system, the class sizes, the lack of support, of discipline. The parents. She sighed. She didn't want to go back. David's offer would mean she didn't have to—

Click.

Pushing herself up from the desk, she spun round to the noise.

"Robert?" But there was no one, and the door was closed again now. Must have been the air from the fan, or the night breeze. The old boards outside creaked. She felt a flicker of fear, before she caught herself. She was getting jumpy, but it would just be a mouse, or a cat, perhaps. Or just the cooling wood giving up the last of the sun's heat.

Her eyes had grown used to the gloom and she could now make out the posters on the walls, even carved initials on desktops. She walked down the aisle, giving her class instructions in her head.

Books out, children. There'd be a clatter of desk lids and a burst of chatter as they hid behind them, using them as shields against the teacher.

Quiet now, please. Settle down. And miracle of miracles, they would.

If only.

She crouched down to look at the books that had been left forgotten on the shelves at the back of the room, picked one out and sat cross-legged on the floor as she turned the pages, trying to make out the words, the images, in the half-light.

Click.

She snapped the book shut and turned her head, her view obscured by the desks.

Click.

She pushed herself inelegantly to her feet. The door was still shut. Had she imagined it? Probably just the branch of a tree creaking in the night breeze or more creaking from the floorboards. Even so. She'd wait outside.

She replaced the book on the shelf, yawned and rolled her shoulders, then walked slowly back through the ghostly class towards the door, saw a flicker of movement under the teacher's desk in front of her. She stooped, peered into the darkness. A mouse? Or a rat? Nothing, except—

Lexy gasped, jumped back at movement in the shadows beneath the desk. She bent down but could see nothing. Imagination? She *was* tired. Over-tired.

The leg of the desk was moving, spreading over the floor, and a dark shadow was seeping towards her. Like a snake.

"Uh!" She breathed in sharply, stumbled back against a desk as the slim, sinuous body curved and slithered its way around the legs of the teacher's chair. She froze. She knew very little about snakes, but enough to realise that being alone with one in a confined space probably wasn't a good thing.

Get out. Now. She started slowly forward, pressing herself against the pupils' desks, not wanting to take her eyes off the creature, frightened of losing sight of it in the dark. If she could just get to the door then she could get out, get help, get someone to deal with it or at least shut it into the schoolroom. But it was moving out from under the desk now, slinking nearer the end of the aisle between the desks, occupying the space between Lexy and the door.

Windows. Could she get out a window? She looked up at the narrow panes running the length of one wall. Thin, and high. Very high. There'd be quite a drop on the other side even if she could manage to climb—

She jerked her gaze back to the floor as she heard a soft *puhushhh* sound and saw the reptile sweeping its way slowly, hypnotically under a desk just two rows ahead of where she stood. Then its head reappeared and it was flowing down the aisle. Towards her.

"No. Oh, God." She pulled herself up onto the nearest desk, folded her knees into her chest, marooned herself like a castaway on a very small island, realising too late that she could no longer see the snake, had no way of knowing if it was still between her and the door. Where was Robert? Why wasn't he here yet?

"No! Oh please no . . ." The snake had reappeared, reached her desk, was gliding beneath it, winding itself around the legs. What was it? A boomslang, puff adder? Did it even matter? She was breathing in short, sharp gasps, blood thundering in her ears as she pulled her legs in tighter, made herself as small as she could, saw the swaying tail disappear beneath her. She craned her neck to look behind her, to see if it emerged, but she was too scared to move in case she overbalanced, tipped the desk, ended up on the floor with the—

A broom. Just behind her. Leaning against the wall between the rows of desks. A weapon.

Goosebumps erupted along her arm as she reached out slowly, carefully, fingers trembling as they touched wood. She scrabbled for purchase and felt the handle move, slip towards her and—

It clattered away from her, hit the desk behind and was sliding out of her reach. Then it stopped, its head caught against one of the desk legs. She exhaled. At least it hadn't slipped to the floor. She still had a chance. She reached again, further this time, felt the desk tilt beneath her but snatched the broom handle and pulled back before her weight tipped the desk over. She held the broom tightly to her, trying to slow her breathing, silence the roaring in her head, listen for the soft swish of the serpent's tail. Where was it?

There. It slithered away towards the back of the room. This was her chance. Dropping down softly from the desk, she backed towards the door, eyes locked on the reptile, tears blurring her vision. She held the broom out in front of her with rigid arms ready to strike if the snake started towards her. How did snakes attack? *Would* it attack? She had absolutely no idea. She had to get the door open.

The snake disappeared into the shadows at the far end of the room, but she was at the door now. Still staring at the spot where she'd last seen the snake, she stretched out a hand behind her, feeling blindly for the handle, finally grasped the cool metal. She pushed it down, the squeak of the mechanism piercing against the soft hum of the ceiling fan. She pulled. Nothing. The handle didn't move. She rattled the handle again, tugged it again. And again, and again.

"No, NO!" She was repeating under her breath as she dropped the broom and turned to the door, wrestling with the handle, grasping it with both hands as she pushed and pulled. But the door stayed fast.

"Help! Help me!"

She knew there was no one to hear her. The surrounding bungalows were either empty or used as storerooms – either way, there'd be no one. Unless Robert? Why wasn't he here? He should be, he—

The snake – where was it?

She whirled round just in time to catch its tail disappearing under a desk in the block furthest from the door. Nearer, though. It was coming nearer. She had to stay calm. She slowed her breathing then crouched, eyes firmly fixed on the shadows beneath the desks as she reached out for the broom handle again. Her fingers grasped the worn wood and slowly, slowly she pulled it

221

towards her as the pointed reptilian head appeared from under the teacher's chair and leisurely swerved to the left and the right, each movement bringing it closer to her.

She was sobbing now. If it struck her, how long would she have before the venom entered her system? Long enough to make a run for it? To get to the hospital and get help? *Idiot.* What did that matter? She couldn't get out of the room. She was trap—

The snake flicked out from the shadows, moving faster now, coming for her. Screeching like a banshee, she raised the broom high and crashed it down onto the shimmering head. It hissed and its tongue flicked out, narrowly missing Lexy's ankle. She darted back and brought the broom down again as the creature slithered round to follow her.

'No, no, no!" She was screaming the words again and again as she lashed out with the broom, ignoring the sickening crunch of bone, the squelch of flesh. It twisted at her feet in a flickering dance, until the writhing slowed and stopped. Lexy continued to beat at the mess on the floor, her arm like a metronome keeping time as her breathing slowed.

"Lexy!" She spun round. Robert was in the open doorway, a look of utter shock on his face. "What on earth— Oh my God." He grabbed her arm and pulled her back behind him as he took in the scene, the dead snake, the now upturned desks. "What . . . How did that get in here? Are you okay? Lexy? Lexy, speak to me!"

Lexy was shaking and sobbing, her gaze fixed blankly on the bloody mess at her feet.

"It's all right, Lexy. It's dead. You killed it. Here, give me that." Gently, Robert took the broom from her and stood it against the wall behind them. He turned her to face him and ducked his head to look up into her eyes.

"Lexy, look at me. You're safe. It's dead. Lexy?" Her sobbing had slowed but she was still shaking as he pulled her into his arms and held her tight against his chest. "Shh, now. I've got you. You're safe now. Shh." He held her, crooning as if to a child until the shaking stopped, until her breathing came more evenly and the tension began to ebb from her taut frame.

He led her out of the schoolroom, cradling her in the crook of his arm, and pulled the door shut behind them.

"Here, sit down," He drew her down beside him on to the steps of the porch. "Tell me what happened."

She just shook her head wearily and looked down at her hands, clasped tightly in her lap.

"Lexy? What happened? Why are you here?" A tinge of annoyance shaded his questions as his arm fell from her shoulders. "You shouldn't be here on your own, you know, not at this time of night. Anything could have happened to you!"

Lexy looked up at him, surprised and hurt by the irritation in his voice.

"But the note . . ."

"What note? For goodness' sake, Lexy! What were you doing? And what in God's name possessed you to attack it? Didn't anyone ever tell you discretion's the better part of valour?"

Yes. Her mother. Frequently. Lexy's breathing was returning to a more regular rhythm, her head clearing.

"Why didn't you just get out? If you see a snake, back off. Anyone would think you had a death wish or—"

"It was locked."

Robert stopped his tirade abruptly. "What was locked?"

"The door."

"No, it wasn't."

"Someone locked me in." Lexy saw doubt come into his eyes.

"Don't be ridiculous. Why would anyone do that? But it wasn't locked, anyway. Jammed, maybe, but it opened perfectly—"

"It was locked, Robert. I tried to get out. Of course I did! But it wouldn't open." She was shivering again. He rubbed her arm,

223

then helped her to her feet and started to lead her back towards the hospital.

"Look, you were in a state of panic. It was probably just stuck and—"

"You don't believe me."

"Well, it doesn't seem very likely, does it? And it certainly wasn't locked when I got here."

Lexy took a couple of steps down the path, hugging herself, shivering still despite the warm night.

"Lexy, think about it. Why would it be locked? Who would . . . That would mean . . ."

The cicadas chattered away in the pause that hung heavily in the air.

"That would mean someone deliberately shut me in the schoolroom. With a snake." She turned and faced Robert. "And no one knew I was coming here. Except you."

"What? I didn't know you were . . . I was at the research lab and—"

"Read it." She thrust the crumbled paper at him, watched him frown as he read the words.

"You think *I* did this? Is that it?"

"You sent the note."

"No, I didn't." He held his hand up as she tried to interrupt. "My name, Lexy, not my writing."

She scrabbled in her bag, pulled out a pen. "Prove it."

"What? No! Why would I have shown up like that if I'd . . . if I was . . . How can you think I'd do something like that?" He sounded indignant, but Lexy wasn't buying it.

"So I'm just lucky you happened to be passing and came to rescue me, then?"

"I didn't rescue you, Lexy. You'd already killed the snake. You didn't need me." His voice was cold. "I'll take you back to your hotel, arrange for someone to come over from the hospital first thing in the morning to clear up that mess." He jerked his head back towards the schoolroom as he stood and took her elbow. "My car's out front."

She stiffened but let him lead her along the path, trying to make sense of what had just happened. Why had Robert denied that he had written the note? And why had he been there at all if he hadn't sent it? She didn't believe he'd been in his lab. Nobody, not even this man, worked in a dinner suit. And that door had definitely been locked. Yet strangely unlocked when Robert had appeared.

As they neared the lights of the hospital, she shook off his arm and picked up her pace.

"Wait, where are you going?"

"Taxi rank. I'll make my own way back, thanks. I'm sure you've more *research* to do."

"Lexy, wait!"

But she didn't look back. And he didn't follow.

22

The Residence, June 16th

Lexy woke feeling woozy. It was still dark, but she could just make out the beginnings of the green dawn through the slats of the shutters over her windows. She stretched and rolled over. Consciousness came slowly, memory returning, and then suddenly she was sitting up, one fist jammed into her mouth to stop the scream she felt rising to her lips as she remembered the night before, the snake, the terror. Her heart raced and she curled up into a ball, pulling the cotton sheet over her head. Tears sprang to her eyes and she felt sick, bile rising in her throat.

Someone had tried to kill her. And made it look as if it had been Robert.

By the time she'd got back to the hotel, last night, she'd realised it couldn't be Robert. Not just because she didn't want to believe it of him, but because he wasn't that stupid. That careless. He hadn't sent the note. She was sure of it now. Why summon her and then turn up to save her? But that didn't mean she could trust him. What had he really been doing there? Following her? Why? Why would he care where she went, what she did? He'd made it quite clear he wasn't interested in her, and disapproved of the time she spent with Evie.

No, Robert wasn't behind this. He had no reason to be. She got up and opened the shutters, stepped out onto the balcony, arms folded across her chest, eyes gazing unseeing over the gardens that had so enchanted her when she first arrived. There was only one person with a reason to want her dead: David. David Buchanan, her new-found uncle. He stood to lose everything if she found a way of proving her birthright. Perhaps he wasn't as sure as he claimed that he had all the bases covered, that there was no way she could prove the incredible story of her past.

She'd seen Robert getting into David's car yesterday morning at the hospital. Yet Robert had told her he hadn't spoken to David since he'd refused to help with the Blantyre case. Had made it clear he disliked him. Had lied to her.

And yet . . . She remembered Robert's face. The look in his eye, the look of . . . what? Regret? Disappointment? She'd thought she could trust him, maybe even be something more than friends with him . . . She cringed with embarrassment remembering how she'd misread that situation. Blame it on the rebound. *Oh, Danny.* She never thought she'd miss his steady predictability as much as she did. So why *had* Robert been there?

The phone rang and she let out a short scream. Was she really that jittery? She snatched it up.

"Yes?" Her voice was shrill even to her own ears.

"Lexy? Did I wake you?" Robert's voice was even, steady, as if nothing had happened. "Evie's been asking for you. She wants to talk to you. I've advised against it, of course." *Yes, of course,* Lexy thought bitterly. "But she's adamant. Will you come? I can pick you up."

"No." Lexy was thinking fast. "No, don't come. I . . . I'll make my own way."

"But you will come, won't you?" Why was he so insistent?

"Yes. Of course I'll come." She had to hear what Evie said, but the thought of being alone with Robert in his car, at his mercy, was frightening. She really didn't know if she could trust him any more.

"She's very weak, Lexy, but they can't wait any longer. They're operating later today . . . So no more histrionics. Give me your word."

"Of course not!" Lexy knew, though, that her behaviour so far had done nothing to suggest she could be trusted to be gentle.

"She wants to make you see why you have to leave this alone and go home."

And Evie would succeed where attempted murder by snake had failed, would she? Lexy swallowed the retort.

"The only thing that will do that is the truth, Robert."

"That's what she wants to talk to you about. Against my better judgement, I should point out."

Well, of course, Lexy thought again.

23

Evie had been waiting for her, the words tumbling out of her like a river in full spate the moment Lexy had entered the room, scarcely giving her time to sit down before the recollections began. Lexy was shocked at the evident pain in the older woman's voice as she spoke.

That evening in early June 1963, just as she had every evening since the news, Evie was trying to distract herself, to stop the relentless flow of bittersweet memories that left her exhausted and hollow. Bereft. Sleepless. Just as she'd been after Douglas had died. Helen had been with her every day, then, to help her, hold her together, soothe her. Now there was no one and Evie was struggling, still reeling from Helen's death, ten days after the awful news had reached them in Blantyre of the devastation at the lake, of the dozens of lives lost. Four days after the search for survivors had been called off, hopes destroyed, families forced to face their losses.

She'd been sitting reading, looking at pages, turning them occasionally but not taking in a single word, until she'd snapped the book shut, slapped it down on the side table, the lamp shuddering and sending shadows dancing across the walls.

She'd looked out into the night garden, found no comfort there so come back to sit at the piano, stroked the keys, but found herself distracted by the photograph looking down at her. Three young women, standing on the deck of the *Aurora*, so eager, so excited, so different, but each so certain this would be their promised land.

"It was extraordinary," said Evie, leaning back in the pillows of her hospital bed, "the three of us becoming such friends. We weren't at all alike, you know. Helen . . . oh my, but she was dazzling, Ursula and I anything but. Poor Helen. She'd changed so much, since those days. The sparkling young woman who'd captivated Blantyre society, Zomba too, she'd dimmed, but her spirit never weakened, her heart never shrank. So generous with her love. She loved Ursula's child as fiercely as she loved her own, never betraying our secret even when . . . even when that vile man . . ."

Evie turned her head away, but Lexy knew there were tears in the old woman's eyes; she could hear it in the quivering voice.

"It was so unfair. That he should live when Helen didn't. And to have the sympathy of everyone we knew for his loss, their admiration for his desperate attempt to save his wife, battling against the wind and the rain, the river and the mud. Quite the hero. I didn't believe a word of it.

"Well" – the voice sounded steadier – "now three had become two, and we two were a world apart. Small comfort to each other at such a distance. Ursula so busy being the impeccable professional in Scotland, determined to leave the past firmly behind her, and me still here in Malawi, unable to go 'home' because it wasn't home any more. Father was long dead, of course, and, growing up as the minister's daughter, I'd not had too many friends. Piety and adolescence rarely sit comfortably together, you know. So here I stayed, busy with my charities – my interfering, as Robbie likes to call it – and I'd just have to get used to things and carry on. *No use crying over spilt milk*, Ursula would have said, I expect, or something equally stoic. That woman had steel inside her, not breakable bones like the rest of us. And dear Helen, what would she have said, I wonder? Nothing, most likely. She'd just have been there. Her presence soothing enough, her silence saying it all."

Evie coughed and Lexy leapt up to get her water, desperate for her to continue her story, realising she had to be patient. This was a frail body, no matter how strong the spirit that still clung to it. Evie sipped gratefully. Leant back and closed her eyes. Just as Lexy was about to despair, believing Evie had fallen asleep again, she continued her tale.

There'd been a tap at the door, and the housekeeper had appeared, wanting to check Evie was alone, before pulling the door open wide, her sturdy body stepping aside to reveal another: slimmer, taller.

"Evie?" Helen said. "Evie, it's me."

Evie had grabbed the piano for support as the room blurred around her. "Helen?"

Helen stepped fully into the room and the housekeeper disappeared into the darkness of the hallway, closing the door behind her.

Evie rushed forward and wrapped her friend in her arms, felt her living, breathing warmth.

"It *is* you! It's really you."

They were both laughing and crying as they hugged each other.

"Helen, I can't . . . I thought you were dead. I thought . . . Oh sweet Lord, you're alive!"

Helen disentangled herself and took Evie's hands in hers, exhaustion, desperation etched on her face.

"I'm alive, yes." Helen took a deep breath. "But I'm not sure I want to be."

"You can't possibly mean that."

"Yes, I do. But not in the way you think. If I'm not alive, I'm free."

"Darling, I don't know what's happened, but it's obviously been

231

dreadful." Evie led her towards the sofa. "You're not thinking clearly. Shock or whatever, but—"

"I know, I know. But that's why I've come to you. You're always so calm and practical and know what to do and right now I . . . I don't. I don't know what's best . . . if I'm being selfish . . . or . . ." Helen was struggling to keep her composure, her breathing tight, shallow gasps that tore at Evie's heart. She held her while her friend's frail body heaved and tears dampened the fine cotton lawn of Evie's blouse.

"Shh, Helen. You're safe. I'm here. I won't let anything happen to you, I promise." Evie comforted her friend, trying to sound reassuring, not really sure what she was promising but knowing she needed her help. That was enough.

Eventually, the sobbing eased and Helen's breathing became more regular. Tears still slid down her cheeks, but she was calmer. She pulled herself upright and leant back against the cushions of the sofa. Evie clasped her hand and the friends sat in silence as the tree frogs sang their night songs.

Evie waited, her mind racing. Why was Helen here, alive, when Cameron had told everyone she was dead? She was impatient to know, but knew her friend needed time. She poured them both a large Scotch and came back to the sofa.

"Drink."

Helen looked up at her blankly.

"Take it. It will do you good."

Without a word, Helen took the crystal glass, looked at it for a second and then drank the contents down.

"Errgh!" she spluttered.

"I know, darling. But it's worked. You're back."

"Yes." Helen nodded, attempting a smile. "Yes, I suppose I am."

Evie took the empty glass. "I suspect you could do with another."

"Oh, no, I hate Scotch—"

"Medicinal. Sip slowly. You'll get used to it."

Evie sat in the chair opposite the sofa and crossed her legs. She swirled the contents of her own glass round, sipped it delicately and then sat back. She watched Helen raise the glass to her lips, but not drink, just inhale the fumes, tears welling again, but whether from the sting of the whisky or whatever she was remembering, it was hard to tell.

Helen closed her eyes and began to speak.

"I'd warned him," she began, "the last time he'd tried . . . 'Touch me again and I will kill you,' I'd said, but I knew he didn't believe me. Thought I was bluffing. Said I wouldn't risk being branded a murderess, being locked up, hanged. That I loved the children too much to do that to them. And of course he was right, or I'd thought he was, until . . ."

Evie heard Helen's teeth chink against the crystal, watched her face grimace as she swallowed.

"Why would he believe me, Evie? Everything I've done, ever done, has been for the children. To protect them. It still is. Only I've failed. Dreadfully. And now I can't . . . I don't know how to save David from his father."

Helen seemed to have forgotten Evie was there, and Evie had to lean forward in her chair to hear her friend.

"I hadn't seen him for nearly two weeks. God knows where he'd been. In the early days, I'd have been angry, shouted at him about damaging our reputation, the business, the children's future. But it made no difference, so I stopped asking and he stopped telling me where he'd been, what he'd been doing once he realised he couldn't provoke a reaction any more. I ignored him. Kept the children from him as much as possible, and kept him away from Buchanan's. I did my best to pretend he didn't exist."

She drained her glass, looked down into it as she clasped it in her hands. Evie reached across and gently took it from her, worried that the tightness of her grip would make it shatter.

"There was a madness in him that night. That madness I'd

always feared, known, was there. But I'd never seen in full flow before. It frightened me. Truly frightened me. But at least I had the gun."

"Oh Helen." Evie reached for her friend, but Helen shrank back, her eyes unfocused, staring straight ahead, one hand rubbing the wrist of the other where Evie could see yellowed marks, old bruises where Cameron's fingers had grabbed her.

"No. No sympathy. I don't deserve it."

"But of course you do."

"The storm was already fierce. The servants said the river had burst its banks north of the town. There was real danger of flooding. I'd told them to pack bags for us, had sent the children to pick out a few toys and books, gone up to my room to pack a few things myself. Just in case. I didn't hear Cameron come in, didn't even know he was in the house. Then I heard my bedroom door close and there he was leaning against it and grinning.

"'I've been thinking,' he said, 'We should spend more time together, you and I.' His timing was always incredible. 'We have our children to think of,' he said. 'My son, yours, Izzie. But we need *our* son, to bring us all closer together.'

"'To secure your stake in Buchanan's you mean,' I'd snapped before I could stop myself, but really, I was ... dumbfounded. There was a storm raging, a flood threatening ... But nothing gets in the way of Cameron's ambition, his greed ... And he didn't deny it, just leered at me.

"'I've told you,' I said, 'you even try to touch me again, and I'll kill you.' But he laughed. Laughed.

"And do you know what he said? He said I might enjoy it. Said he could teach me a thing or two his boring old brother wouldn't even have ... Kept saying how women adored him, how Ursula ... It was disgusting, Evie, unbelievably disgusting. He was ranting, mad, bragging like a ... a ... but I wasn't listening, I was thinking how to get out. I edged over to the dressing table, leant against it, pulled open the drawer behind me, just a little.

"The storm was wild now. Wind and rain lashing at the windows, thunder rumbling overhead so loudly the house shook. There wasn't much time. We had to leave or the roads would be impassable, the lake too rough for the boats.

"I told him we needed to get the children and leave, but he wouldn't listen. He came over, tried to grab me. And that's when I pulled out the gun, pushed it into his chest. For a second I thought I would pull the trigger, and I think he thought I would too because he stumbled backwards, fell into the armchair.

"That's when . . . Oh dear God. That's when Ross . . . *Ross* . . .

"I heard him screaming for me, turned as the door swung open and his little figure ran into the room, arms outstretched, calling for me. Cameron sprang up – I'd no idea he could move so fast, the state he was in. He pushed me away, grabbed Ross, picked him up off the floor so swiftly his little legs were still pumping and he was still running, running through the air. The shock seemed to wind him, but then he yelled, howled, louder, and he was more frightened, more panicked, than I'd ever seen him. Calling me over and over. But Cameron had him locked tight against him, one thick forearm around his neck, the other crushing the tiny chest. He was using him as a shield, for God's sake, Evie. A child as a shield. And he was laughing, dancing around me, taunting me. 'Still going to do it Helen? Still going to shoot me?'"

Helen was sobbing now, her words barely coherent. "My boy, Evie. He had my *boy*."

Evie couldn't bear it, moved across to the sofa and put her arm around Helen's thin shoulders, but couldn't think what to say that would help.

"He was terrified, Evie. My boy was terrified, and all the time Cameron was laughing, imitating him, his squeals of panic, until . . . until he put his hand over Ross's mouth, his nose. Ross couldn't breath. I tried, Evie, I tried to line the gun up to Cameron's head, and I would have killed him if I could. But Ross . . . Cameron was lifting him up and down, waving him at me, so I couldn't shoot in case . . . in case . . . It happened so fast. I . . . I was lowering the gun, but Cameron lurched forward, threw Ross at me and the gun kicked and his little body was falling . . . thudded on the floor and he didn't scream, but there was blood, blood streaming from his head, covering his face. Blood everywhere, and I was screaming. I dropped the gun and screamed; Cameron pushed me away, kicked the gun across the floor. And then there was a noise . . . the most almighty groan I've ever heard and I knew, we both knew, the slip had started. I didn't know what to do, I couldn't think, I . . . Ross . . . on the floor . . . but Izzie, David . . .

"Cameron shouted at me to get David, get to the car. But I couldn't. I just wanted Ross to move, wanted to touch his little crumpled body, but Cameron wouldn't let me, held me back as he felt Ross's neck, his wrist, put his ear to his tiny chest.

"'Forget this one,' he said. 'He's dead.'

"But he couldn't be. Not my Ross, my son, Gregory's boy.

"But then he was pushing me towards the door, shouting at me that Ross was dead, telling me to get David.

"I tried to get to Ross. We had to take him, too, couldn't leave him there alone . . . But Cameron kept shouting at me, saying did I want to be charged with murder, that no one would win, just as if I'd tried to kill Cameron himself, only this was worse, I'd be a baby killer. He said he'd help me, that I had to do as he said . . . I couldn't think straight, Evie, I didn't know how . . . and all the time, Ross was lying there not moving.

"Then there was another groan and this time a cracking, ripping sound and the house quivered and then juddered as the roof at the back caved in.

"Cameron pushed me out of the room, telling me to run, to get David and to run, and suddenly I was shouting David's name,

Izzie's, running towards Izzie's room and there she was. I picked her up still shouting for David, but he wasn't there, in his room or . . . I ran down the stairs still calling him, Izzie crying in my arms. The servants were in panic and I yelled to them to get out, to leave everything, just go, and then I was at the car, and David was there with Cameron. 'Get in,' he said, pushing me round to the car door, but before I opened it I looked up to my bedroom window, to Ross, and there were flames leaping at the curtains. Then Cameron had the back doors open and was pushing the children in and shouting at me to get in, too. Then he was gunning the engine and we were moving forward and Izzie and David were crying, calling for me, shouting for their brother.

"'Want Ross,' Izzie was sobbing, her heels drumming against the seat, little fists clenched, and David looked at me as if . . . as if . . . he *knew*. But how could he? I looked back, at the window, shattered now, black smoke billowing out from the room where . . . where . . . and all I could see was the little body I'd left on the floor behind me.

"God forgive me, Evie, I shot him. I killed my son."

Evie closed her eyes. Lexy sat in stunned silence, questions, for once, stilled as the full horror of Helen's tale wiped out all other thoughts. That meant . . . that meant . . .

"Your grandmother shot her son, your uncle." Evie was watching her again now. "I was shocked to the core. Not that she'd shot him; I don't believe she really did. Oh, she was holding the gun, but it was Cameron who orchestrated it. And whatever I felt, I knew it was nothing, *nothing*, compared with what Helen must have been feeling."

"But why didn't she . . . I don't know . . . tell the truth? Surely everyone knew what he was like, what *she* was like. No one would believe she ever *meant* to shoot her own son—"

"Helen took the loaded gun out of a drawer and aimed it. She'd been close to firing it at Cameron. So there'd been murderous intent, and there was a body. Not the body Helen had intended, but a body nonetheless. All too risky. Courtrooms are not predictable places. Trusting in truth, innocence, reputation is a dangerous game, my dear, particularly when the enemy have friends in so many high places. No. Helen wanted to stay dead, to stay free and spare her children more pain. If Cameron believed her dead, he wouldn't denounce her as a murderess. She was devastated that she couldn't think of a way to get David away from Cameron. She said her only consolation was that I was close by. I could take care of him. But I don't think I did a very good job of that. I let her down. Cameron wouldn't let me get close to him, did everything he could to keep me away. And, in time, it worked. David didn't want anything to do with me."

"I still don't understand. Surely . . ."

Evie shook her head. "Believe me, Lexy, we tried between us to think of a way and there wasn't one. Helen was convinced that if she reappeared she would go to prison and she believed that would be worse for the children. David would no sooner have got her back than he'd lose her again to prison, or a noose. And there was Izzie, too, of course. Your mother. Helen couldn't bear the thought of her with Cameron. Nor could I. No. Izzie was safer with Helen."

"Only she wasn't, was she? With Helen? Helen gave her to Ursula. Gave her away, like a . . . like a toy a child grows out of, or a pet that gets tiresome. How was that better? And why just Izzie? What about David? She just *left* him?"

Evie's face was grey. "It wasn't like that. I'm not sure I can make you understand. Forgive me, my dear. I'm so very, very tired. I think I . . . need to rest a little now . . ."

"No! Don't you dare sleep, not yet. How did Helen survive the accident, the boat?"

"She wasn't on it."

"What? Well, the mudslide or whatever?"

"I don't know. I'm sorry, I'm so very tired, now. I need—"

'But you must know! Surely she told you?"

"Lexy, I'm too tired . . . I . . ."

"Tell me!"

"She was so . . . traumatised . . . Her housekeeper . . . Please, Lexy . . ." Evie sighed and closed her eyes again, shutting out Lexy's questions.

"No, wait. Don't sleep. You have to—"

Lexy felt the strong hand grasp her arm, pull her up from the chair, knew it was Robert even before he spoke. "Get out of here." He bundled her out into the corridor, not relinquishing his grip until he'd closed the door behind them and pushed her roughly down onto one of the hard plastic seats that lined the corridor.

"How dare you interrogate her like that."

"I wasn't interrogating her! There was just one last thing, one more question."

"There always is with someone like you. Always something more."

"Someone like me?" Lexy was stung. "You mean someone you've all lied to and spied on and tried to scare off and . . . and . . . You know, if you'd been honest with me when I brought you that letter, we wouldn't be here now. You could have told me everything Evie has and saved her the trouble. So if you're looking for someone to blame here, you don't have to look very far." She stood up and glared at him, a little less impressively than she would have liked given the difference in their heights, but she held her ground. Robert turned away first.

"Fine," he said as he sat in one of the seats, and gestured for her to sit too. She glared at him again, stayed where she was. He shrugged. "So what is it, this one last thing you're so desperate to know?"

"Helen and Izzie. How did they survive? How did they get away that night?"

239

Robert frowned up at her. "I don't know what—"

"Do you want me to go back in there? Wake her up?"

"All right. I'll tell you. But then you leave her alone, okay?"

Lexy nodded, perched on the edge of the seat beside him, her body turned to face him.

"They'd got to the lake, to their private launch, but it was all pretty chaotic apparently. As I told you, one of the company steamers, the *Blantyre*, was in and there were hundreds of people trying to get on board. No way it would have been able to take them all. Helen wanted to let some of them on to their launch but Cameron refused, tried to send her and the children below. But Helen wouldn't go, and Izzie wouldn't leave Helen. Helen saw their housekeeper and tried to call her over, determined that Cameron would let her on board at least. But Adela didn't hear her, so Helen, with Izzie in her arms, ran down the gangplank to get her. Cameron pulled it up behind her and took off, taking David with him."

"My God. The utter bastard."

"Yes, that's about the measure of the man. Anyway, Helen and Izzie got to Adela, but it was clear the steamer was already dangerously overloaded so they weren't going to get out on that, and then Adela's brother appeared and pulled them away. They couldn't hear what he was shouting, but they followed him. They didn't really have much choice. He'd got the keys to one of the company's trucks and bundled them all into it and drove away just seconds before the deluge struck the shore. They didn't get far – trees were down and the road was impassable – but they'd got away from the shore. Miraculously, they'd survived. They waited out the storm in the truck. It blew most of the night so Helen had plenty of time to think. By the time it was over, she knew she wasn't going back. Adela and Joseph took her to their parents, hid her and Izzie and then after a few days—"

"Took her to Evie."

240

"Yes."

"Adela and Joseph. They're the housekeeper and gardener in Ursula's will. I assumed they'd been hers."

"No. Helen's. But between us all we've made sure they've been looked after. They couldn't go back to work for Cameron, and it was little enough really to set them up with some land and a farm of their own after what they'd done."

Lexy swivelled round and sat back in the hard plastic chair, suddenly exhausted. How could someone do something like that? She closed her eyes, tried to imagine the scene at the lake that awful night, the screams, the noise, the rain. And Cameron calmly pulling up the gangplank behind his wife and Lexy's own mother. How could someone do something like that? What kind of man could be that cold-blooded?

And then Helen. Helen had shot her child. No wonder she'd disappeared. Lexy doubted she would ever want to come back.

David was right. He'd told her she might not want to know this family she had been so desperate to find. She was beginning to understand what he meant.

24

Blantyre Hospital, June 16th

"She's awake. She wants to see you."

Lexy looked up, startled. She was still sitting in the same chair Robert had left her in, still struggling to process all that she had learned, to understand that she was a part of this horrifying family. That their blood was hers.

"Now, Lexy. Don't keep her waiting. She's exhausted." Robert held the door back for her, glared at her as she squeezed past him. "Go easy."

"Leave us, Robbie."

"But Gran, I—"

"Go."

Evie had never looked frailer and Lexy was torn between compassion and curiosity, guilt and anger. As soon as the door swung shut behind her grandson, Evie closed her eyes again.

"No, Evie. Please. Don't sleep again."

"I won't. I just don't want to see your face when I tell you . . . I'm so ashamed, you see. So very angry with myself for letting him manipulate me into giving him exactly what he wanted. Power. The power to harm those I loved. I'd no idea, of course, hadn't meant . . . But I did make the mistake of underestimating him, letting him goad me. No one was ever safe from that man. No one."

It had been nearly two weeks after Helen's reappearance and Evie's face ached from keeping it stretched into a polite smile as she pretended to listen attentively to the admiring conversation around her. If she closed her eyes, she might even believe the tale of heroism, love and loss. But her sharp, clear blue eyes were fixed, frozen, on the recipient of this cloying admiration. Cameron.

She had to admit he looked the part. His features held just the right combination of stoic endurance, devastating loss and handsome helplessness. No wonder it seemed the entire female contingent at the consulate soirée was entranced, almost scrambling over each other to stand alongside, place a comforting hand on the muscular arm that had tried so hard to hold on to his wife as the crashing torrent of the storm-swollen water had dragged her from his loving grasp.

Evie felt sick. She knew only too well how those muscular arms had grasped at his petite wife, leaving livid fingerprints embedded in pale flesh for days afterwards. She'd seen her friend wince with pain as spiteful injuries this loving husband had inflicted took their toll.

"Oh my poor, dear Cameron!" Yet another of the young consulate wives joined the group, almost teetering over on her heels in her excitement to clasp the grieving widower's hand and gaze sympathetically up into his amused, dry eyes.

Evie could take no more. Murmuring an excuse she knew no one would hear, she stepped back from Cameron's charmed circle, the enthralled women closing ranks around him as if Evie had never been there.

She stood for a moment, undecided. Should she try to sneak away altogether or was there anyone here she needed to speak to? Her practised eyes scanned the room as if casually but in fact noting everyone who was present and rifling through her mental index to match faces and names to roles and responsibilities. Winston Stanley, chief of police, was entertaining a circle of guests with one of his stories, and judging by the burst of startled laughter, she imagined it was one of his more colourful tales. She wondered what he'd have to say if he knew the truth. His men had been so very quick to accept Cameron's story and she had to wonder if money had changed hands.

Poor Winston. He tried so hard to stamp out bribery and corruption in his ranks, but she feared he was fighting a losing battle. He certainly was the only chief of police she'd known in all her time in Malawi who still lived in a modest bungalow and whose children went to Mission schools. The only one whose surname wasn't Chakanaya, although he'd married one. He was a good man, though, and she was tempted to ask for his help. But it wasn't her place. Helen had made it clear that no one, absolutely no one, was to know.

"Evelyn – how lovely!" Fredi appeared at her side, his appearance as precise and elegant as his command of the English language.

"Fredi, darling!" Evie was genuinely pleased to see the handsome Dane.

"Enjoying yourself, Evie, my dear?" Fredi enquired, a hint of humour just detectable in his soft voice as he leant in to kiss her lightly on the cheek. Evie's raised eyebrows said it all. "Hmm. Thought not. Come with me."

With one hand cupping her elbow and the other clearing a path through the chattering masses, he led her over to a pair of chairs sheltered from the worst of the hordes by an ornamental Chinese screen.

He helped settle her into one of them and then beckoned a waiter over.

"Champagne, Evelyn. Never fails to make the truly tedious just about bearable." Nodding a thank you to the waiter, he took the other seat and raised his glass to her. "To the most intelligent woman here tonight, and the most glamorous."

Despite herself, Evie smiled. "Fredi, dear, you're quite ridiculous and a hopeless flatterer. I was a minister's daughter and am now a doctor's widow. Glamour is what you'll find over there." Her head flicked briefly in the direction of Cameron's circle.

"Ah yes, the heartbroken Cameron and his coterie." Fredi's eyes followed in the direction she'd indicated. "If that's glamour, I want none of it. But intelligence, wit, charm – I have that in abundance right here."

"Kind of you, Fredi. But I fear I'm a little under par this evening."

"I'm not surprised. You must be missing her. You and Helen were such very good friends."

"Yes. Yes, we were."

"And Ursula too. In the old days. How the three of you could make even a young man like me blush!"

"We never made you blush, Fredi." Evie laughed.

"Oh, but you did, I just hid it well. You were quite formidable." Fredi rolled his eyes and Evie felt her spirits lifting a little.

"Were we? I suppose perhaps we were. Young women never really understand the power they have."

"Well, that certainly doesn't stop them using it with devastating effect on a fellow." Fredi was warming to his theme. "You had us all running around like quicksilver."

"I'm sure we never did . . ."

"There was that time you and Ursula—"

A chiming of metal against crystal stopped Fredi's reminiscences and a hush settled over the room.

"Ladies and gentlemen, may I interrupt your evening for just a few moments, please." The consul general's booming voice easily filled the large space. Evie and Fredi stood, straining to see him over the heads of the assembled company. Evie's breath caught sharply as she saw Cameron beside him. Fredi heard her and took his arm in hers, gently patting her hand in reassurance.

"A few weeks ago one of the worst storms this country has ever seen carved a path of chaos through our lives, and we have all been busy trying to recover and to repair the damage it caused. That night was one few of us will forget easily and one which has left us all more than a little shocked. Not least because of the tragic loss of one of the best-loved members of our tightly knit community, our lovely Helen Buchanan-Munro, and two of her children. Nothing, of course, will ease the pain of the family she leaves behind, but, Cameron, I want you to know that I'm sure I speak for all of us when we say we admire your courage, not only in the heroic attempt to save your family, which put your own life at risk, but also the fortitude with which you are bearing her loss and caring for your boy. Good man. And I'm sure again that I speak for all of us when I say that if there's anything at all any of us can do to help you and little David through this awful time, we will do it gladly. Helen was always the first to offer help to a friend in need. It's the least any of us can do."

Murmurs of "hear hear" filled the room and Cameron, jaw clenched as if to contain his grief, looked up from the floor, nodded and mouthed a thank you as the consul general shook him by the hand and clapped him stoutly on the shoulder.

"May I . . . could I say a few words perhaps?"

"Of course, Cameron, dear fellow. Of course."

The room fell completely silent again, expectant faces turned toward the handsome widower.

"I can't tell you how much it means to me to . . . to have your support at a time . . . like this." Cameron's voice was taut with emotion, clipped and precise. "Helen meant the world to me, and the children . . ."

Evie couldn't help herself. "Oh! How—" Fredi coughed to drown her words as a few people turned to look in their direction.

"I know, Evie, I know. But not now," he murmured softly, squeezing her hand. She nodded tersely.

Cameron was still speaking. "I will never forget the horror of that night. But it has shown me the strength of the community we have here in Blantyre. The value of good friends and the importance of supporting each other . . ." His voice cracked. "Thank you."

The guests clapped loudly as the consul general's wife stepped in and led the broken man away to a quiet corner. The room was positively humming with the drama of it all.

"A marvellous performance," Fredi remarked wryly. "He's in quite the wrong profession."

"It's all lies, absolute lies." Evie's voice was low and vehement.

"I know, Evie." Fredi turned to look at her carefully. "I know."

Her stomach lurched. Fredi *knew*? How could he? She stared at him and waited for him to say more.

"A few of us do, in fact."

"Really? Know what exactly?" Evie forced herself to keep calm, although her pulse was racing. They'd been so careful.

"How he treated her. The bruises. She didn't always manage to conceal them completely."

"Oh. Oh those." Evie realised her relief that this seemed to be *all* he knew was making her sound dismissive. "Dreadful. Yes, of course. Absolutely dreadful. She wouldn't say, of course, but one knew."

"Did she ever—"

"Fredi, darling? Would you mind? I've really had enough this evening and would like to go home."

"Poor darling. Of course. You must be feeling awful, and having to listen to that little display can't have helped. How thoughtless of me. Shall I take you?"

"Oh, no need for that. I'll get—"

"I insist. Did you have a wrap? Wait here and I'll fetch it for you when I ask the desk to send my car round."

Evie stood by the open verandah door with her back to the throng. She shouldn't have come. She really wasn't in the mood

247

for socialising, and had she thought for one moment Cameron would have been parading his "grief" like a medal of honour she'd have turned down the invitation point-blank.

She stepped through onto the quiet terrace, and froze. Cameron was bending over one of the younger consular women and was whispering in her ear, that lascivious look Evie hated on his face. The girl giggled and put a pretty, manicured hand up to her mouth. Blowing Cameron a kiss, she wriggled away, looking back over her shoulder at him before she traipsed back into the reception room through the doors at the far end. Cameron watched her go, then turned to look out over the gardens and saw Evie watching from the other end of the terrace.

"Evie. Watching over me, are you? Been there long?"

"Long enough."

"We've not had a chance to talk this evening, have we? And we, the two people in the world who loved her best, should really be comforting each other, shouldn't we, at this dreadful time?"

"Should we, Cameron? Looks to me as if you're not short of comfort this evening."

"I know. Wonderful isn't it? Everyone's being so very, very . . . kind." His smile was taunting her and she breathed deeply. She would not give him the pleasure of seeing her irritation.

"Darling Helen. How I'll miss her." He placed a hand against his heart, playing the part of mourning husband with blatant insincerity now that his audience had disappeared.

"Really."

"Oh yes. She was everything to me. To little David. Life simply won't be the same without her."

"No, I don't expect it will." Evie was seething. How could he? The nerve of the man. Surely he must know that Helen had confided in her? That Evie – and, it seemed, others – had seen the evidence of his brutality.

"Her loyalty, her love. My life will be so empty without it. I can't

248

bear waking up alone every morning without her there beside me, that beautiful head lying on the pillow, her soft skin touching mine—"

"You make me sick."

"Evie!" He pouted at her. "Come now, is that any way to talk to a poor grieving—"

"You can drop the act, Cameron. I know. I know exactly how much you loved Helen. Exactly how hard you tried to save her." Evie hissed as she held him in a steely gaze. He flinched in an exaggerated way, and looked down.

"Oh, I'm hurt! Cut to the very quick! I'm sure I don't know what you mean."

"Yes you do, Cameron. We both do. You didn't try to save her. In fact, quite the reverse." Even in the dusky light she could see Cameron's eyes lose their teasing sparkle and grow dark, but she couldn't stop herself continuing. "You left her there. And Izzie. Pulled up the gangplank and sailed off to safety. If David hadn't been down below already, would you have left him there too? Or did you need at least one son and heir to survive? Oh yes, our brave hero. You *really* tried to save her."

Cameron reached over and pulled Evie towards him, looking intently into her eyes. "How could you possibly—"

"There you are, Evie – got it." Fredi bustled towards them, waving Evie's wrap like a flag of surrender over his head. Cameron sprang back from Evie, dipping his head so his face fell into shadow.

"I say, Cameron. Damned sorry, old man." Fredi nodded briefly in Cameron's direction as he draped Evie's wrap around her shoulders. "Shall we leave you in peace? Shouldn't think you'll feel too much like socialising. Come on, Evie, old thing. Let's get you home." Fredi hustled Evie back towards the nearest doors, leaving Cameron standing silently behind them.

Even with the wrap around her, Evie was chilled. She'd let

him goad her and now she could only pray she hadn't said too much.

Ever since she'd found out that she had, realised the devastating consequences of her indiscretion, she'd lived with the guilt, been unable to forgive herself. Now, lying in her hospital bed, she felt the familiar tears of remorse trickling down her cheeks. She let them run unchecked, grateful for Lexy's shocked silence, and cursed herself for ever presuming to interfere in the lives of others, and for lacking the courage to confess to Helen that it was she, not Ursula, who betrayed her in the end.

25

Blantyre Hospital, 16th June

"Miss Shaw? Christopher Chizumu here. Senior partner at Chiz—"

"Mr Chizumu. Good afternoon. What can I do for you?" As soon as she'd felt her phone vibrate in her pocket, Lexy had stepped out of Evie's room. She pushed through the door from the corridor to the empty stairwell as she spoke, perched herself on the top step of the downward flight and wondered what bombshell the legal profession had in store for her now. She'd thought her business with Chizumu & Chizumu had been concluded, but clearly not.

"Rather more a case of what we can do for you, I believe, Miss Shaw. I've just been speaking to Ms Hamilton in our Edinburgh office." Lexy curbed her impatience. She knew precisely where the inimitable Ms Hamilton worked. "I understand you were talking to Ms Hamilton's assistant about the tenancy agreement drawn up on Miss Reid's croft in the Scottish Highlands."

"Yes that's right, I was. He expressed surprise that it was in the current file when it should have been archived—"

"Yes, yes. Which would imply we legal creatures are mere humans capable of misfiling material. But I'm delighted to say it seems we are not. Ms Hamilton says the lease was kept in the current file at Miss Reid's request. In case anyone should come across it . . . inadvertently, let's say. The correct paperwork sits in an entirely different file. The lease merely acts as a reminder to the lawyer in charge of Miss Reid's affairs. However, in the light of current circumstances, and in view of the speculation surrounding the whereabouts of certain funds—"

"Please, Mr Chizumu, come to the point." Lexy was not in the mood for rigmarole.

"Of course, I simply want to make it clear, that although it's all been a little irregular in administrative terms, we have not in any way been remiss in attending to our fil—"

"Mr Chizumu, please."

"Yes. Quite. Well, it transpires that in fact ownership of the property was transferred for an amount which can only have been a token payment—"

"To whom, Mr Chizumu?" Lexy cut in, proud of her punctilious use of that relative pronoun, under such trying circumstances.

"Ross Buchanan-Munro."

Evie heard Lexy come back into the room but didn't open her eyes, feigning sleep as she replayed the consequences of her betrayal over and over in her head, trying to find the words that would make it more palatable, make herself less culpable. But there were none. The truth, unadorned and unmitigated, was what Helen's granddaughter deserved. Evie knew that now.

She flicked open her eyes, saw Lexy watching her, turning her phone over and over in her hands, before dropping it into the bag that lay at her feet.

"Well? Were you going to tell me Ross survived? I know he did, so don't bother denying it, and I know where he is, too. Are you going to tell me how that happened, or why you said Helen shot him? Has this all been some ridiculous, elaborate lie?" Lexy's voice was low, but her anger was clear, colder now than it had been before. Her posture was cowed, as if she knew what was coming would be bad, not at all what she wanted to hear. *Poor girl*, Evie thought. All she'd wanted was to find a family, somewhere to belong. And instead . . . But there could be no going back. Evie was reconciled to having to tell her it all.

"No, not a lie. He was shot, yes, but he did survive."

"She *left* him there?"

"She didn't know. Cameron had checked for a pulse, said he was dead—"

"And she didn't bother to check for herself."

Evie sighed. How could she make Lexy understand? She'd never met Cameron, never faced the demon.

"Hear me out before you judge her."

Lexy crossed her arms and legs, slouched back in the plastic chair and tilted her chin. "Go on, then, I'm listening."

Cameron, of course, had bided his time, kept away from her until he'd worked out his next move, but then he came to find her, as Evie had known he eventually would.

Evie had been sitting in the garden, her book closed on her lap, a finger marking her place. Impossible to read. All she could think about was Helen. How she missed her. How she hoped their plan would work and keep her and Izzie safe. Sister Agnes had agreed to help, as Evie had hoped, and it had all been surprisingly easy to arrange. Helen was safe now. Evie could relax.

She'd turned her face up to feel the warmth of the early morning sun and tried to still her thoughts. A shadow fell and she snapped open her eyes. The sun was directly behind him and he was just a darkened silhouette to her sun-drenched gaze.

"May I join you?"

The moment he spoke, she sat upright. Those silken tones made her flesh crawl. Cameron sat next to her on the bench, too close for comfort, but when she tried to move away to the far end, his hand grasped her wrist. "If you want to hear what I have to say, Evie, and believe me you will, I suggest you stay exactly where you are."

"You have nothing to say that I want to hear. I'm quite sure of

253

that." Evie tried to pull his hand from her arm, but he simply squeezed harder.

"I think I do. We could start, perhaps, with the fact that we both know Helen is still alive. That you've hidden her away somewhere. I'm sure if I really tried, I could find her."

The sun no longer felt warm and she stopped trying to move away from him.

"That's better." He let go her arm. It throbbed, but she wouldn't give him the satisfaction of rubbing it, of letting him know he'd hurt her.

"Now, where was I? Yes, Helen. Alive. But then you know that. In fact, you told me."

Evie's stomach clenched. Stupid, stupid woman. She'd known he wouldn't have missed it, her carelessness. She'd betrayed Helen, put her in danger. What was Cameron going to do?

"You didn't mean to, of course." He was smiling, obviously enjoying her discomfort. "But you've never been much of a dissembler, Evie. Too much Christian honesty bred into you back in that cold old manse. You shouldn't ever let anger goad you into revelation, my dear. And you did, didn't you? Or was it that you'd had too much champagne? So unlike you. And there I was. So recently bereft and you had no pity in your heart for me, the poor young widower left with a young bewildered boy to care for—"

"Enough, Cameron. I didn't fall for it then and I won't now. You have no audience to impress here. Spare me the performance. What do you want?"

"Why, to chat about the old days. About my darling wife. Her lovely children. My own lovely son."

He was watching her closely and saw her flinch at that.

"That's right, Evie. I know that too, you see. All your little secrets are safe with me. For the moment. But she must have told you I knew about the boy. Quite a scam, really." He laughed with genuine pleasure. "Can't say it was easy resisting the temptation to tell dear old Gregory. Can you imagine, the poor fool. A honeybird in his nest all that time and he had no idea at all. I have to say I was impressed. You all managed the situation very well. But I'm not here to go over old ground. David is mine, but I won't go public on that. I want him to have Buchanan's, you see. No, I'm here to talk about the other one. Young Ross and what happened to him. That's something you don't know and I think you'll be interested, if not a little shocked, to learn the truth."

"I do know, Cameron. So whatever you hope to gain by revealing that tragedy to me, or whatever lies you're planning to tell, save your breath. If it's to make Helen out to be a murderess, a villain, in my eyes, you won't succeed. If anyone is guilty of a crime there, it's you. Pushing a child into a loaded gun. What did you think would happen?"

"Certainly not what did."

"You expect me to believe that?"

Cameron smiled again. "Evie, amusing as our banter always is, we need to cut to the chase. These are the facts – Helen is alive, whereabouts unknown. Ross is alive and staying in a house a few streets from here. Do you think Helen might be interested in knowing that?"

"You're despicable, Cameron. I don't know why you'd say a thing like that, but whatever game you're playing I refuse to be a part of it." Evie stood up to leave him there mired in his rank subterfuge, but he tugged her arm sharply so that she sat heavily again, the planks of the bench jolting her bones.

"Sit down, woman," he hissed. "You will hear me out, and then you will do what I want you to, if you want your beloved friends to stay safe."

"What do you want, Cameron? Just get on with it and say."

"Tell Helen she can have Ross."

"He's really alive? How can that be?"

"The bullet didn't kill him. Richard came back with me to the

255

house that night. Good man, our Richard. Dependable. He was listening outside the room, overheard everything. He hid in the shadows until I'd dragged Helen away, then slipped into the bedroom. He saw the boy twitch so felt for a pulse and found one. Faint, but there. So he took him. When I went back the body was gone, but I saw no need to mention that to Helen. I set fire to the room as a precaution."

"But *you* did that! You felt for a pulse. You said he was dead."

"Oh, all but. And the important thing was to get out of there. Dragging a dying child with us was only going to slow things down."

Evie stood, furious. "You cold-hearted—"

"Spare me your condemnation, Evie. I really don't care. And do sit down if you want to hear the rest of this." He waited until she did as she was told. "That's better. So. Against all the odds, Ross survived. For all that puniness, turns out he was a tough little beggar after all. But sadly, little more than an idiot now, so no use to me. And certainly no use to the company so better if he doesn't surface and muddy the waters. Best he 'dies' alongside dear Helen and little Izzie."

Evie was incredulous. Ross alive.

"But I'm a fair man." Cameron was still speaking, enjoying his moment. "I'm prepared to strike a deal. I don't need to know where Helen is and I don't want to see her again. She stays hidden and she gets her boy back. And I'll arrange funds to make sure they don't starve and have whatever attention the boy needs. I keep David. He's mine, after all. If she ever decides to surface, I have a witness to the shooting who will say she shot the boy in cold blood and turned the gun on me. And Richard assures me his testimony and the gun he recovered from the scene, along with one or two other items he could rustle up if needed, mean we have enough evidence to ensure she will be convicted."

"What items?"

"Does it matter? I'm sure he'll have had the foresight to have 'saved' whatever our lawyers might find they need."

Evie nodded. They would fabricate whatever they needed and with Chakanaya's connections there was every chance their bogus evidence would be accepted.

"So that's the deal? She gets Ross and stays out of jail; you get David and, through him, the Buchanan money."

"Seems fair to me. And what man would want to see his beloved wife locked up in jail for the rest of her life anyway? I'm only doing what any loving husband would do: protecting my wife and her child."

"You make me sick, Cameron, you really do. How do I know you're not lying?"

"Why would I?"

"I really don't know, but you usually do." Evie was all business, determined not to let her confusion and horror overwhelm her. "I'll need to see Ross, of course."

"Of course, I imagined you would. My car's just outside."

Evie started to rise, but he caught her arm again, pulled her round to look at him.

"One other thing. If Izzie survived, I want her, too. As insurance." He was watching her closely, but Evie was ready for him this time.

"Of course you do. Well, sorry to disappoint you, Cameron, but that much at least is true. She died, despite everything Helen did to try to save her. She was drowned along with all those other poor souls when the mudslide hit. She slipped from Helen's grasp."

Cameron raised an eyebrow. "Did she, now."

Evie found it impossible to tell if he believed her or not, but she kept her gaze steady, fought to stay calm.

"You might as well have drowned her yourself, Cameron. Her blood is on your hands, so if you regret it now then you've only yourself to blame. But it's the living we should concern ourselves with. Ross. Take me to him. Prove what you've told me is true."

Richard Chakanaya was waiting by Cameron's car, a slow smile spreading across his features as he saw Evie coming towards him.

"Mrs Campbell. A pleasure as always."

She wanted to slap the obsequious man, but she nodded her head stiffly and got into the back of the car, staring straight ahead as the chauffeur closed her door. Cameron slid in the other side and Chakanaya got into the front.

As the car set off, in her mind she ran through everything Cameron had said. It wasn't possible, was it? The only way to be sure was to see with her own eyes. She tried to think of ways that Cameron might try to fool her, pass off another child as Ross, trick her into believing what felt like the unbelievable. And she found herself wishing she'd stopped to tell someone where she was going, or at least who with, before she left.

But as soon as she walked into the tiny room and Ross turned his large brown eyes up to look at her from under a grubby bandage covering his head, she knew. It was him. No doubts, no subterfuge. Incredibly and against all probability, Ross was alive.

"Ross! Ross darling!" She tried to pull him into her arms, but he ducked and stumbled over to an old woman Evie hadn't seen when she came in. He buried his head against her apron, whimpering.

"I have to warn you, Evie dear. He's not 'whole'." Cameron stepped forward, tipped Ross's chin up so he was looking straight into his eyes. Evie saw the boy tense. "He won't remember you, Evie. Or Helen. In fact, I'm not really sure if he remembers anything at all." Ross's eyes flickered over to Evie and then he wriggled away from Cameron's hold and buried his face again in the apron of the old woman.

"Ross. Ross, it's me, Auntie Evie." She tried to take his hand.

"Ross, look at me." Cameron's voice was bored. The old woman turned Ross to look at Cameron, the little head tilted to one side,

258

his thumb plugged into his mouth like a comforter. "This is Auntie Evie. You remember her, don't you?"

But the boy's face crumpled as if he were about to cry. Then a shout in the street made him scream and he turned to the old woman again, burying his head and sobbing. She crooned and soothed him, as his small shoulders heaved. Evie was horrified. He didn't know her. Would he know Helen? Evie fought back tears. This was unbearable.

But it *was* Ross. And he was alive.

★

"Not wearing her out again, I hope, Lexy."

Robert. Back to check on her.

"Shh." Lexy raised her finger to her lips, smug to be the one issuing the admonition for a change. "She's sleeping and you'll—"

"Robbie?"

"Now, look! You've woken her." Lexy tried to sound exasperated but was secretly pleased. Would there be time before Evie went into theatre to talk some more?

"Hello, Gran. Bearing up? They'll be coming to prep you for theatre shortly."

"Not yet, Robbie, I need to . . . to tell Lexy, is she still here . . . I . . ."

Even to Lexy the voice was thin, too weak. "I'm here, Evie."

"Lexy. I have to tell you the rest, to . . ."

Lexy stepped forward, took the old woman's hand. "Evie, it's all right, I'm here." She looked across the bed to Robert. He was frowning, feeling for Evie's pulse.

Had Lexy done this to her? Worn her out just before the operation? She felt a pang of worry. She'd been angry, of course she had, but she didn't want anything to happen to Evie. It was just there had been no one else to be angry with, or at least there hadn't been, until that phone call had changed everything.

"You should go, Lexy," Robert was saying. "She's too weak to talk, I'll stay—"

"No, I need to tell . . . to . . ." Evie's eyes were darting from side to side, her fingers twitching in Lexy's hand.

"No, Gran, you don't. You have to rest. Whatever it is can wait. Lexy, you have to go now, you're upsetting her."

"But she's the one who wants to talk. I'm not forcing her."

"Robbie, I need to talk . . . Just five more minutes."

Lexy knew she had one last chance before Evie went into theatre. One last chance to find out what she really needed to know. "Evie, just tell me, why did she send Izzie away to Ursula? Why did she abandon my mother?"

"She had no choice. It broke her heart."

"So why do it? Surely it made more sense to keep them together, Ross and Izzie?"

"No. He knew, you see." Evie's voice cracked and her shoulders heaved as coughing racked her body. "He'd have taken—" The coughing took hold once again and small beads of perspiration appeared on her creased forehead.

"For God's sake, Lexy, just leave it." Robert reached over to put his arm around his grandmother's shoulders, lift her into a more upright position. "Easy now, Gran. Let me get you some water."

"Taken what? Izzie? But how—"

"Enough, Lexy!" Robert's voice was harsh, his fury evident. "Get out. Just go. Have some compassion, can't you?"

"Well, of course, but I . . . just . . . One last question before I go."

"*No*," he shouted, then visibly restrained his temper and added more calmly, "She needs to rest."

"No, it's a question for you. Why, after you told me you no longer spoke to David Buchanan, did you get into his car and drive off with him yesterday afternoon?"

"Look, Lexy. I'll explain." He looked at Evie. "But not right now. Later. I'll come to the hotel, after . . . when Gran's out, okay?"

That's right, Lexy thought, *Give yourself time to dream up a story.*

"Fine," Lexy said, though it wasn't at all. "Evie, I hope—"

"Go, Lexy, now. Leave her alone."

Lexy looked at them both for a moment, then walked out, pulling the door closed behind her. No slam. That was good. Although it hardly mattered now. Lexy didn't plan to see either of them again, or at least not until she'd found the answers elsewhere. She had other options now. She had family. Real, blood family. That open ticket she'd bought would be pressed into service as soon as possible. Tonight, if she could make the London flight, and from there, a credit card would get her to Scotland and to her uncle, Ross Buchanan-Munro.

26

Taigh na Mara, Ross-shire, Scotland, June 17th

Helen stood, arms crossed across her chest, staring out at the thin grey ribbon of road winding down the hillside past the peat banks towards the shore, watching, waiting. She'd stood here for hours, days, it seemed, watching, waiting. Each time she saw a splash of colour, a flash of movement, her heart stalled, kicked again when the car turned off to the right at the T-junction, leaving her behind, still hidden, still safe, still dead to those she had run from. Nothing had come her way since she'd begun her vigil, the height of the bracken and shallow ruts on the track a testament to the croft house's isolation. Her sanctuary. Her prison.

In the early days, they'd tried, these scattered inhabitants of the slopes and shoreline beneath Ben Mor Coigach. There'd been the odd curious neighbour dropping by with words of welcome on their lips to mask the inquisitiveness, the intrusiveness, of their uninvited calling. Helen had been cold and distant, relentlessly unfriendly. She'd shrugged off her interest in society, her need for company and conviviality, with the fur stoles and cashmere wraps she'd left behind her in the hills above the lake. No need now to concern herself with pleasantries, with doing the done thing, with the conventions of hospitality. She had no need, no desire, to like or be liked. Anonymity, isolation, secrecy: these were what had come to define her. The croft house had lain empty since she and Ursula had left it, Helen armed with a certainty that deserted her now. No one had stepped over the threshold, seen inside the croft house until she'd returned, almost half a century ago. No one, she'd believed, ever would.

She knew they spied on her. She sometimes caught the flash of sunlight on a metal buckle, or the glint from trained binoculars. But the word had spread and no one came near these days, the lifelines and rhythms of this peninsula community ebbing and flowing round her like snowmelt round a rock.

She could see a face looking back at her, distorted by the buckled glass of the windowpane, like Munch's *Scream*. Gaunt and hollow as a skull, black holes where once there'd been bright eyes, rictus where there'd once been a smile. Who was she? *What* was she, this creature, haunting her like a silent reprimand, a story whose ending would never be told? Helen Buchanan, heiress, socialite, adored mother, happy wife. Gone. Abandoned. Forgotten. She couldn't be, didn't know *how* to be, that woman again, even if she were free, or inclined, to try. Instead she'd turned liar, deceiver, destroyer of lives, become wraith, remnant, more dead than alive. What would her daughter make of her? Would she come, would she try?

Izzie.

Who was she now? Had those blue eyes stayed baby blue, the blonde waves straightened or furled into curls and ringlets? Did she grow tall and strong, like her father, or delicate and slight like her mother, loud as David, shy as Ross? Helen would know soon enough.

Izzie. She breathed the word again, saw it snake like a hiss of steam in the air between Helen and her reflected self, felt the prickle of impatience on taut skin, a fluttering in her stomach. Years of not knowing, not daring to ask, not trusting herself to remember, wiped out in that instant when she'd finally relented, replied to Ursula's letter with a single word scrawled on the back of a postcard of Inverness Castle. *YES.* Her reward: this purgatory of waiting.

Helen turned from the window and looked up at the clock. Nearly midnight. Long days made longer by summer light. No one would come now. She could go to bed, but she knew she wouldn't sleep. She'd stare at the light filtering through curtains, fading but never fully darkening before brightening again into yet another morning. And each time the same thought, the same question: today, this day, would this be the one?

The corners of the room were dim, too dim for reading, so she picked up the single page she'd left on the table by dirty plates she'd yet to clear and took it back to the window. Perching one hip on the wide ledge, she dropped her glasses from the top of her head onto her nose and began to read, as she'd read umpteen times before, searching for clues the words wouldn't yield, answers they didn't hold.

Edinburgh, May 24th 2014

My dear Helen,

She's coming. She's agreed, as I so very much hoped she would, and she will be here in a few days. I am praying that she will forgive us, although I am afraid, truly afraid, that she won't. I have this single chance – we have this chance – to make her understand how much she is, and always has been, loved by us both. Oh Helen. My youthful stupidity has led us both to do so much wrong. But no point in repeating all that here. You know how sorry I am and I know you have forgiven me even though I can't forgive myself. Your generosity and love overwhelm me.

So, to the matter in hand. I have prepared a folder, a portfolio, for her. I will tell her what I can, and provide her with evidence from my diary and our letters for her to read through and keep. It will be too much, I'm sure, for her to absorb, to follow, in a single conversation, and I fear that's all she will allow me when she hears what I have to say. I also fear that Jenny will not leave me alone long. And as you know, I have my concerns about her. In some ways she reminds me of Izzie – quick-witted, funny, gregarious – but she has a level of cunning to her intellect which is unpleasant, and there is something that just doesn't ring true about her. As if she's acting. And that worries me. She is too much the serendipitous helper at times. I am sure she is reading my mail, looking for something, although I don't know exactly what. I pray it is simply a way to establish my worth, to decide if I'm worth robbing or bumping off or whatever. God forbid it is anything to do with all of this. But how could it be? Jenny is a child of poverty, that much is clear, hardly likely to have been brought up on tales of Africa and fortunes. I've promised her a legacy and spoken to my lawyers in the hope that that will be enough to keep her from prying further, but time will tell.

In the folder I show Izzie our deception. My shameful behaviour, Evie's solution. Our trip to Scotland. But from the point where you returned to Africa and I remained here, I will be silent. I died a kind of death when you left. I have no words to express what I felt, if indeed I felt anything at all, until our darling girl brought me back to life with her laughter and love and joy. So the years of hiding are yours to tell, dear Helen. Your story, not mine. Your horror. You tell it as you see fit. And feel no need to hold back on my account. Not a day goes by when I don't blame myself for what I did to you. For what I let Cameron do.

There are some details I will not include in the folder for fear of – I'm not sure what. Superstition perhaps, force of habit, or maybe even Jenny again. I cannot trust her. But I will not write down your location, nor will I commit details of the financial arrangements to paper. There will be nothing in writing that will lead to you or any of the others. If Izzie wants to find you, I will give her details of the croft face to face. If she doesn't come I have arranged for a "clue" to be left with my lawyer. A copy of an old unsigned lease for the croft house in the middle of my current file.

Our Izzie won't be able to resist the questions that will pose and she will find you. Jenny's legacy will serve a similar function. Should I be right in my fears about her, our inquisitive Izzie will track her down, I'm sure, when she comes across a name she doesn't recognise. I leave it to you to provide details of anything, anyone else, if you see fit to do so, when you meet with her. Revelation will, after all, break our side of the pact we made with our very own devil and his henchmen and could mean no further support for you and R. So again, that must be your decision. I am simply a conduit in the matter of the funds.

Dear Helen. Nothing is guaranteed, but I feel certain that she will come to you. She was so disappointed before when you wouldn't let me talk to her. It's why she walked out and refused to speak to me for all those years. All those lost, long years. She wanted to know the truth then and now she can. Whatever has happened to her in the intervening years, I know that desire will not have changed. She spoke of feeling incomplete, and needing this to complete her. Of needing to tell her daughter.

So it is nearly time, and I wait, as you do. This is something I must do if I am ever to rest easy in my grave. And I fear that rest is closer than I would like. For me, Izzie's visit will bring closure, but for you, I pray it will be a beginning.

Your repentant and grateful friend,
Ursula

Helen let the letter drop to the ledge beside her, stared into the half-light and remembered. Another letter, waiting for another child. Another lifetime. The same knot of anticipation. Would it be different this time or would she be punished again? She was afraid to hope for too much, in case she was disappointed, as she had been on that day some fifty years ago. In her mind it was as vivid, as fresh as yesterday had been. No. Fresher . . .

* * *

It had been early afternoon that day he'd come, the air still and calm. She heard the car climbing the slight hill before she could see it tip over its brow. She'd been sitting sewing a button back on one of Izzie's blouses, expected the car to be the battered white Peugeot, to see the florid face of Sister Agnes set in concentration behind the wheel as she brought Izzie back to her from the Mission clinic. Izzie would be tearful and tired, no doubt, after the journey and the shock of the inoculation. Sister Agnes would have done her best to soothe the disgruntled child, but Helen knew Izzie in that mood would take comfort from no one but her own mother. She smiled to herself as she dropped the cotton blouse back into the sewing basket and flipped the lid closed with her foot. She stretched and stood, swallowing a yawn. Her hand shielded her eyes from the sun as she sought out the car.

And there it was. Black. Black and growing bigger as it neared the house. Not white, not whining the way the small Mission car did, not lurching over the bumps and dips, but slithering, gliding, invading.

Helen's hand flew to her mouth as she turned and made for the door. Hide. She had to hide. Whoever this was, it wasn't good. But too late for that: she would have been seen, would be seen disappearing through the screen door. And the house was full of Izzie's things; she mustn't let them see, whoever it was, they mustn't know there was a child. Whatever they'd come for, they could do what they liked to Helen, but not to Izzie. Not her. Her heart was thudding, drowning the sound of the car as it came.

Her eyes flickered over the verandah. Hide anything that suggested the presence of a child. Of anyone other than herself and an absent husband. Brazen it out. She had to. She could do this. She'd practised with Evie. Oh God – she swept up a tiny knitted shoe fallen from Izzie's favourite doll and rammed it into her pocket. She was Anna, she must remember, the Dutch pastor's wife. She spoke little English, heavily accented but just comprehensible enough to send any visitors on to the Mission— No. *No.* She'd have to change their plan. Not the Mission: Izzie was there. She couldn't do that, she'd have to think of—

"Helen, my dear. How nice." She spun round and was instantly mesmerised by cold reptilian eyes. Familiar eyes. But the voice itself was enough to snare her, petrify her.

Cameron.

Cameron had found her.

Helen turned on the light in the tiny kitchen at the back of the house. Its small, north-facing window yielded little enough light at the best of times, and the shadowy, not-quite night of summer was hardly that. The water from the creaking tap splattered against old metal like rain battering the corrugated-iron roof of the workshop next door. She'd found that comforting once, something to break the solitude of her exile as she turned the wheel and threw her pots. Something other than Ross and his childish moods. The rhythm steady and sure in the midst of something so elemental and unpredictable.

She didn't really want more tea, but the ritual soothed her. The feel of the warm mug cupped in her hands thawed the cold, piercing fear that threatened to harden into denial, refusal. To keep the bolts fastened tight against hope. The hope that this daughter might still love her and want her in her life. Helen hadn't realised how badly she wanted this opportunity. This child, her lost Izzie, was the only child who might have the capacity to love her, to know her, to understand and forgive. Ross loved her, as far as he was capable of love, but guilt not innocence was what she saw when she looked into his still childlike face. And her heart lurched not with mother-love but with self-loathing every time he smiled at her in that slightly puzzled, vague way of his.

The mug she cradled was too hot in her hands. Not comforting but scalding. She hooked her fingers through the handle, raised it to her lips, blew tremulous air across the mud-brown surface. A cloud of steam rose, quivered for a moment and then dissolved as she set it back on the table. She'd read Ursula's letter over and over again, before she let herself acknowledge even the slightest hope. She'd been too quick to hope before, all those years ago, and wouldn't make the same mistake this time round. Back then, Evie's letter should have warned her. She only had herself to blame. The clues were all there when she reread it later. But she hadn't seen them. She'd been too distracted by the miraculous news. The promise of the redemption she'd sought even then seemed to lie in Evie's words, but she'd learned the hard way that you can read what you want to read into anything if you're desperate enough. A leopard doesn't change its spots. Nor a vindictive, mercenary brute of a husband either.

She should have known Cameron wouldn't do what he'd promised Evie. There was always a price to be paid with him. A deal to be done, a double-cross. But she'd never been so desperate to believe something before. Now, she was wiser. Expect the worst from everyone, everything, and you're rarely disappointed.

The tea was cooling in the cup now. A thin, darker skin on its surface broke up and floated towards the edges, where they clung to white walls like brown liver spots staining the back of an old woman's hands. Like the spots on the back of her own. All her beauty gone. A relief in some ways, although it hardly mattered here. Beauty: disturbing the effect it could have on people, that it had on her husbands. Both, in different ways, had been overwhelmed by it. Intimidated, even.

She pushed her chair back from the table and went out to the small mottled mirror inset in the uprights of the art deco hallstand. Like all the furniture in the house, it had been here when they came. Someone must have chosen it, liked it once. If it had been old then, it was ancient now. But Helen had grown used to it, had no idea what fashionable decor might mean these days and no interest in finding out. It suited her, this old furniture. It was as familiar, as unremarkable, as her own features had become. She rummaged in the single narrow drawer beneath the stand's shelf and pulled out a hairbrush, pulled it through her short hair, then rummaged further until she closed her fingers round the metal tube of a lipstick. Pulling off the cap, she swivelled the base until a nugget of rose-coloured cream surfaced. Peering forward into the dim mirror, she ran the nub across her thin lips, stretched them, smacked them softly together, dropped the lipstick back into the drawer. That, these days, was as good as it got. But she wanted to make an effort, for Izzie. In case she remembered something of the glamour of Helen's younger years, although lipstick hadn't been a feature of her disguise as a pastor's wife, nor would the nuns at the Mission have approved of sophistication and adornment. But Helen remembered finding Izzie one day looking into the box on her dressing table where she kept her make-up and brushes with awe on her face. "Mummy's box of magic," she'd laughed, and her daughter's eyes had grown wider still.

"Oh for God's sake, woman," she muttered in disgust, turning away from the mirror and pushing the drawer shut with her hip. She dragged the back of her hand across her lips, smudging pink across her cheeks, stretching skin until her lips felt tender and dry. The last thing Izzie would notice would be lipstick and brushed hair.

Back in the kitchen she rubbed the smears from her hand and cheeks with a dishcloth, scrubbing harder than needed. Idiot. She was an old woman. A recluse. A woman who'd given up her daughter to another's keeping. No amount of lipstick could put a gloss on that. She should be wearing sackcloth, smearing herself with ashes not 1960s Dior.

There was a noise from upstairs. Heavy feet thumped across the ceiling above her head. Ross appeared, stumbling down the

270

stairs, not really awake. He passed her without a word, without a trace of acknowledgement. She stood in the shadows and waited, heard the door to the bathroom off the kitchen close, the bolt shot, then the creak and rattle of the chain as it was pulled and the echo of rushing water. A moment later, Ross reappeared, saw her this time.

"Get up?" His brow was knotted in concentration, in puzzlement. This was not part of their morning routine. She shouldn't be standing in the hallway, dressed in yesterday's clothes, not yet. Not when the sky outside was green in anticipation of the rising sun but there was no glow over the slope of Ben Mor, no shimmer off the surface of the sea at its foot.

"No, Ross. I couldn't sleep. You go back to bed now and I'll wake you when it's time."

The frown fell from his face and it resumed its customary blandness. Helen leant forward, pulled the cord on his pyjamas tighter, tied a bow.

"Go on, Ross. Back to bed." She turned him towards the stairs and gently pushed on a thickset shoulder, sighing to herself as she watched his clumsy climb, his feet disappearing up the staircase. What would Izzie make of her brother? What would Helen tell her? The truth? Would Izzie believe her if she did?

The jaundiced pre-dawn light was fading to a cooler shade of yellow now and, driven by a sudden sense of imprisonment, Helen reached up and grabbed the jacket hanging beside the door. She shrugged it on at the same time as she reached for the doorknob, its worn surface cool against the heat of her palm. She needed air, space, escape.

She pulled the door behind her, thrust her hands into deep pockets and lifted her face, eyes shut, to the sky. It was happening again. She couldn't stop it. The horror film playing in her mind. Not the one where a mother shoots her child. Its sequel. The one where she gets what she deserves.

271

She'd struggled to keep her face neutral when she saw he was alone.

"Where is he?"

"Darling," Cameron reprimanded, "no soft words of greeting for your beloved husband after all this time? No passionate embrace? Surely you've missed me?"

"Where *is* he?"

"Not even a little? Oh darling, you do disappoint me. And here's me, absolutely heartbroken at the loss of my adored wife, positively overwhelmed by my struggle to cope with my grief despite, I should say, the very best efforts of the good ladies of Zomba, not to mention the Blantyre coterie, of course. In fact, so many of your pretty little friends, now that I think of it, have been so very, very kind."

His laugh was brittle. He leant in close to Helen, who was standing, fists clenched by her side, eyes fixed on a knot in the mahogany floorboard at her feet.

"Yes, my dear," he whispered, and she felt the heat of his breath on her skin, flowing like liquid venom into her ear. "So very . . . *enthusiastic* in their efforts to comfort me."

Helen winced, repulsed, as he tilted her chin to force her to meet his eyes.

"I wonder what they'll say when they realise I'm not the widower we all thought after all." He laughed again and released her, wandering away towards the far end of the verandah, peering through the windows that looked on to it as he went. "Really, Helen, it's too, too naughty of you to have deceived us all like this."

Helen breathed a quiet prayer of thanks that the bedrooms were at the back of the house, that she always pulled their shutters against the day's heat in any case.

"Aren't you going to offer me tea, dearest? Or some of that divine lemonade you always had the kitchen boy make. So

272

refreshing and it's been such a tedious journey. I'm positively parched."

Cameron settled himself on the rattan sofa Helen herself had only recently vacated. "Do call someone, darling. Have them bring something . . . Unless . . . ah. All alone are we?" He arched an eyebrow in that mocking way he had. She forced herself to look away, not to watch his foot idly swinging above the lid of her sewing basket, the hidden blouse of a child, praying the foot wouldn't dip an inch or two lower, catch and flip the lid.

"Of course. Fugitives probably don't run to servants, do they? Having to get those dainty little hands dirty, are you?" Still the foot was swinging. She had to distract him, get him to move.

"Don't settle, Cameron. You're not staying." She walked over to the top of the steps, leant against the balustrade and extended an arm out behind her towards the car. "If you haven't brought Ross then I want you to leave, now."

"Do you indeed? Don't you want to hear what I have to say? No?" He stood and walked towards her with that same hideous grin on his face. "Well, what my darling wife wants—" He grabbed Helen's outstretched arm and twisted it high behind her back, pulling her in towards him at the same time. "What my darling wife wants," he hissed, spittle flecking her face, "she's not going to get. Not until *I* say so."

"Let go of me." Helen struggled, but the more she moved the harder Cameron wrenched her arm. "You're hurting me—"

"That's the general idea." She saw the gleam in his eyes, the excitement.

"Let me go!" Her voice was thin, shrill, as she struggled against the pain.

"Manners, darling: let me go, *please*." He pushed her away, lowering her arm and pulling on her wrist to spin her round. Stepping in behind her, he grasped the back of her neck and pushed her face into the screen door.

273

"Let's go inside, shall we? We need to talk, you and I. Do what I want and I'll bring you your precious boy. Try to resist me and you'll never see him again. No one will. After all, like you, he's already dead."

Helen's ankle twisted beneath her and the jolt of pain brought her back to the cool Highland morning. The pebbles of the beach crunched beneath her as she sat down heavily and rubbed at the pain, erasing it with gentle rhythmic pressure. She flexed the foot, rotated it and, when the pain ebbed, dropped it back down beside its partner. Then she hugged her knees into her chest and rested her forehead on top of them. It was all so long ago. Still so vivid. Would she have the courage to tell Izzie? Extending her legs in front of her, Helen stretched her hands back behind her and propped herself up, rolling her head on her shoulders, listening to the cricks and creaks snapping as the tension of waiting and wondering took their toll. Breathing deeply, she tried to focus on the serenity around her, let the natural beauty soothe her, heal the memories that consumed her.

The sea was calm and glistened like granite in the dawning sun, islands like lumps of glittering coal scattered on its surface, disrupting the clear line of the horizon. Far out in the distance she could see a single fishing boat chugging out to deeper waters. Even this early, the day held the promise of heat. Not African heat, that deep, drenching, bone-melting fire that seeped through walls and windows, bringing its smell of burnt dust and ripe fruit with it. No. This was different, this Highland heat. A soft glow like the warmth that lingered in a bed, a hug that held you close and then let you go. A heat that let you breathe, that let fresh air wash the spaces in-between its waves, a heat that left shade cool and breezes fresh. Helen had come to love the Highland heat. She no longer pined for the brazen strength of tropical sun. But even more, she'd come to love the wind and the wet. The rain that washed and cleansed, the snow that covered tracks, the gales that howled and screeched in catharsis. She'd been purged clean by the climate of her adopted home and she welcomed the shelter it afforded her. Africa was the past. But when Izzie came, she'd have to allow it room in her present.

Turning her face to the east, to the rising sun, Helen looked up at the croft and its outhouses up on the slope above her. Ross would be up by now, wondering where she was. Perhaps he'd come out front, look for her, call on her in that plaintive, frightened way he had when he couldn't find her. Like a lamb bleating for a lost ewe. She should get back. He needed her. He needed the comfort of the familiar, of the routines they'd established, the patterns they lived by.

Small pebbles gave way to larger, and seaweed crackled under her feet as she climbed up the beach to the machair that edged it, the soft bounce of white clover and yellow rattle beneath her feet muffling her step, a welcome respite from the grating rub of shifting stone. She followed the sheep trail that etched a narrow path through the bracken up to the track. She was fit, but still the climb was hard, and her hip troubled her. She'd left her walking stick in the hallstand, her eagerness to get outside overcoming pain, the distraction of her memories giving her the power to walk unaided for a time. She'd pay for it later, though, she knew, just as she'd paid for everything else.

She paused to catch her breath, caught a shadow slipping between the cottage and the workshop. Ross? Too quick, too slight. But who else could it be? A seagull screeched overhead and she smiled as its shadow flitted over the path in front of her, vanished, then danced across the red roof of the shed. She was jumpy, nerves tight as she anticipated what the day might bring.

She reached the old wooden bench at the front of the house and sat down, reluctant to go into the dim, damp kitchen, enjoying the calm of the early morning, the blank canvas of another day, waiting to begin. A few moments of tranquillity and she would go in, get Ross up and breakfasted, ready for another day of routines and rituals. She sighed. Tranquillity was not, it seemed, to be hers today. Too many memories pushing to be replayed.

27

Upper Shire River, 1963

Helen heard the Mission car wheeze up the slope over the brow of the hill in front of the house. It must have been at least an hour since Cameron had left. But still she sat huddled like a foetus on the rumpled bed, the shutters filtering the fading light of the afternoon, which lay like whip lashes across bare skin and ripped clothes, criss-crossing with the streaks tears had carved on her pale cheeks.

Izzie.

Whispering the word to herself like a mantra, Helen forced herself to move, pushed her limbs away and straightened. With tremendous effort she pushed herself off the bed and into a standing position, only to have her legs collapse under her and land her with a jolt back onto the bed. She should be thankful this room was the first off the corridor from the hallway. If he'd gone further and seen Izzie's room—

Izzie.

The whining of the car was louder now; they'd have started on the downward track. She had to move quickly. Still sitting, she stripped the remnants of the clothes from her, dropped them on the floor and kicked them under the bed. Searching around, her eyes lit on her silk dressing gown, draped casually over the ladder-back chair where she'd dropped it this morning. Was it really only this morning?

She stretched out to reach it, but it was just beyond her grasp. Once again she tried to stand; once again she fell back. Sobbing

277

now, she dropped down to the floor, pushed herself forward onto all fours and crawled over to the waterfall of silk cascading from the edge of the chair. She hugged it to her gratefully, its cool smoothness soothing the fires of pain still burning in her body. Shrugging it on, she moaned, swallowed tears, straightened her shoulders. She gasped as she heard the car doors slam, a child's laugh joined by an older woman's and something else. A yelp? A bark? And then the clattering of the screen door.

"Mama! Mama! Come and see who Sister Agnes has brought to meet you. Mama!"

Helen opened her mouth to call out to Izzie, to tell her she'd be right with her, but no words came, just a hoarse, rasping, choking sound as she felt again the pain of Cameron's hands around her neck squeezing, squeez—

"Mama! Where are you?" The little voice was more strident now, the child not used to being ignored. "*Mama!*"

"Shh, child. No need to shout." Helen heard the measured tones of Sister Agnes as the screen door clattered once again, less violently this time. "Go outside, Isobel, and watch Rusty. He's very keen to dig up your mother's vegetables."

"But I want Mama to meet him!"

"She will, child. In a moment. Now go play with Rusty. I need to talk to your mama."

"But where *is* she?"

Before Sister Agnes could answer the impatient child, Izzie was distracted by a sharp bark from outside, followed by a yelp.

"Rusty!"

"I think you better go and see what he's up to. Run along, child."

The screen door clattered once again and Helen released her breath, unaware that she'd been holding it. Izzie must not see her mother like this. Helen had to pull herself together, put on a smile, behave normally. She heard Sister Agnes moving around the

278

house, a brief squeal of furniture scraping across the floor as it was righted, then soft footsteps in the hallway outside.

"Helen? Helen, where are you? It's Sister Agnes."

The footsteps stopped outside the door and there was a faint knock. Helen's eyes filled with tears. Still she could not speak.

"Helen? Are you in there? I'm coming in."

The door opened slowly and Helen looked up through her tears to see the shape of the nun fill the doorway, block out the hall, the outside world, then come closer. Helen leant against the solid frame of the older woman as Sister Agnes bent down and put her arms around the shaking woman. Saying nothing, Sister Agnes helped her up and onto the chair, placing Helen's trailing hands into her lap with a gentle squeeze before going back to the door and closing it softly. She stood and looked around her, quietly taking in the crumpled bedclothes, the upturned lamp on the bedside table, the strip of ripped calico Helen in her haste had missed.

Crouching down beside Helen, Sister Agnes took her hands in hers, held them firm to stop their shaking.

"You're safe now, Helen. No one will harm you now I'm here."

Helen looked up into the warm brown eyes. Tears were flowing freely now and she struggled to make out the placid features of the nun's homely face. She nodded, trusting the calm words of the steady voice. Helen tried again to speak but choked on the words.

"Shh, Helen. Don't speak. Just sit quietly now. Breathe deeply, slowly. That's it. Just concentrate on that. Time enough for talking later."

Helen's panic began to subside; the nun's presence, her gentle voice, soothed her. The thudding of her heartbeat quietened, the trembling in her limbs lessened.

"Izzie," Helen managed to croak. "She mustn't see me . . ."

"She won't. She's outside playing with one of the Mission puppies we brought over to show you. Rusty will keep her occupied. Don't worry about Izzie for now. Let's see about you."

Helen felt the firm, cool touch of a work-hardened palm on her forehead, then under her chin as Sister Agnes turned her face to the thin light from the shuttered window.

"Hmm. Some bruising to that cheek I expect. But nothing— Oh, Helen, child, your neck!" Already the lividity of bruising was clear, fingerprints imprinted on white skin like the red petals of a winter rose dropped on snow. Without a word, Helen let the silk fall from one shoulder to reveal the angry scratches across her breast, blood all but dried, yet still red and raised.

Without a word, Sister Agnes pulled the robe back up again, sat back on her heels and looked down at her hands for a moment as if in silent prayer. *Much good that will do,* Helen thought, surprising herself by the sting of bitterness she felt. Prayers were no protection against that man. That evil.

She flicked her eyes open and found Sister Agnes looking at her, deep into her soul. Helen blushed with shame, both at her blasphemous thoughts and the certainty that the nun knew exactly what had happened here, what Cameron had done to her, forced her to do. What she'd let him do. She felt a wave of anger, clung to it, needed it to make herself strong again.

"You poor child," Sister Agnes murmured. "I'll bring water, we'll clean you up, and tea."

"Tea?" Helen spluttered as anger, unfocused rage, erupted from deep within her. Tea? Had this woman no idea? Helen felt a calming hand on her arm. "Tea?" she screamed again. "Get your hand off me. What damned good will tea do, you stup—"

"Quiet, Helen." The voice was firm. "Izzie will hear you." The nun's admonition stopped the words in Helen's throat; her steady hands stilled the arms that were flailing, lashing out, wanting to

280

fight back, but the person they wanted to strike was long gone. The nun held her with surprising strength until reason returned to Helen's distraught mind.

Sister Agnes was right, Helen realised a short while later, as she sipped tea and rested back against fresh pillows. She'd sat in the chair dazed and distant as Sister Agnes had gently washed her, found fresh clothes and bed linens, stripped and remade the bed. Then the sister had brought her the tea, and told her to rest and stay calm. Sister Agnes would see to Izzie's supper. Izzie understood Mama was ill and had promised to keep Rusty quiet. When Helen felt calmer, the Sister had said, she would bring Izzie, and Rusty, to see her before putting the child to bed.

Helen had gratefully acquiesced to the nun's plans, thankful to abdicate responsibility for her gregarious daughter for a few precious hours while she regained her strength, her composure. Even now she was playing happily with the Mission puppy, working up, Helen knew, to finding a way to convince her mother and the nun that Rusty should be allowed to stay with her, to become her friend and companion.

It was lonely for her daughter. Brief visits to the Mission afforded scant opportunity to make friends, although Izzie always managed to come home with tales of playing with this child or that, promises to meet again next time Izzie visited. Then disappointments when she found her new friends had moved on and forged other, deeper connections between themselves that Izzie was no part of when finally she did return or, worse still, found that her friends had left the Mission. Helen had worried that her daughter would lose the ability to connect with others, yet worried too that her pixie-like pale face, her blonde curls and sky-blue eyes would set her apart, make her the focus of too much attention, the subject of tales told out of school. That the story given in passing of being a missionary's daughter would not stand the test of deeper friendships.

But now, little of this mattered. Cameron had been here. He would come again, to bring Ross, he had said, "one of these days". He'd do more than that, Helen knew. He'd joked about conjugal rights, a wife's marital duty, a husband's entitlement. Today had shown her what he was capable of, the extent of his depravity and his pleasure in the pain of another, of the power he could wield over another life. If he knew Izzie lived, Helen could only begin to imagine how he might use that to torment her, to keep his wife where he wanted her. Worse was the thought of what he might do to protect David's position as only heir to the Buchanan fortune. To protect his own, as that heir's natural father.

Izzie was in danger. That much was clear. How her mother could protect her, less so. Could they run? But what would happen to Ross then? Her stomach lurched as she thought of her timid, gentle son, of the last time she'd seen him, lying on the bedroom floor, blood spreading out behind his dark head like a witch doctor's headdress, a darkly shining halo. Cameron had told her he was dead. *Dead.* She would never have left her son if she'd thought there was still breath in that tiny body. And now, she was torn. She could have Ross back, but it meant exposing Izzie to risk of discovery. Helen's head spun as she tried to work out a way forward. A way to let her have both her children with her, to keep them safe and out of Cameron's reach.

Helen didn't hear the door open, or the tiptoeing feet cross the polished floor, but felt first the lurch of the mattress as Izzie pulled herself up onto the bed, the splash of cold tea on the back of her hand as the cup tipped in response.

"Izzie, you startled me, sweetheart." Helen was amazed to hear the calm normality of her voice, and smiled at her daughter as much in relief as with the overwhelming love she'd always felt for this, her favourite child, from the moment she'd first held the wriggling bundle in her arms.

"Are you better now, Mama?" The little face was serious. "Sister

Agnes said you were ill. I was ill once, wasn't I? But then I got better. You will too." The head nodded wisely.

"Nearly better, darling. Very nearly."

"I played outside so you could sleep. Sister Agnes said I could keep Rusty for tonight. He's a dog. I know you'll like him, too."

Helen smiled. "I'm sure I will."

"Mama, will you be better in the morning?"

"Oh yes. Why do you ask?"

"Only Sister Agnes said she'll go back to the Mission tomorrow."

"Yes, I expect she will. What's wrong with that?"

"Well, she might take . . . You haven't met Rusty yet and if she takes him you might not be able to." There was a dramatic sigh out of all proportion to the size of the slight-framed child who'd snuggled in under her mother's arm and was leaning against her chest, head rolling restlessly from one side to the other as she let her sentence trail away. "Sister said I wasn't to ask you yet. Not till you're better."

"Ask me what, little one?"

"If I can—" The little body twisted round to face her and laughter broke around them. "No! Naughty Mama! You're trying to trick me into asking you! I promised Sister I wouldn't. But please get better fast. Before she goes tomorrow."

"I'll see what I can do." Helen smiled and pulled the child to her in a hug, kissed the top of her head, thanked God she was still safe. "Where is Sister Agnes? I need to talk to her."

"She's making supper," Izzie said, and wrinkled her nose. "It doesn't smell very good, though, Mama. Not like yours. I don't think we'll like it."

"Nonsense, I'm sure we will." With every word her daughter spoke, Helen felt the steel grip the memory of the afternoon had on her lessen. Cameron would not make her a victim; he would not harm her daughter. Helen would fight back with every breath, with every drop of strength she had. She would find a way to match his cunning, outdo him. Her daughter deserved at least that.

And her son Ross, her boy, her true firstborn, even more so.

Izzie had been right about supper. Helen could only surmise that someone else was responsible for kitchen matters at the Mission. But she'd forced herself to eat a little of the plate the good woman had prepared and brought to her on a tray so Helen could eat still propped up against the pillows on her bed. Helen hoped Izzie had managed to do the same, knew hunger had a way of persuading her daughter to eat most things; and if not, perhaps Rusty would have helped her out.

When Sister Agnes returned to take the tray, Izzie was with her.

"Are you better yet?" she asked.

"Shush," Sister Agnes had intervened before Helen could answer. "Not now, Isobel. It can wait till morning."

Izzie's face had shown her struggle, but obedience won the day.

"Goodnight, Mama." She'd clambered up onto the bed again to kiss Helen and hug her. "Get better *soon*."

"Goodnight, darling." Helen squeezed her daughter tight.

"Rusty's going to sleep outside my door, Sister Agnes said."

"Better that than in her bed." The Sister smiled. "Come on, let's get you off then."

"Sister, I—"

"Later, Helen. I'll get this one to bed and then we'll talk."

"Is she sleeping?"

The nun smiled. "Barely finished her prayers before her eyes closed and I had to lift her into bed. Rusty, too. Sound asleep, the pair of them. She's worn them both out. Perhaps I shouldn't have brought her the puppy, but I'd thought it might be some small protection for you both, living alone here . . ."

Sister Agnes looked down as her voice trailed off. Helen knew they were both thinking the same thing. Too late for protection.

"She'll want to keep the dog anyway, I imagine," Helen said. "But I'm not sure we can. I'm not even sure we can stay here. We're not safe here any longer. Izzie isn't safe. He was here. This afternoon. He did this. He'll be back."

"Yes."

"I don't know how he found me. But he thinks it's just me. If there's anything to be thankful for in all of this, it's that Izzie was with you. He doesn't know she's still alive."

"Are you sure?"

Helen hesitated. How could she be sure? She'd spent the morning tidying after Sister Agnes had taken Izzie, so there had been no toys or traces of her in the sitting room. She'd hidden the shirt she'd been mending out on the verandah, picked up the tiny knitted doll's shoe that had lain on the floor and stuffed it into her pock—

"My clothes. Where are they?"

"My dear, they're not fit for—"

"Where, Sister? I need to check the pockets." Helen struggled to throw back the sheet, pushed herself to her feet, clutching at the Sister in her effort to stand.

"Now, now, Helen. I'll fetch them. You stay in bed."

"No. Let me see them. It's important." Helen lurched to the door, leant against the frame until she found her balance, then pushed herself off towards the kitchen, feet thudding heavily on the bare wooden floor.

"Shh, Helen. You'll wake—"

"In here?"

"No, I've put them out the back. I was going to burn them later, when Izzie was asleep. Sit, Helen. I'll fetch them." Sister Agnes turned to push the kitchen door shut behind them, but not before the clack of claws on wood announced the arrival of Rusty. The puppy sat at Helen's feet, looked up at her expectantly.

"Oh, that dog. Keep him here. We'll lose him in the darkness if he gets out." Sister Agnes disappeared into the night.

Helen and the puppy looked at each other. Then the dog whimpered, ears rising then falling again, flat against its head. The tail wagged once then stopped. Another whimper and it ducked its head forward and down, nudging Helen's leg, before starting back and up onto all fours. Rusty danced back a step or two, then forward again.

"He wants to play."

Helen hadn't heard the door open, looked up to see a sleepy Izzie rubbing one eye and yawning, her doll, minus one shoe, tucked trailing from her free hand.

"Izzie. It's late. You should be sleeping."

"I heard you talking to Sister Agnes. Then Rusty wasn't there so I came to find him."

"Take him then, Izzie, and go back to bed."

"But he wants to play—"

"*Izzie.* Just do as you're told."

The young girl's eyes widened at the sharpness in Helen's voice.

"Oh darling, I'm sorry. I— Come here." Helen reached her arms out to her daughter, lifted her onto her lap and pulled her close, inhaled the soapy smell of her, the mint from recently brushed teeth still lingering on the ragged breath.

"Sing, Mama. Sing me to sleep." The thumb tucked into the pink lips, the flushed cheeks dipping as she sucked. Helen reached down and gently pulled the thumb from her daughter's mouth, then leant forward and kissed the blonde head nestled against her chest. There'd be no need to sing, Helen knew. In seconds Izzie's breath had evened to a rhythmic pulse, the slender limbs had fallen relaxed and heavy against Helen's own. The doll dropped to the floor, where Rusty was sniffing at it with interest. Careful not to disturb the sleeping child, Helen reached down and picked it up, safely out of the dog's reach. If only it were so easy to put the child herself out of harm's way.

"Here—"The nun stopped abruptly as she took in the Madonna and Child-like tableau at the table. She closed the outside door gently behind her, dropped the pile of soiled and tattered garments onto the far end of the table and came towards them, arms outstretched. "I'll take her back to bed."

"No. Not yet." Helen spoke softly, held her daughter closer, eyes filling with tears. "Look in the pockets. For a shoe. A doll's shoe. Like this one." Helen's free hand lifted a leg of the doll she'd laid in front of her on the table.

Frowning a little, Sister Agnes pulled the remains of Helen's dress out of the bundle, shook it out. One patch pocket hung ripped and open, the fabric folding back like the corner of a page turned over to mark the reader's place in an unfinished book. Helen held her breath as the nun reached into the other, shook her head.

"Are there any other pockets?"

Helen shook her own head now, slowly, heavily.

"You didn't see it when you were . . . the bed . . . or . . . or . . ."

"No." The nun was frowning still, as she tried to work out why Helen was so concerned about a doll's shoe.

"He's taken it. He knows."

Helen pulled her daughter closer still, the tears that were now sliding down pale cheeks dropping softly onto the dishevelled curls. After a moment she looked up at Sister Agnes. Helen knew what she had to do.

"Take her."

Helen's arms crossed over her empty chest as the nun carried the sleeping girl away.

★ ★ ★

Watching her daughter being driven away the next morning had been the hardest thing she'd ever done.

"Bye darling," she'd said casually, desperate to sound like she did every other time her daughter had climbed into the dusty white Mission car, hardly with a backward glance, excited at the prospect of having other children to play with. Helen had kissed her lightly on the cheek, resisting the urge to pull her in close and hold her tight. Izzie usually wriggled out of her mother's embrace on Mission days, her mind already on the games that she would play, the fun she'd have, the stories she'd have later to tell her mother.

That day, though, Izzie had been a little clingy, almost reluctant. Helen had marvelled at first at her child's intuition, her ability to pick up on her mother's mood no matter how hard Helen tried to hide it. But then the real reason for Izzie's reluctance had scampered out from under the verandah steps, snout dusted red with the dry earth, a forgotten tennis ball clenched tight between drooling, chewing jaws.

"Rusty!" Izzie had raced towards him. "I'll be back soon – promise!" She'd hugged the excited puppy as tightly and as enthusiastically as Helen longed to hug Izzie herself.

"Come on, Izzie," Sister Agnes, said, her eyes locking onto Helen's. "Rusty will be fine here without you today. Mama will look after him."

"Why can't I take him? He could play with the others."

"He'll stop Mama getting lonely." Helen said, her hand rising to her neck as she felt her throat tighten on the words, wincing as she brushed the bruises from yesterday, hidden by the high-buttoned collar of her blouse.

"But I'm only going to the Mission. I won't be long. Mama . . ." Izzie's face took on a puzzled look as a new thought struck her. "Why am I going to the Mission again? I only went yesterday."

"I . . . I know, darling. But you see . . . ." Helen couldn't think what to say.

"There's a special treat today," Sister Agnes cut in, and Helen wondered at the nun's unexpected fluency in the lie. "A trip for you and some of the other children. You're going to go away for a little while."

"But . . . but . . . ." Izzie looked panicked as she turned her head from side to side, from Rusty to the nun and back again to the dog, now hunched down on the shade of the mimosa tree, ball between paws, jaws working at a loose flap of yellowed rubber. Helen's heart lurched. Her daughter didn't even glance in her direction.

"Mama will take care of Rusty, Isobel. Don't you want to go on an adventure with the other children?"

Izzie's face broke into a grin. She ran over to the dog and hugged him and then, in a fit of exuberance, hugged her mother too. Then she took the nun's hand in hers and started to walk over to the car. As the nun turned, she looked back over her shoulder at Helen.

"I'll take care of her."

Helen nodded and stood there watching the dust the car threw up behind it as her daughter was driven away, praying she'd be safe. Praying she'd done the right thing for her in giving her up. Wondering if she would ever be able to reclaim her, would ever even see her again.

It was another twelve days before Cameron came back. It was evening and Helen was sitting, as she'd taken to doing, in the room that had once been Izzie's but which now was stripped bare, robbed of all traces of the presence of a child. Rusty sat at her feet. It was his ears pricking up and the low rumble akin to a growl that emanated from deep inside the small body that had alerted her to the sound of a car. Rusty might turn into a protector yet, she thought, even as her stomach clenched and her skin prickled with revulsion at the memory of the thick fingers probing, pinching.

When Cameron pulled back the screen door, he saw her waiting for him, knife in her hand, small dog at her feet. He laughed. Laughed loudly, his face reddening as his mirth brought tears to his eyes and he threw himself down on one of the sofas.

"Ah, Helen." He dabbed at the tears with a pressed white handkerchief he'd pulled from the top of the cream linen jacket he wore, despite the heat. "You never cease to amuse me." Helen watched the eyes narrow into slits as he looked her slowly up and down, and then he looked down again, to Rusty sitting quietly at her feet, strangely still and cowed.

"What's that? A guard dog?" He laughed again and in one fluent movement rose from the sofa and crossed the room, grabbing her wrist and twisting till the knife fell from her grasp. He kicked at it, kicked Rusty instead, laughing again as the animal yelped and scurried away. "Well, I think we can agree your defences don't amount to much. But there's no need. Fun though it was, I've other things on my mind tonight, and look at you anyway. My, how you've let yourself go. Hardly the society beauty I married. I doubt even Gregory would be tempted now." He tossed her wrist away and turned his back on her as he strode back to the screen door. "No, I've a pretty young thing tucked up in bed – our bed – back in Blantyre, waiting for me later tonight. So relax. It isn't you I've come for this time."

He slid a hand into a jacket pocket and pulled out the tiny shoe. Helen couldn't suppress the small gasp that escaped her lips. She heard Cameron chuckle. He turned to face her, threw it down on the floor between them, a parody of a gauntlet but the challenge clear nonetheless. "A deal, dear Helen, a straightforward trade. A child for a child. What could be fairer than that? Oh and of course, you and Ross stay dead."

"I don't know what you mean—" Helen began.

"Don't provoke me, dearest. You know what I'm like when I'm cross." He picked up the shoe, rubbed it between thumb and forefinger, then crumpled it into his fist. "I won't ask politely again. Bring her out."

"I . . . Who?"

The slap was sudden and harsh, the force of it spinning Helen's head round until a yank on her hair stopped its momentum. Cameron pulled harder, forcing her head back as he loomed over her and spoke through clenched teeth.

"Fetch her. Now." He released her and pushed her in front of him towards the corridor leading to the other rooms in the small bungalow. Helen tripped over the edge of the rug and fell onto her knees, but he caught her arm and pulled her upright before pushing her forward again. She shook her head, pulled back, refused to move.

"Come on. Move." He dragged her behind him as he started down the corridor, kicking open her bedroom door, striding in and pulling at the wardrobe handles, wrenching back the mosquito net and lifting the cover to look beneath the bed. "Izzie? Izzie, sweetheart! Uncle Cameron's come to take you home."

Pushing past Helen where he'd discarded her on her knees at the threshold of the room, he kicked open the door to the bathroom opposite, then strode on to the next room, where Rusty sat growling in front of the door. Cameron's foot swung and the dog yelped again as it slid over the floor to collide with the dresser standing in the corner.

"Guarding your little mistress, are you? Very noble." The room was empty. Bare. The bed not made up, the mosquito net knotted and hooked back, the shelves and surfaces clear. And clean, Helen realised with a start, as she stepped into the room behind Cameron and scooped up the whimpering puppy.

291

Too clean for an empty, unused room.

"Well, well. Had a bit of a clear-out have you? Pity. Looks like you've nothing to bargain with, doesn't it?"

"Wait, Cameron." Helen grabbed his sleeve as he pushed past her, dropping Rusty as she did so, tripping over the puppy as he danced to run from their feet.

"What have you done with her?"

"I . . . She . . . Izzie died. In the mudslide. I tried to save her but—"

"Don't make the mistake of taking me for a fool, Helen. I know she was here. Was she hiding when I visited last time? Did she hear us? Hear her mother screaming in passion and lust?"

"No! No, she was . . ."

"Was where? Same place you've hidden her now?"

"She was killed in the—"

"Mudslide. Yes, you said. Only problem is, Helen dearest, I don't believe you. You always were a hopeless liar."

"I saved the doll. I . . . sometimes . . . help with the Mission children. They, one of them . . . I gave her the doll, you see, just that day you came. Sister Agnes had been here with some of them. And the shoe, it must have fallen off and . . . and I found it. I know it's stupid, but I wanted to keep it. It reminded me—"

"Is that where she is, then? The Mission?"

"No! Aren't you listening? Izzie's gone, *dead*." Even saying it made Helen feel sick. But she had to convince him. Had to. Or he'd never give up. He'd find a way of—

"Wait! Cameron, where are you going?"

"I will find her, you know. Wherever you've hidden her. Right now, though, Ross and I are going to the Mission. Seems as good a place as any to start looking."

"Ross? He's here?"

"In the car. A child for a child." The pause hung between them, like an empty noose dangling as it waited for a neck. "A child for

292

a child, Helen. The child you tried to kill, your firstborn, in exchange for your daughter."

Helen's mind raced. Why would Cameron want to give her Ross but take Izzie away? It made no sense. Izzie was as entitled to inherit as Ross, both of them her flesh and blood so both of them legitimate heirs to the estate David was set to inherit, unless the truth came out. She forced herself to think, to muffle the static of panic that was interfering with her ability to process information, to work out Cameron's game.

"A wasted journey then. Such a shame. Especially when the boy gets so hopelessly travel-sick, just like his mother. Well, we must away again."

"Is he really here?" She hated the needy desperation in her voice.

"Of course. Would you like to see him?"

Helen couldn't speak, bit her bottom lip to stop it from trembling.

"Come on then." He led her out to the verandah. Pushed her down into a rattan chair. "Stay there. Move and you won't see him." Helen realised he was being literal. She was to see but not touch or kiss or hold her son.

"Richard," Cameron shouted into the growing darkness. A passenger door opened at the back of the car and a slim, tall man emerged. Helen recognised him instantly. She should have guessed. Wherever Cameron went, his trusty fixer Richard Chakanaya was never far behind. Had he been there last time Cameron had come calling? Had he heard, watched, laughed at her humiliation, her pain? Had they joked about it on the journey back to Blantyre, chinked glasses and smirked at the Club as Cameron told and retold the thrills of his conquest? She was sickened. These men had Ross, her innocent, darling boy.

"Show her the boy."

With a mocking half bow in her direction, Chakanaya slammed

his door shut, sauntered slowly round to the other side and reached in. He dragged out a boy, but whether it was Ross or not was impossible to tell. The car was almost the same height as the boy. All Helen could see was the crown of a dark-haired head, dropped forward onto the boy's chest so she couldn't make out the features. Was it Ross? It could be anybody.

"Bring him round. Let her see."

Chakanaya pulled the boy round to the front of the car.

"Show his face."

Chakanaya stood behind the boy, one hand on his shoulder; the other grasped the boy's chin and raised the face. Helen felt the colour drain from hers.

Ross.

But the face was distorted, the eyes even from this distance unfocused black wells. What was wrong with him? She stood and took a step forward.

"Ross! It's Mama!"

"Sit." Cameron snapped the command as if to a dog. In her shock she obeyed, hearing the rattan protest as she dropped back down into her seat.

"You want him, Helen?"

"What have you done to him? Why is he so . . . so . . . ?"

"Vacant?" Cameron laughed. "Well he never was the brightest in the pack now, was he? He's still a bit under the weather from the accident, you know, and the sedatives help keep everything under control."

"You're drugging him?"

"Richard and I do our best of course, but we haven't the time or the skills – or the inclination, to be honest – to mollycoddle better. And we can't have anyone else come in and find out our secret now, can we?"

"But Evie's letter said there was a woman . . ."

"That addled alcoholic? She rather overdid it one night so we had to . . . let her go. No. Poor lad. He could do with a bit of motherly love. So what do you say, Helen? Your choice."

"I don't have a choice. I've told you. I don't have Izzie."

Cameron's eyebrow raised as he looked at her. "Interesting. You don't *have* Izzie. A few moments ago, Izzie was dead; now, you simply don't have her."

"*Because* she's dead, Cameron. Dead. How many times do I have to tell you?"

"Don't distress yourself, dear Helen. Take some time. Calm yourself. I'll be back." Cameron waved a hand in Chakanaya's direction and the tall man bundled the boy back into the car. Ross showed no emotion, barely moved of his own volition, allowed himself to be pushed and prodded like a piece of meat. Senseless. Unfeeling.

"Why are you doing this, Cameron? Why are you bartering like this with our children's lives?"

"But they're not *our* children, are they, Helen? They're yours. Yours and dear old Greg's. Which means I might not get a look in. David, on the other hand, now there's a son a man can be proud of, a chip off the old block. We had an interesting conversation the other day. You know he's just at that age where he really begins to grasp things, to understand the wider implications, the nuances of what's being said. No child any longer, that one. No. Not at all."

"You've . . . Oh God, no Cameron. You've told him."

"Well, I rather think he had a right to know, don't you? There he was, the poor lad, mourning his mother, or so he thought. He needed to know. Soften the blow of your loss if he realised you weren't his mother at all. So of course I told him. And do you know what he said? The first thing he asked when I'd finished our sorry little tale? 'Who else knows?' he asked. 'Who else knows?'"

Cameron's laugh was chilling to Helen, who was still watching the sleek black car, all its doors now firmly closed, the tinted windows as black and concealing as the night-time sky that was even now beginning to darken around them. *Ross*.

"We'll work well together, me and my boy. He's a bright kid. More like me than I'd thought. But more . . . obedient. And young enough still to mould. I like that."

"So why would you want Izzie?"

"If she were alive, you mean?" he mocked. "Backup. Insurance. Never does any harm to have a Plan B. I'd love that child as if she were my own, of course, and I'm sure she'd do everything she could to keep her dear father happy. Including letting me control the small matter of the family fortune. And a daughter can be useful in cementing an alliance. A Chakanaya alliance, perhaps."

"No, Cameron. I won't let you do this."

"Really? And just how are you going to stop me?"

"I'll come forward. I won't stay dead. Then the company's mine, the money's mine, the children too."

"And much good it will all do you from a prison cell." Cameron smiled at her. "Attempted murder of your own child. That I'm sure will carry a very, very long sentence. And make for a particularly unpleasant time of it inside. I understand the criminal sorority are not too keen on baby killers."

"That's not what happened, Cameron, and you know it. I'll tell the truth. That you fired the gun—"

"That the gun discharged after you recklessly pushed your child at me, using him as a weapon at worst, a shield at best. That I did everything I could to help the boy after you'd dropped the gun and run off, intent on saving your own skin as the mudslide began, without a second thought for any of your children—"

"But that's nonsense! You threw Ross at *me*—"

"I did? So you fired the weapon directly at your own child?"

"No. No, that's not it at all. I was trying to save him!"

"Not sure a jury would see it like that."

"It'll be my word against yours, and with your reputation—"

"Don't forget the eyewitness account, my dear."

Helen felt icicles stabbing at the back of her eyes. What was he talking about?

"Ah. I see Evie didn't tell you about that. Yes, Helen. That's right. A witness. Someone who saw the whole thing through the door little Ross left wide open when he came running in, too frightened to knock or to push it to behind him."

"But the door . . . it wasn't . . . Who could have . . ."

"Darling, surely you remember? Richard had brought me home, hadn't he? He was coming up to warn us of the danger, urge us to make good our escape when he happened upon our little domestic drama. Saw everything, didn't he, heard every word. And you know what that man's memory is like – astonishing. Verbatim, photographic, whatever."

"Richard wasn't anywhere near the house that night."

"Well, his written affidavit says otherwise."

"His *what*?"

"And we can't really expect you to remember very clearly. You were very distraught, darling, and we had been having cocktails, maybe one or two more than we should have done. And then there was all that laudanum you'd been taking for your nerves as well, as Dr Tembe will testify. Made you forgetful, and temperamental, as your poor maid Felicia knew only too well. Who would have thought someone as gentle and caring as you would strike a servant? Amazing what drugs and alcohol can do to a person. And amazing too how much people can remember when you ask them nicely, motivate them well, to think very, very carefully."

"What are you saying? You've *bribed* these people?"

"Heavens, no. What an ugly word. No, no. They only needed a little encouragement, support, in advance of their testimony. After all, it's only right that the truth be properly recognised. It takes courage to come forward and speak out against someone of Helen Buchanan's standing." He smiled, leant back against the verandah

297

railing, feigning an interest in his perfectly clean nails. "Incidentally, darling, you were right. Felicia's son is a bright boy and he'll make a marvellous doctor, I'm sure, with that scholarship to medical school in the States. Dr Tembe was only too happy to provide a reference, and as the newly appointed chief medical advisor to the government, his word was probably what swung it for the boy. Did you know old Tembe was Richard's uncle on his mother's side? Amazing, that family, they're simply everywhere."

"Anyone who knows me would know I'd never harm a child, hit a serv—"

"Really? Would you risk your future, your children's future, and very possibly your life itself, on that? And if so blameless, why have you been hiding out here the last few months? How do you explain that then, Helen, hmm?" He sucked air in between his teeth. "No, doesn't look good. Ask Richard, if you don't want to take my word for it. He knows everyone in the legal system, from high court judges to clerks to prison officers; he knows how these things can go. And believe me, he'd advise you to keep a very low profile. These things can be so very . . . uncertain."

"You can't frighten me. I know I'm innocent—"

"Yes, innocence. The last bastion of the naive. Or the downright stupid. Wake up, Helen. You're dead and staying that way for as long as it suits me. And that, from where I'm sitting, is highly likely to be the rest of your life. Rise up from the dead and you'll simply exchange one life sentence for another, or maybe even a noose. Either way, you won't get your old life back, or your children, unless I say so."

Helen pushed herself up from the bench reluctantly. Time to start the day. A day exactly like the one before, and the one before that. The relentless monotony of their life here would continue unabated until Izzie arrived. There was no knowing how, but that all their lives would change was certain. Hand on the doorknob,

Helen stopped and turned her face to the sky before closing her eyes and hanging her head, not quite able to go in, to wake Ross, to get them through another long, empty day. Ross needed her, needed her more than the others did, always had, even before. And she loved him, deeply, but not a day went by when she didn't remember . . .

And Izzie. How much did Izzie remember? Of her life in Africa, her escape from it? How much had she suffered? Had she cried? Had she called for her mother? For Rusty? Oh God. Helen felt the familiar guilt wash over her, burning like acid, searing its way through to her very core. Thank God for Fredi. Dear, frivolous, dependable Fredi. Helen breathed deeply, let the cool morning air fill her lungs, soothe her. He would have charmed her, distracted the little girl with some ridiculous magic trick or by inventing some outrageous drama: dressing up essential, dramatic talent optional. Yes, Izzie would have loved Fredi. But still, such a journey for such a small child. Her daughter, she knew, was a fighter, a survivor, possessed of an inner strength that had passed both her brothers by, but even so, Helen hadn't slept properly for days, not until the Mission car had wheezed over the hill again and Sister Agnes had got out, her face beaming. She'd heard from Denmark. Fredi had done it. He and his "niece" had arrived safely and had already booked passage on to Scotland to visit relatives there. Oh, what it was to have friends in the right places. Diplomatic immunity made light work of officialdom and border controls. And then he'd done it all over again, coming back for them when Ross was well enough to travel. He would have already been ill, although he'd hid it well, and she'd had no idea. The "African disease" as they'd euphemistically called it then. She'd wept when Ursula told her he was dead.

28

Ross-shire, June 17th

The single-track road coiled like a lethargic serpent beneath the craggy peaks of Stac Pollaidh and the shores of Loch Lurgainn. Lexy had seen no other vehicle for the last few miles and was beginning to wonder if she'd somehow lost her way. The possibility of taking the wrong road seemed remote, though, as there'd been no alternative to this for several miles. Indeed, the last turning that was anything but a track or glorified footpath had been over half an hour ago. Nonetheless, she pulled into a passing place in the unlikely event that there'd be anything coming behind her on this godforsaken road and opened the map she'd bought when she'd filled up with petrol before leaving Inverness, a prudent move she was relieved she'd made, as roadside service opportunities had been as non-existent as traffic jams. Or traffic lights, come to that. There'd been none of those since Inverness either.

She pulled the map across from the passenger seat but instead of opening it let it rest in her lap as she looked around her. She rolled her neck and heard the cracks of tension snap like kindling. She'd been travelling for nearly twenty-four hours and the inside of her eyelids felt like they'd been pebble-dashed, as if she'd been drinking too much caffeine, even though she'd had nothing but half a polystyrene cupful of lukewarm watery tea on the train from King's Cross. She was exhausted but too jittery to sleep.

But perhaps she should just rest up for a little, anyway. This road was treacherous to the uninitiated, and that was certainly Lexy.

She woke up with a start as a rusty red pickup rattled past, a blast on the horn suggesting annoyance at finding her parked at the side of the road. It was a passing place, not a parking one, and perhaps the locals took badly to tourists using them for snoozes.

The cricks in her neck were even louder this time as she rolled her head from side to side to help her come to. The sun was in her eyes now, lower on the horizon. Seemed she hadn't been too jittery to sleep after all. Nearly an hour of unconsciousness hadn't improved things, though, and if anything she felt worse. The hangover without the party.

She shook herself awake and checked the map. As far as she could see she hadn't taken any wrong turnings. There had been none to take. It looked like it was straight ahead to the end of the road, or a T-junction at least. Things might get a bit trickier after that.

She turned the key in the ignition, and as the engine kicked into life, she glanced at the digital clock on the dashboard: 20.53. Long late evenings this far north. She was thankful for that. The road was anything but straight ahead as it meandered up and down and through twists and turns that alternated between being mesmeric and nauseating. Occasional sheep slowed her progress and she had to concentrate hard. This wasn't a style of driving her city upbringing had accustomed her to, nor was the road itself in any condition to encourage speed. She juddered and jolted past shimmering lochs and the green lower slopes of mountains she could see in her peripheral vision, but nothing was encouraging her to take her eyes off the road.

Eventually the mountains fell behind and the landscape opened into flatter terrain. The car rattled over a cattle grid and then a small bridge over a river tumbling its way down to the open sea on her left. The road widened so Lexy slowed and risked a sweep of her eyes over the open country. The road was straighter here,

301

stretching like a grey ribbon across a flat plain. Far ahead of her she could see the red pickup again, all but throwing up clouds of dust in its wake as it sped through the green expanse, silhouetted against the low evening sun. As the thin ribbon of road swept down toward the promised T-junction, the pickup turned left and she found herself mildly disappointed. She'd seen no other cars, no sign at all of any living being, for the last hour and there was something comforting about knowing she wasn't entirely alone, even if its horn had shattered her slumber.

But at the junction Lexy turned right, driving into a blood-orange sky streaked with purples and deep blues as the sun glowed and dipped behind a headland. She wondered how long she had before darkness fell, *if* it fell at all this far north. She was regretting her gung-ho decision to leave Inverness so late in the day. She should have checked in to a hotel for the night and then headed out in the morning. Still, the Cul Beg Hotel, the only hotel Google had offered her on this remote peninsula, couldn't be far now.

And there it was. A weather-blasted green board with almost illegible gold letters rusted by rain, a hand-painted white arrow on a thin piece of ply tacked to the post beneath it and another murderous shriek from a cattle grid at the foot of the track leading up to the small hotel, and she was finally there. She hoped she wouldn't be too late for dinner. She'd seen nothing resembling a shop of any description and doubted it would be the kind of hotel that had a room-service menu. She pulled her bag out of the back seat and reached in for her jacket. As she shrugged it on she was surprised to hear the sound of a car. She looked up and saw a red pickup slow down and pause at the entrance to the hotel and then speed away again. Strange. Disconcerting, in fact. How many vehicles of any description had she seen since she'd turned off the main road, and what were the odds of seeing two rust buckets like that in such a remote area within ten minutes of each other? Probably about the same as her getting locked in a room with a snake, or her mother being killed in a hit-and-run, or Ursula falling down the stairs.

She pulled her jacket tighter around her. Had she been followed all the way from Malawi? *To* Malawi?

She didn't want to pursue that thought. She wouldn't let her own suspicions intimidate her, scare her into giving up now. Not when she was so close to finding out the truth, the last piece of her particular puzzle. She was tired, overwrought. Maybe it *was* just coincidence. After all, it was a rural area, hardly affluent, and perhaps strangers were such a rarity that any unrecognised car merited a second look. But she doubted it.

With one last look back down the driveway, she picked up her bag and walked briskly into the sanctuary of the gloomy hotel.

An hour later she scraped the last of the lukewarm cream of tomato soup onto her spoon and swallowed, grimacing as she did so. Never one of her favourites, but there had been little choice. None, in fact. She crammed the last triangle of sliced bread spread with margarine into her mouth and reminded herself to be thankful. The night porter or whoever he was hadn't offered anything other than the restaurant opening hours, which were long past. She'd had to push hard for this impromptu supper, for which she would no doubt be charged a king's ransom, but, as Izzie would say, *beggars can't be choosers*. Nutritional content zero, but at least she wouldn't feel guilty about ordering the full Scottish breakfast in the morning. She'd need all her strength to confront her uncle and, she hoped, her grandmother.

29

Taigh na Mara, June 18th

Helen stared at the door. The echo of the knocker still reverberated around her in the cold stone-floored hallway.

It wasn't Izzie.

For a moment she'd thought it was, the long curls swinging, the features blurred with distance, slowly coming into focus as the woman walked up the track from her car towards the house. But as she drew nearer, Helen's mind began to work. This woman was too young. This wasn't Izzie. It couldn't be. It was a version of her, perhaps, but it wasn't Helen's baby girl. She rebuked herself – of course it wouldn't be. In Helen's memory Izzie was a toddler, but in real life that toddler had grown into a woman, a middle-aged woman, with a child of her own.

Helen had gasped and stepped back from the window, stumbled into the windowless sanctuary of the hallway. It was Izzie's daughter. That woman had to be Izzie's daughter. Why? Why hadn't Izzie come? Was she so angry, so unforgiving that she wouldn't come herself, that she'd sent this young—

The knock on the door had stopped her thoughts. She had a decision to make. Izzie would have known she was expected, so Helen couldn't very well pretend not to be there. Or could she? No precise date or time had been arranged. But what if Ross appeared from the workshop? He was usually so absorbed in his work that he was hard to distract. But this. A car, then a knocking at the croft door. It was so unusual even he—

The knock came again, louder this time, more impatient. What should she do? She pressed herself back against the wall behind the coat stand as the letter box rattled and lifted.

"Hello? Hello? Anyone in?"

The letter box flapped shut again. Helen's heart was racing, her hands shaking. Why was she so frightened? She'd agreed to see Izzie, so why was she so reluctant to see Izzie's daughter, her own granddaughter?

But this woman was a stranger. And even though Helen knew Izzie, the grown Izzie, was a stranger to her too, there was a connection. She'd held Izzie in her arms, loved her. And Izzie had loved her back. This woman at her door had no reason to love Helen. The woman who had abandoned her mother, refused to reclaim her, let her grow up an orphan when all the time—

More knocking. And the letter box again. Then a voice.

"I know you're in there. Please! Just open the door. Let me speak to you."

Helen knew she wouldn't give up. She had no choice really. But she didn't have to admit to anything.

"Yes?" Helen's voice was cold, her head tilted as she peered down her nose to the woman on the doorstep below her.

"Oh. Thank you. I'm looking for . . . Are you . . . are you Helen Buchanan?"

"No."

"Oh." The younger woman looked surprised, lost for words. Helen took her chance, stepped back and started to close the door.

"No!" A hand shot out to hold the door back. Helen looked at it pointedly, avoiding the eyes that were so like Izzie's staring up at her in puzzlement, doing her best to keep her face completely expressionless, to suppress the curiosity that was surging through her. Praying all the while that Ross would stay where he was.

"Please, wait. I . . . I think you are."

Helen didn't move.

"I've seen photos, you see. Old ones. And . . . and . . ." The

305

younger woman swallowed, cleared her throat. "And I can see my mother in you. I'm Lexy. Izzie's daughter, you see, and I just want to—"

"I've no idea what you're talking about. I don't welcome visitors. Take your hand off the door and leave, please."

"But I'm your granddaughter!"

"I don't have a granddaughter. And I've asked you to leave."

The younger woman's face moved from puzzlement to anger, as quick to change mood, as revealing of that mood, as Helen knew her own face used to be. Until she'd mastered the mask she now presented to the outside world.

"No! I won't. Why are you being like this? I know you were expecting my mother."

Helen caught her breath, and the younger woman leapt on it.

"See? I'm right. You were, and I've come because . . . I've been looking for you and because . . . she . . . My mother . . ."

Tears welled in the visitor's eyes. Helen watched her struggle to contain them, struggle to find the words to finish her sentence. Despite herself, Helen felt compassion. She wanted to reach out and touch this girl, this woman, comfort her. Yet she couldn't, was too afraid.

"You're mistaken," Helen began. "I can't help you and I think you should leave."

"My mother's dead."

The words fell like stones onto the doorstep between them. The young woman dropped her hand from the door and turned away as she wiped tears from her eyes. The hands dropped to clench in fists at her side. Helen watched this as if in slow motion as her own brain struggled to take in the words. She knew, of course she knew, this was Lexy, Izzie's daughter, so if this woman was saying her mother was dead, then it meant Izzie was—

Helen slammed the door, pressed her back against it, breathed hard. It couldn't be true, could it? Izzie dead? Why wouldn't

Ursula have told her? Why would Ursula have arranged for Izzie to visit, hounded Helen until she agreed to meet her daughter? Why?

There was a thudding at the door.

"Open up! Don't shut the door in my face! I need to talk to you. I need to understand. Why did you do this? Why did you all lie to me?" The voice was shrill, ranting, shouting.

"Go away!" Helen shouted back through the door. "I don't want you here!"

"Please! I need to know. I . . . There's no one left to ask. My mother . . . Ursula . . . they're dead. I don't know . . ."

The words faded as Helen shook her head to try to clear it. Ursula? Ursula was dead too? What had happened? Why? How? This wasn't happening. It couldn't be. If Ursula was dead, and Izzie too . . . Oh God. She couldn't deal with this. She needed time to take it all in.

"Please! Open up. I'm not going to leave until I've talked to you. I'm going to sit here on this bench all day, all night if I have to, but you will talk to me." The woman was clearly crying, her voice catching as she forced the words out. Helen was stunned. Unsure. Frozen to the spot.

★

Lexy shivered. Despite the watery sun on her face, the air was cool and damp and chilled her. She wasn't sure how long she'd been sitting there, but her legs were stiff and her back was beginning to ache. The wooden slats of the bench groaned as she shifted her weight, stretched out her legs, wondered if she'd be able to make good on her threat to stay here until Helen agreed to see her. She knew Helen must have worked out who she was, so why wouldn't she speak to her? If she'd been prepared to talk to Izzie then why not to Izzie's daughter? It didn't make sense. But then very little about this whole crazy scenario made sense. She opened her eyes, let them settle on the mountain ridge in the distance, a faint shimmer of silver on the sea beneath them in her peripheral vision. It was so peaceful here. If she could just stop her mind racing and relax, if she could just pretend none of this was happening, if she could—

A movement to her left snapped her out of her reverie. Sitting upright, she swivelled round, just in time to see the door of the low adjacent building click shut. Someone had been watching her. She shivered again, not from the damp this time. Hugging her coat tightly around her, she stood, waited.

The door creaked a little, then opened a crack. Fingers appeared bent round its edge, then a head stooped to peer out at her. A man. Middle-aged, yet . . . It had to be him.

"Hello, Ross," she said, gratified to see the face break into a smile. If she'd needed any further proof, she had it. Helen couldn't keep up this pretence. Not if Lexy had Ross on her side, and he looked a good deal friendlier than Helen had. "I'm Lexy."

The man's grin spread even wider and he pulled the door fully open, stood filling the doorframe. He was tall, broad, thick-haired, with just the beginnings of grey at the temples. They might have had different fathers, but there was a clear similarity between him and David. Ross was what a fit and healthy David might have been and David what a pampered, monied Ross could have become.

Ross was twisting something over in his hands, looking down at them, with just occasional glances up at Lexy. Shy, she realised. But then, how often did visitors come to this remote hideout? Or was it something more . . .

"What's that?" Lexy asked, starting towards him, stopping abruptly as he clasped his hands to his chest and stepped back from the threshold, shaking his head vigorously.

"It's okay." She realised she'd frightened him. "I won't come any further unless you say I can. I'd just like to talk to you. I'd like you to be my friend."

Ross kept his head down, but Lexy could see that he was grinning again.

"Would you like that, Ross? To be my friend?"

He looked up at her, nodded briefly, then dropped his head again.

She took a step nearer to him, holding her hands up in front of her. He swung his head to one side, looked up at her. The grin was gone, but he didn't look frightened so she took another step, and another.

"Can I see that?" She pointed to his clasped hands. "Is it something special?" He opened his hands a little, looked at whatever it was he was holding, turned and stepped back into the narrow building.

Lexy paused at the threshold, then pushed the door fully open. It was a workshop, a studio of some sort. She slowly took it in. Canvasses: blank, half-finished, full of rich and exotic colours that were a far cry from the landscape that surrounded them. A smell of turpentine and something else she wasn't familiar with but which seemed appropriate to the setting. A greyish dust covered most of the floor; her eyes followed it to where it was thickest and saw a potter's wheel, and then noticed the shelves running across the back wall, packed with small figurines, some painted, some glazed, some still pale grey, almost all of them birds.

"Can I come in?"

Ross looked at the object in his hand, then up at her again, head on one side. Then shook his head.

"Please? I won't touch anything. I just want to look. You have such beautiful things here. I'd like to see."

Ross was looking down into his hands again, mumbling something Lexy couldn't make out, but her heart leapt. It was a start.

"I'm sorry, Ross, could you say that again?"

"See-cret." He said the word slowly, two distinct syllables.

"Secret?" Lexy prompted.

"See-cret." Ross was nodding now. "In-side."

"Oh I see. But I can keep a secret. I won't tell anyone. I promise. I just want to look. Can I come in?"

Ross frowned for a moment, then smiled and nodded his head, stepping back to let her pass him as she walked towards the centre of the room. The low ceiling had had glass panels fitted along its rear, south-facing slope and the watery sun filtered through dust to fill the room with as much light as possible. Lexy recognised the other smell as her eyes landed on the gas heater in the far corner, its heat welcome but having little effect on the overall temperature of the room, on the damp of years that had seeped into the thick walls.

She stepped over to the birds clustered on the shelves like migrating flocks on telegraph wires. Like starlings, she thought, but they were seagulls and puffins, mainly. She realised as she stood closer that there were other items too, not just birds. Small bowls and plates decorated with thistles and heather; miniature croft houses and byres, not dissimilar to this one, in bas-relief against mountains and hills; even a few sheep and the odd Highland cow. Tourist fare, she thought, wondering if this was how Helen survived if money ever failed to arrive from Malawi. And another shelf near the bottom was filled with familiar green-and-blue vases, thistles freshly glazed, and exactly like the one on Ursula's draining board, the one in Izzie's hallway.

The paintings were different, though. Not at all what she would associate with the Scottish Highlands. These, she realised with a shock, were African. A more refined version of the prints that had adorned the walls of the hotel in Malawi. Leaning forward to look more closely, she was surprised to see the initials in the corner were not those she'd expected but "RM".

310

"Did you do these, Ross?" she asked, looking back at him over her shoulder. He nodded. "They're very good." He nodded again, then came over towards her.

He opened his hands, and on his palm sat a figurine of a small bird. No seagull, this one. No stranger either: she'd seen one before. Two, in fact. Identical birds. Honeybirds, she now knew.

"Ross! This is . . . Where did you get this?" She looked around her. There were no others like this in the studio. "Ross?"

Ross put the bird down on the bench in front of them. He stepped back. Watching him carefully, Lexy reached a hand tentatively towards it.

"May I?" When he didn't react, she picked it up, turned it over in her fingers. It was exactly the same as the ones she had seen in—

"I asked you to leave."

Lexy spun round, felt colour flood her cheeks.

"I was just—"

"You should leave. Ross, come here. Give me the bird. You know you're not allowed to play with that one."

"She. Asked."

"Did she." Helen's eyes were black as she kept them fixed on Lexy; she reached her hand out to Ross and drew him in beside her.

"I'm sorry," Lexy began. "I did. But I was curious. I've seen one before. Two actually. My mother had one. And there was one in Ursula's flat. Identical. So I wanted to look. Bit of a coincid—"

"It doesn't mean a thing. I've been making and selling birds for years. All over the place. Anyone could buy one."

Lexy looked around her. "Birds, yes. But not honeybirds. It's special, isn't it? Why would Ursula and my mother both—"

"Leave us alone! Just go. Get out. I don't want you here." Ross

311

began to whimper. "Shh, Ross. It's all right. I didn't mean to frighten you. Let's go into the house. Come on, darling." She turned the hunched man towards the door, pinned Lexy with one more glare. "See what you've done? Get out. And don't come back."

Helen waited outside the door, Ross hiding his face in her arms, until Lexy reluctantly stepped outside. Helen then locked the door, pocketed the key and led Ross slowly into the house, without another word.

Lexy looked after them, angry and frustrated. But above all, puzzled. It wasn't the reception she'd expected. None of it had gone quite as she'd thought it would. And the honeybirds had really thrown her. She'd assumed they were some souvenir Ursula or her mother had acquired in Malawi. But what if they'd been made here, in a croft in the Highlands? Didn't that prove that there was a connection between them all? How could Helen deny it?

Lexy walked back down the track to her car, deep in thought. She leant against the bonnet and looked back up at the small, low croft house, thinking about the people inside. Her grandmother and her uncle. She was sure of it. She'd find a way of forcing Helen to acknowledge her. Her grandmother owed her that much at least. She sighed and pushed herself off the bonnet, turned towards the driver's door, searching her pockets for keys. As her fingers clasped the metal, though, she realised she was too restless, too upset to go back to the hotel. She needed to regroup, work out what to do next, true, but she'd been cooped up in lawyers' offices, planes, cars, hospital rooms for days. She looked around her at the towering mountains, the wild expanse of heather-tufted slopes, and out over the glimmering ocean towards islands as quiet and tranquil as a lazy Sunday afternoon. She could think while she walked. She needed air and space and to feel free for a while. Dropping the keys back into her pocket, she brushed her hair back off her face and turned down towards the beach that curved like a smile beneath her.

An hour later and she was feeling better as she climbed up the path back towards her car. Her breath came in heavy spurts as she planted one foot above the other, hands pressing down on thighs to give herself leverage. She still didn't know what she was going to do, but she felt clearer, more confident she'd find a way of making Helen acknowledge her. As the track toward the car evened out, so did her breathing. Up ahead, she noticed for the first time the bank of rhododendrons to the left of the croft. Not azaleas, blazing in glorious colour in her imagination in African sunshine, but Scottish rhododendrons peeking round the corner of a white-washed Highland croft house. This was where the photo of Helen and Ursula holding a baby between them had been taken.

The car was silhouetted against the trees, the fading sun playing over the bonnet as the leaves and branches danced in the breeze that had sprung up. As she watched the patterns swirl ahead of her, she saw one darker patch that didn't move, a small speck just ahead of the wing mirror. Intrigued, she quickened her pace. There *was* something there. It wasn't until she had nearly reached the car that she realised what it was: one of the birds, the first one Ross had shown her. She picked it up, turned it over in her hand, then looked around her.

"Ross? Ross, are you still here?" she called softly, stepping towards the thicket of trees. "Is this for me? Ross?"

The trees danced and shadows swayed, but she couldn't see anyone, until there was a sudden burst of cracking undergrowth and her uncle's childlike face appeared from behind the trunk of an oak.

"Present," he said, and laughed. "You." Then he disappeared and she heard him running back towards the house.

313

Back at the hotel, Lexy lay on her bed, hands above her head, counting the circles that had been painstakingly crafted in the Artex ceiling. Wondering why. Trying to focus on anything except the fact that her grandmother didn't want to know her. That her last living relative, her mother's mother, had refused to acknowledge her. Weeks of grief and trauma, of death and shocks, of sweltering African sun and relentless Highland mist, and it had come to this: lying alone on a lumpy bed in a draughty room in a faded hotel in the middle of nowhere. Not even counting sheep, for God's sake.

It would be easy to cry, to give in to the despair that gripped her gut, twisted it, wrenched it when she least expected it. It would be easy to feel sorry for herself, to howl out her anger, her fear. Easy to give in. But there was no one to hear her. No one to care. If she got herself into a state, she'd only have to get herself out of it again. Life didn't just stop. Although right now she almost wished it had. Before she'd had to accept that her last living relatives had rejected her. Blood wasn't thicker than water, although it was certainly more impenetrable. Why had she even begun all this? It was her own fault that she was lying here miserable and alone. She couldn't blame her mother, or Ursula, for this. She was the one who'd gone haring off on her heroic quest to find the long-lost son, and look where that had got her. Idiot. She wanted to wave a white flag at the universe, at everything she felt was conspiring against her. Give up.

Light was still glowing outside her curtains. Twilight now. Or the gloaming, as her mother had called it. Izzie had loved it. Said she'd missed it so desperately, the years she'd been in Africa.

"No time to readjust," she'd explained to Lexy, "One minute it's blazing sunshine and the next it's darkest night. Like a switch has been flipped. Always one thing or another. I like things to merge a little, to let day seep into night, gently, so we can get used to the idea of change."

Lexy had always throught she'd been black or white, one thing or the other, but now realised she would have liked to have had the chance to get used to the idea of change too, to say goodbye to her mother, to come to terms with her death, with the discovery of a family she'd known nothing about. She would have liked, most of all, the chance to ask them all why. Why had no one told her who she was? Why had she been lied to all her life?

She felt her brain chug into motion again, churning the same questions over and over, like a hopper straining to throw out an answer, a grain of truth or hope she could cling on to and feel it was hers. Not letting her give up and lie quiet. Exasperated, she rubbed her eyes, then flung an arm out to the bedside table to put on the lamp, banish the shadows that were gathering in the corners.

Water splattered over her arm and the bedcover as her hand struck the heavy glass she'd left there and sent it tumbling to the ground, her phone straight after it as her clumsy hand tried to snatch the glass back.

"Damn!" Throwing her legs round to stand, her foot kicked the glass and what remained of its contents, sending it spinning across the floor, leaving a darkening trail on the fuschia carpet, like blood splatter in a horror movie.

"Bugger, bugger, bugger and blast!"

It felt childishly good to vent her rage with words her mother would have pulled her up on. She caught sight of herself in the mirror above the chipped pink enamel sink in the corner of the room. She looked ridiculous. Her face pouting like an adolescent, panda eyes from the mascara she'd forgotten she was wearing, hair frizzed from the omnipresent dampness.

She sighed. Picked up the glass and set it down on the edge of the sink, looked for her phone. She sat back on the bed with it resting in her hands on her lap. She looked down at it.

No.

She couldn't.

She threw it down on the bed behind her. Sighing again, she walked over to the window, looked down to the water in front of the hotel, then over to the mountain ridge that separated this small bay from the next, from the red-roofed workshop and the low white croft house where her grandmother and uncle lived. She was sure of it. She had to find a way of getting through to Helen. Ross had seemed to like her, as far as she could tell. That was a start, wasn't it? Maybe that was the way to reach Helen. Through her son. Her damaged son. Was that why she stayed hidden here? To protect him from ... from what? Life? He seemed happy enough, making pots, painting the birds, his pictures. African scenes, locked away in his memory. How could he possibly know about those if he hadn't lived there as a child? Helen must have known Lexy had seen them.

She looked round for her bag, pulled out the small ceramic honeybird, so familiar, identical to her mother's. She ran her finger over the white initials on the base. HBM. *Honey Bird Malawi*, perhaps? Or something else? Did her mother's have that on the base too? She'd never looked, but that would prove it, wouldn't it? That they were connected somehow. It wasn't chance. Her mother and Ursula had got their birds from Helen. She was sure of it.

She strode over to the bed, snatched up the phone and pressed the contacts button.

No. She couldn't. It wasn't fair. But she didn't want to go all the way back to London. She couldn't risk it. What if Helen took Ross away somewhere? If she was really rattled and thought Lexy was going to expose her, she might do something drastic. No. Lexy had to stay here. Had to go back to the cottage tomorrow to try again. With or without the bird. But better, so much better, *with*.

She tapped a contact, put the phone to her ear, paced up and down as it rang.

"Danny? Danny it's me, Lexy."

316

"As it says on my screen."

"Danny, I want—"

"Fine, thanks for asking. How about you?"

It really irritated her when he did that, but she ignored it. He'd learnt it from her.

"Yes, sorry. Danny, hi, how— Oh, I haven't got time for this. Danny, I need your help."

"Now why doesn't that surprise me?"

"Danny, please. Look I know you don't have to help me. That you're probably still angry with me. And that I deserve it, but please, I really need you to help—"

"Stop it, Lexy. I can't bear it when you beg. You know I'll help. Boringly dependable, you always used to say, right? What is it?"

She sighed with relief. She wouldn't have blamed him for hanging up on her. But was so glad he hadn't.

"Remember my mother's honeybird?"

"No." He sounded puzzled.

"Yes, you do. The little ceramic bird that used to sit by her bedside. The one I took with me the day we . . . When we were there after the hospital . . . I think I left it in the car."

"You did. I boxed it up with the other bits and pieces I had of yours. With your mother's ashes." The rebuke was clear. She ignored it.

"Good, so it's with Mrs B then? Do you think you could get it and send it up to me?"

"Up? In Malawi? Where the heck are you now?"

"Scotland. It's urgent, Danny. I wouldn't ask, but it's really important. Can you send it by overnight courier? Here – I'll give you the hotel address. Got a pen?"

She picked up a tea-stained piece of hotel stationery and rattled off the address, which was little more than the name of the hotel and a postcode. She could imagine him frowning as he painstakingly wrote the details down.

"I'm scared to ask, Lexy, I really am, but what in God's name are you doing?"

"It's complicated."

"Of course it is. And I thought running off to Malawi was weird. What do you want a ceramic bird so urgently for in the Highlands of Scotland? You weren't that bothered about it before, just left it to roll under the seat of the car."

"I need to know who made it. I want to see if it's got any initials on its base." Lexy thought she could hear scrabbling in the background.

"Well it does. HBM."

"Really?" Suddenly it fell into place. *HBM*. Helen's initials, just like on the other one. "That's fantastic. I still need it though. Can you send . . ." Her voice trailed off as a thought occurred to her. "How do you know, Danny?"

"Because I'm look—" She heard Danny's sharp intake of breath.

"Where are you, Danny?" She could hear nothing. She knew he was still holding his breath. "Danny, are you at Mrs B's? What are you doing there?"

"I . . . she gave me the key . . . asked me to move the box . . . so I've put it in the hall . . ."

"Oh my God. You're in my flat. What the hell—"

"Technically, it's still *our* flat," Danny interrupted. "You haven't signed the papers. Just one of the many bureaucratic chores you left undone when you ran away to Malawi."

"Danny, don't be so bloody pedantic, and I didn't run—" She registered she was swearing again but was too rattled to care. "What the hell are you doing in my flat?"

"Well, after the burglary, I said I'd clear—"

"That was days ago, Danny. How long does it take, for Christ's sake?"

He sighed. She waited, her mind trying to make sense of this latest turn of events.

318

"I moved back in."

"*What?* Oh, don't tell me . . . not in my flat. I don't want that woman anywhere near my—"

"On my own."

"She chucked you out?" Lexy gave a snort of laughter although she was far from amused, then immediately regretted it. "Oh Danny, I'm so sorry. What happened? The baby . . . ?"

"There is no baby."

"Danny, that's awful, I'm—"

"Turns out there never was. She just wanted to make me make a commitment, she said. I'd no idea someone would make up a thing like that. It never occurred to me . . . anyway. When the associate professorship went to Paul Manders, she realised I wasn't the love of her life after all. He is."

"You didn't get tenure? But I thought it was in the bag?"

"Apparently not. I'm as bad a judge of faculty politics as I am of women, it would seem."

"Don't say that, Danny. You're not a bad—" Despite herself, Lexy found herself feeling a little sorry for him. She knew how much his work meant to him, and she also knew how hard he tried to do the right thing. But then he should never have slept with Fizz in the first place. Her anger came back with a vengeance. "Danny, you can't just crawl back to *my* flat when you have a tiff with your adolescent girlfriend."

"I know, I'm sorry. I just need a place to stay for a bit until I can find somewhere to rent. And Mrs B was really pleased the flat wouldn't be empty. She's still a bit shaken about what happened. That's why she gave me the key. Well, that and I told her you were okay with it."

"You *lied*?" Lexy's shock was more to do with the fact she hadn't thought him capable of subterfuge than outrage at him blagging his way into her home. She was almost impressed.

"Yeah. Sorry. I know I shouldn't have."

"I want you gone before I get back."

"And when exactly will that be? When exactly are you going to stop running around the place like a . . . a . . . a . . . oh, I don't know! But when are you going to face up to what's going on here? Sort out your burgled flat, your mother's ashes, the whole damned shooting match of responsibilities that entails, not to mention tying up the ends of our relationship. Hmm, Lexy? When exactly will that be?"

"I don't know!" Lexy shouted, surprised by how much he'd wound her up. "You know what? Just go. Go now. I want you out of there—"

"Before or after I send up your precious little bird by overnight courier to the arse end of the country?" Danny shouted back. Danny *shouted*. But she hardly registered it in the maelstrom of her own emotion.

"Just send it and get out!" But it was too late. The line was dead.

30

Ross-shire, June 19th

It wasn't quite eight o'clock, but the dining room was empty. Crumbs of black pudding and the deepening orange of drying egg yolk adorned the empty plates at the next table, turning Lexy's stomach. She was too wound up to have much appetite, but breakfast had seemed a way of killing time until the courier arrived with her mother's ceramic honeybird. She knew Danny wouldn't let her down, no matter how angry he'd been with her. She helped herself to muesli from the Victorian sideboard that had been pressed into service as a breakfast bar, hesitated at the few remaining fragments of tinned grapefruit before moving on to pour herself a half glass of pale apple juice. Diluted, she was sure.

Not that it mattered. She pushed the muesli around with her spoon, sinking sultanas beneath the surface of too much milk and watching them pop up again, finally putting the spoon back down on the tacky place mat. Propping her chin on her hand, she gazed out of the window at another dreich day. *Dreich.* The only Scots word she knew, but one that Isobel had taught her, especially, she'd said, for their trips to Edinburgh. It had made the bad weather, the relentless damp of the haar in from the sea, more exciting, exotic somehow, something they were privileged to experience and never could at home in London. Lexy smiled. Nonsense, of course. Just another of the half-truths her mother had told her. The smile faded. Half-truths. Lies. What was the difference? Had her mother ever been totally honest with her?

The door to the kitchen swung open and for a few seconds the sound of the dishwasher burst into the silence as the only member of staff Lexy had so far encountered that morning came in with her tea.

"Has there been anything delivered for me?" Lexy asked anxiously as the teapot was dumped in front of her without a word from the waiter, or even a smile. Lexy didn't care. She didn't have time for small talk either.

"Like what?"

"I've arranged for a package to be couriered to me from London. Overnight."

"Oh well, that won't be here till tomorrow then."

"No, no. I arranged for it yesterday, to come overnight *last* night," Lexy explained impatiently.

"So it will be here tomorrow." He finally smiled at her, no doubt amused by the consternation on her face. "We don't have overnight services up here. It all goes to Inverness and the couriers all hand it over to Archie's lot. They're the only ones that come this far north – consolidate it, you see."

"But . . . but that's not overnight then . . . I mean . . ."

"It does fine for us and it's the best you get up here. Nothing's ever really that urgent anyway, is it?" He disappeared through the swinging door, his exit again accompanied by a fanfare of mechanical humming from the dishwasher.

Yes it is, Lexy wanted to scream after him. She had to have that bird. She pushed back her chair, coffee spitting from the spout of the pot as she did so, and glared out of the window. At the nothingness of this godforsaken wilderness. No wonder the couriers wouldn't come. Who would? What had seemed so beautiful and free when she'd arrived was now inhospitable, as confining as Alcatraz. She didn't want to lose another day. She could go back to Helen's today, but if she didn't have the bird to show her, to prove—

322

"Hello, Lexy." The voice was weary but still instantly recognisable. She spun round.

"Danny! Oh Danny, thank God. Did you bring it? They just told me the overnight couriers don't—"

"They don't." He cut across her. "Why do you think I'm here?"

"Have you got it?"

"Yes." He held up a backpack, dangling it by a single strap.

"Let me have—"

Danny threw the backpack down in front of him. It hit the carpet with a thud, but, Lexy noted thankfully, no crack of smashing ceramic.

"Jeez, Lexy. Aren't you even going to ask me how I got here?"

"I . . . Sorry, Danny . . . I . . ." Her eyes were darting between his and the backpack at her feet. She was desperate to snatch it up and open it. She felt his hand close around her wrist and pull, forcing her to look at him, to connect.

"Lexy, you're behaving like a . . . like a . . . You're manic. What the heck is going on with you?"

She looked at his familiar face, shadowed with unfamiliar stubble, at his blond hair, rumpled and falling over his forehead. His clothes, too, were rumpled and he smelt a little stale. Yet, somehow, the overall effect was surprisingly good. Attractive, even. He looked like his own wilder, younger brother.

Lexy nodded, looked down, forced her racing pulse to slow. She put her hand over his on her wrist.

"I'm . . . I'm fine. Long story. But you, you look all in, Danny."

"I am. Drove all night."

She reached up and touched his face, fingertips feeling the bristles on his chin, the coolness of his skin. He hated driving. Especially at night. He leant slightly into her cupped palm. She

323

could feel the warmer air of his breath brush her skin. It was too intimate. She stepped back, dropped her hand.

Danny made a sharp sound, more snort than laugh, nudged the backpack towards her with his toe. "Take it. I'll get a room, sleep. Leave you to it, whatever it is."

Lexy grabbed his arm as he started to turn. "No. No chance. Take mine." For a moment something flickered in his eyes. "No, no." She rushed on. "I mean there are none. Hotel's full." Danny looked around in obvious disbelief.

"German tourists. Serious about bagging Munros or whatever. Out at crack of dawn."

"There must be something."

"Just come up to mine. I'll be going out and you can sleep all day."

"And be gone before you get back, right? Yeah, I know the drill. Okay. I get it."

Lexy was hugging the backpack to her. "Hmm? No, not at all. Come on, the other bird's upstairs; we can compare them."

"Are you going to tell me what's going on?"

Lexy considered him. He was exhausted, his eyes bloodshot and black-ringed. He was standing hunched, hands in the pockets of the Superman hoodie she'd bought him when they'd first started going out. She'd had no idea he still had it. But that was Danny for you. He clung on: to things, to people, to her. Refused to let go. It had driven her mad, this stubbornness, this resistance to change. But right now, she realised his steadiness, his groundedness were just what she needed.

"Yes," she said and started up the stair, knowing he would follow.

An hour later and they were both sitting on her bed, Lexy leaning against the headboard, knees drawn up to her chest, arms circled around them, Danny sitting at the foot of the bed, shoulders slumped forward, hands clasped and dangling between his legs.

"So you're saying this woman is your grandmother, and that you're her heir? Lex, it just doesn't make sense. Your mother . . . I knew her, Lex. She wouldn't have kept something like this from you. She just wouldn't."

"Unless she didn't know. Look, Danny, I know I'm right. And that little bird there is going to help me prove it."

Danny turned and picked up the bird that was sitting on the bed between them.

"And, uh, this Robert guy. He fits into this all how, exactly?"

"He's Evie's grandson. He lived with Ursula when he was studying in Ed—"

"Not what I meant."

Lexy felt colour spring to her face as she realised what he was asking. "Oh Danny, for Chrissakes! My mother's just died, I've just found out I'm not who I thought I am—"

"You can say that again."

"—and you think I have time to go falling at the feet of the first man I—"

"So you found him attractive?"

"Danny! That's not what I said and anyway I don't think you've got any . . . Oh, you know what? It's none of your business. But for what it's worth, no. Okay? No. No Robert and me, all right?"

Danny started to nod, then stopped and looked down at the small bird in his hand. He turned it over and up towards the grey light from the window.

"That's odd."

"What? What is?" Lexy scrabbled to her knees and crawled over towards him, bedsprings groaning as her weight rolled over them. She put her hand on his shoulder to pull it back a little so she could see. His finger was rubbing back and forth along the base.

"There's a ridge here. It feels slightly . . . I don't know. Almost as if it's been mended. Must have been broken at some point, I guess."

"Give me that!" Lexy snatched it from him and leapt to her feet in one fluid, feline move, as Ross's words came back to her.

See-cret, he'd said. *Secret inside.*

She tapped the bird against the top of the old chest of drawers.

"Lexy what are you doing? You'll break it!"

Danny tried to grab her arm as she raised it high above her head, ready to bring it crashing down.

"No, Lexy, don't. It was your mother's. You'll— oh!"

Lexy yanked her wrist free, stumbled backwards and tripped as her ankle banged against the leg of the heavy winged chair next to the window. Twisting as she tried to stay upright, she clutched at the chair's arm to break her fall but succeeded only in pulling it down on top of her as she landed hard on her stomach with a thud that set the bedside lamp shaking and the honeybird flying from her hand. She was sprawled on the floor like a chalked corpse in a police procedural.

"Lexy! Lexy, are you okay?" Danny was beside her in an instant and the chair was lifted away. She could feel him crouching over her, knew his forehead would be creased in a frown of alarm.

Lexy couldn't speak, couldn't open her eyes. All her energy was focused on the struggle to get air down into her lungs.

"Oh God, Lex." Danny slapped lightly at her face. "Speak to me, say something, Lex." She managed to lift a hand to stop his as she opened her eyes.

"Winded . . . Can't . . ."

Danny gently rolled her over onto her back, then stood and righted the chair before stooping down, sliding his hands under her shoulders, scooping her up and settling her gently back in the armchair. He knelt on the floor beside her, stroking her hand, the worry dancing across his face as he fussed over her, undermining the Danny-as-Tarzan fantasy that had started to take shape in her mind.

"Easy now," he was murmuring, over and over. "Just stay calm." Lexy found herself wishing he'd take his own advice.

"W . . . w . . ." She tried to speak but the sound was less than a whisper.

"Shh, don't try to talk."

"W . . ." She tried again, more urgently.

"Water? Yes, yes, of course," Danny stood looking around him. She caught the hem of his hoodie as he started toward the pink basin.

"Bird," she finally croaked. "What . . ."

"Oh, the bird . . ." They were looking around them, scanning the room, couldn't see it. Danny bobbed down onto all fours to check under the bed, the chair, the—

"Got it." His hand disappeared beneath the bedside table, retrieved it from where it was nesting against the skirting board.

"Think it's okay," he said, handing it to Lexy. "Ah. Maybe not." He handed her the beak, which had fallen off in his hand. "But a bit of glue and you'd never know."

She wasn't listening. She was peering into the hollow body of the bird through the tiny spyhole left by the broken beak.

Before he could stop her, she dropped it and stamped down on it hard. She looked at him, then slowly moved her foot. Together they looked down at the shattered bird, and saw the folded, yellowed paper that had been hidden in its shell.

Lexy's colour was returning to normal now and her breathing was shallow but strengthening.

Danny picked up the paper, shook it to remove ceramic dust and handed it to her. She shook her head.

"You," she whispered.

He sat back on his heels and slowly unfolded the paper, looking up at her for reassurance.

"Get *on* with it, Danny." Her impatience was back, along with her breath.

"It's . . . I think it's . . . a birth certificate."

"Whose?" she asked, although she thought she knew what the answer would be.

"Isobel Buchanan-Munro's."

Lexy nodded, pushed away Danny's hand as he tried to give her the paper, pushed herself out of the chair and reached into the bag she'd left on top of the chest of drawers. She pulled out the other bird.

"So what about this one?" she mused as much to herself as to Danny. Running her fingers over its base, she felt the ridge. Smiled as she turned it towards Danny. "Same thing."

She came over to the table, lifted her arm again to smash this bird too, but Danny stood.

"No, Lex. Don't smash it. This one isn't yours."

"I hardly think that matters in the circumstances."

But she let Danny take it nonetheless, her eyes widening as he pulled out a Swiss army knife from his jeans pocket. She shouldn't have been surprised. Danny the Boy Scout. Always prepared. But a Swiss army knife wasn't really something she'd expected him to possess. It was a bit too . . . rugged.

"Danny," she laughed. "Where on earth did you get that?"

"Had it for years. Thought I better bring it in case . . . in case I needed . . . Well, you know."

"Danny, this is Scotland, not the jungle," Lexy said, choosing to ignore her own earlier broodings on the hostility of the environment as she succumbed to the temptation to tease him with familiar ease.

"Yeah well. Better safe—"

"—than sorry," she finished for him, as she always had, and they both laughed briefly before an awkward silence descended.

Danny cleared his throat and sat on the bed, resting the bird on his lap as he opened a blade on the knife. Carefully, he began to scrape at the ridge, blowing the dust away from time to time and then scratching the blade a little deeper, a little deeper.

Lexy, fully recovered now, paced up and down in front of the window, dying to wrench the bird from his hands and just smash it as she'd originally intended to do. What did it matter? Helen wouldn't care – not when Lexy confronted her with the truth. She'd have much more important things to care about.

"Oh, come *on*, Danny!"

He paused briefly, then returned to his painstakingly methodical scraping. *Good grief, he's annoying,* Lexy thought. No wonder it hadn't worked between them. Look at him, chip, chip, chipping away, when all she wanted to do was grab it, smash it, get to its heart at once. Chalk and cheese, they were, night and day, tortoise and hare—

"Gotcha." Danny dropped the knife, twisted his hands in opposite directions and the bird fell neatly into two pieces, a folded yellow square falling down onto Danny's lap.

Lexy snatched it up, no longer afraid of what it might contain, anxious to read the name on what she knew would be another birth certificate. David's, it would be David's, and then she'd have all the proof she needed.

She felt the colour drain from her face, sat down in the armchair as heavily as if she were winded again.

"Lex? Lex, what is it?"

"It's not him. It's not David." She was speaking slowly, eyes running over and over the words on the page as she tried to understand them, tried to force them to spell out what she'd expected to see.

Danny came over and sat on the arm of the chair, took the paper from her.

"Sen . . . Senga? Who the hell is Senga? And what kind of a name is that anyway?"

"It's another one."

"What?"

"Another child. A fourth child. Helen had another child. Look." She pointed to the mother's name: Helen Munro. "That's her. It has to be."

"No Buchanan this time, though."

"No, and no father's name, either."

31

Taigh na Mara, June 19th

Helen had had another sleepless night. She'd been in the workshop since the small hours, glazing pots, something she usually found soothing and therapeutic. But not today. Her hands hadn't been steady and she was sure she'd spoilt at least three but wouldn't know for sure until they'd been fired. They'd start the kiln later. Ross always liked to help with that. She wiped her hands with a damp cloth, dried them on her dusty apron. Breakfast. Ross would be hungry. She paused for a moment outside the workshop, looking at the islands in the distance, sun bouncing off the water all around them. She wished she were on one of them, sometimes. This island she'd tried to maroon herself on here on the mainland not enough to keep the world at bay. Alexis had found her. Lexy. She regretted sending her away. It was the shock. She'd been expecting Izzie and hadn't known what to say to the vibrant young woman. Her granddaughter. Helen found she was hoping Lexy wouldn't give up, would try again.

The door creaked its welcome as she pushed it open.

"Ross?" she called, craning her neck up the stairs behind her as she slung her jacket over its hook. "Ross, darling? Are you up? Breakfast."

She was answered by a thump and scratch of a chair from the kitchen. "Ross? Everything all right?" She sighed. He'd be trying to make tea, to surprise her. Sometimes he managed, other times he struggled, dropped or smashed cups, spilt hot water on his hands, threw milk across the room in frustration. The metallic clatter of the kettle lid falling onto the kitchen flagstones told her which it would be today.

"Ross, I'm just coming, darl—"The kitchen door swung open and she saw Ross sitting at the table, panic on his face, and a young woman standing behind him, one hand on each of his shoulders pressing him down into the wooden chair, a smile of sorts on her face. A smile Helen felt she'd seen before.

"Ross, are you—"

"Oh, he's fine. For now." There was menace in the voice, a familiar undercurrent.

Ross whimpered. "Dropped kettle," he said.

Helen saw the water pooling near the door as it trickled its way across the uneven floor.

"Not really a good idea to leave the kitchen door unlocked, even out here. Never know who might happen along. I gave you a bit of fright there, Ross, didn't I?" The woman squeezed Ross's shoulders as she leant forward and placed her head alongside his, her eyes never leaving Helen's face. "But we're all right now, aren't we, Ross?"

Seeing the two faces side by side, one dark and puzzled, one light and smiling, Helen's eyes widened. The resemblance was there and yet . . . she was young, this woman. Too young.

"You're not . . . You can't be . . ."

"Who? Who can't I be?" The hand slid off Ross's shoulder, cupped his upper arm and pulled him closer. "We're going to be such friends, Ross, aren't we? You'd like that, wouldn't you, a friend?"

Something about her tone alarmed Helen, but Ross looked back at the smiling face and grinned, nodded vigorously. "Friend."

"That's right. Friend. Good, Ross. Very good."

Helen took a step forward, picked up the kettle lid that lay upside down at her feet, held it in both hands in front of her like a miniature shield.

"Who are you?" she repeated, although a slow nausea was building in her stomach as she began to wonder if she might already know. "What are you doing in my house?"

"I've come to visit. Family should, after all."

Helen kept her face still, her eyes steady, anything to fight the growing tide of realisation that was sweeping through her body, a physical pulse of disgust and horror. But she was too young . . . like the other one yesterday . . . Oh dear God.

"Nothing to say, Gran? Don't you even want to know your granddaughter's name?"

"You're not my granddaughter." This could not be. It wasn't possible.

"Yes, I most certainly am."

"You . . . you're . . . Alexis is my granddaughter."

"Lexy?" The woman laughed. "So she is. And I'm sure she'll be along soon, too. She's not one to give up, that cousin of mine. She's been beavering away, dig, dig, digging to get to the bottom of the scam you and your friends put together all those years ago. All I had to do was follow on behind. I feel I've come to know her quite well already. Trust me, she'll be back."

Helen slid down into a chair across the table from her son and this . . . this stranger. The cold metal lip of the kettle lid was digging into Helen's hands, the pain helping her keep her focus, take in what this familiar stranger was saying. Her mind was trying to fight what she was hearing, find a way of making it all lies . . . and yet . . . Helen knew.

"That's better, take a load off. Don't want that hip playing up, do we? Thought we could have a little family reunion later, when Cousin Lexy gets here. You'd like that, wouldn't you, Ross, a party? And Gran can tell us more about her adventures in Africa, won't that be fun?" She leant in to the bewildered man, squeezed his arm, too tightly, smiled at his yelp of pain and surprise.

"Leave him alone." Helen's voice was steady, despite the

333

adrenalin crackling through her veins. "Get out. I don't know who you are or what you—"

"Oh Gran." Even the pout was familiar, Helen realised with horror. "Don't be mean. You know who I am. Think. Think back to Malawi, to a time I know you've a tendency to forget. But I'm sure it's all still in there somewhere." She leant over, flicked Helen's forehead and laughed again as Helen gasped in shock. "Come on, Gran. You can do this."

Helen's mouth was dry, speech impossible. She shook her head slowly.

"I can see it's all coming back now. Good, good. No point in denying it, Gran, now, is there? Blood will out and all that. But how rude. I haven't told you my name. I'm Jenny, Jenny Kennedy, although that name won't mean anything to you yet, I expect."

But it did. Ursula's letters, Ursula's fears. Blood buzzed in her ears. She grabbed at the edge of the table, pushed herself back to stand, the chair legs scraping on flagstone as it fell behind her.

Jenny darted round the table, righted the chair and pushed Helen back down into it.

"No, no, Gran, don't you worry yourself. I'll do that, shall I? Put the kettle on?" Jenny plucked the kettle lid out of Helen's hands, picked the drum up from the floor at her feet. "Nice cup of tea should see us right. After all, we've a fair bit of catching up to do, haven't we?"

32

Ross-shire, June 19th

Danny watched from the window until Lexy's car disappeared over the ridge. He really wished she'd let him go with her. But as usual, he'd given in to her. And he could understand why she felt Helen might not take kindly to an audience when Lexy confronted her. He just hoped Lexy would keep her temper in check. It worried him to see her so tense, so brittle. Ready to go off on one at the slightest thing, ready to break down into tiny pieces. He was glad he'd come. Even if she wouldn't admit it, he knew she was glad he had too. But he was no fool. He knew this didn't mean she'd have him back. Whatever happened, though, he had to make sure she was okay.

He lay down on the bed, closed his eyes, but his body could still feel the juddering of the steering wheel as he'd driven at speed on motorways, more cautiously on single tracks, thumping over potholes there was no room to swerve and avoid, his eyes straining against the darkness and, later, the mist that had tumbled down off the hills rising up to either side of him as he'd neared his destination and a green-tinged sun had risen slowly behind him. And now his mind itself was still running on at a hundred miles an hour.

Was Lexy right? Was she really related to this odd woman and her retarded son, to some corporate fat cat in Malawi? Was she really an heiress to a fortune? It was so far-fetched, she might as well have claimed to have won the lottery.

Everything she'd said, every outrageous twist in her story just put her further out of his reach. And into the arms of that man Robert, no doubt, no matter what she said.

It was no good. He wasn't going to be able to sleep. Too much to think about, too unused to the barbs of jealousy snagging at his thoughts every way he turned. The flask of black coffee he'd used to fuel him during the night drive probably hadn't helped either. The light, dull and grey though it was, filtered through the thin curtains and kept reminding his overactive brain that it was day. Not sleeping time. Lexy laughed at him, called him a creature of habit, was irritated by his love of ritual and routine. And here it was again. Couldn't sleep if it was day; couldn't stay awake if it was night.

He wondered how Lexy was doing. He picked up his phone, wondered if he should call her. She'd probably only be annoyed with him, but even so . . . He tapped the screen, watched the light snap on, the screensaver resolve.

It wasn't his phone.

The cuddling kittens screensaver told him it was Lexy's. She must have taken his by mistake because he'd definitely seen her drop a phone into her bag. Typical. Never paid enough attention. Fine, he'd phone himself then.

His finger hovered over the phone icon as he hesitated, looking at the red circle protruding from another icon at the top of the screen. The green message icon. Three unopened texts. He tapped. Three unopened texts from Robert.

He dropped the phone, steepled his hands and pressed them against his lips. It took every ounce of his integrity not to read them. But what good would that do? And Lexy was right. It was none of his business any more. He stepped backwards, away from the phone to stop himself picking it up again and scrolling through it. Would there be voicemails? Emails from him? God, this was unbearable.

As if to taunt him further, the phone buzzed; the opening bars of something new, tribal, African, played loud in the quiet room as the phone danced and span on the bedspread, telling him who it would be before the name appeared on the screen spinning round to face him: Robert.

He picked up.

"Hello? Lexy? Why haven't you answered my messages?" The voice was deep, strong, clearly irritated. Danny felt a nip of smugness: not just his messages she ignored, then.

"Lexy?" The voice was getting sharper. "There's been a . . . development. And . . . and Gran, she's . . . Lexy? Lexy!"

"She isn't here."

There was a sharp intake of breath at the other end. "Who the hell are you? Where is she?"

"I'm Danny, her—"

"Her ex. I know. Put her on the phone. I have to talk to her."

"She isn't here." Danny didn't feel inclined to be helpful.

"I haven't time to mess around. This is serious. Let me speak to her."

"She isn't here."

"Then why have you got her phone and where the hell is she?"

Danny was taken aback by the other man's anger.

"She's gone to see . . . ." The unhelpful inclination returned, swept in on a wave of Danny's own anger. "It's none of your damn business, actually. I'll give her a message for you, but that's it. She'll tell you anything she wants you to know herself."

"For Christ's sake, man, this is serious. I know she's looking for Helen, her grand . . . I've got David Buchanan here with me and he's just had a call from the chief of police. . . Hugh Pendleton was arrested for defaulting on his gambling debt to Richard Chakanaya—"

"Who?"

"—and tried to get out of it by making some pretty wild accusations. But the upshot is he's been working for Jenny Kennedy."

"What? Slow down, man."

337

"Jesus. Where to start? He'd been spying on Lexy, trying to scare her into leaving. He even . . . It was him, the schoolroom and snake and—"

"The *snake*? What the—"

"Just trust me, okay? She's in real danger. I know she's looking for Helen Buchanan. But if she finds her . . . You *have* to stop her! Someone else is looking for Helen too, and she's dangerous, armed, we think, and she's—"

"Senga," Danny cut in. "Senga Munro."

"Not Senga, her daughter . . . But how the hell . . . Do you know who she is? Danny, she's really dangerous. You have to get to Lexy. If she's gone to Helen's, get her out of there!"

*

Lexy's hand rubbed the smooth head of the ceramic honeybird in her pocket like it was a talisman, patted her bag where the other one, in pieces, was wrapped in a polythene bag. Helen couldn't deny her now. She'd have to acknowledge her. Lexy fleetingly wished she had the third honeybird from Ursula's flat. But it didn't matter. Two had to be, surely would be, enough to break down Helen's denials.

Lexy took a deep breath, exhaled, rolled her head and shoulders like a prize fighter about to go into the ring, which wasn't too far from how she felt. She banged on the croft door; her ears pricked, listening for sounds from within. She'd seen Helen's old car at the back of the house as she'd driven down the track, and she'd peered into the workshop window to check, but no one was in there. So they had to be in the house. The absence of smoke from the chimney concerned her, but it was a milder day today so perhaps there was no need of a fire.

Or perhaps there was no one there.

No, there would be, there had to be. She banged again, more

338

heavily and with more determination. Then she tried the handle and was amazed to find it turned, but before she could push open the door it was pulled back a few grudging inches and Helen's face appeared in the crack.

"You! Go away. I told you, you're not welcome," she hissed, eyes flicking back and forth between Lexy's face and the shadows of the croft's hallway over her shoulder.

Lexy put a hand on the door to stop Helen closing it. "I've come to return something of yours. Something I know is important to you."

"You can't have anything of mine. Just go. Keep whatever it is, but just go."

"It's something Ross gave me."

"Ross." Helen laughed bitterly. "You've done enough harm there."

"Has something happened to Ross?" Lexy was surprised at the concern that swept through her.

Helen's head jerked round as if she'd heard something behind her.

"What's the matter, Helen? Can I help?"

Helen snapped her head back, her voice now no more than a hoarse whisper. "You have to leave. *Please*. Just go aw—"

Helen stopped as she saw the honeybird Lexy had pulled from her pocket, nestling in the younger woman's palm. What little colour was in the thin cheeks drained away.

"Where did you get that? I told you yester—"

"Ross gave it to me."

"And I took it back. Did you *steal* it?"

"No. He left it on my car for me. After you'd thrown me out. Why do you think he did that?"

"I've no idea." Helen drew her breath in sharply as she snatched a glance behind her again. "Keep it, but for God's sake just get out of—"

"I've got another one." Lexy held up the transparent bag containing the broken pieces of her mother's honeybird, let it dangle in front of Helen's eyes like a hypnotist's pocket watch. "I know where there's a third one too. And most importantly, I know what's inside."

"Please. You must leave!" Helen's voice was pleading now and Lexy felt a sudden shiver of premonition. This wasn't the controlled, arrogant woman she'd met yesterday. This Helen seemed frightened, as if there was more to her insistence that Lexy leave than—

"Let her in."

The words came from the dark hallway. Helen jerked upright as if she'd been nudged by a cattle prod. She looked at Lexy with something unspoken in her eyes, then took a step back as if in surrender.

Lexy felt adrenalin prick her skin. There was something wrong here. Very wrong, but she couldn't quite—

"I said let her in." It was the voice. It was familiar, and yet not.

A hand reached for Helen's shoulder, pulled the old woman back into the hall, and the owner of the voice stepped forward.

"Hello, Lexy. I was hoping you'd drop by."

"Jenny?" Lexy struggled to work out what Ursula's carer was doing in Helen's house. "What . . . how did you—?"

"Yes, puzzling isn't it?" Jenny laughed coldly. "But don't stand there on the doorstep. Come on in. This is turning out to be just the reunion I'd hoped for."

There was none of the garrulous warmth of Jenny the carer now and Lexy realised what it was that had made her uncomfortable with Jenny in Ursula's flat. She'd been acting. Playing the part of the cheery home help. But *why*?

Stunned into uncustomary silence, mute obedience, Lexy stepped into the hall, saw Helen standing beside Ross, who was sniffling, heard the door shut heavily behind her.

340

"In the parlour, I think," Jenny was saying as she pushed open the door to the cold room. "Fewer utensils and stuff. Don't want anyone falling on a knife or anything like that, do we?"

Like automatons, they all followed Jenny into the small room, took the seats she indicated for them.

"Ross, you beside me." Jenny pulled the bemused man down next to her on the sofa. "Isn't this cosy?" Jenny took Ross's hand and squeezed it, hard, smiling again when Ross yelped. "Oh dear, did that hurt? Best just sit still then, hadn't you?"

"Leave him alone." Helen seemed to have recovered a little of her spirit, sat forward on the edge of her seat. "Whatever you want, it's nothing to do with him."

"No, you're right. He's no use to me. Other than as a little incentive for you to cooperate. Now, Lexy, have you worked it out yet? Why I'm here?"

Lexy shook her head. She sat clutching the honeybirds and her bag in her lap, a parody of a confused little old lady.

"Oh, and there's me thinking you were a bright one. Just goes to show a fancy expensive education isn't everything. Perhaps Gran will explain. Lord knows our poor dear uncle can't, can you, eh, Ross?" Another squeeze, another yelp, panic evident in the simple face.

Jenny smiled at them all, clearly enjoying herself. All Lexy could hear in the silence was the steady ticking of the grandfather clock in the hallway, the slight metallic ring to it like the echo of a percussion triangle. She looked at Helen.

"What's going on? I don't understand."

"I don't know who you are." Helen stood, raised her hand to stop Jenny interrupting, walked over to the window. "Oh, I know who you claim to be. But there's no proof, is there? Not a shred of evidence that you're anything but a fantasist." Helen turned to look at Jenny. "And that's exactly what you are."

"Oh, Gran, how hurtful." Jenny threw her arm around Ross's

341

neck. "And here we are getting on so well, uncle and me. As for the lack of evidence, I think we all know that's bullshit. You did what you could to destroy your traces, although it was a bit sloppy not seeing to the paperwork at the Mission, and then Cameron and that man Richard had their own reasons to bribe and bully their way to ensuring their version of events became official record. But you couldn't see it through, could you, Helen? You couldn't resist leaving a little bit behind. So sentimental for a woman who just abandons her children left, right and centre. And now look, Lexy here has done the legwork and brought your little mementoes home to us. Tell us what you found in the honeybirds, Lexy, why don't you?"

"I . . ." Lexy was still holding the small ceramic bird in her hand, the plastic bag of broken pieces on her lap with her bag.

"Don't be shy, Lexy. You've found proof, haven't you? What, some kind of confession, signed statement . . . What? What is it?"

"No, I . . ."

"For fuck's sake, you stupid cow!" The force of Jenny's anger shook them all. Ross began to whimper; Helen stepped forward to comfort him. "Back off, Gran. Don't want your firstborn to . . . Birth certificates." She looked pleased as she saw the slightest twitch of alarm in Helen's face. "Of course. That's what you found in the birds, wasn't it, Lexy?"

'Yes." Lexy's voice was low.

"Well, of *course*. Honeybirds. Very clever, Gran. And to think I wasted all that time running after you to Malawi, Lexy, searching your room while Hugh kept you entertained and then had to hightail it back to London to do your flat."

"That was you? But how—"

"Yeah, a lot of airmiles that week, quite a schlep, but Ursula's stash paid for First Class, so not really a problem, was it?"

"But . . . Hugh? You and Hugh Pendleton . . . ?"

342

"God, no. The man's an arse. He'll do anything for money. Got him to help me with the Mission job first time round and then had him keep an eye on you. Cut him loose when he got greedy, though. Idiot was freelancing, sending everyone little cryptic anonymous notes to see if anyone got scared enough to stump up some readies. He really had no idea what he was playing with. Loose cannon, that one. Or a loose end at least . . ." Jenny's eyes drifted to the fireplace as her words trailed off thoughtfully. Lexy felt a frisson of fear. She had no idea what Jenny had in mind, but she was sure it wouldn't be good for Hugh Pendleton.

"So." Jenny snapped her eyes back to Lexy, all business once again. "The certificates. Whose?"

"My . . . my mother's. Isobel Buchanan-Munro's."

"Interesting . . . Not that we need it, now that she's so conveniently stepped out of the way."

Lexy was horrified. "Oh no. Please. That wasn't you."

"No, some kind drunk saved me the trouble. Didn't even know where she was, my auntie Izzie." Lexy's hackles rose at this disconcerting woman claiming kinship with her mother. "No," Jenny continued, "I had no idea then that you and your mother were inhabiting a parallel universe just over a couple of miles from my own, but then there's a lot more in real terms than a couple of miles between a Battersea tower block and a Putney terrace, isn't there? Do you think we ever sat next to each other on the Tube, brushed shoulders on a bus, Lexy?" She laughed harshly. "Nah, doubt it. Taxis for you or one of Boris's right-on bikes. Leaving *public* transport to the likes of me. Yeah, and don't imagine we hung out in the same pubs either, and wouldn't have bumped into you shopping in the Arndale, would I?"

"I still don't know who you—"

"Getting to that, Lexy, getting to that. Now, where was I? Yeah. Didn't know where Izzie was so that's why . . ." – she wiggled her head from side to side, searching for a word – "why I *persuaded*

Ursula to take the initiative, to call her and talk her into a visit. And then you turn up. Couldn't have worked out better if I'd planned it." Jenny looked pleased with herself. Lexy felt the temperature in the room drop. "But what about the other one, the other bird? What did you find in that?"

"Another birth certificate, but I don't know whose it is."

"Oh my." Jenny's face lit up; her smile widened. "Helen knows, though, don't you, Helen? Why don't you tell us? Tell us about *my* mother, Gran."

"Your mother?" Lexy was feeling a bit at sea now.

"Yes. Tell us, Helen. Tell us about Senga Munro."

Lexy's last mooring line snapped. How could Jenny possibly know that was the name on the other certificate?

★

Danny was frantic. He'd turned the room upside down. It was now in a mess that would astonish even Lexy, but he still hadn't found anything that would tell him where this croft house was. He should have asked her before she left, made her call him when he got there . . . She'd have laughed in his face. Called him an old woman. And besides, it was easy to be wise after the event.

But he had to find her, warn her. She wasn't answering her phone. His phone. And he knew he hadn't much charge left on it anyway. *Think, Danny,* think. But he couldn't. All he could focus on was that someone was trying to harm Lexy.

Grabbing his jacket from the back of the chair, he patted the pockets, pulled out the car keys. He'd just have to go looking. There was only one road in and out of this peninsula, so how many crofts could there be? But even as he was running down the stairs he knew that was ridiculous. Maybe not many, but they'd be scattered, hidden: it would be impossible to cover the ground quickly. He had to stop, think, approach this systematically.

To hell with that.

Lexy. He was sick at the thought of anything—

Police. He needed to speak to the police.

Was that the right thing to do? Hand over to them? No. They'd be too late and Lexy could be . . . Someone might—

"Morning, Sir. Going out?"

Of course. *Ask.*

"I . . .Yes. I don't know how to find the . . . the croft . . ." Perhaps this wasn't gong to work after all. He didn't even know what it was called, what name Helen went under.

"The one Miss Shaw was asking about?" *Oh, thank you, you angel.*

"Yes. Please. It's urgent. I have to get there before . . ."

The receptionist was looking at him oddly but seemed to move just a little faster than she had been. She pulled out a map and showed him.

"There's only the one road, so you won't get lost. The trick is to find the turning, of course," she laughed. Danny didn't share the moment. "Right, yes." She was flustered now. Not helping. "Well, left, actually. It's a small turning on the left just after the second bend. There's a sheep grid about a hundred yards before it and if you get to the crossroads you've missed it."

Danny snatched the map. "Get on to the police. They need to get there too, fast. And an ambulance," he added, finding himself praying to a God he hadn't thought he believed in that it wouldn't be needed.

The receptionist's eyes widened.

"*Now*, dammit!"

Danny raced for his car, scarcely registering the fact that he'd just sworn at a stranger. But Lexy was in danger. Normal rules didn't apply.

★ ★ ★

345

The car groaned as he scrunched gears, sending small stones flying as it lurched forward, stalled.

"Buggeration!" Danny yelled as he hit the steering wheel, turned the key in the ignition again, thrust it into gear and kicked the accelerator pedal. Lexy. He had to find her. Save her.

Robert's words were running amok in his mind. Senga Munro had a daughter, a daughter who had been on Lexy's tail from the start of her mad quest. A daughter who wanted it all, all Helen's money, Buchanan's, everything. A daughter who had no intention of sharing with anyone. A psychopath who they thought had a gun.

Danny slammed on the brakes. Crossroads. *Concentrate.* This wasn't the time to get lost. He ground the gearstick into reverse and twisted his head back, spun the wheel too fast, too far, hit the grass verge and stalled again. God, he hated driving. Breathe. Slowly. No good to anyone in a ditch. Turn round. Not exactly a three-point turn, but eventually he was heading back the way he'd come. The track on the left— No! On the right, now, not the left. Take it slow. Steady. But get there, get there before . . . before . . . There it was! The car bucked like a newborn lamb as he forced it to start up the potholed track, bounced down hard on the ridge in the middle, stalled. *Dammit.* The ignition rasped, juddered as he turned the key once, twice. Then he was out the door and running uphill, stumbling but determined. Lexy. He had to get to Lexy.

★

"You're Senga's daughter?" Lexy's voice was thin, quavering as she turned from Jenny to Helen. "And you're Senga's mother?" Helen was still silhouetted in the window, still staring at Ross, no movement giving any indication of acknowledgement.

She'd been right. There was a fourth child. Helen had had a fourth child. Lexy's head swivelled back to Jenny again, as her

346

mind tried to keep track of this dreadful game playing out in front of her, shot by shot. "And Cameron . . . was your *grand*father?"

"Finally, she gets it. Yes, Lex, which makes me your long-lost cousin. How about that?"

"But, Helen" – Lexy appealed to the woman who was standing, arms crossed across her chest, expressionless, eyes never leaving her son's face – "you *hated* him, you ran away—"

"None of this proves you are who you say you are. Either of you."

"For God's sake, Helen." Lexy's nerves made her snappy, impatient, more than a little frightened of what was happening here. "You can't still deny that my mother, Izzie, was your daughter?" Just the faintest flicker of something stirred in Helen's face. "And not your only daughter either." Lexy ploughed on, determined to get a response, a reaction. "What kind of a woman are you?"

"I wanted her to be safe."

"Safe?" Despite the flicker of victory Helen's admission gave her, Lexy was incredulous. "First you abandoned my mother and then—"

"You abandoned mine." Jenny took control of the conversation again. "If I'm not who I say I am, Helen, how could I possibly know as much as I do? Why, *how*, would I know any of it?"

There were small pink patches now on Helen's pale cheeks; her hands were clenched tight, white-knuckled, at her sides.

"When my mother died – which she did, Helen. That's right, your youngest child is dead. I got up one bright morning to find her slumped on the sofa, needle still in her arm. Pretty picture, huh? But I'm sure you'll contain your grief. When she died, I decided to . . . keep her alive for a while longer. The opposite of your scam, really. There was money, you see. Every month, an envelope on the doormat. I didn't know who was sending it, so I didn't feel any obligation to try to inform them. And no one was

347

going to miss her. She was a junkie and a whore, Helen, your youngest, and I think we can fairly put that down to you. Abandoning her to the 'mercy' of the nuns without a second thought."

"That's not true, I—"

"Spare us, Helen. A little late for all that, don't you think?"

"He *raped* me."

"Don't be such a drama queen, Gran. He was your husband. It's what they do."

Helen's face registered something Lexy couldn't quite make out before the mask fell again.

"I didn't have a choice. It was hard enough to get Ross out, I couldn't risk exposing a newborn—"

"Oh, whatever." Jenny cut her off with a hand gesture. Helen looked about to protest but then dropped her head, her face hidden as Jenny continued.

"So I decided to" – that wiggle of the head again – "keep things quiet. No announcements anywhere. No one came looking. Well, her dealer turned up once, wondering what had happened to one of his best customers, turned tail when I spun a yarn about police and rehab. No one else came. None of her many boyfriends, none of the 'friends' she'd bring home with her from the pub, none of the neighbours who never did anything anyway but bang on the walls and shout at her. No. I just kept it to myself, disposed of her, got on with my life."

"Jenny, I'm so sor—"

"Sure you are, Lexy." Jenny didn't even look at her, kept her eyes on Helen. "You with your perfect little life and all that shit. Your loving mummy and daddy, although, sob, sob, he kicked the bucket when you were just a tiny little tot, didn't he? Ah, poor little Lexy. I don't even know my father's name; my mother *definitely* didn't. And look at us now, both here, both messed up by Grannie and her games. Still think you're better than me? How does it feel to know they lied to you all the time? Never told you who you really were? At least my mother, drunken slag though she was, didn't lie. She had no idea. Stupid cow was too addled half the time to wonder why the money was coming in every month regular as clockwork. The only time I asked, she said it was the nuns. Like that'd be right. Stupid mare."

"Where *was* it coming from?" Helen was watching Jenny again now, a strange expression on her face.

"Same place as yours, Gran. Same place as yours."

"David."

"Cameron. David never knew, doesn't even now. Oh, he'll know there's a slush fund somewhere to smooth wheels and buy silences, but that's what he pays Chakanaya for and he won't want to know the details. Small change to a man like him. Wonder what he'd say if he knew he'd been funding his usurper under miscellaneous expenditure? I'm looking forward to telling him that."

"But why would Cameron—"

"Patience, Lexy. Didn't Mummy teach you it was rude to interrupt? I'll come to that. So. After a while, I get curious. This money. Been the same amount for years, and we all know what the cost of living's like these days. Maybe, I think, maybe it's time for a little review. A pay rise if you like. But before I can get to tracing the source, I have a visitor. And my, what a story he had to tell me. And what a proposition. Think you'd better sit down again, Gran. This is where it gets really interesting."

33

Mortlake Crematorium, London, September 2013

Jenny had been the only mourner at her mother's funeral, which hadn't surprised her. She'd told no one. She almost hadn't come herself. She sat alone in the crematorium chapel and felt nothing. It wasn't numbness, shock. It was just that there was nothing left to feel. As a child, she'd poured so much love and hope and care into her mother before she realised it was like a black hole. Everything disappeared and nothing came back. Her mother had no time or interest or energy for anything except her addiction. Even her daughter had never been anything more than a means to that particular end. Senga's "gentlemen callers" had rarely been gentle and Jenny had learned early on not to expect her mother to protect her. So she'd found her own ways of taking care of herself, of ignoring her mother's slow suicide.

So no: no tears.

Jenny had waited until the curtains swished together again behind the cheap box, until the hum of the electric tracking ended with a click and she could imagine the heat, the fire, the flames licking their way through to the sallow-skinned corpse that lay within. She wanted to be sure her mother would be consumed entirely, before allowing the slow smile that was spreading across her face to take hold completely.

As she turned to leave, she saw movement in the shadows at the back of the near-empty room. The flash of a white cuff, the click of a cigarette lighter, then the brief flare of a flame. The man stepped out ahead of her into the outer vestibule, his well-tailored back presenting itself to Jenny, the smoke of his cigarette hovering in his wake. Intrigued, she followed.

"Jenny, isn't it?" The man spoke without turning as Jenny caught up with him. "I'm here on behalf of your grandfather."

Jenny had barked out a laugh, shock more than humour, incredulity uppermost.

"Yeah, and I'm friggin' Cleopatra."

"You don't believe me. Of course. Why should you?" The man turned slowly until she could look directly into his eyes, startling against the deep blue-black of his skin. "What would it take to convince you? Or perhaps the real question is, how much?"

Jenny said nothing. Felt her eyes narrow. Her mother claimed never to have known her parents. Been born illegitimate, she once said, put out for adoption immediately, like a discarded puppy.

The man was smiling at her, seemed to be appraising her. "More than your mother, I imagine. You don't look as if you share her . . . tastes."

Jenny snorted. "Do I look like a loser?"

"No . . ." There was a thoughtful tone in the voice. "I hadn't expected you to be, of course, but neither had I expected someone quite so . . ."

"So what exactly? Look, I don't know who the hell you are or what you want, but if it's anything to do with my mother, I don't give a toss. I'm only here to make sure the bitch is really gone, so don't make the mistake of thinking I give a damn because I don't. Now move. You're in my way and I'm out of here."

"Forgive me. I'm sure you must be busy." The man's smile didn't falter as he stepped back and to one side, his arm extending to indicate a long black car gleaming in the autumn sunshine. "Perhaps I can give you a lift? Anywhere you need to go. We can talk en route, become better acquainted."

Even Jenny with her limited experience of cars knew a top-of-the-range Mercedes when she saw one. And there was a uniformed

351

chauffeur standing to attention beside it. Thoughts rattled round her head like the beads on an abacus as she weighed up the possibilities. Whoever he was, he was loaded. If he was looking for someone's lost granddaughter and thought she'd fit the bill, well, maybe she would oblige. No harm in listening to the old geezer anyway.

Jenny nodded sharply once. "Battersea, then."

"Ah, your dear mother's flat, I assume? Well, your grandfather's actually, if we're to be entirely accurate."

Jenny's head swivelled involuntarily in the stranger's direction.

"Oh yes, my dear. Although he'd arranged for your mother to live there rent-free for as long as she wanted. The least a father could do for his own child, make sure she had a roof above her head, particularly one with such extensive needs. Don't disappoint me so soon, Jenny. Surely you must have wondered how your waster of a mother came to have a flat like that?"

Actually, she had. It wasn't exactly Knightsbridge, but Jenny knew enough about the property market in London to know that even a two-bedroom flat in the depths of south London was worth a bit. She'd tried to get her hands on the deeds to find out if her mother did really own her flat. Certainly, no landlord had ever come knocking demanding rent, even in the leanest days. Despite herself, she was intrigued.

As they neared the car, the chauffeur sprang to life and opened the rear door.

"Shall we, my dear?" The stranger stepped aside to let her slide in first along the smooth leather upholstery before he settled in beside her, his movements making the leather groan. The door closed with the softest of thuds and a moment later the car purred into life, leaving the solemnity of the crematorium behind them.

352

34

Ross-shire, June 19th

The track was steeper, longer than he'd thought, and he couldn't see the croft house yet. He prayed it was the right track. Should have stayed with the car, tried to start it again. Danny stopped, bent forward, hands on his knees, gasping for breath, trying to loosen the tight band constricting his chest, his lungs. This wasn't the kind of activity junior academics usually went in for; in fact, the most exercise Danny normally undertook was carrying armfuls of books up and down the back stairs to and from the library.

Sweat trickled from his hair down his forehead, stung at the corners of his eyes. He flicked his hair back from his face as he straightened up again, wiped the back of his hand across his forehead, driving even more salt into his eyes, caught a glimpse of red between the banks of gorse shielding the left side of the track. He pulled back branches, cursed as the thorns dug into his palms, snagged on the sleeve of his jacket. A rusty red pickup truck, tracks on the soft ground showing where it had left the road. But not by accident. This was deliberate: someone had hidden this. His heart thumped, and he was pushing up the track again, thorn scratches, stinging eyes, tight chest forgotten. *Lexy, I'm coming.*

★

"Blood. Your blood, Helen. That's all that matters right? Whether I'm the bastard child of a bastard, the discarded daughter of a drunken bitch, or the Queen of bloody Sheba doesn't make any

353

difference. It's all about the blood running through these veins being directly connected to yours, isn't it? And he said he could prove I was your granddaughter and that would be enough."

"Enough for what?"

"Oh, Lexy, keep up, you're boring me. To get rid of David. Put me in his place. Stop him ruining the company by fessing up to the whole Blantyre 144 thing. Who would have thought Uncle Dave would turn into some kind of bleeding heart in his old age? Don't expect anyone would have seen that one coming."

"But Robert said—"

"*Robert said*" – Jenny mimicked Lexy – "Robert, cousin mine, is a prize asshole, but one whose Christmases are about to all come at once. Uncle Dave was dithering, you see, despite what the official line was. Getting all morose about his solitary, ageing state. Wanting to leave a mark and all that shit. Chakanaya believed at any moment he'd pick up the phone to his old school buddy's son Robert and say let's meet, sort out the world over a jar or two – or a magnum or two, given the old fart's pretentious crap. That he'd cave in and pay off the niggers for the mudbath. But what the hell. If we got in quick, I'd get my due, finally, I'd get everything that you three old witches with your child-swapping schemes had taken away from me. My kindly visitor assured me any other claimant was either dead, mental – as in you, eh, Uncle Ross?" A nip this time, another yelp. "Or ignorant, and that, cousin dear, would be you and the lately departed Izzie."

"My mother didn't know?"

"When she went out to Malawi, they'd thought she'd worked it out somehow, watched her like a hawk. But nothing happened. She didn't have a clue. Just lived in that nurse's hostel, then in a tiny bungalow in the hospital grounds when all the time it could have been five-star all the way, Buchanan House as her Blantyre pad and not a bedpan in sight." Jenny's laughter was taking on a slightly hysterical edge now but Lexy ignored it as she let relief

354

flood her mind. Her mother hadn't known she was a Buchanan, hadn't lied to her. Izzie was as innocent as—

"Not until later anyway." Relief stalled, threatened to ebb as quickly as it had come. "The way she told it, seemed old Ursula tripped herself up, made some comment about you, Lexy, looking like your grandmother and Izzie was on it in a flash. Ursula had always claimed she'd never met Izzie's mother, the missionary woman, just her father, some pastor or something. When the old bird wouldn't talk, Izzie stormed out and that was that for years."

Lexy exhaled. Izzie hadn't known who she was. She hadn't kept that from Lexy, hadn't denied her family, hadn't known she *had* a family. All her mother had done was keep Lexy from knowing Ursula was a liar. Her mother had been protecting her, trying to spare her all the anger and uncertainty and sadness Izzie herself must have felt at discovering she'd been lied to all *her* life, deliberately denied the simple right to know who she was, where she'd come from, those same feelings Lexy herself had felt these last two weeks and which now she could let go. Izzie hadn't betrayed her; her mother hadn't let her down.

"She was on to you, you know." Helen's voice cut through Lexy's racing emotions.

"No, she wasn't," Jenny snapped. "I had her fooled; she was eating out of my hand!"

"No, she wasn't. She didn't trust you. She'd taken precautions in case . . . You didn't find any addresses, did you? Nothing that you could use to trace me, trace Lexy, come to that. Nothing useful, apart from all those old photographs, but you didn't know—"

"I found the money!" Jenny sounded triumphant. "I found all that cash in her flat, hidden in a book for Chrissake. Took it as a kind of advance on what I'm owed." Jenny laughed. "It was for you, wasn't it, that money? Might have found you lost a bit of this,

Uncle Ross, when that didn't come through." She pinched the roll of fat just tipping over Ross's belt, and he yelped again.

"Leave him alone!" Helen shouted, standing and starting towards her son.

"Oh sit down, Gran. He's fine. Nothing happens to him if you do what I want."

"Then why did you murder her?"

"Murder? Oh, that's a little strong isn't it? She fell. Those stairs, you know, for a woman like her." Jenny smirked, shook her head and tutted.

"Why?" Helen persisted.

"Stupid cow. Always checking up on me, nagging me, never satisfied with anything. I'm not a bloody housekeeper after all and it wasn't as if she was paying me. Ungrateful bitch. She'd sneak around in those minging slippers of hers. Came in just as I was counting out the notes. Said she'd call the police" – the smirk was back again. "Ended up it was me called them, though, wasn't it? After her little tumble down the stairs." Jenny twirled her hand over and over before she brought it down with a splat on Ross's thigh, her laugh drowning his whimper of pain.

In the silence that followed, Helen and Lexy exchanged a glance, but Helen's face was still impassive. Lexy knew hers wasn't as she struggled to keep her shock under control. She looked back at Jenny, sitting smiling at her from the sofa, looking triumphant, amused, carefree.

"Oh come on, Lexy," Jenny was saying, "don't look like that. It wasn't like you cared. You'd not seen the old cow in years."

"I don't think that's quite the point," Helen chipped in.

"Who was he, this man that came to you?" Lexy had been trying to piece it all together. It wasn't David, and Cameron was dead—

"Richard Chakanaya." Helen spat the words out like sour milk.

"Top marks, Gran. Your husband's Mr Fix-it. Who, you may be

interested to know, now holds a significant number of shares in your company. Not enough to stop David, of course, which is why he came for me, but he still stood to lose an awful lot of money if Buchanan's went under. Wasn't wild about that." Jenny sniffed, crossed her legs and shuffled to make herself more comfortable before continuing.

"After he'd gone, I got to thinking. As long as there were any other claimants, ignorant or otherwise, and as long as he knew where they were and I didn't, I reckoned I'd have to dance to his tune. And I wasn't sure I wanted to do that. Didn't see why I should dance to a tune played by some native, by my grandfather's lackey for God's sake. And I didn't fancy any long-lost relatives coming out of the woodwork at a later date. No. Ignorance doesn't always last forever and I like to know where I am with things. Incapable, like Uncle Ross here, I can live with; no way this boy's making any kind of recovery. But otherwise, dead's best. Chakanaya wouldn't tell me where my relatives were; why would he? So I told him to shove it and decided to sort things out all on my own. Only without his 'proof' of my identity I needed something else. Someone to verify that I really am entitled to Buchanan's and all the rest of it. Which is basically why we're here today, Helen, enjoying our nice little family reunion."

"I won't do it, you know. I'm not that woman now. That Helen Buchanan died fifty years ago, and I'm ... someone else altogether." Helen's voice was flat, her eyes on Ross, an unreadable expression on her face.

"You're forgetting the birth certificates." Jenny's face was smug, her eyes flashing with triumph.

"I'm not sure a piece of paper found in such strange circumstances will do you much good when there's so much at stake. And there's no corresponding record anywhere official. Cameron saw to that. The certificates were never meant—"

"So you admit it," Lexy chimed in. "You admit you—"

"You will do it, Helen. You owe me this. All you need to do is sign a statement and make a brief return to the world to validate my entitlement. Then you can come back here and live out the life sentence dear Uncle Ross has imposed on you. Although you did shoot him, but what the hell. No one cares about either of you. They'll all leave you alone. I'll be the one everyone is interested in; it'll be me in the headlines, the magazines. *Me.*"

"Do you really think David will stand aside and let you do this?"

"He can't do anything – he's an imposter, taken what's mine!"

"And Lexy's, if what you claim is true."

Jenny spun round to Lexy, a hard, cold look on her face.

"I don't want a penn—"

"Don't take me for a fool, cousin. You'd say anything right now."

"I don't. I don't want it."

"Maybe not now. But what happens when you change your mind, as you most definitely will the first time those little brats in that school play you up and you start to think of all that money, all that freedom it can buy you. No, Lexy. Can't take that risk."

Jenny's hand disappeared into the bag at her feet; it emerged clutching a bundle wrapped in hessian. Lexy looked at it, horrified. Jenny's face split into a tight grin, as she slowly sloughed the cloth off to reveal a dark, shiny weapon. A gun. Helen gasped and her eyes flickered between Jenny and Ross, Ross and Lexy.

"My, Helen, you're looking a little agitated there. Wondering what this is for, perhaps? Why a sweet young thing like me should have one of these handy? You should know. You had one yourself. Self-preservation, isn't it? Protection of what's yours, what you care about, remember? Well, same for me. This guarantees my future. One bullet removes the . . . competition . . ."

The gun barrel twitched in Lexy's direction.

"The other provides you with the right motivation to do what I tell you." Jenny swung the gun round to point at Ross's forehead. The confused man blinked wide eyes, unaware of the danger the weapon posed.

"Leave him alone!" Helen's voice was shrill, sharp. "What possible harm can he be to you?"

"None at all, Helen. Unless you decide not to cooperate, he'll be perfectly fine, I assure you. He's a simpleton. No legal standing, so quite irrelevant in all this except for his worth to you."

Jenny was nudging Ross with the gun, watching Helen while she did, taunting her. Lexy edged forward in her seat: this was her chance. She glanced at the door. Could she get to it, open it, run . . . But then what? It was clear the gun's immediate purpose was to dispose of only one person in the room, and it would only take a second for Jenny to turn the barrel on her, squeeze the trigger . . . But she had to get out, get help. Jenny wouldn't harm Helen or Ross, not yet at least, not while she still needed Helen's cooperation. Lexy's heart was racing. Oh God, Jenny was going to kill her; even if she got to the door, could she get away? Jenny would come after her—

She saw something move outside the window. The outline of a figure flashed past, indistinct against the feeble glare of sun in the cloud-thick sky. Who? Did Jenny have someone outside, waiting, ready in case—

"Time to go, Lexy."

Lexy's head snapped back to Jenny's face, to the gun that was now pointed steadily at her, as Jenny walked towards the door, took the old-fashioned key from its lock, stood with her back towards it. Lexy's head was buzzing, like hornets swarming, and she struggled to fight the panic, the terror, the disbelief.

"You" – Jenny jerked her head towards Helen – "over there with the idiot, keep him calm while Lexy and I take a little walk outside. I'm sure you won't want him to see what's coming next. Might bring back the memories of his own . . . trauma. Don't want him having nightmares, do we?"

Lexy felt heat flushing her throat and face, veins boiling with blood, burning like touchpapers either side of her neck. Yet she was frozen, mesmerised by the coldness, the emptiness of Jenny's gaze, aware in her peripheral vision of Helen watching them as she sidestepped across the room towards Ross, who had started whimpering again. This wasn't happening, couldn't be happening. She didn't want to die . . . not without . . . not now. She felt a sob gather strength, try to force its way up from the very core of her being, but she wouldn't give Jenny the satisfaction. All she'd wanted was to find family, but not this, not—

The door burst open, knocked Jenny hard and she stumbled, fell to her knees, dropping the gun, sending it skittering across the floor, stopping as it collided with Ross's foot.

"Danny!"

He spun round to where Lexy was standing behind the door, reached towards her.

"No – her!" Lexy shouted as Jenny lurched to her feet, went for the gun. Danny hesitated for a second, then roared and flung himself towards Jenny, but Helen was faster, threw herself in front of her son, pushed back at Jenny and then there was a bang and everyone, everything, stopped.

"What the . . ." Danny was the first to come to, turned and grabbed Lexy, pulled her in to him, as he searched her face.

"I'm fine, I— Oh God!"

Blood was spreading like an emerging star from the centre of Helen's chest, her face registering surprise, disbelief and something else: a calmness, a stillness. Her hands fell from Jenny's arms, and then she was falling, slumping to the ground, revealing Ross sitting on the sofa behind her, the gun hanging limply from the fingers of his left hand.

"Jesus!" Jenny pushed the injured woman away from her,

sending her sprawling onto her back, stepping over her to grab the gun from Ross.

Danny roared again, flung Lexy aside and caught Jenny in a rugby tackle, bringing her down, cracking her head on the coffee table as she fell.

"Gun, Lex, get the gun."

"Drop it, Ross," she shouted and he did, shuffling back into the cushions, hugging himself as the gun bounced on the carpet and disappeared under the sofa.

"Good boy, Ross, that's right, just sit still." Lexy put one hand out to pat his shoulder as she shuffled past to get to Helen, lying on the floor, the faintest of smiles on her face.

Behind them, Danny was struggling to get Jenny under control, sitting on her back, grabbing her wrists and pinning them down above her head. Jenny was trying to resist as she came to, kicking and fighting as she recovered from the knock to her head, gaining strength and raging at finding herself captive.

"Get off me, you bastard, let me go!" Jenny was screaming, gasping for breath as Danny threw the full force of his weight onto her.

"Lexy, do something! This is . . . like riding an effing . . . bucking . . . bronco . . . here."

But Lexy was trying to stem the bleeding from Helen's chest, to keep Helen awake.

"I can't, I . . . Ross! Ross, help us. Help Danny. Sit on her, you sit on Jenny too, you can do it, she won't hurt you now, she can't. Go on, that's right," she encouraged, trying to keep her voice steady and soothing. "Good, Ross, yes, that's it."

Danny reached a hand up quickly and pulled the heavy man down. Jenny grunted loudly as the air was forced from her lungs by the extra weight, but not before she'd managed to reach up with the hand Danny had released and scratch the side of his face, drawing blood and making Danny roar again with a rage Lexy hadn't known he had in him. But Helen's gasp drew her attention quickly back to the woman she was kneeling beside.

"Helen, don't close your eyes. Look at me, please, Helen. Oh God, don't . . . you can't . . . I've only just found you . . ." Lexy was crying now, as she stroked the woman's forehead with one hand, keeping the other pressed to her chest to staunch the flow of blood, her hand sticky with the warmth of the life slipping away beneath her palm. Helen exhaled, inhaled shallowly; her lips formed shapes but no words emerged.

"What? What are you saying? Helen, please. Don't . . . You can't do this to me!" Lexy's fury, frustration at the discoveries and lies and betrayals and shocks of the last few weeks welled up and she was shouting, shouting at a dying woman, shouting at her grandmother to stay. She felt a hand on her shoulder, looked up into Danny's worried face, saw Ross beaming proudly as he sat on Jenny's back, her hands and ankles tied with curtain cords, her struggles ineffective and losing momentum.

"Danny, she's . . . Don't let her . . ." Lexy was sobbing as she looked into his concerned face, then turned her gaze back to the dying woman.

"Ah . . . lexis." The voice was a breath, a sigh. "My Izzie's . . . girl . . . her little . . . Lexy . . ."

Lexy's sobs stalled in her throat at the words, the acknowledgement, the relief.

"Don't go . . . Not yet . . ." Lexy's voice was tight, her throat aching as she held the woman's hand, felt Danny lift her other hand away, replacing it with his own in pressing on the wound, the flow of blood undiminished, seeping into clothes and carpet as Helen slipped out of Lexy's reach.

"Ross." The word was sibilant, no more than a wisp of air released from her slack mouth. "Please . . . lexis . . . Ross."

Lexy was nodding, stroking Helen's face, smearing traces of blood on to the loose, weathered cheek, but then she felt the fingers she held in her other hand relax, saw the eyes cloud over, dim. And she knew her grandmother had gone.

They heard it then, the sound of a car, a siren, then another car coming up the track, fast, but for Lexy, as she looked around the room at the farcical staging of her grandmother's demise, the cavalry was arriving too late.

Aftermath

Lexy watched Danny cross the room and sit down opposite her. They were alone in the tiny hotel bar. The German tourists had long since retired ready for another epic climb the next morning and the barman had returned to the front desk leaving them instructions to ring if they needed him, after Danny had persuaded him to leave the bottle on the table, in exchange for a credit card.

"Did you get through to him?"

Danny shook his head. "No. He's at the hospital. I spoke to David, though. He'll pass the information along."

"To Robert? Since when did they become such great buddies?"

"David's agreed to compensation for the mudslide victims."

"He has?"

"You persuaded him, apparently."

"Me? I only spoke to him once, and it wasn't exactly amicable."

"Well, seems you can be very convincing when you're unfriendly. David took Robert to meet his lawyers to get things started."

Lexy remembered the car at the hospital, seeing Robert get into it, her suspicions. "I thought David was trying to kill me, you know. That Robert was in on it too, somehow."

"Nope, that was all down to cousin Jenny and her sidekick Pendleton."

"Just Pendleton, actually. She'd ditched him by then. Probably thought his snake trick would get him back into her good books."

"There has to be an easier way to impress a woman." Danny picked up the whisky bottle, turned it to the light to check the level of its contents. "Do you want something to eat?" Lexy shook her head. "I think you'd better, if you're going to keep on drinking at that rate." Lexy threw Danny a look. "Okay. Just saying. Look, I'm just going to see if I can get us some sandwiches or something. For later. Just in case."

Lexy watched him disappear back out into the lobby, curious to know if he'd fare any better than she had. She couldn't face tinned tomato soup again. Red, thick, congealed. She shivered, drained her glass, clattered it down on the table and looked down at her hands. They'd been covered in her grandmother's blood a few short hours ago. *Blood is thicker than water*, her mother's voice whispered in her head. It certainly was.

By the time Danny returned, empty handed but for a wrinkled apple and a blackened banana he'd found in a bowl in the deserted hotel kitchen, Lexy was deep in thought, the whisky bottle considerably lighter, and her mood considerably darker. She took the banana, peeled it, then dropped it uneaten on the table between them.

"Come on, Lex. You have to eat something."

She ignored him. "You know, I've been thinking. Everyone I've ever loved, everyone I trusted, lied to me. How can I believe anyone again?"

"That's a little overdramatic, Lexy." Danny pushed the banana to one side, went back to nursing his whisky. He didn't like whisky, but Lexy had insisted he join her and for once he hadn't argued. She hadn't wanted to drink alone.

"And you'd know, would you? You with your comfortable Cheshire family, stretching back to Magna bloody Carta, your predictable WI chairing, home-baking mother and your ... and your ... your ... I don't know! But you have no idea—"

"Don't be angry, Lexy." This didn't sound like one of his lectures. The patronising tone was missing. "You have to start forgiving." *Oh, wrong. Here we go,* she thought. "If you stay angry

365

with everything and everyone, you'll destroy yourself, and it won't change anything."

"You would say that, wouldn't you?"

"What do you mean?"

"You're just trying to get off the hook. You betrayed me, too, didn't you? You lied."

"That's different. I . . . Yes, I slept with Fizz, but . . ."

"Don't make excuses."

"But I didn't stop loving you and I never lied."

"Oh don't be—"

"No, I didn't. There was no affair, really, no secret love nests, no pretend conferences or out-of-town seminars. I'd slept with her precisely once before you found out. And to be honest, if you hadn't found out, I think I would have slept with her *only* once. Ever. I didn't love her, Lexy. You knew that."

"I . . . Only once? I didn't know . . . but that's not the point! The point is you betrayed me."

"No. The point is I was angry. And I did something I regretted more than I can tell you *because* I was angry."

"You were angry?" Lexy laughed bitterly. "You don't know how to be angry, you don't have the passion." Even as she said it, though, she remembered his roar as he flung himself at Jenny, her astonishment.

"Well, it seems I do. And it seems I have a very self-destructive way of expressing it."

"So this is my fault."

"No, I'm not saying that. We were . . . broken. Fractured. I wanted to make it right and I couldn't. You shut me out. Sniped at me when I tried to get close. Oh, I don't know. This isn't about who did what when. Recriminations. I know I did wrong and I'll have to live with that. But I didn't lie, Lexy. I didn't lie to you."

"Bloody nitpicking academic. It comes to the same thing.

366

Betrayal. Just like my new-found family, my murderous, conniving, lying—"

"Don't, Lexy, let it go. Forgive—"

"Forgive? Who? Oh, I suppose I should start with you, should I? The hero rushing in to save me. Is that how you see it? Don't think I don't know what you were doing. Trying to get back into my life."

"You didn't need me, don't need me, to save you. But would that be so wrong, anyway, wanting to look after you?"

"You betrayed me!" She wouldn't listen to this, wouldn't let him distract her from her anger, this rage bubbling like lava, desperate to erupt, escape, be purged.

"Fine. Forget about me. But forgive your mother. Your grandmother. All those people you're so angry with. You're angry because you loved them, you know. So angry you can't see what's clear as day."

"Oh yeah, and whaz that, Mr Smartass?"

"That they did what they did because *they* loved *you*."

"Oh, can't listen to any more of this. Really, Danny, for a supposedly rising star in academic circles you do a good line in Jemy . . . Jeremy Kyle melodrama. What d'you know about any of this anyway? You're such a cliché, but for all your degrees and journals and . . . and stuff, you know nothing! Such a fool, such a . . . an *innocent*, falling for the 'little pregnant woman' thing."

"That's enough, Lex."

"No it's not. Not even nearly enough." She grabbed the bottle and poured herself another healthy slug, drops splattering the tabletop around her glass as heavily as monsoon rain.

"This isn't my fault, Lexy." Danny screwed the top back on the whisky bottle, put it on the bar behind him, out of reach. "You're angry because you think you've been betrayed, but—"

"You did it too! You betrayed me. You *left* me—"

367

"You threw me out, Lexy. I've told you. If you hadn't made me leave, it wouldn't have gone anywhere with Fizz. As it was—"

"As it *was* you were quite happy to believe you'd got her pregnant and play happy fam—"

"I most certainly wasn't happy. I was just trying to do the right thing."

"Oh, right. Only you. Only you would fall for the oldest trick in the book. Always the honourable man."

"What's so wrong with that?"

"How could you be so gullible? How? I mean surely you . . ."

"Lexy, does it matter? I've no idea. You know more about the gynaecology of it all than I do. What did you expect me to do, ask her for proof?"

"Yes!"

"I'd slept with her and she was pregnant and what else can I say? It doesn't matter. It was all a huge mistake, anyway. I'm . . . I'm relieved."

"But the child . . . your child. You wanted—"

"You're such an idiot at times, Lexy. Yes, I wanted a child, I *want* a child, but not with Fizz. Never with her. With someone I love. With you."

"Don't you dare. No." Lexy was finding it hard to string the words together, her enunciation becoming more deliberate as she struggled to say in control. "Danny's dumped so he comes running back to me?"

"That's not it."

"It is. It's very mushit from where I'm sitting. You can't do that. You can't betray me and then walk right back into my life and 'spect me to—"

"I don't expect anything. I just want you to know I love you. That I'm here. And that I didn't sodding lie—"

368

Lexy cut him off as she stood up, pushing over the little table, and stomped out, slamming the door behind her.

There was something satisfying about stomping along a pebble beach. The groan and crunch of the stones under her feet were like the screams she was screaming in her head, the blows she was aiming at imaginary punchbags. She was slowing now, though, her calves protesting at this unusual punishment. She stopped, hands on hips, breathing heavily, and looked back at the mountain towering above the beach, the hotel a Monopoly piece dropped from its board.

How dare he. How *dare* he. But already it was slipping away from her, her anger. What was she so angry about? The fact that Danny had slept with Fizz? The fact that he was a gullible idiot? The fact that he still loved her when she'd behaved like a first-class b—

Her phone, her *own* phone was beeping. She pulled it out of her pocket. Robert.

"Hello?"

"Lexy?"

"Yes. Robert—"

"She's dead."

Lexy sank down onto her knees on the unyielding pebbles, oblivious to pain.

"Lexy? Are you there?"

"I . . . Oh God, Robert, I'm so sorry."

"So you bloody should be. You with your histrionics and making her drag up the past like that. She was in no state to go into theatre in the first place."

"No! You can't blame me for this. You're the doctor. If she wasn't up to it why did you let her—"

"And then the news about Helen, it was all too much."

"But I thought the operation was straightforward—"

369

"It was, but she was too weak. *You* made her too weak. She couldn't fight the infection and . . . and . . ." She could hear his voice crack, knew he was crying.

"Robert. I'm so very, very sorry." Evie. Oh good God. Evie was dead. And Lexy had left in such a rush, let Robert hustle her out when she should have taken the time to say a proper goodbye, to wish the old woman well. Evie had helped her so much, and Lexy knew it couldn't have been easy for her to trawl through the past like that. She'd never even told Evie how grateful she was. Hadn't thanked her for telling her what she needed to know, probably would have been happier not knowing, but yes, needed to know. But it wasn't just guilt Lexy felt, it was loss. Another thread connecting her to her mother's life had been cut. And she knew, had she had the chance, Evie, her mother's godmother after all, was someone she would have grown to like, even perhaps to love.

"You should never have come here, Lexy. None of this would have happened if you hadn't been so determined to rake it all up. Well, I hope it's worth it. I hope your new-found wealth, your precious family, are worth getting Helen killed for. And Gran . . ." She heard him choke, struggle for breath. "I hope you can live with that, Lexy." The line went dead.

Lexy crumpled forward, curled into a ball, feeling the pebbles hard beneath her now, relishing the pain, no more than she deserved, as she started to cry.

Cold and aching, head thick and heavy now that the buzz and fire of the whisky had abated, Lexy trudged back up the path to the hotel. Relieved to find the door unlocked, she slipped in past the empty reception desk in the dark hall and up to her room. She shut the door softly behind her and slid down to sit on the floor.

She watched Danny sleeping, his chest rising and falling, its steady rhythm mesmerising, the soft murmur of his breath as soothing as a lullaby. Tears welled in her eyes, again. Now that she'd let the tears begin, she wasn't sure they would ever stop. She knew Danny loved her. He'd proved that beyond any doubt over the last few days. The question was . . .

She shut off her thoughts, blinked and wiped away the tears. She stood and tiptoed over to the window, peeped out from the side of the chintz curtains to watch the dawn spread its green tinge across the blank canvas of an empty sky. She'd always loved sunset more than sunrise, but as she watched the clearer yellow of the morning sun push its way over the summit of the mountains in the distance she realised it was every bit as beautiful, the palette every bit as rich and complete as the hotter shades that heralded the coming night, every bit as exciting. Just different. Dawn and dusk, light and dark. Both had their place.

She looked back at Danny.

"Oh! You're awake." She wondered how long he'd been watching her, propped up on one elbow, his blond hair tousled and half covering his still unshaven face.

"What were you thinking about?"

"Do you have to ask?"

"Yes, Lex, I do. I'm not sure I know how to read your moods any more. Not sure I ever did."

She nodded thoughtfully, then shrugged her shoulders, walked across to sit beside him on the bed. She took his free hand in hers.

"Danny, I'm sorry. I didn't mean to fight, to say those things. It was the whisky . . . No, no that's not true. It was . . . I needed to lash out . . . to hurt someone . . . which is awful and you were there and . . . but after everything you've done for me—"

"It's okay. I can take it, you know. I'm not the total wimp you think I am." He managed a half grin, looked rueful and tousled, boyish almost, and Lexy knew he meant it. He'd forgiven her, like he always did. He was like a rock. No, a big, strong tree, an oak, or a willow, buffeted by the wind but so grounded it could bend and

371

flex then stand strong again when the storm had passed, give shade and shelter. It would be so easy to stay safe beneath the branches.

"Danny, I . . ."

"Don't. Don't say it."

"I've decided I have to go back to Malawi."

"Oh God, Lex, why?"

Danny took his hand back from hers, pushed himself up to lean against the pink padded headboard, reached for his glasses, avoiding her eyes.

"I need to . . . find out who I am. What it means to be Helen's granddaughter. A Buchanan."

"A wealthy woman."

"No, Danny." Lexy was stung by the unexpected bitterness in his tone. "None of this is about money. It's about family. My family."

"After the last few days, you really want to be a part of that family?"

"I don't have any choice. I *am* part of it. I need to make my peace with that. So I'm going back. And . . ."

Lexy felt her voice catch on the lump in her throat, swallowed, tried again.

"And I want to . . . to go to Evie's funeral. Pay my respects."

"She . . . ? Oh, Lexy."

"Robert rang. He blames me."

"But that's ridic—"

"No, it's not. I can understand why. And I can understand that he needs to be angry with someone, too." He raised an eyebrow as she smiled apologetically. "So why not with me? It doesn't matter, Danny. One way or another, I deserve it. I've behaved so badly."

"Extreme circumstances—"

"Are no excuse. I should be there. Take my punishment."

"I'll come with you."

Lexy shook her head. "I want to – have to – do this alone. Make amends."

"With Robert." He scowled, looked distractingly rugged for a moment.

"What? No. Well, yes, partly, but not in that way. But really to a hundred and forty-odd families who lost loved ones because of *my* family, and who deserve compensation."

"With Robert." Danny was a dog with a bone.

"I told you. This has nothing to do with Robert. It's about family, and whatever I think of him, that's David. And Ross. I need to find a way of bringing us together, of taking care— Danny!"

Danny had thrown back the bedclothes and was grabbing at his clothes, stumbling as he caught a foot in his jeans, cursing as he fell back on the bed.

"Danny, take it easy." Lexy had so rarely seen Danny angry that she had to fight the urge to laugh.

"Don't lie, Lexy. Whatever else, don't bloody lie to me. You, of all people. You've just been ranting about how you hate it that people have done it to you, so just don't. I deserve better than that."

He pulled himself up to stand again, reached for his T-shirt.

"I get it, you know. The African dream, you and Robert righting the wrongs of a colonial—"

"Danny, will you listen to me? There *is* no me and Robert."

"Then why won't you let me come with you?"

"Because you'd hate it." She tried to smile, lighten the moment. "And you know what you're like about foreign food and—"

"Don't patronise me, Lexy. And don't trivialise what I'm saying. I would do anything for you. Surely you realise that by now? I love you, dammit, Lexy."

"I know you do, Danny."

"Yeah right." He shrugged on his jacket, turned up its collar.

"I know you love me, and that's why I want to do this alone. I

373

want to make my peace with . . . myself and then . . . I have to do this for myself. I need you . . ." He was looking at her warily. "I need you to stay here." He snorted looked away, zipped up his jacket, pulled car keys from a pocket.

"Danny." She put her hand on his arm to stop him. "Listen to me. I need you to stay here because you are my reason to come home."

Acknowledgements

The first draft of *Ursula's Secret* won the *Sunday Mail* Fiction Prize 2015. For the opportunity to be published, and for their tremendous vote of confidence, my sincerest thanks to the judges: *Sunday Mail* writer Heather Greenaway, author Daniela Sacerdoti, Waterstones Scottish books buyer Angie Crawford and Alison McBride, marketing director of Black & White Publishing. My thanks too to the rest of the team at Black & White Publishing, and in particular editor Karyn Millar for guiding me expertly through my first foray into this new world and helping make this book the best it can be.

Thanks also to all who've helped me along the way from the birth of the idea in a short story to its final expression here. They are many, but for timely words of wisdom at Moniack Mhor, my thanks to Isla Dewar and Morag Joss; to Sophie Cooke, Director at Skriva Writing School, for sustained encouragement and always asking me the right questions; and to my writers' group, Marianne Paget, Emily Dodd and Louise Kelly, for empathy, honesty and humour. To Anne and the team at Casa Ana in Spain, thank you for taking the chores of everyday life away from me while I finished the first draft. Look what happened. I'll be back.

Finally, special mention to the friends and family who encourage me, listen to me, put up with me. You know who you are. I am so grateful and don't say it often enough, so here it is, in print: thank you.